THE
HUNTER

THE HUNTER

A Detective Takako Otomichi Mystery

Asa Nonami

Translated by
Juliet Winters Carpenter

KODANSHA INTERNATIONAL
Tokyo • New York • London

Originally published by Shinchosha, Tokyo, in 1996,
under the title *Kogoeru Kiba*.

Distributed in the United States by Kodansha America, Inc.,
and in the United Kingdom and continental Europe
by Kodansha Europe Ltd.

Published by Kodansha International Ltd.,
17–14 Otowa 1-chome, Bunkyo-ku, Tokyo 112–8652, and
Kodansha America, Inc.

First edition, 2006
15 14 13 12 11 10 09 08 07 06   10 9 8 7 6 5 4 3 2 1

          Library of Congress Cataloging-in-Publication Data

Nonami, Asa, 1960-
  [Kogoeru kiba. English]
  The hunter / Asa Nonami ; translated by Juliet Winters Carpenter. -- 1st ed.
    p. cm.
  "Originally published Shinchosha, Tokyo, in 1996 under the title: Kogoeru kiba"--T.p. verso.
  ISBN-13: 978-4-7700-3025-2 (hardcover)
  ISBN-10: 4-7700-3025-8 (hardcover)
  I. Carpenter, Juliet Winters. II. Title.
  PL857.O494K6413 2007
  895.6'35–dc22
                         2006023086

www.kodansha-intl.com

PROLOGUE

At dusk the north wind suddenly picked up. As night came on, the streets lost color; leaves danced in little eddies at the corners of buildings and out-of-the-way places, and passersby screwed up their faces to keep the sand and dust from getting into their eyes. An air of festivity had pervaded the area a week earlier, during the New Year's holiday, but the herd of commuters now hurrying home looked gray and spiritless. After rush hour peaked, the moon came out in the east. As it rose higher in the sky and the night wore on, a kid with a guitar and a white guy who sang nothing but Beatles songs took up residence in front of the station, unbothered by the gusting wind. The singing, the guitar strains, and the sporadic applause were swept up into the sky along with the moaning of the wind.

Masayo Kizaki, a part-time waitress, was the first person to notice the man in the doorway of the restaurant. It was a family restaurant on the edge of town, bordering the highway, which perhaps explained why it was crowded even when the trains would soon stop running for the night. The restaurant was filled to about sixty-percent capacity. Masayo, who had spent her entire New Year's holiday on the slopes, and who intended to go skiing twice more before spring, was nineteen; she was a student at a vocational school.

Ten minutes before midnight, Masayo, whose shift had begun at ten, was carrying a large coffee pot past the cash register as she headed toward the tables of customers when she felt a chilly gust of wind. There were two doors in the front of the restaurant, and every time someone came in or went out wind would blow in, along with dust, leaves, and the noise of traffic. Masayo was wearing a light-cotton, short-sleeved uniform, so the cold air immediately raised goose-bumps on her arms.

"There'll be two of us," said the customer casually to Masayo as she turned toward him. His voice was husky and, for a man, rather high-pitched. Masayo did not want to escort him to his table while carrying the coffee pot, but the cash register was unmanned and no other waitress was coming over to say

"This way, please." The late-hour shift operated with minimum staff.

"Smoking or non-smoking?" Masayo asked.

"Smoking."

Masayo turned around, coffee pot still in hand, and pulled out a menu from the slot by the cash register. She had gone by the book in asking him his preference, but she definitely remembered this customer. His face rang no bells, but the minute she heard his voice, she knew: he was a regular, probably in his late thirties, and no ordinary salaryman—you could tell that from the color of his suit, gray tinged with purple, and from the heavy gold bracelet glittering on the wrist of the hand holding a zippered briefcase. He wasn't wearing a coat, so he must have come by car. He usually came pretty late, and he always laid his cellphone on the table. The restaurant had too many customers for Masayo to have either the inclination or the time to commit to memory, but this man's voice was distinctive; that and the bracelet were hard to forget.

She led him past the oblong case used for a salad bar at lunchtime and over to a window seat with its back to the highway, placed the menu in front of him, and said the words specified in the restaurant manual: "As soon as you're ready to order, please let me know." The man slid onto the curved, pink-upholstered bench that wrapped around the circular table, paying no attention to Masayo, and picked up the menu in silence. Most customers didn't bother to respond to every little thing you said to them. Wait staff didn't expect a response every time either, so after reciting her line, Masayo proceeded to ask the other customers if they wanted a refill of coffee. When she returned to the man a few minutes later, he ordered a beer and fries.

Doesn't he have to drive home?

The thought entered her mind, she recalled later, as she took the menu and said reflexively, "One moment, please." After that, how many minutes went by? With another burst of cold air, two new customers came in; after seating them, she set a bottle of beer and a glass on a tray and started toward the man's table. The words "Sorry to keep you waiting" were in the middle of her throat when it happened—flames shot up, right before her eyes. At the same moment, a howl, like the war-whoop of an enraged beast, filled the restaurant.

At first Masayo was too stunned to realize what was happening. The next instant, she was screaming in horror. She threw the tray down and, leaping back, slipped and fell. The flames roared, consuming the man in a flash. Masayo's mind went blank. From all around she heard shrieking, chairs being knocked out of the way, dishes breaking. Still on the floor, she stared wide-eyed at the scene before her.

"I'm on fire! I'm burning up!"

The cry emerged from the middle of the flames. The upper body of the man, now a human torch, was twisting and turning. Masayo slid backward. The man was up on his feet, sparks cascading.

"Help! Somebody, help me!"

It was as if the flames themselves were speaking. Masayo stared up, seeing the silhouette of a man waving his arms wildly from within the flames. The fire raged, black smoke billowing. The stink was terrible. Masayo's eyes stung as she watched the fire spread to the curtains and the padded bench where the man had been sitting.

"I'm burning up! Help me!"

The next moment, the pillar of flames toppled over and rolled on the floor next to Masayo. She screamed and scrambled away. There was a crackling sound in her ears, and the stench of protein charring filled her nostrils. There was a dull pain in her right arm. With every jerk of the man's body, flames scattered, new offspring of the flames leaping and spreading of their own volition. From her position on the floor, Masayo, dumbfounded, just stared. Though her mind was blank, incapable of thought, for an instant there arose in one corner of her consciousness something like a thrill: the flames moved with such vitality, gave off such radiant light, they were beautiful.

"Fools! Run for your lives!"

Behind her came this shout. As soon as she heard it, Masayo jumped to her feet as if released from a spell. The carpet was catching fire. The fire moved with amazing speed, flames licking everything within range like a famished monster. Customers ran screaming for the exit. Desperate, Masayo joined the stampede, getting stepped on, then herself stepping on and clambering over fallen customers.

"Customers first!"

She thought that was what she heard someone cry. A hell of a time to say something like that. Forget it, man, I only work part-time. No sooner had this thought crossed her mind than she felt someone grab her shoulders from behind.

"You heard me. Customers first!"

Masayo was flung to the back of the onrushing crowd. She fell hard against a corner of the cash register and once again sank to the floor in a daze.

This can't be happening.

Slowly she turned around. She saw the man wrapped in flames, writhing, black smoke rising from him. He was no longer whooping. He was crumpling over, looking like an actual beast.

"Hello! Hello! Somebody's . . . somebody's on fire!" Over her head the manager was screaming into a phone.

The stampede of customers out the door had allowed a strong gust of wind into the restaurant, fanning the flames enveloping the man. The fire now had free range; the air grew thick with smoke and crackle and stink.

"Somebody's on fire, and the fire is spreading!"

Whipped by the wind, the flames spread across the curtain even as Masayo watched. There was a loud *crack*, followed by the plate-glass window falling and shattering. The lights went out. More screams. With wind blowing in from the gaping hole, the restaurant swirled with flames and smoke. It was not about the man anymore.

Gotta escape, gotta get out of here!

Trampled by customers, listening to the roar of flames that drowned out all the screams, Masayo began to crawl for all she was worth. The smell of the fire was everywhere, her eyes stinging so badly she could barely keep them open, her mind incapable of rational thought. Instinct alone propelled her in the direction of safety, toward the air blowing in from outside.

ONE

1

As she opened her front door, her nostrils were assailed by the obnoxiously artificial perfume of air freshener. She had been duped into buying it by the advertising; far from refreshing, the scent was cloying and annoying, thought Takako Otomichi as she took one boot-clad step indoors.

It's like my front door opens right into the bathroom.

The thought of encountering this irritating scent every time she dragged herself home from work was unbearable. She groped around for the switch. A soft orange light lit up the small entryway and the kitchen beyond.

"What it is, is fake," Takako muttered to herself. With a gloved hand she reached up for the small white jar of freshener sitting on the shoe cupboard. Cuteness, aimed at a universal appeal. By itself the thing was trim and attractive, but no matter where she put it, it looked out of place; the thing had no style.

That's what you get for swallowing the ad, dummy.

Takako slid open the cupboard door and stuck the jar of air freshener inside, next to a pair of black pumps she never wore. That was the right place for it, hidden away. She peeled off her gloves, then removed her helmet. With the pressure off her ears, the sound of her breathing echoing inside her head suddenly stopped. Placing her gloves and helmet on top of the shoe cupboard where the jar of freshener had been, she bent over to take off her boots. She felt a numbness in her lower back. After spending all day in the same position, small wonder that her back muscles were in knots, that her body was so thoroughly chilled.

Take a hot bath, get something to eat.

Her condominium, a one-bedroom apartment with a combined dining room–kitchen, was on the top floor of a five-story building; as it was on the corner, it got plenty of sun. With a six-mat tatami room and an even bigger kitchen, the place was plenty big for one person. The reason it seemed so cramped was that, ever since she moved in, an entire corner had been taken up by a heap of cardboard boxes. She knew very well she should get cracking and clear the mess away, use a day off like today to tackle the pile a little at a time—packing had only taken a matter of hours—and yet somehow she could never get started. The boxes had sat where they were for almost a year. But even without unpacking them, Takako found she did not really lack anything, so there couldn't be much of value in there anyway. The kind of knickknacks you were happy to get as presents but would never buy for yourself, porcelain mugs in saccharine colors, old junior high textbooks, . . . Her old judo outfit must be in there, too.

Well, doesn't do them any harm to sit there.

Giving herself the same old excuse, she walked around the apartment turning on all the lights. Then she checked her phone for messages, but the green light that flashed on and off when she had a message was not blinking.

On her ride home that evening the wind had picked up, and Takako had used up all her strength. Her legs felt heavy, her neck and shoulder muscles rigid. She ran the bath; while the tub was filling, she peered in the refrigerator and clucked at the slim pickings. Whenever she was out on her bike, she didn't stop to eat or drink, so now she was good and hungry. She had hoped to find something for a quick meal, but the spinach and chrysanthemum greens she'd bought before New Year's were now yellow, and the cucumbers, still inside their plastic bag, were turning to mush. The ham and tofu were both past their shelf date. That left *natto*—fermented soybeans—that had been in there for god knows how long, some ketchup and mayonnaise, and several cans of beer.

Wasn't smart enough to pick up something on the way home.

Disgusted, she shut the refrigerator door. No way was she going out shopping now.

"Hello, I'd like to order a large plain pizza. Corn salad and fried chicken on the side."

It took Takako only a few seconds to decide to call the pizza place; she knew full well it was going to cost her. But soba noodle shops and sushi places sometimes wouldn't deliver for just a single order—and besides, you had to wash out the bowl afterward and leave it outside for them to come pick it up. Too much trouble. Pizza was fine. All she really wanted was something to put in her belly.

Piece by piece, she stripped off her leather riding suit and then, leaving the bathroom door open, she stepped into the filling tub. She couldn't wait to get in the hot water, even if it was just her feet. Slowly she lowered herself into the water, careful to avoid touching the cold sides of the tub, then sat down, arms around her knees, as the hot water gradually rose around her chilled body, engulfing her, warming her. The steady sound of the water pouring out of the tap was soothing. By the time the water level was up to her breasts, Takako's shoulders had begun to relax; she stretched out her legs full length, closed her eyes and let out a deep breath, resting the back of her head against the tub. She could feel the tension draining from the very marrow of her bones, and a tingling sensation ran through her. In a voice like a middle-aged man's she murmured: "Sweet ride."

Behind her closed eyes, scenery of the day's ride passed vividly by. She saw road after mountain road. The scenes beyond the guardrail, Mount Fuji draped with snow, . . . Beautiful, all of it beautiful. At sunrise, riding through a village tucked in the mountains, she felt a touch of spring in the air. Yes, today, even as she sped through the bone-chilling cold, Takako had definitely felt that spring was near.

One year.

Slowly Takako opened her eyes. She reached out and turned off the tap. Quiet filled the room, and amid the clouds of steam she could feel the pores in her face opening. Scooping up the silky water, she scrubbed her face, filthy from exhaust fumes and dust, as she played back the events of one year ago.

She had gone for a long, solitary bike ride, coming home after dark. And then, alone in the bath, she'd found herself weeping. She hadn't meant to do anything of the sort, but when she gave her pleasantly tired body over to the warmth of the bath, the tears had just flowed, and flowed, and flowed.

It's been a whole year.

Never had she wept such bitter tears. Never had she dreamed she would cry so pathetically. That day, with her face half submerged in the water, sobbing, Takako made up her mind: She was going to get a divorce. She knew her lying husband wasn't coming home that night. She knew where he was, and she knew it wasn't the first time.

I thought I was going to sink right to the bottom.

And now, nearly a year later, here she was in the bathtub again. What was strangest to her, looking back, was that for four and a half years she had lived with someone she called a husband. That she had ever been any man's wife. Having never lived alone before, on first moving into this apartment she'd felt a kind of vertigo—an enormous sense of helplessness and insecurity. It felt as if a cold wind were constantly blowing. And yet, the days had gone by.

It hadn't been too late to start over. Much better than sitting around clinging to the past.

After the divorce, she heard all kinds of rumors about her ex. "I wouldn't have said anything before, but you may as well know it now." That's how people would preface their remarks, and then tell her something rotten he'd done. None of it was easy to believe, and sometimes there was nothing she could do but laugh—or else cry. Each time Takako made a point of telling herself: This is why you're better off. The loneliness is nothing compared to the humiliation of being treated like that. It hurts, but you're far better off.

The deeper the wound, the longer to heal. Fear of healing just deepens the wound.

This year, for the first time in her life, Takako had spent the long New Year's holiday alone. Somehow she had found the energy to prepare the traditional New Year dishes, or a reasonable approximation of them. The year before, she'd done the year-end shopping with her husband. She remembered this as she saw the New Year in by herself this year, breathing a sigh of relief that the normal rhythms of life were resuming. But now, feeling sorry for herself, she wondered if she alone in the city had missed the New Year. There was nothing new or good about it. One look at the calendar was enough to bring back the taste of tears; was January always going to be bad for her? That was exactly why she climbed on her motorcycle this morning.

Strange to be thinking these things. To be discovering only now how exhausted she really was.

Her thoughts starting to fog over, Takako suddenly realized that her forehead was covered in perspiration. If she didn't hurry and get out of this bath, the pizza delivery would come and she'd miss it. She was starving. She stepped out of the tub, swiftly shampooed her short hair under the shower, and washed and rinsed herself all over. In a corner of her mind lingered the image of herself a year ago when, sobbing, she splashed her face with cold water. She had not forgotten the despair. How much better it was to be giving herself a quick shampoo while waiting for a food delivery. That's the way to look at it.

Just as she was slipping into her sweat suit, the food arrived. Takako laid the pizza out on top of her small *kotatsu* heater, along with the salad and fried chicken, got a can of beer from the fridge, and settled down to her meal.

On her motorbike, she had wanted nothing but a cup of hot coffee; now the cold beer felt good sliding down her throat. She exhaled and took a bite of the still-hot pizza. She relaxed and then, not liking the quiet in the room, switched on the TV with the remote control. She found a program that wasn't too demanding, and continued munching in silence.

What am I going to do with all this pizza? she thought. It won't taste any good tomorrow. Well, so what. I'll just eat it anyway. That settles it: pizza for breakfast.

You ordered this large pizza knowing *you wouldn't be able to eat it all.*

This was true. Not wanting to give the impression that she was eating alone, she had purposely ordered a large pizza.

Polishing off the beer in no time, she padded into the kitchen in her bare feet and brought back another. She changed the channels randomly, drank her beer, and poked at her salad—the same kind you could get at the convenience store—with a plastic fork. As her hunger abated, she slowed down; when she stopped, full, a good half of the pizza was still left. By then it was just after nine. The top of the kotatsu showed the remains of her feast for one: the half a pizza, most of the slightly greasy fried chicken, one empty salad container, and three empty cans of beer.

"My stomach!" she groaned. "Agh—I ate too much."

No one was around to order her to clean up. Feeling quite satisfied, slightly intoxicated, Takako looked around the room.

"What a dump."

When she first moved in, she'd been rather enthusiastic about taking care of the place. It represented a fresh start in life. She even thought that, in order to make it fully her own, she would put out only things she really liked. But work had kept her so busy that the apartment looked like it belonged to a college kid newly arrived in Tokyo from the countryside. The one saving grace was the curtains, a soft, pale pink.

It's just a place to sleep, after all.

She was thoroughly warmed now, sitting cozily on the floor with her legs under the heater. She lay all the way down. Wonderful to have no worries, no nagging problems. Her body was tired, her mind empty. The past was past; this was paradise.

Things seemed to unfold without connection to her. Life in society and TV dramas alike—none of it seemed to have any meaning for her. It all washed over her. Lying stretched out, her eyes on the uninteresting television show, she could not resist drowsing off.

As her eyes closed, the road through the mountains came back to her. The comforting vibrations of the motor, the rounded tank between her knees. The road stretching on and on, the center line, the bikes behind her glimpsed through the rearview mirror. Come to think of it, there had been somebody behind her for a good long way. When she pulled over at a scenic spot for a rest, a biker discovering that she was female registered curiosity, acted like he wanted to come over and talk.

I've got no time for kids. How old does he think I am? If he knew, oh boy, would he take off.

"Can you see it from this angle? Flames are shooting out of the building! The windy conditions have made things worse. Despite the valiant efforts of fire-fighters, the fire is raging out of control!"

Takako jerked awake, thirsty, and found the TV screen filled with the scene of a fire. She stared at it foggily.

"At one point the fire was starting to die down, but a short while ago it picked up strength again. A ladder truck has arrived on the scene, and while firefighting operations continue below, a search for people trapped in the upper floors is also going on. On the ground floor is a restaurant, and various small businesses occupy the building from the second floor up. It was past midnight when the fire broke out, and so except for the all-night restaurant, there were few people in the building, we're told. From where I stand, I don't see anyone crying for help."

Fire? Where? Was this broadcast live?

Takako tried to focus, but she was just too sleepy. About to drift off again, she told herself, no, mustn't sleep here, and managed somehow to drag herself out of the kotatsu.

"That's all from the scene of the fire in Tachikawa in Tokyo."

Tachikawa?

A lousy place for a fire. Tachikawa was where Takako worked—at the government building in Midori-machi, Tama, which housed the Eighth District Headquarters of the Tokyo Metropolitan Police Department, along with the local Traffic Riot Squad, Automobile Patrol Unit, and Mobile Investigative Unit. Takako was a member of the Third Mobile Investigative Unit. Takako was a cop.

So, what this news meant for her was, things were going to be crazy tomorrow. She took a long drink of water. She wasn't going to think about it. She staggered into the bedroom, set her alarm clock, and fell into bed. She'd better get some sleep while she could.

"A fire in Tachikawa. Oh boy," Takako mumbled to herself in the dark. She exhaled deeply, once, and then she was asleep.

2

At 12:05 A.M., Tamotsu Takizawa, the sergeant on call at the Tachikawa Central Station of the Metropolitan Police Department, got word of the blaze. An officer at the local police box was reporting in from the site: Fire had broken out at a popular family restaurant, and even though it had just started, the flames were spreading with surprising vigor. It had the potential of turning into a five-alarm fire.

"Rotten luck."

"Damn right. Who wants to lug bodies in this freezing cold?"

Takizawa and the two young detectives with him had not relished being on call tonight. One step outside the station and a keen, cold wind sliced through you. Riding shotgun in the patrol van, its siren screaming, Takizawa kept on grumbling, "Damn it all." His waistline had ballooned of late, and he found himself sitting on the edge of his seat. He was wearing a leather coat over his uniform; if he didn't get busy and lose some weight, by next year the coat would be like a straitjacket.

"Was it an explosion?" he asked.

"The report didn't mention any," answered Wada, the greener of the two young detectives, who until now had been spending most of his time on larceny investigations.

In that case, maybe there wouldn't be any bodies to deal with, Takizawa hoped as he sucked noisily on a molar. The noodles he'd had as a late-night snack were full of thinly sliced green onions, some of which were now stuck between his teeth. Matter of fact, his whole mouth tasted kind of oniony. On the other hand, he told himself, on a windy night like this, the damage could be bad.

For Takizawa, after twenty-seven years on the force, fifteen spent as a detective heading investigations of violent crimes, a big fire was nothing out of the ordinary. But no matter how used he was to them, no matter how many times he went through the drill, he always got depressed. People who came to gawk could stand around during the height of the fire and then go home. They might stop to think what it was like for those who had to hang around to clean up. It wasn't ever a pretty sight.

"It's a big one, all right," Wada said as he gripped the steering wheel.

Sure enough, the sky before them was stained bright red. At this rate, there was no chance it was going to be put out before they arrived.

"Was that a four-story building, or what?" asked Takizawa.

"Six, I think. There's also an underground garage."

"Well-informed, aren't we. Don't tell me you eat at a place like that?"

"At a family restaurant? Why not? Nothing wrong with that," Wada replied, glancing at the sergeant with surprise, then smirking to himself. All Takizawa knew about where to eat around here was the ramen and soba noodle shops that delivered, or the little joints that served one cheap special-of-the-day; other than that, he never went anywhere but places to drink. "That one does a good business, even late at night."

"I know. Full of kids hanging around all night till the trains start up in the morning."

"Well-informed, aren't we."

"Go jump in the lake."

How long ya think I been working this beat, Takizawa was about to add, and then swallowed the words. They were coming up to the site of the fire. From every gap in the building, bright red flames leaped and writhed like devils' tongues, reaching up to the night sky. A siren was wailing, and the sidewalks were filling with people running toward the fire. Even if the building didn't burn to the ground, damage would be severe.

"We may hafta bring headquarters in on this."

Putting the fire out looked like it was going to take some time. If it turned into a really big-scale fire, somebody from headquarters would definitely have to come out.

Ordinarily it was only five or six minutes to the restaurant, traveling swiftly by patrol car, but as they drew closer, the traffic was starting to jam. "Isn't anyone directing traffic yet?" groused Takizawa.

"No. It's a big intersection. They could be short-handed."

Wada maneuvered the car through the crowded streets. By the time they pulled up in front of the restaurant, the area was clogged with people who'd fled to safety and others who'd come to gawk, many with a coat tossed over their pajamas. Among them were several nicely dressed young women with disheveled hair, standing staring up at the fire, their expressions rigid. The first floor was wrapped in flames, and the blaze was starting to work its way up to the second floor and part of the third.

"I'll be damned," Takizawa said to himself, shuddering at the building belching black smoke and flames. This was much worse than any house on fire. The three officers quickly piled out of the unmarked police van.

In case of a fire, the police investigators first on the scene had to start gathering evidence immediately: taking down eyewitness testimony, verifying who called 119 to report the fire, identifying the wounded, . . . If it was arson, the arsonist often hung around, mingling in the crowd, so the onlookers had to be carefully photographed. But until the fire was out, the firefighters' work took priority; all the police could do was handle traffic and control the crowd.

Sorimachi, the other detective on emergency duty with them, now spoke up: "I'll go take some pictures."

"OK, and I better ask headquarters to send backup. This fire is gonna hang around for a while."

Takizawa watched the uniformed policemen running around, and then turned to Wada, standing motionless at his side, entranced by the flames. "Don't stand there like a dummy. Bring me a witness, the person who called emergency, somebody. Get a move on."

He slapped Wada on the back, and the words "Yes, sir!" came out in response. Wada made as if to run off.

"Before you get lost, ask the guys in uniform! While you're at it, find the cop who first reported the fire."

Wada looked hastily back, said, "Yes, sir," again, and then dove into the crowd.

"The fire is dangerous. Stand back! Stand back!" A voice roared over the loudspeaker on the fire-truck. Firefighters dressed in silver suits ran to the right and to the left, getting drenched from the spraying water. The ladder truck was there, along with a rescue squad and a special squad in case the fire spread to the underground garage. The scene was so bright it didn't seem like the middle of the night, but it wasn't only because of the fire. Lights from the media lit everything up like a film set; the building spouting flames and smoke, with water being sprayed on it from all sides, was a dramatic centerpiece. Standing at a considerable distance from the fire, Takizawa could yet feel the heat of it on his face; that's how powerful it was. He'd seen fires like this more than a few times. It was always a picture of hell.

Using the wireless radio in the patrol van, he called for backup.

A uniformed officer, pushing through the crowd, came to inform Takizawa that witnesses, including workers in the restaurant, had been rounded up; Takizawa told him to get their names and addresses.

"So far, seven people with injuries are being treated in two different hospitals," another officer reported; he was in radio contact with the ambulance team.

Yet another officer ran up to say, "According to witnesses, the fire started in the seating area."

"The seating area?" Takizawa frowned, perplexed. It was one thing for a fire like this to start in the kitchen; for it to start where the customers sat, and reach these proportions, didn't make sense. Even supposing a customer started the fire with a cigarette, or dropped a lighted match, how could it develop into an inferno like this? An electric short was possible but seemed unlikely out where the customers were.

"I don't like it," mumbled Takizawa, watching as the billowing smoke gradually turned white. In the darkness and confusion, separating out the witnesses from the curious was not going to be easy.

A little after 1:00 A.M., a representative of the arson team arrived from headquarters. At about the same time, a report came in from the officer who went to the two hospitals tending to the injured; there were twenty-two casualties. Most had suffered burns, but others had also sustained external injuries as they fell, trying to get away. All had been identified. Only one person was too badly burned to speak.

At 1:50 A.M., the fire was extinguished, leaving the surroundings soaked as in the aftermath of a flood. Here and there, white smoke continued to rise, and depending on the direction of the wind, you could still smell the stench of the fire. The temperature reverted to the bitter cold of midwinter. One fire truck drove off, then another, bells ringing to indicate that the fire was over.

The remaining vehicles from the fire department belonged to investigators who would survey the scene alongside Takizawa and his colleagues. The officers from the neighborhood police box speedily roped off the area to preserve the scene. A rigorous search would begin in the morning. In the meantime, Takizawa and other officers from the Tachikawa office, along with several backup investigators from headquarters, waited for the last group of firefighters in the building to finish their final check.

The other investigators were divided into teams, some to get statements from the wounded in the hospitals, others to question building residents, restaurant workers, and other material witnesses who'd been assembled nearby. It was official policy to get the statements as soon as possible, while people were still in a state of excitement; once that initial excitement wore off, people tended to avoid saying anything that might reflect poorly on themselves.

"Here they come!"

It was after 2:10 A.M. when the last group of firefighters began to emerge from the building. Most of the crowd had dispersed by then. That was when Takizawa felt his stomach muscles clench. He nodded knowingly, slowly, signaling with his eyes to Wada and Sorimachi, who were standing next to him; they grimaced, their faces stiff with cold.

The body was brought out on a stretcher covered with a blanket. You could tell from the shape of the lump that it displayed "boxer's stance," the forward-leaning posture peculiar to victims of severe burns. The firefighters set the stretcher down on the ground before officers gathered around and removed the blanket.

"What the hell is this?" said Takizawa, pressing a handkerchief to his nose. One thing was immediately clear to him: the burns were unnatural. "What happened to him?"

The body revealed burns of particular intensity from the waist up, mostly fourth-degree burns showing carbonization. Below the waist the burns were much milder, with fragments of clothing stuck to the skin. A victim showing so much difference in degree of burns between the upper and lower torso was unheard of.

"Looks like suicide, eh?" said Sorimachi, leaning in from the side for a better look, holding his nose. Takizawa quickly replaced the blanket, and then he and Sorimachi began to carry the stretcher to the police van. This should have been Wada's job, but when Takizawa looked around for the younger detective, he was off in a dark corner, vomiting.

"Gimme a break. This his first time?"

"Yep."

Those on emergency call had to report for duty regardless of what unit they were on; Wada, who usually spent his time chasing petty thieves, could only lament his bad luck tonight. Removing the bodies of burn victims from the still-hot ruins was the job of the fire department, but from then on the police took over. After this, the three of them would have to transport the body to the station morgue, examine it and clean it up, and light incense.

"Well, he'll get used to it."

As Wada drove back to the station, Takizawa clapped him on the back. Wada responded weakly, "I'm OK," but his face was drained of color and he remained downcast, obviously uncomfortable.

Takizawa had a good idea of the young investigator's feelings, a confused welter of embarrassment and revulsion. The first time he ever saw a corpse, Takizawa retched. Even if you became accustomed to death, you retched when a decomposed body came along, and you retched again when you saw your first drowning victim. By experiencing the same thing over and over, you maybe got used to it.

"You never see burns like that in an ordinary fire. You think it was a suicide, or what?" Sorimachi asked, repeating his original theory.

Sorimachi was an officer with plenty of experience around death. Sitting in the back seat, he blew his nose loudly, then lit up a cigarette and took a drag. A cigarette dangling between his own lips, Takizawa leaned his head to one side and said, "I dunno. Think what would happen if you doused yourself in kerosene or gasoline."

"It would all run down."

"Exactly. The burning would concentrate on the lower part of your body. Besides, this was a crowded restaurant! Hard to imagine somebody deliberately picking a place like that to set himself on fire, in front of all those people. Even supposing he doused himself outside and then walked in— something weird about it."

The minimal damage to the lower half of the body made it plain at a glance that the deceased was male. Unless he left a car in the parking lot, if he was someone who just wandered in for a meal, establishing his identity might take some time.

"What if he had a grudge against the place?" Sorimachi persisted.

"A death protest. In a family restaurant?"

"Maybe he had a grudge against the owner."

This was not impossible. But only one thing seemed certain to Takizawa: the deceased was near the seat of the fire. With burns that severe, whether he had other injuries—whether, even, he was alive or dead before incineration—would be hard to determine.

In assessing burns, Takizawa and his colleagues adhered to the "rule of nines." Assuming the genitalia accounted for one percent of total body surface area, the remainder of the body was divided into eleven sections: head and neck, right arm, left arm, upper trunk front, upper trunk back, lower trunk front, lower trunk back, left leg front and back, and right leg front and back. Each section was allotted nine percent, the numbers altogether adding up to one hundred. Depending on the placement and extent of burns, you determined the multiple of nine. Generally speaking, burns covering two-thirds or more of total body surface area resulted in death, burns covering one-third or more were life-threatening, and burns covering one-fifth or more were considered critical. But burns on the head and face were potentially serious in any case, and in the case of children, the rule of nines did not apply.

Today's victim had suffered burns all over his body, so death was probably inevitable. Still, there was something about the nature of his burns that Takizawa didn't like.

We're gonna be busy on this one.

That was Takizawa's instinct talking. This incident, it was telling him, was more than a simple fire in a restaurant. Perhaps it was just as well that he was going to be absent from home for the next few weeks: he had a kid at home studying for college entrance examinations.

At 3:00 A.M., the backup team returned to the station with eyewitness testimony.

"A customer? You mean the guy was a customer?"

Takizawa, with the help of Sorimachi and Wada, had just finished rinsing off the body with cold water in the morgue. Rubbing his freezing hands, Takizawa stared vacantly at the investigators as the group convened. They had gotten started with the barest of greetings, scarcely introducing themselves. This one guy, who looked to be in his late thirties, peered into his notebook with a serious air and nodded slowly. He spoke: "Witnesses say he burst into flames all of a sudden. Until then, he was sitting like a normal person at his table."

Along with everybody else gathered in the meeting room, Takizawa cocked his head at this.

Another investigator added: "Doesn't seem much chance it was a suicide.

We've got testimony that the guy rolled around on the floor, yelling 'Help! I'm burning up!'"

Takizawa, feeling worse and worse, blew his nose; he still couldn't get rid of the stench of the fire. His heart ached to think that he had just cleaned the body of a man who, hours ago, had no idea he was about to wind up as a blackened corpse.

3

At 9:00 A.M., a joint inspection of the fire scene was undertaken by the heads of investigation of the Tokyo Fire Department and the arson unit in the First Investigation Division of the MPD, along with Takizawa and his colleagues on emergency duty the night before. Because of a flurry of testimony indicating that the flames had originated on the person of the one victim who burned to death, the group was joined by a forensic scientist from the physical evidence division of SRI, the Science Research Institute.

"Damn, it's cold." As soon as he set foot back on the site, Takizawa screwed up his face with displeasure.

Wada, who the night before had been ashen-faced and silent, was now in a different mood. "What's the matter, didn't bring your pocket warmer?" he teased.

Why shouldn't he feel the cold more than Wada? The kid was twenty years younger than him—and then some. "Wise guy," he said, and made as if to jab Wada in the ribs as they walked across an area already ringed by reporters. They ducked under the perimeter tape. A rank odor still pervaded the ruins. The ground, heavily soaked in water the night before, was covered in puddles that glistened in the weak winter-morning sunlight.

Other investigators were deep in conversation.

"You're saying we can rule out the possibility that the fire broke out in the kitchen or somewhere else in the restaurant?"

"We can't say that for sure yet. The fire could have started beneath where the victim was sitting, or nearby."

"Hard to believe there was any electrical wiring around there."

"Anyway, a simple short circuit wouldn't give you a firestorm like that."

"According to eyewitness testimony," the MPD arson unit head now began, "the victim was seated at a window table. He burst into flames, writhed in agony, and rolled on the floor as far as the salad bar." After peering at a roughly drawn map of the fire scene, he pointed out the relevant locations to the group. Within the First Investigation Division, the arson unit was charged with ascertaining a fire's origin and its cause, whether accidental or intentional. They were professionals in fire disaster.

The group then prepared themselves. They wrapped a towel around the lower half of their faces and the neck of their jumpsuits. They put on helmets, slipped on heavy gloves. Because of the danger of treading on nails, they wore steel-soled boots. Each had a rake.

All told, there were fifteen men, including Takizawa and his Tachikawa colleagues, who now proceeded into the site of the fire.

"The waitress who took the victim to his seat hasn't recovered her eyesight and wasn't able to show us the exact place, but she did say it was a window table, fourth from the rear, next to a round pillar, and had a curved bench, so it's probably . . . ," the arson unit head paused, standing with the group in the restaurant now destroyed beyond recognition, his feet set on fittings reduced to rubble, looking from his map to the premises and back again before pointing, ". . . right around there." He went on: "The victim fell over and rolled on the floor. Taking into account where the body was found, he must have come along here."

Finding the seat of the fire was the most important question in a fire investigation. It could be difficult to pinpoint, especially if the building had been deserted, but that was not a problem in this case where there were so many eyewitnesses.

"Common sense tells you people don't just spontaneously combust, so there's got to be some clue right around where he was sitting."

More than seven hours had passed since the fire was put out, yet the site still gave off a lingering heat. Exercising caution where they stepped, the investigators walked around what had until last night been a colorful restaurant serving dinner to an array of customers.

"I'm going to pour water."

"Easy now."

When water was poured on a certain spot, the soot ran off, exposing the degree of incineration beneath. Just as the MPD officer had predicted, a curved bench next to a thick pillar near a large, shattered window showed particularly intense incineration; even the urethane filling was charred. Further, where the man had presumably rolled on the floor, the carpet was severely burned; just one place the approximate width of a human back was spared. This, then, was where the man expired.

The investigators then focused on the distance between the curved bench that the victim had been sitting on and the spot where he came to an end, seeking any kind of evidence. Nothing was to be overlooked, however small; with utmost concentration, they sorted out even tiny particles. If kerosene or gasoline was used, there would be an oily residue; if there was an explosive device, there would be remnants of it; if an electric wire had shorted out, there would be telltale signs of the live current.

"Hey, take a look at this," Wada beckoned to Takizawa, who was engrossed in examination of the bench and its surroundings. Wada had donned a surgical-like face mask, the kind sold for protection from pollen, that he'd cleverly brought along. Takizawa walked over to him, giving wide berth to the other investigators, and when he saw what Wada had uncovered from the cinders, he immediately called the forensic scientist from SRI over.

Wearing thick glasses that gave him the appearance of an insect, the scientist crouched down and picked up the item with tweezers, examining it meticulously. Takizawa stood behind him, leaning forward, studying the object. One by one, the others gathered around.

Leaning farther forward, Takizawa asked, "Now whaddaya suppose *that* is?"

Hearing Takizawa's voice in his ear, the scientist gave a start, but he answered thoughtfully, "Well, let's see." He brought the object to his nose and sniffed it, then held it up so the rest of them could see. Less than two inches long, it looked, at first glance, like a charred section of the body of a snake.

"Part of a belt, I should think. Probably belonging to the man who burned to death," the scientist pronounced, his voice muffled behind the towel over his mouth. Recalling the severity of the victim's burns at the midriff, Takizawa was amazed that any part of the belt could have made it through the fire.

"Whaddaya make of that?" Takizawa said, pointing to a part of the item that was completely carbonized and so fragile-looking that it seemed the least amount of force might cause it to disintegrate.

The scientist nodded. "See the tarry substance, over here?"

"Yeah."

"I can't be sure, but . . . Let's look around again. I'm wondering if there's anything in this area that could be part of an ignition device?"

At these words, spoken as the scientist got up from his crouch, an excitement ran through the team of investigators. Takizawa also straightened up, stretching his sore back. Several investigators were already crouched down again to begin a new search.

"Part of an ignition device, you say?" Takizawa asked the scientist.

"At this stage, I can't draw any hard and fast conclusions, of course. But just for argument's sake, let's say—"

Long years of experience gave Takizawa a pretty good idea what the other man was thinking. But the scientist tilted his head to one side as if deep in thought, and chose his words carefully. Resisting the impulse to tell the guy to stop sounding so self-important and just spit it out, Takizawa looked up at this scientist, who, fortyish, still seemed to have something of the student about him. Takizawa had never thought of himself as particularly short in stature, yet lately it had occurred to him that no matter who he was talking to, especially if they were younger, he was the one looking up.

"There is a possibility that a chemical was used."

"A chemical," Takizawa repeated.

That much he could understand. The problem was, it was on the belt. The scientist was holding the blackened object up in his tweezers and sniffing it.

"Is it possible to rig something like that up on a belt?"

"That would depend on the type of chemical. But there's nothing on the inside of a belt that would burn like this, and we do have multiple witnesses saying the fire erupted from the victim himself, so it fits the facts."

The same suspicion had occurred to Takizawa straight away; the moment he saw the blackened object held up by Wada, alarm bells had gone off. That was precisely why he had beckoned the scientist over. Yet even if the theory fit the facts, the notion of attaching an ignition device to a belt still seemed incredible.

"People will do the goddamnedest things."

Until now the scientist had looked distinctly out of sorts at being dragged out of bed so early in the morning, but with the discovery of the belt fragment, his attention seemed all at once to quicken. He, too, began searching the floor with care, his eyes darting around.

One investigator had taken a broom and swept up debris around where the belt fragment was found; he was now going through it painstakingly. Suddenly his voice rang out: "Hey, this could be it!"

"Aha," said the scientist, as he picked the item up with his tweezers.

It was about a quarter inch thick, an inch and a half tall, and an inch and three-quarters across—a perfectly ordinary belt buckle, on the surface of it. On closer examination, however, there was a tiny hinge along one side of the buckle. Carefully, the scientist pried the face of the buckle open, and lo and behold, inside there was a digital monitor. It had not burned evenly; of the four corners, only one was severely damaged.

"This means—"

It meant that suicide could be ruled out. One, someone determined enough to immolate himself would not immediately cry out for help. Two, here was evidence of a timed incendiary device. And three, if the point of origin of the fire was not the bench or any other place in the restaurant, but the belt the victim was wearing—assuming that the device had somehow been implanted in his belt—then this was no accident. It was premeditated murder.

"What a convoluted plot," said one investigator.

Takizawa's sentiments exactly. If this was intended as an act of terrorism, maybe you could say there was a kind of logic to it. But this planting of a timer to blow the poor bastard up was . . . Well, it certainly wasn't common. So the question was: Who was this guy? Who were his enemies? Was he some kind of bigwig? And what the hell was he doing at midnight in a family restaurant?

Takizawa stepped away and called the head of the Criminal Affairs Division at the Tachikawa Central Station to let him know the latest development, then returned to the area where the buckle was found; he walked around, muttering. The division head who received Takizawa's report would pass it on to the First Investigation Division of the MPD. Then, instead of the arson squad, a homicide squad would be brought in on the case. If they found a likelihood of murder, a homicide investigation would be set up.

"The next thing we do is hurry up and ID this guy," Takizawa said to himself.

The autopsy would have started at 9:30 A.M. The crime scene investigation would last till noon. Around the time he got back to the station, the results of the autopsy would be getting in.

The homicide investigators from the MPD came scuttling over as soon as word got around, and they went over the site thoroughly; after listening to the opinions of the SRI scientist and the arson investigators, they agreed with the general opinion: This was murder.

"There are definite signs a timed incendiary device was used, and if it was fastened directly to someone's body, that's pretty compelling."

"Its going off here could have been coincidental. For all we know, it might have had an even bigger impact somewhere else."

What kind of person would do this—fasten a device to the victim's belt and burn him up like kindling? What coldhearted monster lurked behind this crime?

The other investigators spoke together in horrified undertones.

"You ever see an MO like this before?"

"I've heard of dousing your victim with gasoline and setting him afire."

"One thing to burn the body after you killed the guy; they burned this guy alive! That's cruel, man. He was fully conscious the whole time."

Takizawa, too, had no experience with a crime the likes of this. He had encountered several cases of self-immolation, when the suicide victims had poured kerosene or gasoline over themselves; each time, staring at the frozen agony of a hideously burned body shriveled into a boxer's stance, he couldn't believe that anyone could do it. But at least there it was self-inflicted.

"Sure is no ordinary murderer," Takizawa mumbled as he raked the rubble, as if tilling a barren field. "Who the hell would do a thing like this? It's beyond belief." He was getting tired, too. His paunch got in the way; he couldn't stay bent over very long. His legs, he realized, were getting numb, and his ass was freezing.

Working beside Takizawa, Wada said quietly, "You know, if the murderer's only intent was to kill the victim, then destroying this restaurant, this whole building, was just a bonus. Nice, huh?"

Wada's getup reminded Takizawa of a clam-digger. But what he said was true—if the dead guy had just happened to stop in here and have the device go off, it would be a cruel trick of fate for everyone else who'd been injured or wiped out by the fire. "Dumb luck," said Takizawa. "Sheer chance, coincidence. Happens all the time."

"That's profound."

"All right, genius, lay off!" Takizawa jabbed Wada with an elbow, and continued his raking.

It was not until early afternoon that they got back to the station. Before that, every cinder around the point of origin of the fire had to be sorted by size. Only when it was all gathered was their survey done. The belt fragment and buckle covered with the tarry substance were turned over to the forensic scientist; determination of the ignition device and detonator would be left to the First Investigation Division.

Detectives who had observed the autopsy returned to the station about the same time. After reviewing the collective eyewitness testimony, all agreed that, while the possibility of accidental death or suicide could not be definitively ruled out, the evidence pointing to murder was persuasive. They were unanimous in recommending the incident be classified a homicide. Even if some doubt remained, it was far better to launch a thorough investigation now rather than to be too sanguine and have the case develop into a major problem later.

At 3:30 P.M., it was resolved to establish a special investigation headquarters at Tachikawa Central Station.

4

At 3:40 P.M., Tachikawa Central Station sent out a fax to the entire MPD jurisdiction. It outlined the case, announced the establishment of a special investigation headquarters, and called for members of a special investigative team. Such a team was always headed by the chief of the Criminal Affairs Division, and so the fax went out in the name of division chief Nagumo.

By 4:30 P.M., the headquarters had set up its operations in a large, well-equipped room. The convening team included, among others, members of the Criminal Affairs Division of Tachikawa Central Station, which would house the headquarters; the MPD Violent Crimes Unit, First Investigative Division; and the MPD Identification Division.

Detectives were mingling in the corridor as Takako arrived for this late-afternoon meeting. As a member of the Third Mobile Investigative Unit in the Criminal Affairs Division, she had been recruited for the special investigation. Her unit, which usually worked with police in the early stages of a case, accompanying them in unmarked patrol cars, followed a system of prolonged split shifts. Officers reported in the afternoon and were on duty for eighteen hours, working straight through the night and going home in the morning to crash in bed, exhausted.

The officers replacing them remained on duty for the next eighteen hours, and so on. Ordinarily, Takako, who had been off the day before, would remain on the job tonight; but once you were put on a homicide investigation, you went to work in the morning and you went home at night. She was glad for this, but the rhythm of her life was going to be interrupted all the same. And she was going to miss those regular days off.

At the door to special investigation headquarters, Takako did as she was asked, which was to write her address and contact numbers on her name card, which read:

"Is it Officer . . . *Ondo?*" the young detective at the desk asked tentatively, looking back and forth between Takako and her name card. The ideographs for Takako's surname were not common, nor was the fact that Takako was a woman.

"It's pronounced Otomichi," Takako said straightforwardly, then turned away to join her five colleagues who had just met up with her. As they walked off, from behind her she heard the young detective say, "Thank you for coming."

"Don't let it bother you," the lieutenant, her supervisor, said to her in a low voice.

Takako glanced toward him and smiled. "I'm used to it."

If she got upset every time she was slighted or stared at for being a woman, she would never succeed as a detective. That was the first thing she learned on transferring from the Traffic Division to the Criminal Affairs Division. Come to think of it, this very same lieutenant, now taking her side, had not shown a whole lot of enthusiasm himself when Takako was placed in his unit last year.

They filed into the large meeting room and sat down. Takako glanced casually around the room. Most people present seemed to be from the MPD, but other than her five colleagues, there was no one she knew.

At 5:00 P.M., the meeting began. There was a brief greeting from Criminal Affairs Division chief Nagumo, who made an appeal for a swift solution to the case. Then Wakita, head of the Tachikawa First Investigative Division, summarized the case, reading from a script:

"As we indicated in the fax that you received, at the site of a fire that broke out early this morning within our precinct, one unidentified male body was found. The upper part of the body exhibits severe burns, some of them fourth-degree; on the lower half of the body the burning is far less extensive."

He cleared his throat.

"The location of the fire was an all-night family restaurant. There were a considerable number of eyewitnesses, and we have obtained multiple testimonies that the victim himself burst directly into flame. Furthermore, the onsite investigation this morning uncovered a piece of belt worn by the victim, along with what appears to be a timer made to look like an ordinary belt buckle. Based on these facts, this case has been declared a homicide in which the victim was killed by thermal trauma inflicted by the trigger of a timed incendiary device. Also, the origin of the fire was in a popular gathering place, and while there were no other deaths, twenty-two people were injured, some seriously. The incident could easily have escalated into a major disaster with enormous impact on society. The killer set out to take a precious human life by cruel and cowardly means, yielding to malicious, selfish urges, and is an enemy of society. This crime can even be construed to be a direct challenge to all of us gathered here as members of the police force."

It was clear, judging from their age and the way they comported themselves, that these men running the show were elite career officials. For Takako, they seemed to be from another world. There was Nagumo, the division head; Chief Wakita, in charge of the actual investigation of the case; Inspector Miyagawa, who had command of the crime site. They all sat atop the hierarchy.

Who wrote this script anyway?

As she listened to Wakita's impassioned speech, Takako entertained brief, sarcastic thoughts in a corner of her mind. She had no desire to antagonize the higher-ups, yet their speechmaking was always the same: easier said than done. And the presence of a meddlesome commanding officer on the site only made it worse; in the end, it was the ones who did the real work who would suffer. All she could do was pray that Miyagawa, who was listening impassively to Wakita go on, would prove smart enough not to get in the way of detectives in the field.

When the top guns finished their speeches, it was time to give the case a name. This name, a virtual signboard and doorplate for the investigation headquarters, would be released to all MPD stations and the media, and would be retained for posterity in police files, so it needed to have a certain cachet.

Still, what a horrific thing to do—fasten a timer to a belt to blow somebody up.

Watching Nagumo sit with arms folded and a severe look on his face—trying to come up with a name for the case?—Takako played with the ballpoint pen in her hand, lightly tapping it against the pages of her notebook. The profile of the perpetrator was elusive. Was he or she a specialist in explosives,

TAKAKO OTOMICHI

OFFICER

THIRD MOBILE INVESTIGATIVE UNIT

CRIMINAL AFFAIRS DIVISION

TOKYO METROPOLITAN POLICE DEPARTMENT

or an ideologue? But either way, a crime of this nature could only be carried out by someone with a fairly high level of education. Someone who was persistent and cautious. Someone precise and determined, not a rough-and-tumble type who flew off the handle.

Thinking about the cruelty of the act sent a cold chill down her spine.

Selfish. Cruel. Takako jotted down thoughts as they occurred to her.

A maniac? A terrorist? No ordinary person would go to such elaborate lengths. What about motive?

At length Nagumo made his decision about the name of the case: "The Tachikawa Timed Combustion Belt Homicide Case." Takako recrossed her legs, tugged down the hem of her skirt, scribbled down the official name and drew a square around it.

"Name's got a real ring to it," deadpanned the older officer next to Takako, leaning toward her.

Takako gave him a sidelong glance, barely lifting an eyebrow. "Yes, much better than 'The Family Restaurant Homicide Case.'"

The man smiled, amused. This led Takako to wonder if he had noticed how nervous she was. His unobtrusive kindness was nice.

But do I look nervous? Enough to make someone take pity on me?

Although she was never aware of giving anything away, her colleagues always claimed that they could tell right off when she was nervous. Well, this time the circumstances of her being in the room were alone enough to make her nervous. It was a tough case, and her abilities were going to be tested. Even the older officer next to her was sitting with a tense expression on his face.

Usually, it was the question "why?"—spoken with head quizzically to one side—that summed up her colleagues' response to her. She was clumsy, unfriendly, incomprehensible. Especially incomprehensible. I don't get it, they would say, why do you care so much about this? Why does something like that bother you? Why are you so gung ho? Why, why, why? Over the past year they had warmed to her, a little, but behind their protests of "I don't get it," she could still hear the unspoken words: "I don't get women." Why did they obsess about it so?

Gung ho? After all this time? Give me a break! I'm not that much of a greenhorn.

Once the name of the case was settled on, headquarters staff were selected. Staff were charged with organizing the materials collected by the investigators, keeping communications flowing, and performing various subordinate tasks. Until the case was solved, it was likely they'd be too swamped with work to go home much.

Five were chosen, including a policewoman from the Tachikawa station, who immediately went into an adjoining room and returned with a large piece of paper on which she had written the name of the case. This policewoman, who was in uniform, was the only other female present.

At the end of this meeting, it was then announced, all members of the investigation would be assigned a partner to work with. Usually, those from the local precinct were teamed with backup from the neighboring precincts, and detectives from the main police office, who were professional investigators, were paired with officers from patrol units. So from this point on, she would be working constantly with a partner—who it might be was a question that loomed large. After all, until the case was solved, they would have to spend the better part of each day in each other's company. In the past, officers paired with her had made a face the moment they realized Takako was female. So naturally Takako felt herself getting even more tense. Already, she was feeling the pricks of stares as she sat there.

It's not the first time you've ever seen a woman, is it? Are your wives all men?

What would they say to that? Would they even know what she was talking about? There was little one could do. These cops were just not used to working with women.

With opening formalities wrapped up, Captain Watanuki, who would conduct the meetings from now on, got up and proceeded to write on the whiteboard the points of the investigation:

VICTIM'S IDENTITY AND ACQUAINTANCES

SUICIDE OR HOMICIDE

ARSON OR ACCIDENTAL FIRE

ONSITE INVESTIGATION

INVESTIGATION OF EVIDENCE FROM SITE

PREVIOUS OFFENDERS WITH SIMILAR MO

MOTIVE

ANALYSIS OF CHEMICAL AND PARTS OF INCENDIARY DEVICE

While Takako was copying the list down, a screen was set up. Through a wireless mike came the gravelly sound of Watanuki's voice: "OK, I'm going to start with a rundown on the case and a damage report, and then I'll move on to the forensic examiner's report and the results of the autopsy."

The lights were dimmed, and a slide was projected onto the screen. First was an outer view of the building destroyed in the fire. Windows in the ground-floor restaurant were shattered, outside walls darkened with soot. The flames had reached as far as the fifth floor of this six-story building.

"It's something of a miracle that in a blaze of this intensity, there were no other deaths besides the intended victim. The reason is that most of the building was occupied by small businesses, and few people were there late at night."

There was a *click*, and the interior of the building showed on screen.

"The victim was found in the seating area of the fire scene."

The empty interior was burned black, and from the force of the water used to extinguish the fire, most of what remained of the chairs and tables lay heaped in a corner.

Click. A close-up of the seat.

"The back of the curved bench on which the victim is believed to have been sitting—but not the seat—was burned far more severely than any other bench in the restaurant. Note where even the stuffing has carbonized."

The slides continued, with more explanation of the main features of the fire.

"The victim's body was found in the approximate center of the seating area, at a considerable distance from the entrance. The eighty or so customers and eight employees who were in the restaurant at the time of the fire made a speedy evacuation. During the rush to exit the building several people were injured, but only one seriously. Putting these facts together, the circumstances in which the body was found disallow any assumption that the victim, an able-bodied male, was so overcome by smoke that he alone failed to escape."

Takako was already familiar with the general conditions of the fire, yet seeing these photographs made it brutally vivid. She peered hard at the screen, determined to commit to memory all she saw.

"Eyewitnesses in the restaurant have testified that the victim burst suddenly into flames, and that he collapsed on the floor after stumbling around crying for help."

After several shots of the restaurant interior, a slide of the victim was projected on the screen, and Takako felt something rise from the pit of her stomach. The slide showed the burned body lying curled on a stretcher, just after it was carried out of the site. Bits of badly burned clothing were glued to the lower half of the body; on the face, which was completely blackened, no expression was discernible.

"As you can see, the victim was covered in second-degree to fourth-degree burns. Observe how the most severe burns occur on the upper torso. No fingerprints or handprints were obtainable, and thus the man's identity remains unknown."

Next came projections of photographs taken at the Forensic Medical Institute prior to autopsy. A dead body stripped of clothing and washed clean was by now a familiar sight to Takako. There was in fact a great difference between a dead body encountered in the course of daily life and one mounted on a stainless steel counter; the latter was a mere object awaiting examination. The screen was filled with an enlarged view of the corpse, the specific details now apparent. It was far less disturbing to Takako than the first on-site photo had been.

"The victim is male. Height determined to be approximately five feet eight inches, weight approximately one hundred thirty-five pounds. As you can see, the body is curled into a classic boxer's stance and burned all over in varying degrees. Again, note how the charring is far more extensive on the head, face, chest, stomach, and back, as well as both arms, than below the waist."

The next slide was an enlargement of the victim's face, which like the entire head was almost completely carbonized, with almost all the hair burned off. The eyes were shut, and out of the half-open mouth protruded an elongated tongue. Virtually nothing of the ears remained. From this photograph, it was impossible to guess what the victim had looked like in life; without seeing the entire body, even the gender would be uncertain.

"Charring is particularly severe in the abdominal area, at the waistline, with significantly less damage below. The feet and legs show heat damage including fluid blisters and erythema of intravital origin. The autopsy found tissue necrosis due to thermocoagulation in the mucous membranes of the upper respiratory tract. From all of this, we can definitively say that the victim was burned alive.

"No oil traces were found in the vicinity of either the body or the bench where the victim was sitting. Nothing was found that could suggest suicide."

Watanuki then repeated what had been in the original communiqué: that a fragment of a belt and belt buckle, presumably worn by the victim, had been retrieved; that it was covered in part with an adhesive, tarry substance; and that the buckle was implanted with a timed incendiary device.

"Given all this, the possibility of suicide or accidental death by fire is infinitesimally small. Accordingly," Watunuki declared, "the case will be treated as a homicide." He then turned to the whiteboard and drew a line through the words SUICIDE OR HOMICIDE and ARSON OR ACCIDENTAL FIRE. "Our first priority is establishing the victim's identity."

Once they knew that, thought Takako, the case might just resolve itself right there. If they had the MO correct, once the investigation turned up someone able to hotwire the belt, the case would be closed. Probably, going down the list of his social connections, they would find someone who sent him a belt as a gift.

Watanuki was going on about the need to gather evidence from articles that had survived the blaze, and saying that a door-to-door survey of the neighborhood would proceed at the same time because information from the public was invaluable. Takako jotted down notes, but it was what he said next that grabbed her attention.

"On the victim's body, fairly recent scars were found on the right thigh and left ankle. These scars were detectable because of the lesser degree of burns on the lower half of the body, and may be key clues to the victim's identity. They appear to be bites made by a fairly large breed of dog."

Nothing about dog bites had been mentioned before.

Bitten twice, and then burned to death.

Poor guy. Talk about lousy luck. Takako mused: Did he think to himself, why me? Or did he maybe think, I reap what I sow?

What kind of man was he to make someone want to light him afire like that? What could he have done to incur that much enmity? What about the dog bites? Were they accidental, or some part of the plot, too? Was it a wild dog? In Tokyo that'd be bizarre.

"After this, we'll announce partners and the tasks each team is assigned. When your name is called, stand up and see who your partner is, and then get moving. Wrap up by 10:00. We'll meet back here again at 11:00. This meeting is adjourned."

The newly designated desk sergeant began to call out names, the room echoing with the sounds of men getting to their feet. It was 6:00 and day had turned to night. Since they were getting this late a start, they weren't likely to come up with much tonight.

"Officer Otomichi, Third Mobile Investigative Unit," the sergeant called out, and Takako stood up. When the next name was called, she found a short, stout, middle-aged man standing and looking at her. His mouth was twisted, as if he were out of sorts. Would he come on hot or cold? He didn't seem the in-between type.

Giving him a tentative smile, Takako made her way to the exit. In the corner of her eye, she saw the short figure heading the same way. In the corridor, she and her partner would meet and confirm their assignment, along with everyone else; then they would all fan out into the night.

"I'm Otomichi," Takako said to him. "Pleased to meet you." She offered him her name card and bowed politely.

He accepted the card without a word and stared at her, unblinking. "You're huge," he finally said.

It was his only comment. The short, heavyset man proceeded to walk ahead of her, a black leather coat thrown over his shoulders.

5

As soon as she got back to her apartment that night, Takako rushed to the john. It was just rounding 1:30 A.M. When the meeting ended, it was already past 12:30. Now she was sleepy and tired, and even colder and hungrier than she'd been the day before—but worse than that, after going so long without peeing, she was putting herself at risk for a bladder infection. Already there were signs.

Just what I need.

When she was twenty-three or so, just getting started as a police officer, Takako had come down with a bladder infection. After that, whenever she got chilled or her resistance was low, the infection would come back. It wasn't worth staying in bed over, and the discomfort was nothing she could complain about out loud; yet if she ignored the prickly, dreary symptoms, they wouldn't go away. She had suffered quite a bit over this. A friend told her of an effective Chinese herbal medicine, and she kept taking it for more than six months until, she thought, she was cured. To have the condition recur at a time like this would be a nightmare.

Be that as it may.

Rubbing her cold lower back, Takako let out a small sigh. What a guy to get stuck with! That old veteran Takizawa seemed to think she was the enemy. After mumbling "You're huge," he managed to go all evening without addressing another word to her. She had given him her name card, but he never bothered to give her his. Typical male behavior in this male-dominant society; rare to find someone so blatant about it, though. Thanks to him, from the time they left headquarters at 6:00 P.M. till they stopped four hours later, she had not been able to say she needed a toilet break. If she came down with a bladder infection now, it was his fault.

Try saying a thing like that. Moth to a flame. That's just what he'd love to hear.

Coming out of the john, Takako stepped right into the tub. As her body warmed, she was able to breathe more deeply, and then she succumbed to a great big yawn. Takizawa had called her "huge," but at five feet five inches she was certainly not a towering figure, not nowadays. Her body shimmered palely in the silken hot water. She ran her palms over her body, from her breasts to her belly, and then grasped her feet by the toes, stretching her legs, saying out loud, "It's because *you're* a shrimp, isn't that it?"

This weariness she felt was due less to the investigation than to mental exhaustion. Tonight, all their poking around in the vicinity of the fire had yielded nothing important; didn't look like anybody else had any success either. What would tomorrow bring? The desk personnel would be sleeping over at headquarters tonight, no doubt, reviewing all the reports and yanking their hair out. Anyway, before things really got hectic, she needed to get a grip on this incipient bladder infection.

I'll be damned if I let that old fart get the better of me.

The short, dumpy Takizawa had to be in his mid-forties. He was just about the same height as she, but when he stood in front of her, she got an eyeful of his thinning hair plastered to the top of his head. He might not be taken with her, but she for her part felt a visceral aversion to types like him.

His skin was rough and oily, his teeth stained yellow with nicotine, and over a bulbous nose, his eyes looked sneaky. He gave off an air of suspicion and an annoying doggedness; you could just tell he was one of those crusty cops who worked his way up the hard way. His style of walking, hurling himself along with his coat open at the front and his paunch sticking out, made him look like an emperor penguin. The short legs only added to the effect. Or maybe he looked more like a seal standing erect? Not, in any case, somebody she would ever want to be caught dead with, if she had the choice.

Why did they pick him for my partner? No way we can be any good together.

Takako did have a policy of doing what she could to establish a bond with the detectives she was teamed with. Sometimes she even allowed herself to form a quasi-romantic attachment. That way, she felt a renewed vigor in her attitude toward work and was able to tolerate the strain more easily. This time, liking the guy was not going to be so simple. Besides, if she tried too hard to act friendly toward him, it would backfire. A man like that was incapable of seeing a woman as anything but not a man. He would never see her as a partner, only as a freak.

I have to make sure I don't let him get anything on me.

Resting her head on the edge of the tub, Takako sighed. Starting tomorrow, she would put on thick long johns and take a disposable pocket warmer with her. Good grief, men and women were made differently, so what was the big deal if a woman took longer in the restroom? And yet she dreaded being told, "That's the trouble with a woman."

She was going to have to come up with some way to communicate with this emperor penguin. Find a way he would accept her as a true partner, not as a woman but as a colleague.

How can I wear him down? His family? A hobby? Don't fawn, but don't come off as stubborn.

What a bore, hammering out a strategy just to get along with a man like that.

If she had to think about men, why did it have to be about one who was burned to a crisp and another who was a little emperor penguin? Why not somebody normal? Yet she couldn't afford the luxury of girlish daydreams. New cases were always cropping up, she couldn't lose her edge. Her friends from junior college seemed to assume that, surrounded by men all day every day as she was, she had her pick of the lot, but she had neither the time nor the inclination for any entanglements. Having once been betrayed by someone she loved, even if Takako did come into daily contact with responsible men with a strong sense of justice who did their jobs faithfully and had firm physiques—very models of masculinity—she was rarely moved by them. Her ex had been the classic athlete type who traded on his charm.

They're all the same under their skin.

The next day, at 9:00 A.M., there was a half-hour meeting, after which everyone took off in teams. For the most part, investigators were continuing to work on learning the victim's identity, or searching for previous offenders with a similar MO, or trying to trace the manufacturer of the explosive device. It fell to Takako and Takizawa—who wore the same scowl on his face, same cigarette dangling from his mouth—to compile the eyewitness reports. Once again, Takizawa started to scurry off by himself; today, in rumpled clothes not changed from yesterday, he seemed soiled, even oilier in appearance; maybe he'd been out drinking last night. He offered no response to Takako's "Good morning."

Bet he was out complaining to his buddies about getting stuck with me.

As she walked alongside him, hurrying her stride to match his pace, Takako completely forgot that the night before, she had spent time trying to figure out how to start a conversation with this man, how to draw him out. He was beyond her; he was someone she could never learn to like.

They were on the way to the two hospitals where restaurant workers and customers injured in the fire were undergoing treatment. Of the twenty-two originally hospitalized, three had been released the previous day. Takizawa and Takako had traveled to interview each of them at home last night. All three had been customers at the restaurant, and because all three lived far from Tachikawa, the pair had been unable to accomplish anything else.

The two hospitals were near the scene of the fire. By noon, Takizawa and Takako had to file an interim report with the desk. At that point, depending on what new information came in from other teams, the investigation might take a new tack, so questioning of the remaining patients needed to be finished this morning; she assumed Takizawa understood the urgency.

But who knows—since he won't say a word to me.

Takizawa, the senior partner of their team, had been proceeding according to his own judgment, and all Takako could do was follow along. She had made up her mind that when he did speak to her—whenever that might be— she would be prepared to give a clear, concise answer. Until then, she would silently go wherever he did.

Six customers—four male and two female—and two male restaurant workers, all with relatively mild injuries, were staying in the first hospital. After introducing themselves to the attending physician, Takizawa and Takako visited each of the six. All said pretty much the same thing:

"What did he look like? I don't know. Just a man."

"By the time I saw him, he was already in flames. All I could think about was trying to escape."

"The first thing I heard was—I think it was a young waitress screaming. I thought, what's going on, and I tried to see. Stuff was beginning to catch fire."

A college student who had broken his arm escaping the fire kept glancing at Takako as he answered Takizawa's questions. "I was in the no-smoking section, you know, way across the room? So I couldn't really tell what the hell was going on. I never thought it would turn into such a big deal—then before I know it, somebody's on fire, jumpin' around, and I'm like, wow! It was like a TV show or somethin', know what I mean?"

Everyone, whatever the level of language used, was of the mind that the fire had indeed erupted from the person of the victim himself. Interestingly, when they spoke of their surprise and terror, all of the witnesses, not just the student, seemed oblivious to the physical pain they themselves had suffered.

"So, yeah, I almost lost it," the student went on. "I mean, it got really wild in there. Pretty soon there's all this screaming, and black smoke coming out of everywhere. It stunk to high heaven, and my eyes were, like, all scratchy."

"Did he say anything, the man who was on fire?" asked Takizawa.

"I already told all this to somebody yesterday."

"Run it by me again, will ya? I'm hearing it for the first time."

"He kept shouting 'I'm on fire! Help!' Over and over. But there was nothing anybody could do."

"'I'm on fire! Help!' Got it. Anything else?"

"Um—he made a sound like a wild animal. A kind of bellow, like *Uaaugh*."

"*Uaaugh*."

"You're writing that down, too?"

"Yep. Now tell me this—how was it you happened to be out getting something to eat at that time of night?"

Takizawa conducted the entire interview by himself, without the least regard for Takako's presence. She took her own notes and stood behind Takizawa, observing the student's demeanor as he talked. It was better if she kept her mouth shut and her eyes open. By standing at a distance and watching, she might pick up something from an expression or a gesture.

When he finished answering Takizawa's questions, the student looked over at Takako. "What about her? Is she a cop, too?"

Takako crinkled her eyes in a smile, but Takizawa didn't turn around. "Yeah, you could say so," he mumbled.

"Wow. A woman cop." The student stared at her with frank fascination.

Then Takizawa closed his notebook loudly and said, "See, it's like this. John Q. Citizen is such an old goat, he won't talk unless it's to a pretty girl."

The student absorbed this absurd explanation with great seriousness. Takizawa, checking the gold watch on his thick, hairy arm, added, "The police department has to offer good customer service."

"That makes sense," the student said.

"Even if she is just an ornament, it's better having her around than not, am I right?"

As they left the hospital, Takizawa again took off at top speed. Takako thought she heard him mutter something under his breath about a "smartass kid," but she didn't ask him to repeat it. He kept up such a fast pace, it was as if he wanted to wear her out.

Ignoring me wasn't enough, now he has to harass me? I know, as far as he's concerned, I'm not even a shadow. I'm an ornament.

Takako was determined to keep pace with Takizawa. Along the cold back streets, the only sound was the echo of their quickened footsteps. This was his turf, he knew all the shortcuts. Of course, he didn't bother to tell her whether they were turning right or left. This stubborn cop would just as soon lose her along the way.

There were still remnants of New Year's in the stores and in front of the prefab apartment buildings. As Takako noticed their shadows on the walls, for some reason her family came suddenly to mind. After her marriage, her parents and younger sisters moved from the overcrowded, older area of Tokyo where they used to live to a new housing development in Saitama Prefecture, where lately Takako had made herself a stranger. That town, that neighborhood, would never feel like home to her.

She and Takizawa went down several alleys and across a trunk road to the second hospital, where among the remaining casualties from the fire, four were being treated for serious injuries. Among them was the part-time waitress who'd taken the victim to his seat. She might well be his last human contact before he died. So it was especially important to see her today. And the other three, too, because they might have been close to the action.

Before knocking on any doors, Takizawa again sought out the attending physician, but the reception they were accorded was much less cordial here than at the previous hospital.

"I cannot have this," said the doctor testily, showing signs of strain. "It was bad enough yesterday with you people demanding answers from casualties who were still in shock."

"Come on, Doc, don't be mad, okay? This is hard on us, too. Please. Let's work together, all right?"

With an ingratiating smile, the likes of which he had never favored Takako with, Takizawa attempted to clap the slender physician—a good four inches taller than him—on the shoulder. But the white-coated physician, who looked to be under thirty, dodged his hand as if it were filthy.

"You people want the answers you want, but our job here is to look after the patients. Now, listen. Of the four patients from the fire in this wing, two are severely burned. If we're not careful, they could go into secondary shock any time."

"Yes, sir, I understand. Secondary shock"

"It could easily be fatal. And Masayo Kizaki, in particular, is suffering great emotional shock."

"I understand. You mean that on top of her emotional shock, she could now go into secondary shock."

"Of course, we'll do everything in our power to keep that from happening. Which is exactly why I cannot have you prowling around at a time like this."

"Absolutely. Of course not. All I need is ten minutes—five—with each person. It'd be really helpful if I could see Kizaki. Please, Doc. She is conscious, isn't she?"

"I'm saying, wait—until—her—condition—stabilizes." The young physician punched his words out.

Takizawa, although he kept his eyes down respectfully and repeated, "I understand," was not about to admit defeat. "Nobody wants to see her go into shock, that'd be terrible," he said. "By all means, Doc, take good care of her. But you gotta understand—we have a job to do, too. We gotta get her statement as soon as we can, so we can go out and nail the guy who did this to her."

Ignoring the young doctor's undisguised scorn, Takizawa looked up at him and plowed right on. Was this insensitivity, Takako wondered, or sheer audacity? "Down the road, there's no telling how crucial Masayo Kizaki's testimony could be. You read the papers, don't you, Doc? That fire was no accident. It was a homicide, and there could have been a lot more victims than one. We won't take long, I promise. Five minutes—ten, tops—that's all I ask. From each of the four under your care."

Takizawa's bearing was mild, and yet he had no intention of backing off, something that the young doctor could see; sourly, he glanced in Takako's direction. She bowed her head reflexively, not averting her eyes. That expression of sour disgust was familiar to her and her colleagues. It was the role of a detective to thrust himself forward insistently, without regard for the convenience of others—even, as now, to make unreasonable demands. No wonder people were always taking offense. In the past, Takako had felt apologetic and embarrassed in situations like this, but now she took it all in stride; everyone had a duty to perform.

"Incidentally, Doc, what would you say were Kizaki's chances of looking normal again? She'll be permanently scarred, will she?"

The answer came stiffly, after a pause. "You mean, assuming she pulls through the shock?"

"Naturally."

Again the pause. "She probably never will regain her former looks."

"That's tough. What about her eyes? Will she be able to see?"

Pause. "With time, she should recover her vision."

In the end, Takizawa succeeded in drawing the doctor out concerning Kizaki's condition and was even granted permission to visit her, "but only for a short time, mind you," as well as the other three patients. Takako mentally tipped her hat to Takizawa for his tenacity, and for the suave smile that was so unlike the self he presented to her. She was inclined to doubt that a woman could have been so successful. At her young age, it would have been impossible to carry off the same degree of pushiness and cheek.

"I can't be in the room with you, but I will see that a nurse is present."

With this parting shot, the aggrieved doctor walked off, his white coat flapping. For whatever reason, of all professionals, doctors were the least in awe of police. They often looked down on them.

"Take the stick outa your ass, ya little bastard," Takizawa muttered under his breath, scowling, as he watched the doctor walk down the corridor. Takako had the feeling that she had just witnessed the skill of a master of subterfuge. And without her knowing, he had also somehow gotten the room numbers of the casualties he wanted to visit. He consulted his notebook, and began to walk down a long corridor that smelled of antiseptic. Takako followed behind.

As Takizawa knocked on the first patient's door, his facial expression softened.

"Hello, sorry to disturb you again at a time like this, but I'd like very much to talk to you for a little while, if that's OK. I'm a detective."

What a terrible disaster that was, he went on, entering the room and ignoring Takako as usual. She remained self-effacingly in the background, now and again smiling at the patient's family members while saying not a word, only watching as Takizawa conducted the interview.

They took statements from the three most seriously injured casualties. By the time they arrived at the room of Masayo Kizaki, it was almost noon. There was a red-lettered sign saying NO VISITORS. "Please promise to do this quickly," said the nurse, evidently under orders from that doctor. She seemed a bit scared as she looked at Takizawa.

Takizawa was sitting in a window seat, jiggling his leg and staring moodily out the window, beyond which lay a dusty landscape. This was the first time he'd been in this ramen shop, which faced a chronically jammed thoroughfare of dump trucks, semi-trailers, and other oversize vehicles. The poor excuse for a sidewalk that led here was so close to the street that when you crossed paths with someone coming from the other direction, you worried the oncoming traffic might slice off a body part. Even though it was noon, the ramen shop was deserted. Takizawa was not surprised.

This beats everything. Of all the lousy luck.

Takizawa's leg-jiggling was a nervous habit that came on when he was upset. He had never noticed it himself until his colleagues pointed it out; now when he found himself jiggling a leg, he made pointed efforts to calm himself down. He wasn't a hothead, not really.

In front of him sat the female detective, expressionless as ever. This tall woman whose neck, arms, and legs were so long and slender looked to be around twenty-seven, maybe twenty-eight—no, make that twenty-eight or twenty-nine. She had small tits and a small face that didn't seem to have on much makeup, but her skin was nice. From Takizawa's point of view she was hardly more than a kid, yet she showed total calm, following him around since yesterday without a peep.

How come it's gotta be me?

When the special investigation headquarters was set up, Takizawa for the first time in a while felt a surge of excitement and energy. He himself had been the first to see the burned body carried out of the fire scene, and the moment he did so, the oddness of the burns made him suspicious. That his powers of observation and his instincts were so dead-on had given him secret delight. But then to be paired with a woman was like having cold water thrown in his face.

"*Tanmen* coming up!" The thin, fortyish man running the place by himself brought each of them a big bowl of hot noodles.

When Takizawa sat down and ordered *tanmen*, noodles in a salty broth topped with stir-fried meat and vegetables, the female detective simply said, "Two, please." After that she said nothing at all, just looked around the place as they waited for their food. Her face wore an extremely unconcerned look. For Takizawa, nothing could have felt more awkward.

Now Otomichi took a pair of wood chopsticks out of the upright container on the table and began to poke at the noodles gently. "Mmm, looks good," she said quietly to herself. She brought some noodles to her lips, blew the steam off vigorously, and ate them with a faint slurping sound. Takizawa reached for his own set of chopsticks, and watched as she ate with her head down over her bowl. There seemed to be a touch of a wave in her hair, which looked fine and soft. Her hand plying the chopsticks was delicate; there was a raised vein on the back of her hand.

And yet she's so inconsiderate! Takes out chopsticks only for herself.

A woman ought to demonstrate a little more consideration for others than that. With scarcely a glance at him, she just went on eating. Was she unaware of what she was doing, or was this a subtle way of busting his balls? Either way, it did nothing to endear her to him. Takizawa's leg jiggled as he poked his chopsticks into his bowl of noodles.

He had his reasons for not talking to her. First off, he didn't trust women. They were flighty. They let their emotions run away with themselves. They lied. They stabbed you in the back. Being a detective required mutual trust and teamwork. There was no way he would ever choose someone like her as his partner on the job.

Second, Takizawa basically did not approve of female detectives. This was a man's work, a man's world. Danger lurked around every corner and the work was demanding. You saw the dark side of the human psyche. Stress built up, the hours were irregular, and the job called for quick decisions and quick action. Anybody who signed up for a job like this had to have the guts and determination to stick it out. This was no job you could take as a temporary expedient.

Besides, women's inferior physical strength and deficient fighting instincts made them ill-suited for the job. If, despite everything, a woman still wanted to be a detective, then she should find something less risky to investigate, like larceny or intellectual crimes. But the woman in front of him was in a patrol unit, of all things. Even granting that society today promotes equal rights for the sexes, what in god's name was the brass thinking? Takizawa was getting more and more pissed off.

Third, women were just a lot of trouble. Things like going to the can. They couldn't go anywhere, like a man could. And when they went home late at night, you worried about them walking dark streets alone. You even had to watch how you talked; you couldn't just say what you wanted to in a free and easy way, like you could with another man. And since she was young to boot, naturally she would end up respecting Takizawa's opinion on everything, relying totally on him. He'd end up feeling like a teacher taking a student on a goddamn field trip. Who needed that?

Fourth—actually, this reason weighed surprisingly heavily on Takizawa— when Takako Otomichi had first appeared in headquarters, a wave of murmurs had gone through the officers around him:

"Since when did we have such a looker on the force?"

"Wouldn't mind having her as a partner a coupla times."

Truth is, Takizawa himself had thought she was an attractive woman, just to look at. That's how much she stood out. If she had a physique that would put a man's to shame, or a face that evoked only grimaces, he didn't know if she would still attract that much attention; but as it was, one look at her and you could see she was a different kind of creature.

"How come I get a desk job now, of all times?" young Wada had lamented, seemingly full of sincere regret. Takizawa had joined in the laughter, never dreaming what his luck of the draw would be. But when he found himself paired with Otomichi, it was no laughing matter. He felt as if every drop of blood had drained from his body.

"That was good," Takako said, finishing up her meal.

As he sat staring vacantly, suddenly her chopsticks entered his field of vision as she laid them across the top of her bowl. Seeing traces of her lipstick on the end of the chopsticks, Takizawa began to feel even more foul. He glanced at her as he brought some noodles to his mouth, and caught her in the act of patting the corners of her mouth with a handkerchief. Her creamy-white cheeks were flushed, and there was a touch of perspiration on her forehead.

Ate too fast, eh?

This is one stubborn female. Takizawa figured maybe it was a point of pride for her not to take longer to eat than him, but again, such behavior was hardly endearing. He deliberately took his time, and paused to slurp the broth. Before he was done, she excused herself, got up, and disappeared into the ladies' room. Watching out of the corner of his eye as she walked by, her legs long and slim, he nearly sighed out loud. This stoicism of hers was hard to take. A girl who burst into tears would be better; at least then you could yell and scold.

A few minutes later, as he was laying his chopsticks down, she came back. Right away she started to slip into her coat.

"What's your hurry? The meeting's not till 1:30," he said gruffly, reaching out for a toothpick. When he phoned in at the set time, right around noon, headquarters had informed him that the victim's identity was now established. A full meeting was scheduled for 1:30. That's how come they had time to sit and have lunch like this.

Expressionless, the female detective sat back down.

Takizawa, cigarette in his mouth, stared her in the face. He was brazenly cool. "I know what you think," he drawled, blowing out cigarette smoke.

"Yes?" said Otomichi, looking directly at him.

"What you think deep down."

"And what would that be?"

"That if it wasn't for you, Masayo Kizaki wouldn't have talked." Jiggling his leg, Takizawa looked hard at her with his eyes narrowed.

A little flushed, Otomichi scarcely reacted, apart from a tiny frown. After a moment she spoke slowly: "I'm glad I could help." Her voice was restrained and unemotional. "It's true that we needed to get her story today if at all possible, and since it worked out that we did, it seems like a good outcome to me."

The girl named Masayo Kizaki, whom the doctor had been so reluctant to let them interview, had demonstrated abnormal fear about everything in her environment, due perhaps to damaged eyesight. Takizawa had spoken to her gently enough, he thought, but the girl screamed and kept saying she was scared.

"I had nothing to do with it! Why do the police keep coming back to me over and over again! I didn't do anything! All I did was try to bring him his order!"

She was trembling, a sign of shock. Takizawa did not want the girl to panic, so he stepped back; if she went into secondary shock, she'd be no use and the police would be held accountable. That was when Otomichi stepped forward and grasped Kizaki's hand, which quieted the girl down immediately.

"It's all right, you're all right now. There's nothing to be scared of. You're safe here, and your injuries are going to heal in no time." Otomichi had spoken slowly and calmly, as if to impress the words on her listener. Bending down by the bed, she ran her fingers lightly over Kizaki's bandaged arm and said things like: "It must have been terrifying," and "You must have been in such terrible pain." A few minutes later, little by little Kizaki began to tell Otomichi her story. Sounding like a little sister relying on her big sister for support.

"Well, if all you did was walk behind me, I guess you'd be stealing your pay, wouldn't you?" Takizawa said, his leg jiggling. He averted his gaze from Otomichi as he spoke.

She said nothing.

"You're not here for decoration. You gotta pull your weight."

Still nothing.

"Well, here's hoping from now on we run into nothing but women and children who are afraid of men, and guys who dig chicks."

Takizawa was astonished at the harshness of his own words. Yet Otomichi's eyes never flickered. Wishing she would cry or sulk or something, Takizawa got up with a clatter. Leaving Otomichi behind as she paid the bill, he strode outside where a dusty wind was blowing, and started walking without a glance back. She was just a chit of a girl and yet she was a lot more collected than he was. That was really galling.

The longer you go on bein' a cop, honeybun, the more you're gonna have to put up with this shit. Why don't you go get married or something, have a kid.

The next thing he knew, from behind him came the sound of her footsteps following him at the same tempo he was walking. Feeling for some reason a desire to escape, he walked on toward the station as if being driven by a whip. Having to think about all this on top of the murder investigation was enough to wear a guy out.

TWO

1

On the thin sheet of paper, the image was of a man standing, leaning slightly to one side, a smile playing on his lips. A stray lock of hair on his forehead, a gaze of invincible cool. He was staring straight into the camera, in perfect control. His slanting eyes and too-thin eyebrows were rather effeminate; had he been ten years younger, he might have passed for a second- or third-rate teen idol. His smile conveyed the sense that he was fully aware of his attractiveness, took pleasure in his looks. But this man would never smile again. His body was now a shriveled, black crisp, split open from cranium to belly, and stored in the city morgue. As yet no relatives had come forward to claim his remains.

"He went by the name Takuma Sugawara, which is an alias. Real name is Teruo Hara. Age 34, not 30. When he was 20, he committed assault with intent to commit bodily harm, but punishment was deferred and he was released on probation."

It was 8:00 P.M., the setting was special investigation headquarters, and the voice of the chief investigator, Captain Watanuki, filled the room.

Two days had passed since the noon hour when Takako sat across from Takizawa eating ramen. This night meeting had been called to bring everyone up to speed. Exhausted and half-frozen, Takako had dragged herself to the station at 7:00 to spend the hour sitting next to Takizawa as he wrote up the day's report without a thought or a peep from her. While struggling with the drowsiness that threatened to engulf her as she warmed up, Takako retraced the last couple day's activities in her mind, trying to connect any dots she might have missed. But the only picture that popped up in her mind was the hateful sight of her partner's backside.

Takizawa still had made no effort to adjust to her presence. Again today, while continuing to interview the witnesses in the hospital, he had ignored her, as if she were thin air. Perhaps, like an artisan in the old days, he meant that she had to learn by watching and copying his techniques—although by now she found it impossible to believe that anything he did was out of solicitude. He never once asked her opinion, and no matter whom he was interviewing, he would thrust himself forward and shove her to the side. If she said anything to him, he scowled in annoyance. Now, back at headquarters, by rights she, as the junior member of the team, should be writing the report while he went off and had a cup of coffee; yet here he was grumpily twisting his head left and right as he appropriated the task for himself.

I'd think whoever reads it would be happier reading my *writing—that's unless the reader is a numskull who thinks you can't trust anything a woman wrote.*

As long as her partner maintained this attitude, Takako found herself putting a negative spin on everything. Although there was precious little fruit of their labor to report, Takizawa pressed down heavily with his ballpoint pen, writing in an oddly square ideographic style developed no doubt from years of presenting written evidence—a cover for lack of results, she thought sarcastically. She gazed at Takizawa, bent over his desk with the posture of a bad student cramming for an exam. Deep down, men like him, who made such an issue of their masculinity, were just a bunch of chicken-livered fools, with all the heart of a flea. That was Takako's humble opinion, arrived at after staring day and night at the rear end of this emperor penguin.

And that wasn't all: she couldn't imagine he was any good in bed.

I bet he goes through the motions, managed to knock his wife up a time or three. God, I wonder what she *looks like.*

Unless she focused on inane thoughts like these, Takako was liable to let out a huge yawn at any moment. But just then the meeting that would end their long day began, and all thought of sleep was instantly swept aside. A photograph of the victim was passed out.

"The photograph you have in your hands was shown to Sadako Kitayama, a person of interest in the case, yesterday, and she confirmed that it was Takuma Sugawara beyond a doubt."

Two days before, when someone had contacted investigation headquarters saying she had an idea who the victim might be, and the name Takuma Sugawara first surfaced, everyone expected the hunt for the killer to take on new life. By the end of the day, the photograph of Sugawara had been obtained, and yesterday morning an in-depth probe of his background and situation was ready to be launched. What held things up was the discovery that Sugawara was not his actual name.

"Kitayama had no knowledge of the name Teruo Hara. She claims she had no idea he was using an alias, but didn't seem surprised to hear about it. All she said when confronted with that information was, 'I see.'"

Sadako Kitayama was a forty-four-year-old housewife who had arranged to meet Sugawara at the restaurant on the night of the fire. She had managed to avoid the conflagration by arriving a half hour late, but when the next day came and went without word from him, she grew worried and on a hunch went to the police. She insisted that the victim was a "mere acquaintance," and that all she really knew about him was his cellphone number. Why didn't she check on him right away? Why wait till two days after the fire to report him missing? What was there to hesitate about? Her answer was, "We didn't have a close relationship."

"She's meeting a younger guy at that time of night. What for, if not to fuck him?" whispered a detective.

The comment was met with muffled laughter. Takako thought the detective was probably right, but she pretended not to hear. Suppose she turned around to express her agreement, what then? They would only stiffen with awkwardness and clam up. After all she'd been through, words like "fuck" were hardly enough to throw her off balance, but male detectives had a tendency to worry about her tender sensibility.

"Our person of interest also said she never knew that the one means of contact she had with Sugawara, his cellphone, was actually registered in the name of another woman."

Because of the extensive damage to the corpse, Kitayama was not asked to identify the body. Instead, she was asked to describe the man she was supposed to meet, noting any distinctive physical characteristics. Kitayama testified that she believed Sugawara had two gold lower left molars, and she added that about ten days earlier, he had been bitten on the leg by a stray dog. These descriptions matched the body in the morgue. Nothing about either the bite marks on the victim's thigh and ankle or about the false teeth had been released to the media. And so it was concluded that the man whom

Kitayama was to meet that night was in fact the victim. Thanks to her testimony, the previously nameless corpse was identified as Takuma Sugawara, age around thirty, employed as manager of a model agency.

Yes, it all fits.

Staring at the photograph of the victim when he was alive, Takako surmised that he was just the kind of person to set up a rendezvous in an all-night restaurant with a frustrated housewife dreaming of an amorous fling. He had the looks, for one thing. And if he was juggling two names like that, and carrying around the old charge of assault with intent, he probably was up to no good. But what had he done to get himself killed in such a bizarre and cruel way?

Watanuki continued his report: "Sugawara, or rather Hara, came from Shioya-gun, in Tochigi Prefecture, a little mountain village near the Fukushima border. His parents and a married older brother still reside there. They are farmers who do forestry work on the side. Police in Shioya-gun report that Teruo Hara ran away from home at age sixteen; he never returned or bothered to contact his parents. That might explain why no family member has come forward to claim the body."

That Takuma Sugawara was the alias for Teruo Hara was discovered in this way: Sugawara's cellphone number, obtained from Sadako Kitayama, was found to belong not to Sugawara but to a woman owner of a bar. Said bar owner confirmed that Takuma Sugawara was a friend who was borrowing her phone. Since she had gone so far as to lend him her cellphone (naturally, she was questioned about the terms of her friendship), she had apparently known Sugawara rather well, perhaps more intimately than did Sadako Kitayama. The bar owner provided Sugawara's home phone number. That number was registered in Sugawara's name, and it also yielded his home address.

The lease for the apartment at this address was made out in the name of Takuma Sugawara, but through the woman who had signed the lease as his guarantor—a manager of a beauty salon with several branches—the name Teruo Hara came to light. His certificate of ward residence also turned up the name Teruo Hara, at the same time revealing his place of birth.

"Hara lived about an eight-minute walk from the JR Kunitachi station. His apartment was expensive, with a monthly rent of ¥260,000. He lived alone, and judging from the furnishings and décor, he maintained a rather extravagant lifestyle. The apartment, however, gave no clues as to his life history or his private life; in that way, it was like a hotel room. There was no date book, no photos, or anything of the kind. No driver's license, no passport, no health insurance card."

Even getting this one photograph of him had not been easy. After questioning, a woman who had had dealings with him found a photo of the two of them together—her image was cropped to maintain her privacy. But there was nothing else to go on.

People, in the course of going about normal life, left traces of their lives behind wherever they went—a daily flow of rubbish that could be used as clues to the life they lived. But the search of the victim's apartment failed to produce any clues to his identity, leading one to think that either he had reason to be careful about leaving such information lying around, or he had a hideout somewhere else.

Hearing all this, Takako felt a pang of jealousy; while the team tracking down the victim's identity had been running around and discovering all these details, she and Takizawa had been mired in taking down statements from injured witnesses. But fruitless effort was part of every investigation. Even if you finally came across a loose end in the big ball of yarn that constituted a case, and tugged on it for all you were worth, it hardly ever led anywhere. In order to reel in the one thread they were after, the investigators had to unravel numberless threads to no avail.

". . . and when the photograph of Hara was shown to residents of his apartment building, barely one or two could make a positive identification. Further, the building has electronic security at its entrance, so there is no superintendent who could speak about his comings and goings."

After running away from home at sixteen, why had Teruo Hara changed his name, and what sort of life had he led thereafter? How could he afford to live in an apartment costing ¥260,000 in rent? What kind of man was he that he was surrounded by so many different women?

You really had something going for yourself, didn't you? I bet a whole bunch of people had it in for you.

That night, as soon as she got home, Takako flopped down on her bed and lay there, face down, without thinking. Her legs felt heavy, and her toes throbbed with pain. Her lower back ached. This morning before setting out, she had stuck a disposable pocket warmer under her clothes to fend off the cold, so she shouldn't have gotten chilled; still, it felt as if her pelvis were out of joint. They had walked around all day long, so it was only natural—and yet at such times Takako couldn't help thinking ruefully how she was growing older. She could tell she didn't have the resilience she'd had in her twenties. Back then, even if she came home tired, she would never have fallen into her bed right away like this. As the years wore on, it would only get harder to maintain her stamina. What a gloomy thought.

It's partly mental, too, that's for sure. Who wouldn't be a wreck after spending all day with that guy?

She felt so tired it was like her body was made of cotton; and yet as she relaxed a bit, thoughts of the victim, Hara, whom she had spent all day thinking about, to the point of exhaustion, began gnawing at her again.

Stupid man. Who would give you a belt booby-trapped like that?

Takako turned over, emitting a sound that was somewhere between a cough and a sigh, almost a groan; lying on her back, she looked up at the ceiling. Once again the muscles in her shoulders all the way down to her loins were taut, like a drum. She worried that one big yawn might send her back muscles into a cramp.

Was it a woman? I bet a woman gave it to you.

He seemed like a man used to receiving gifts. The owner of his cellphone, for starters, plus the guarantor for his apartment and the person he went to meet on the day of his death—older women, all of them. That isn't entirely normal.

What had until today been only a pathetic, charred victim now had a name and, thanks to the photograph, a face, and the secrets of that man's life were now starting to be laid bare. Whether he wanted them to be or not. The investigation would pool all the team efforts together, and he would be stripped naked, his hidden life revealed. How strange it was, she thought. The first time she learned his name, his life was already over. And from now on, however familiar she might become with the minutiae of his life, she could never come in actual contact with him.

Imagine spending all this time thinking so hard about a dead man!

It was a wretched business. It would be different if she were consumed with worry on his behalf, but the man was a charred crisp. Mentally she addressed him: "I've got to get serious and find out who did this to you— because until I do, I'm stuck with that awful old man."

Takizawa was maddening. He hardly ever opened his mouth unless it was to be snide. It was always "Bully for you" or "Thanks for caring"; he had no idea how to treat a person decently. If he'd only let her have even one happy memory of being his partner, she would be satisfied, and her opinion of him would soar; but he was too short-sighted, or just too set in his ways, to think of such a thing. He was an ass, a tight ass, that's what he was.

There's a man for you. What did I expect?

Sighing, she pulled herself out of bed. The suit she had on didn't need cleaning yet. Then she spoke the words out loud: "It's for your sake, Teruo Hara, that I stay well groomed and walk around with that penguin!" How many women friends Hara may have had, there was no telling; but it made her feel funny to think that she, more than any of them, would probably come closest to understanding his true self.

It was not until Takako was about to turn off the lights that she noted the blinking light on her answering machine. In her exhaustion she'd forgotten to check.

"Hello, Takako?" It was a familiar voice. "This is your mother. New Year's came and went without any word from you, so I got worried. Why don't you come home to visit us once in a while? Your father and Koko would love to see you, and Tomoko is . . . well, call me back, all right? I'll tell you about it then. Anyway, how are things? Are you OK? I know you won't listen to me, but you're not doing anything dangerous, are you? You know, really, I just wish that when you first said you wanted to be a policewoman I had put my foot down, because lately I—"

The tape ran out while she was still talking. Her mother's messages were always like this, but she never called back to finish what she'd been saying. Her mother no doubt found it frustrating, too, but for Takako, listening to such half-finished messages was unsettling, like a bout of indigestion. That was her mother's way.

Takako arranged a cushion at the foot of the bed to prop up her legs. This was the best way to get rid of the heaviness and swelling in her feet. What could be going on with her youngest sister, she wondered. She and Tomoko, who was five years her junior, had always gotten along well.

Call home. I have to remember to call home.

When Takako first suggested becoming a policewoman to her family, her mother opposed the idea violently. It was quite common for members of the family to work as civil servants or in the medical or teaching profession; that's what almost all of them did. Apart from the stability of such careers, it was part of the tradition of not overtly chasing after profit, not living for monetary gain. Takako's father was a government employee, and her parents had met at work.

From the time she was a little girl, Takako had assumed that she, too, would be a civil servant one day; only later did she make up her mind to become a policewoman. Not because she had it in for bad guys, or because she wanted to fight for justice. Nothing like that. Rather, she liked the idea of doing something with her aikido, which she had taken up as a way of steeling herself against asthma; in addition, the uniform appealed to her. Sitting all day at a desk didn't. If she could, she wanted to be active, lead a life filled with variety. Such had been her motivation in the beginning.

When Takako graduated from junior college and entered the police training academy, her mother was half hysterical in opposition, standing beside her as she packed to move to the dormitory and weeping bitterly. Her father had no problem with her decision. Although for all she knew, he may have thought that as long as she was a civil servant, anything would do.

Women who sought to become policewomen generally were strong-willed and had a mean streak, Takako soon discovered. Even though the academy was an all-female environment, it was worlds away from the peaceful, fun-filled, and easygoing atmosphere of junior college. These women lacked a shred of any kind of fellowship. Beneath the protective armor of a strong sense of justice or mission, they were startlingly feminine. They traded on an integrity rooted in a deep inferiority; they put on high-minded airs that were filled with vulgarity and greed; they used filthy words without the least embarrassment. Full of swagger and self-consciousness, they acted with the conviction that they alone were right. They were a jealous bunch of bullies. What on earth made them want to enter the police force, Takako wondered. During her six months in the dormitory, it was made abundantly clear to Takako, more times than she could count, that the enemy was not the opposite sex; it was her own gender.

What kept Takako going, besides her own stubbornness, was the merciful presence of a few inspiring friends and seniors. One in particular had continually displayed qualities of single-minded purpose, seriousness, and purity, teaching Takako by example that it was possible to be a first-rate policewoman without ceasing to be ladylike. If not for her, Takako would probably have given up long ago.

On graduating from the police academy, she was transferred to a new dormitory near the police station where she was assigned. After further training, she had gone out on patrol in a squad car, as a member of the Traffic Division. While other young women her age were continuing their studies, or dressing in pastel suits and learning to apply natural makeup, Takako was starting out at the bottom of a rigidly disciplinarian and hierarchical world.

"So now you're a cop! Actually, it kind of suits you."

That's what her junior college friends would say, with a mischievous smile, when they got together. And then they would reveal how they used to be surprised by her obstinacy, or how inflexible they always thought she was. Aghast to hear this, and saddened to discover the gap between them—after all this time, they were still like fluttering butterflies—Takako was at the same time reassured that her becoming a policewoman was not a mistake. As a fledgling, dewy-eyed officer, she was full of ideals; she was on fire with a sense of mission, determined to uphold the law—even if that meant being somewhat inflexible—and to maintain social order.

But as she patrolled the streets in her Traffic Division vehicle, certain things that she had been blind to as an ordinary citizen now became clear. She discovered that simply riding in a black-and-white car, and wearing her uniform, caused men's attitudes toward her to undergo a drastic change. They would either assume a very low profile, or come right out and tell her that since so-and-so in such-and-such a division was a pal of theirs, she'd better back off. Or when she preparing to have a car towed, they'd protest that they were just trying to make a living, sister, and what was the big deal.

Really, it took all kinds. Back when she was enforcing no-parking laws, she experienced all sorts of horrors that she could laugh about now. True, her senior officers had often been spiteful; one had been the perfect picture of an ogress. Yet overall, her first experience on the police force had been enjoyable. She and her like-minded colleagues would get together and talk about the pitiful cases they came across each day, always finding something to laugh about. They had talked about the normal things that interest young women, too: which male officer was especially good-looking and whom he was going out with, or which spinster officer was having an affair with a younger patrolman. Even if they wore police uniforms, inside they were scarcely different from your average young O.L., what they called "office ladies."

We were embarrassingly, scandalously young.

When she thought of her life since then, it seemed like police work had controlled her destiny. From the time she followed the recommendation of her boss and put in an innocent request to join the women's motorcycle corps, her life started to change. Right away, while commuting to the training center in Asaka for motorcycle lessons, she met her future husband, who was also working in the Traffic Division. Her prospects were rosy; of this she had no doubt. Those were days when she'd been her most audacious, exultant, confident, positive. She'd been utterly carefree; scoldings from her superiors rolled off her back.

The women's motorcycle corps had been part of a campaign to soften the image of the MPD. Rather than law enforcement, their work consisted of ornamental tasks like providing a motorcycle escort for marathons and public events; they were sent strictly to safe environments where, as women, they would stand out. Even so, in the beginning it seemed festive and exciting. Takako got calls from friends who'd seen her in a telecast of the marathon; once she was written up in a magazine. Even if former colleagues from her days as a patrol officer looked on her with jealousy, and male officers treated her like a fifth wheel, still she felt on top of the world. Love had made her strong and bold.

After a while, as her relationship with her then-boyfriend settled into permanency and she could turn her mind to other things, a pleasant sort of boredom had crept over her. The idea of staying on as a figurehead member of the motorcycle corps held no magic. The work lacked excitement. She needed more challenge.

"Everybody says you're doing great," her boyfriend tried comforting her. "Your motorcycle skills are getting up there, too. Why don't you enter a tournament? You're good enough to join the top ranks."

But while she stayed in her rut, he was gaining valuable experience as a member of a mobile riot squad. She might be wearing a uniform like him, but she could not share his experiences; one might think they were walking side by side, but in the end she would be left behind.

Takako felt a growing impatience. Wanting to test her abilities, she requested a transfer to the Criminal Affairs Division. She'd made the request lightly, not expecting it would go through quickly, if at all—but surprise surpise, she was assigned to the larceny investigation section and ended up undergoing training to become a detective.

Takako could still remember the look of astonishment on her ex's face. "You mean you're gonna be a dick?" he said. Then, with a resigned laugh, he added, "Imagine, a wife who's a dick." That, in effect, had been his proposal of marriage. And so, when she was twenty-six and he was twenty-eight, they had wed.

After her marriage, Takako had begun assisting at crime-scene investigations, and she learned to make the rounds of pawnshops looking for stolen goods. In the beginning it seemed like a game; there was fresh stimulation in her work, but more than anything else she felt free and alive. When she came back to their newlywed home after work, those times when they could eat dinner together, she would chatter incessantly about the events of her day. But after a while, from around the time she began to work in the detention rooms of police headquarters, the situation changed. When she was put in charge of guarding the women's cells, for the first time she came into direct contact with actual criminals, encountering women of all ages and backgrounds.

Why would someone like this do a thing like this? Day after day, she asked herself this same question. Some of the women were openly hostile to her, others spoke to her with a trace of something like a fond memory. Thing was, they struck Takako as rather like herself. They were separated only by a trick of fate—and yet there was a great, unyielding difference: the difference between the captive and the captor. Takako did not speak about these women to her husband. Not because of her professional duty to preserve confidentiality, but rather because as a fellow woman, to do that seemed thoroughly inappropriate.

In time she was assigned to the homicide section, where her thinking was forced to undergo yet another dizzying change. Now she found herself in an all-male society which no longer treated her with distant politeness but stood rudely in her way. There were six female police officers in the entire Criminal Affairs Division, but they did not band together for mutual support; differences in the work they were assigned, as well as in their ages and personalities, contributed to an atmosphere which, as had been the case at the police academy, kept them from becoming best friends. Besides, among the roughly 1,200 investigators in police headquarters, a mere handful of women would have been virtually powerless.

Day after day, surrounded by men, Takako ran around performing unfamiliar tasks, studying how to write reports, and learning the ropes of actual investigation, all the while being told things like, "Get out my way, will you?" At home, before she knew it, she and her husband were spending less and less time together. Without realizing that the hours he was keeping were odd, she put up with bald-faced lies. Finally the day came when it hit her:

I'm being played for a fool.

If she had listened to her mother and become a nursery school teacher, or something feminine like that, what would her life have been like? Would that have been any guarantee of happiness? By now, she'd probably be the mother of at least one child, but would she be satisfied passing the time schmoozing with the other mothers? She would never have learned to ride a motorcycle or to fire a gun; she would never have gotten so tired she was ready to pass out; she would never have had to worry about bladder infections or spend so much time staring at the ugly butt of human nature. Without somebody like the emperor penguin snapping at her, she might have gone on secure in her belief that men were protectors of women. It might have been a fine life. Better than this one, definitely. Peaceful, laid-back, carefree. But there was no turning back now. Besides, when had she ever wanted a life like that?

Takako craved stimulation. And in her current position in the homicide section, it had become a thing with her to expose the truth about people.

Hate the sin but not the sinner. She had no intention of making any such noble declaration—and yet it was true that hatred for perfect strangers was far from easy to sustain. Hatred took energy. With case after case always cropping up, and a ceaseless flow of offenders passing through, it was impossible to go on feeling such callow emotion. There simply wasn't time.

Gotta call home. Tell them I'm fine, nothing to worry about, all that stuff.

A phone call she could manage, but for now there was no way she could get time off for a visit home. No need to tell her mother that. She wouldn't complain to her, wouldn't discuss her work. That, she was sure, set her mother's teeth on edge. And yet, judging from that message, something was going on with her little sister, in which case her mother's anxieties would not be focused just on Takako. That would actually be a relief. Anyway, must call home. *Call home . . . call home . . .* Repeating the words to herself, Takako drifted off. As if her body were being dragged into a marsh, her consciousness sank into blackness.

2

Takuma Sugawara. Born Teruo Hara, 28 March 1961. Father, Motoharu; mother, Hideyo; both living. A brother seven years older has succeeded to the family business, and a sister five years older is married and living in Kori-yama. After graduating from the local middle school, Teruo went to the prefectural high school but dropped out after one year. Thereafter he repeatedly ran away from home but was brought back each time until, at the age of sixteen, he disappeared and never returned. Four years later, at the age of twenty, he was caught in the act of assault with intent to commit bodily harm; under questioning, he revealed that after running away from home he had gone to Tokyo, moving frequently from place to place, living in Ueno, Kinshicho, and other parts of town before getting work in a discotheque in Roppongi and settling into that area. To the authorities, he didn't seem like a thug, and as he had no prior convictions, he was let off with a warning. His activities since that time are not clear. His most recent occupation is yet to be established.

Investigation headquarters put top priority on discovering Teruo Hara's last known occupation and his social contacts. Examination of the timed ignition device would of course proceed simultaneously, focusing both on chemical agents and on parts used in its construction. Although the lab was working overtime to identify the chemical agents, full analysis was expected to take more than a week; moreover, as the mechanical parts were all widely available, there seemed little chance of tracking down a suspect based merely on the physical evidence. The MO was perplexing—no investigator could recall a similar method of killing, and the police computer databank drew a blank as well. In other words, the profile of the suspect was extremely hazy. The only recourse was to flush out the killer from the victim's surroundings. Only by hitting the pavement—walking and walking and walking around town—could they hope to find a clue that might break the case open.

Takizawa and Takako revisited the witnesses they had interviewed and showed them Hara's photograph. The response was uniform: never seen him before. Masayo Kizaki, the severely burned young woman, was the only witness who remembered what the victim had looked like; unfortunately, she still had not recovered full vision.

With no knowledge of Hara's employment or his sphere of activity, it was difficult to proceed. Other investigative teams concentrated on the women in Hara's life and his social contacts from the Roppongi disco. Still, days were going by without any light being shed on his recent activities.

Takizawa and Takako next checked with other tenants of the building that had housed the restaurant. There was a superintendent's office, but as it happened, the fire had occurred not long after the previous superintendent quit, so the super on duty knew little.

"You know, I do have a feeling I've seen this guy somewhere."

"Where? Try to remember."

The man Takizawa was talking to, the owner of a beauty salon just above the burned-out restaurant, stood with his arms folded, looking stumped. "I can tell you one thing, absolutely," he said, rubbing his cheek with one hand. "He wasn't one of our customers. If he was, I *know* I'd remember."

"You mean, you have male customers, too?"

"Well, of course we do, silly. No offense, Officer, but you must be a real old-timer to even ask such a thing."

The beauty salon was not the only business forced to suspend operations because of the fire. There had been an English conversation school and a photography studio on the second floor. On the third floor, there was a dental clinic, a health appliance store, an astrologer, and an acupuncture and moxibustion clinic; on the fourth, the office of a sporting goods store, an accounting firm, an architectural firm, and one office the nature of whose business was unclear from the name alone. On the fifth and sixth floors was more of the same—another architectural office, a massage parlor, an event-planning firm, an interior designer, and a fortune-teller.

Damage from the fire was concentrated on, besides the restaurant, the second, third, and fourth floors, and more narrowly on the fifth and sixth. But essentially, with the basement garage burned out as well, the entire building had been rendered useless and would have to be torn down. This was the verdict of the beauty salon owner Takizawa and Takako were now sounding out.

The beauty salon owner had come to the shop by to see what he could salvage from the fire. The acrid smell of smoke was still strong. Looking at the photo in Takizawa's hand, he asked, "Is that the guy who did it? . . . Oh, he's the one who burned to death. What a terrible thing." And that was when, after a moment, he said the guy looked familiar.

"I don't know where I've seen him," he went on. "I have to say, it's quite chilling to hear he's dead. All in all, I think it would be better if he was a stranger, don't you? I mean, if it turned out he was someone I knew even a little, I couldn't be this offhanded about the whole thing, could I?"

Once the man started talking, he rattled on, perhaps a habit ingrained from his line of work. If she were interviewing him alone, thought Takako, she would cut the pleasantries short, ask him point-blank what she wanted to know, and then move on. She had no use for men who were so blatantly shallow and glib, real chatterboxes. He seemed the type who had no real information to offer but was full of curiosity, eager just to keep the conversation going.

"You suffered a lot of damage here, didn't you?"

"Oh, did we ever. I'm scouting around for a new place now, but who knows how much it's going to end up costing me. I had a really, really nice setup here, but now I'll be right back in the hole."

Too bad, but what about the face in the photograph? Takako had to bite her tongue to keep from butting in. If he remembered, he remembered; if he didn't, he didn't. She just couldn't bear the way he kept going on. Now he was starting on about the early days when he was a live-in employee.

After spending the better part of a half hour in conversation, Takizawa finally lifted a hand. "Well, if anything comes up we may be back to ask your help, but in the meantime, you hang in there."

The guy looked deflated, apparently not yet done talking, but he nodded and said, "Mm-hmm."

Every little gesture of his struck Takako as effeminate.

He and the penguin would make a great couple.

No one was in the remaining stores and offices, all the way to the top floor. The elevator out of use, Takako and Takizawa trudged up and down the stairs, knocking on doors. Nearly half the places had notices posted giving contact information, an address and phone number. Undoubtedly, they were all out hustling for new quarters. Her hands numb with cold, Takako copied down every bit of the information. As she did so, Takizawa stood aside smoking a cigarette, not bothering to open his notebook; he must think this is women's work.

Sure, sure, I'll do it all. God knows if you wrote it down we wouldn't be able to read it later anyway.

The building was draped in white plastic sheeting on the outside, like a construction site; inside, the passageways were freezing cold, and sunlight filtering through the white sheeting created the effect of bright snow. On the upper floors the wind was stronger, and the sounds from the sheeting as it bellied out or pressed in toward them were eerie. Takizawa finished his cigarette and tossed the butt to the floor. Such insensitivity made Takako cringe. She loathed people who carelessly threw trash alongside a road—and this was worse: it was the scene of a fatal fire, for heaven's sake!

As they came back down the frigid stairs to the second floor, suddenly a shrill voice sounded behind them: "Oh, there you are! Officer!" The beauty salon owner was waving a long, thin arm at them.

Takako looked reflexively at Takizawa, who greeted the guy like an old friend. "What's up?"

Takako sighed and tagged along.

"You know, I just happened to remember where I saw the gentleman in your photograph. I'm *so* glad you're still here."

Was this guy gay or what? He laid a hand on Takizawa's arm and smiled at him in a creepy way. His smile had the coyness of a young girl—it was not at all becoming. But of all the people she had seen Takizawa interview so far, no one else had shown this much eagerness to talk to him.

What appalling taste.

The beauty salon owner glanced toward Takako, tilting his head a trace and smiling. She steadily returned his gaze, unable to bring herself to smile back. Even if he came out and said, "Ooh, a scary policewoman!" she did not care.

"A customer once was telling me about how, on one of the upper floors of this building, there's a . . . what do you call it? You know, a date club."

"A date club?"

Takizawa's face was turned away from Takako. From his tone of voice, however, the term meant little to him.

"The kind of place where they set up a date for you with high school girls. They say the girls make good money. Well, the elevator in this building was always chock-full of people. High school girls in middy-blouse uniforms, mostly. We always used to see them when we were going home at the end of the day, so at first I thought there must be a cram school on the upper floors."

On the guy's large, sinewy middle finger there was a silver band. He waved his hand in the air as he went on excitedly. "Then, I heard it was a *date* club, of all things. Well, you could've knocked me over with a feather. I mean, from the outside, you can't tell at all. Anyway, in my shop, whenever a customer leaves, I always accompany her to the elevator to see her off. So there we are by the elevator talking, this customer and me, when the doors open and there he is! My customer does a double take. 'It's him,' she whispers. Then she turns to me and lifts her eyebrows—like this."

His hollowed cheeks slightly flushed, spraying spittle from between too-large teeth, the hairdresser lifted his eyebrows in high arch. Then pausing, he cooed, "Could I possibly trouble you for a cigarette, Officer?"

No doubt about it—the guy was queer as they came. Takizawa offered the guy a cigarette, lit it for him, and urged him on: "So then what happened?"

"At first I didn't have the *foggiest* notion what she was trying to tell me. I just thought, hmm, such a good-looking man! So she walks into the elevator, greets him nonchalantly with something like, 'Oh, hello, you're the owner of the date club.' The gentleman *ran* the place!"

The beauty salon owner pursed his thin lips and blew out a cloud of cigarette smoke. Then he gazed into the distance theatrically, as if trying to re-envision the event. "That man . . . Officer, could I take another peek at the photograph, please?"

Takizawa obligingly showed him the photo again. Frowning, the guy studied it intently.

"Yes, I *thought* it might be him. I had a feeling at the time that I'd like to see him again or, you know, meet him, should I say, but I never did. You see, in our profession, the working day starts surprisingly early, and we hardly get out much. But he was *awfully* good-looking. I do remember him quite well, after all." Besides, he added with a touch of pride, it was part of his job to remember people's faces. "And if it turns out he *is* the one, you should be able to verify it with the building maintenance company."

Another investigative team had already checked with the maintenance company. They'd had the photo, and the real name to go with it, so if Hara, or Sugawara, had been a tenant, there would have been an ID. Yet Takizawa responded as if impressed, "Ah, the building maintenance company!" Takako could not tell if he was serious or simply going out of his way to be nice to the guy.

"You know where it's located, Officer? Out in Hachioji. But you know, I have to tell you—this is the first time in my life I have ever met a real live police detective. All I can say is, I didn't know that in real life there actually were such people! It's like a TV drama. Police officers are so *masculine.*"

The guy kept chattering on happily. Takako said nothing, thinking that after having to listen to him prattle on, she could only hope that his recollection was on the money, whether by coincidence or by miracle.

When they were finally free of the beauty salon owner and left the building, the winter sunshine was dazzling. Takizawa lit up another cigarette and, addressing Takako for once, muttered, "The building maintenance company in Hachioji. Might as well go there next, ya think? All the tenants have scattered to the four winds anyway."

Takako hesitated, surprised to be spoken to, wondering whether this called for a response.

He shot her a glance. "OK?" he asked.

"Umm, OK. Shall we go to the maintenance company now, then?"

Takizawa took the cigarette from his mouth with an indecipherable grunt. "Look, you," he said, "however we do it is OK by me, but would you please smarten up a little?"

"I beg your pardon?"

Takizawa skewed his face into a scowl. "You want to stand behind me all the time, fine, whatever, but I've had it up to here with you on your high horse, giving people dirty looks."

Instantly, Takako felt her face flush bright red. She was about to speak, but Takizawa cut her off.

"I'm not telling you to make nice just because you're a woman, but on the other hand, why not turn it around, make it work for you, huh? Would it kill you to give out a smile now and then? What's the point in acting like such a goddamn sourpuss around a well-meaning citizen? Who are you to be so condescending, anyway? It interferes with the work. Or have you got something against his type? Maybe you don't care about what his kind has to say, is that it?"

"No, that's not true."

"Oh yeah? Well, good. I figured maybe a young lady like yourself couldn't bear the thought of being around queers."

"You're wrong."

"Or else that you had a stick up your ass. You made up your mind nobody was going to look down their nose at you for being a woman." Takizawa narrowed his eyes, smiling out of a corner of his mouth. His eyes had a reptilian look that made her skin crawl.

"That's not true either."

"Good. Yours truly doesn't have to worry about the sensitivities of a little princess then."

Takako drew in her chin and bit her lip, staring at Takizawa. She could feel the color draining from her face. The hand gripping the strap of her shoulder bag clenched into a fist.

"Now we've got that settled, let me ask you one favor."

Takako smothered the impulse to turn away. At the same moment, she understood what it might be like to be interrogated by this man with his cunning gaze trained steadily on you.

"Yes?" she said.

"Could you keep your mind on the job? Walking around all day with nothing to show for it comes with the territory. If you think it's boring or stupid, then quit."

With that, Takizawa strode off. Takako chased after him, feeling her heart pound a drumbeat in her ears. Her hands and feet were shaking, and it was not from the cold. Takizawa had acted completely oblivious to her—she never dreamed he would say such a thing to her.

You old fart. How dare you?

As she walked to the station, Takako felt her blood begin to boil. Adrenaline coursed through her. She hadn't felt fury like this in a long time. From the core of her being rose stinging, wordless retorts. Struggling with the urge to shout herself hoarse, let out all she'd been feeling, Takako followed Takizawa through the wicket, showing her badge to the monitor to get in.

As they stood alongside each other on the platform, Takizawa glanced at Takako. She gazed unwaveringly back at him, waves of emotion roiling in her.

"What?" he said, looking at her expectantly.

She said nothing.

Takizawa's face, slack-skinned and reddish-brown—whether from suntan or booze, who could say—bore a cold smile: "If you have a complaint, now's the time."

You bastard. What is it with you and that look you give everybody? You're a fine one to talk. Besides, when did I ever complain about my job? Don't I spend all my time tagging along after you without a word? If it wasn't part of my job, do you think I'd ever get within ten feet of your sorry ass?

"I apologize."

On the crowded platform, Takako lowered her head in a profound bow. Just then the train came sliding into the station, riffling the hem of her coat. She kept her head down long enough to get a good look at Takizawa's grubby shoes. Then there was the sound of the train doors opening, and Takizawa's shoes began to move. Finally Takako lifted her head and followed after him, muttering under her breath as she entered the heated car: *But not because of anything you said.*

Certainly there was room for reflection on her part. But right now, she wanted to savor the sensation bubbling up inside her. It felt familiar and good. She felt unaccountably happy.

To act aggressive and wild without thought of consequences, and yet to be honest and alive, crackling with energy—not so long ago Takako had experienced that kind of excitement often, whether at work, out on her motorcycle, or at home. But when her emotions burst out from deep within, it could sometimes lead to trouble. The flare-up was like a sudden storm, stirring up arguments and inflicting pain.

That's how I used to be.

When for the first time in her life she had experienced an internal storm of jealousy, that most intractable of emotions, she'd been dismayed; unable to control the storm, exhausted by the effort, she forced herself to lock the jealousy and rage away. Until then, no one had ever told her she was "incomprehensible." Inept, maybe; but only after her divorce did people began saying she was grumpy and incomprehensible.

"I hope you got the address of the maintenance company," said Takizawa all of a sudden.

Takako quickly turned and nodded at the face beside her, eye to eye. Takizawa looked as if he would have liked to say more; but then, blinking several times, he turned his cold, reptilian eyes away and faced forward again.

Maybe I should thank you. For making me remember what it's like to feel this way.

Now that she had regained her edge, she did not want to lose it again. She knew better than to let her feelings show like a child; but between this emotional swirl and a heart that was cold and quiescent there was all the difference in the world.

Newly defiant, Takako sat swaying with the motion of the train. One of these days she would knock the wind out of this man's sails. Or if not, she would dearly love to take out her frustration on whoever was behind this crime.

3

That afternoon, there was a break in the case. The gay beauty salon owner's memory proved accurate.

Tenant records in the building maintenance company's office contained neither the name Takuma Sugawara nor the name Teruo Hara. Even when shown the photograph, the office worker didn't recognize him. Disappointed that beauty salon owner had been mistaken, Takizawa was just about to leave when there was a telephone call from the one tenant yet to phone in since the fire.

Apparently this is what the caller said: "I've left everything for Sugawara-san to take care of." The office worker, surprised, said, "Sugawara?" And Takizawa's ears perked up.

"The office is sublet, so I didn't want to say anything," said the woman on the phone when Takizawa grabbed the receiver. She ran a bar in Kyushu, but she associated with the victim when she lived in Tokyo, she explained, and she sublet the office space to him when she moved away. The office space was originally rented out as a model agency, and Sugawara had declared the setup "perfect" for his purposes. After taking down the woman's particulars, Takizawa faxed the victim's photo to the police station in Kyushu nearest to the woman; the upshot was that, as expected, Sugawara was positively identified.

Although it was on the fourth-floor, the office he sublet had sustained no damage in the fire, and so Takizawa and Takako had not entered its premises. But Takizawa remembered the door. It bore a mysterious hand-lettered sign that read only CHERRY BOOM-BOOM. He had wondered what kind of business it was, but it made sense now: Sadako Kitayama, the woman who was going to meet the victim at the restaurant, had said he managed a model agency. Takizawa hastily contacted investigation headquarters and instructed them to prepare an application for a search warrant and submit it to a judge.

When the investigating team walked through the door of Cherry Boom-Boom, what they encountered first was a wall covered with black paper. At the top, written in large gold letters, was this: ALL BONA FIDE HIGH SCHOOL GIRLS! WE WILL BE YOUR DATES!—with a pink heart dancing at either end. Beneath the banner, about an inch and a half apart from each other, were some eighty snapshots of girls, each with a number in the lower right-hand corner. Some had large hearts drawn around them, inscribed with NUMBER ONE FOR DECEMBER and the like. This might have been no different from any whorehouse or massage parlor except for the fact that, in every case, the smiling face in the photo belonged to a girl in a high school uniform. Below each picture were notations describing the girl, like SECOND-YEAR STUDENT AT A MUNICIPAL H.S. or FIRST-YEAR STUDENT AT A PRIVATE H.S. Some of the girls appeared so young they had to be in middle school.

In response to Takizawa's call, investigators and a crime-scene unit had been dispatched from headquarters, and the group stood fixated by this wall of pictures. Takizawa searched involuntarily for the face of his younger daughter. It seemed impossible she could be there—and yet every photo showed a young girl more or less like his daughter, innocent, not tough, not brazen or showy. Had her picture been on the wall among the others, it would not have seemed out of place in the slightest.

The employee from the building maintenance office who had opened the door for them was deathly white—not just from the cold, thought Takizawa—and he kept repeating bumbling explanations: "If the previous superintendent was still around, he might have been able to answer your questions, but he got sick around two months ago and quit. . . . We only ask that tenants pay their rent promptly each month. . . . Actually, subletting is a breach of contract. . . ."

After listening to the employee, Takizawa glanced at Otomichi and signaled with a jerk of his chin, then proceeded right into the office. Behind him he heard Otomichi say to the employee, "Please wait right here." She was a girl, but not so dumb after all. Before, when he came down on her harshly, she didn't cry or wail or talk back like he thought she would; she had apologized politely immediately. Maybe, even though she looked soft, she was a tougher adversary than some bungling greenhorn.

The office of Cherry Boom-Boom had a short hallway extending straight from the entrance with two doors on the left, one on the right, and another straight ahead. The first of the doors on the left had a carved wooden sign that read WC; it was exactly the sort of cute thing that appealed to young girls. The second door was fixed open, with a short curtain of plastic streamers in the doorway. What would be the combination kitchen–dining room if this were an apartment, had been converted to office space: there was a small refrigerator next to the built-in sink and on the counter were packages of instant noodles, instant coffee, and an electric kettle; but instead of cupboards and a kitchen table, there were a desk, filing cabinets, and a telephone. The investigators would concentrate their search here.

The other two doors both led into a large room that had originally been two rooms, the dividing wall removed. Apart from a pink wall-to-wall carpet and a low white table with cushions scattered around it, here the only furnishings were some boxy shelves. Takizawa's eye took in a tall stack of magazines, bags of sweets, boxes of tissue, and a CD player. A sweet, vaguely fruity or flowery scent filled the air. So, Takizawa surmised, the room must have been sealed shut since before the night of the fire; if the door been opened even once, the smell of smoke and soot would have gotten in here. The flames had come up as far as the moxibustion clinic one floor down, and the architectural design firm next door; yet this room smelled like it could have been filled with young girls only minutes ago. This was probably where they spent their after-school hours, waiting for some dimwit with a thing for young girls to choose their photo from the lineup.

So basically this was the next thing to a brothel. Get a thumbs-up or thumb through your homework while you wait your turn.

Takizawa walked around the room, picking things up and examining them. He flipped through magazines of the sort his daughter probably read. He felt sick. What a hell of a world.

Once Takizawa stepped out of this room, the building maintenance employee, who'd been waiting as instructed by Otomichi, rushed up to him.

There was a look of agitation on his face. "Um, if you like, I could leave the key with you. I really have to get back to my other work."

From the time they first met him, this guy had acted anxious; now he looked like a nervous wreck. He might be the timid type, but his reaction, for a member of the general public, was probably normal. Police investigators were no grim reapers, but neither were they lady luck.

Eventually, one of the other detectives took him back to the station. There was a good chance that the victim's occupation had run afoul of the Anti-Prostitution Law. That might have nothing to do with the case at hand, but if the maintenance company had knowingly leased space for that purpose, they would have to answer for it.

Several hours later, the detectives left, taking with them stacks of photographs of young girls, a list of customers, and a pile of receipts, as well as a large cache of what seemed to be personal possessions of the victim. Teruo Hara had stored his important papers here, not in the luxury apartment he was renting. His bankbook, passport, and other documents—things feared to have been burned on him in the fire—were all found in the safe.

On the way out of the building, Takizawa exchanged comments with another detective as they descended the stairs.

"I'm getting the idea this guy was a real nut case."

"Enough to justify a murder like that?"

"That's the thing. It doesn't seem like the kind of thing a female would do."

As they walked along, shooting the breeze, Takizawa was struck by the realization that he hadn't had such easy conversation in a while. Come to think of it, when he and Otomichi walked along she never said a peep; no wonder he felt this way. He twisted his neck around casually, looking for her, and a little ways behind them there she was, descending the stairs with her head bent down.

"So what's it like having a woman for a partner, eh?" Following the line of Takizawa's gaze, the detective leered and dug him in the ribs. While bristling at this treatment, Takizawa put on a game face and said, "Don't even ask."

"That much fun, huh?"

As the officer yukked it up, Takizawa smiled with as much irony as he could muster and shrugged his shoulders in a deliberately exaggerated way. No point in speaking too frankly and having his remarks get back to the ears of the wrong person.

"Why, it's so much fun it brings tears to my eyes."

After Takizawa delivered this pithy remark, his companion snickered with amusement. Who the hell gave him the right to laugh, thought Takizawa; he doesn't know anything about her. But Takizawa went right on smiling sardonically.

Based on the material they had retrieved from the office of the date club, the investigation now branched out in new directions. First, investigators had to pin down exactly what Cherry Boom-Boom was all about. Every girl involved with the operation, and every customer, would have to be tracked down and interviewed. Had Hara run the establishment by himself, or did he have assistants and staff? Had he had financial disagreements with any of the girls or any of the patrons? Had there been any simmering jealousies or resentments? Where had he learned the nuts and bolts of operating a date club to begin with? Hara had been renting the space for some eighteen months, it was learned; what had he done before that? Who knew anything about his private life?

With the new load of evidence, detectives scattered in all directions. One team was assigned to find out whom Hara had made payments to from his bank account, and who had deposited money into his account. Takizawa and Otomichi, along with several other teams, continued to interview the tenants of the building. The beauty salon owner's testimony had led to a huge break in the case, which was all the more reason why they needed to hear what the other tenants might have to say. It was essential to cover the same ground more than once.

"He put those girls to work and then sat back and raked in all the profits. What a low-life." Takizawa said his thoughts aloud as usual, and then, with a sideways glance at Otomichi, caught himself. Damn.

She was beside him again, being her usual glum self. Perhaps she had felt the weight of his eyes; in any case, without a change of expression, she replied flatly, "Yes, that's right."

The woman did not have a shred of likeability. She was straightforward, which was fine, and intelligent, which he appreciated; but he found her presence stifling. Still, unable to think of any pretext for lodging a protest, he walked along in silence.

They were able to interview people from the English conversation school located on the second floor alongside the beauty salon, and from the photography studio next door to it, with little difficulty. But none of them recognized the victim from his photograph, and none knew anything about the date club on the fourth floor. The language school personnel were furiously searching for a new location, yet were efficient and willing enough to comply calmly with the investigation. The photography studio, in contrast, was run not by a company but by an individual, who was beside himself at the loss of expensive photographic equipment. He appeared at the entrance of his swanky condo, on which he no doubt still owed a lot, looking worn-out, and had this to say:

"I mean, just think about it. I busted my butt from the time I was a kid, and finally opened that studio. After all I went through, then to have it go up in smoke, literally . . . I'm sorry for the guy who died, but I sure wish he hadn't been in that particular restaurant at that particular time, you know what I mean?"

"What about insurance? You didn't have any?"

"I did. Of course I did. But who knows if they'll reimburse me for everything, and even then, it's sure to take time. In the meanwhile I'm going to have to shut down the business. This is pretty devastating."

He was angry about the fire. But on learning that it was neither the fault of the restaurant, nor arson, but the byproduct of a murder, he seemed unsure who should bear the brunt of his anger.

Takizawa made himself listen attentively to the photographer's story, but found himself getting more tired than usual. Murder investigations and fire investigations were known quantities, but this case fell into a category all its own. Besides, the thought that the dead guy was far from an upstanding citizen made the suffering of the others much more unfortunate.

On hearing that the acupuncturist on the third floor could not be reached, Takizawa, eager to hear testimony from someone who wasn't in such a bad way, said to Otomichi, "What places didn't get burned?"

"On the third floor, only the astrologer's place. Also the accounting firm and the sporting goods sales office, both on the fourth floor. The floors above that are mostly intact. The closest one from here would be—"

"The astrologer. Let's start there."

"All right."

"That oughta be right up your alley. Women go in for that kinda thing."

He knew this sounded inane, but it was the best he could manage. If he ever softened up on her she'd take advantage of him, start walking all over him. Women were like that. Anyway, before you could talk to someone, you had to be interested in them.

Yeah, right. What about this female could ever interest him?

There was one thing he might be able to work up a little interest in, but what was he gonna do, ask her about the men she'd slept with? With another guy he could joke around about it, but with her it could turn into an unmitigated disaster. Still, if she was his partner, she was an important factor in the equation; he wanted to talk things over with her—to the extent necessary—but when everything he said got no reaction out of her, he couldn't help adding a few barbs.

"How about if you do the talking this time?"

"Is that all right with you?"

"Suits me fine. I have a thing about fake fortune-tellers. Kinda like you do about queers."

"Well, let me see how he reacts to us, and then I'll decide. If it seems like I would be better suited to handle him, then I'll take over."

Now she was being weirdly cautious. Of course, there were times when a woman *was* better suited to ask the questions. There were people like that patient with the bad eyes, the one who couldn't deal with men. But work was work—you couldn't pick and choose. About the only time he was glad to have a woman partner for work like this was late at night, when visiting a woman who lived alone.

If only we were interviewing those harebrained high school girls.

Takizawa was curious to know what girls his daughter's age could be thinking, what reason they could have for working at a date club. If they had been assigned to investigate that angle, it might have been a strain, but Otomichi might have done herself proud.

"Date clubs, huh."

As they walked along, the words slipped out of Takizawa's mouth. Quickly he glanced over at Otomichi, but seeing that she showed no reaction, he clammed up, feeling slightly irked. It made him mad that she would ignore him, without so much as a "Pardon me, did you say something?" Anyway, today was as good a time as any to lay down the law to his younger daughter: Don't be an idiot, don't do anything you'll only live to regret.

4

Teruo Hara did not have a bad reputation. Regardless of how he made his living, there was no sign he had connections to *yakuza* or ran up huge debts. His relations with women were complicated, but the women he was involved with had nothing worse to say about him than "I turned all my money over to him." No one seemed to bear him any particular grudge. Surprisingly, he had been saving money regularly, and he had taken out a life insurance policy with his mother as beneficiary; he seldom used his credit card, and had apparently been a reliable guy despite appearances to the contrary.

"He got women to shell out all the money he needed, so sure, his earnings could go into savings, or whatever," one investigator said. "No decent man would run a date club."

True, thought Takako, very true, and yet this seemed like a kind of prejudice, plain and simple. Not that she was anyone to talk. She'd been prejudiced against the gay hairdresser from the start.

The date club's books were balanced, there were no reports of disturbances, and neither the girls nor the clients had anything bad to say about Hara. In fact, detectives were surprised to learn the girls had affectionately nicknamed him Taku, short for Takuma. More than a few of the girls—not just a handful—testified that they were able to tell Taku things they couldn't tell their parents or teachers, and that he listened and gave them helpful advice.

The girls had learned about the date club by word of mouth, and they came to him by themselves. Once they joined the club, he would lend them cellphones for free. The cellphones were for the purpose of contacting the girls when they had been selected by a client; but the girls were free to use them as they liked, and could give out the number to whomever they pleased. Many of the girls had joined up just so they could get a free cellphone, and had been further tempted by the chance to make easy money on the side.

"Some of them were earning more than their old man."

That night, after the meeting was over, several detectives had stayed behind at headquarters, and this bull session just seemed to evolve. They put together a simple meal, had a few drinks. It would have been easy enough to go out somewhere, but the case was not a topic that could be discussed openly and conversation would be constrained. It was more relaxing to hang around headquarters, kick back, have a few, unwind. Four days had passed since Takako and Takizawa pinned down Hara's office.

"What the girls did after the date was up to them. If they let the client fool around with them a little, they could make a bundle."

"What I don't get is, here you got a guy who's taking advantage of them, preying on them, right? Why would they trust him so much? Why would they go to him with their problems?"

"Maybe because he had so little connection with their ordinary lives. Maybe that made it easier. Even a son-of-a-bitch can be like an older brother."

After tapping each other's drinks in plastic cups, the detectives had started to express their opinions. Gradually the victim's profile was beginning to emerge, but there was nothing that tied in with his murder. It was the business of the date club that really got to them.

"They were kids! The guy was involved in prostitution since he was a teenager, if you ask me. He made his living off women. These girls sound precocious, worldly and all, playing around with men, but this Hara guy was a pro. Him getting these high school girls to do his bidding was child's play. Don't you see that?"

Teruo Hara became Takuma Sugawara when he started working at discos as a *kurofuku*—literally, "black suit"—serving as watchman or scout, keeping track of clientele and girls. In that line of work, going from one joint to another until he was twenty-two, twenty-three, he was never hard-up for women. Then he quit the disco life and went to work in a host club; at twenty-seven he persuaded an older woman to finance a small place of his own. That was back in the days when the whole country was caught up in the bubble economy, so things went swimmingly for a while, but after a year and a half he was bankrupt. Then he went back to the host club business, working as a pimp on the side. At thirty-one he started a "telephone club," a place where guys sat around waiting for women and girls to call up and chat and, maybe, get together; but that went under as well. And then, eighteen months ago, he opened the date club in Tachikawa.

Looking at his life overall, there was no sign of any male friends. Rather, once one female entered his life, other females just materialized. That had been the pattern, investigators found; in fact, since the break in the case, a team of detectives had been doing nothing but going around talking to women of all ages and occupations who had known Hara.

"High school girls aren't the only stupid females here. Look at that Sadako Kitayama. And one of the women I talked to was fifty-four; her husband is the director of a hospital!"

"Yeah, or look at that mama-san of the bar in Kyushu, the one who sublet him the apartment—she must be pushing sixty."

* * *

As their drinks began to take effect, the detectives forgot about Takako's presence among them. She had no intention of taking offense at a phrase like "stupid females," so she let the remark pass unchallenged. It was true—some females *were* stupid.

"He must have been really something with the ladies."

"You can say that again. I don't know about the high school kids, but to seduce those old bags, he'd have had to—"

As the detective was tipsily going on, his eyes met Takako's and he stopped mid-sentence. He was a guy in his forties, someone she knew only by sight; but seeing her, he clammed up, embarrassed. Takako couldn't very well say "Go right ahead, don't mind me." Nor at her age could she pretend she didn't know what they were talking about. Takako did her best to look casual.

"Uh-oh. Keep it clean, guys, keep it clean," somebody stepped into the breach to make amends. For a while there was an uneasy silence. Takako was never sure how to react in these situations. From the corner of her eye she could see Takizawa, grinning at her with his reptilian eyes.

"Well, I figure," someone else spoke up, "one way or another he musta made plenty of enemies among the women, but if ya ask me, no woman is gonna use a trick like that to get rid of him."

Agreeing, Takako nodded slightly, and was finally able to look away.

Actually, I bet a man like Hara didn't *make enemies among women all that much. He met them smoothly, gave them pleasure, and then left them smoothly.*

Otherwise, how could he have lived like such a Don Juan? There was probably good reason why the high school girls liked him so much.

"Otomichi, you ready for another drink?" A young detective had come up to her holding a large bottle of saké. He filled her plastic cup without waiting for an answer and gave her a genial smile, then continued on his way. She followed him with her eyes as he went around the room offering saké to the group of men, bending down before the veteran members of the force to refill their cups.

"Anybody want some soy sauce?" asked another young detective. "It's right here." This guy had to be about Takako's age. His sleeves were rolled up, exposing his hairy arms, his tie tucked between the buttons of his shirt; he was waiting on the others with ease and skill.

A world where women aren't needed.

When she first transferred to this division, Takako had felt self-conscious at times like this, wondering if she was expected to go around waiting on everyone, serving tea, pouring drinks. But when she did, she found the men either became uncomfortable or, as they got drunker, started treating her like a bar hostess. Anyway, these guys were surprisingly good at throwing a meal together and serving drinks. Years of working in an environment without women had probably made it necessary. The sight of these men waiting on each other so capably and affably was charming. And so after a time, she had made it her policy to sit tight on such occasions and do nothing.

As the night wore on and the drinks flowed more freely, the men began raking through memories of old cases.

"Right, right, that old investigator could cut through the shit like nobody else."

"That's what I heard too. Even among the pros, he was head and shoulders above the rest."

"But apparently his instincts weren't like they used to be when he was in his prime. He was always calling for more data."

Takako found these tales fascinating. But no one ever bothered to explain the details to her. She was still a relative newcomer to homicide, and with her limited experience, much of what they said went right over her head. Then the conversation came back round to the current case.

"The killer's got brains, though, that's for sure. Who would come up with the idea of a timed ignition trigger? He's got to be some kind of a professional or crazy geek."

"What about a political activist?"

"Why would a political activist want to kill a pimp?"

As the conversation rolled along, Takako looked around, and her eyes fell on Takizawa, sitting almost directly across the table from her, among officers he was evidently on good terms with. Looking stumpier than ever, her partner was talking enthusiastically with the guy next to him. Takizawa looked relaxed and friendly, a side of himself he never showed her.

"He's gotta be used to handling chemicals, for one thing."

"The lab results are due in any time now, eh?"

"Once we know what he used, it should be easy to figure out how he got hold of it."

How would they do that? Takako wondered. She would probably have opportunity to find out, but in the city of Tokyo, or in the surrounding prefectures, how many ways might there be of obtaining such chemicals? That was the conversation on her left; on her right, a vigorous discussion of motive was underway. She waited for a chance to join in.

"If it was a crime of vengeance, they picked a hell of a way to get back at the guy. A woman couldn't do it."

"Don't be too sure. As long as you had the know-how, it wouldn't take much physical strength to pull it off."

"But do you think it's in a woman's nature to pick an MO like that? Something that elaborate?"

Everybody was wrapped up in the case. Since they were running a race with no end in sight, they appreciated each other's company and support. Takako, who never once had talked the case over with another investigator, felt the same way. She had her own thoughts about it, but no one to share them with.

Not even my own partner.

Feeling downcast, she took a drink from her plastic cup, which, now that she thought about, looked like the kind used for urine samples. The situation was absurd. She wanted to yell across the room at Takizawa.

How come you won't talk to me? How come you're so nice to other people and not to me? What don't you like about me? Why are you always trying to pick a fight? Is that how you see me—some kind of shadow or mascot trailing after you?

What if I'd said, "Oh, how could you!" that time, and burst into tears—would that have made you happy? Would it have pleased you to think, Yup, that's a woman for you? Don't you think you should try to train your partner, whether male or female? Or do you think your attitude is going to make me a better cop?

The more she thought about it, the more rage she felt. Good, let it burn, let it grow! She wallowed in dark thoughts. But her rage was not aimed solely at Takizawa. It was aimed at everyone here—at the whole police department—at men.

Suddenly Takizawa's grating voice cut through her gloom: "Don't be an idiot. Ever since the headquarters was set up, I—" But the room was getting noisier as the party progressed, she lost track of what he was saying mid-sentence, and he wasn't even talking about her in the first place. She came to the conclusion that it was time to find the right moment for her exit.

"Want some more?" said a voice at her elbow, breaking through her reverie. Takako turned to see another young detective about her age holding a bottle of saké. She'd seen him around, but didn't know his name. As he concentrated on filling her empty cup, upending the bottle, he said, "Takizawa is a great guy, isn't he? He looks out for you, and although you wouldn't know it to look at him, he's really pretty sensitive."

Takako was stunned—unable to muster the ghost of a smile. She didn't say a word.

Sure, you people may think he's a great guy. Male bonding. One big happy family. How nice.

"Of course, he is kind of bashful. With a woman as his partner, maybe he's a little harder to approach."

"Bashful?" Takako stared at the young detective with unfeigned surprise. You call that bashful, she was about to say—but swallowed her words. These men were trained to read people's thoughts. He was studying her observantly, trying to size her up.

"Am I wrong?"

Just as she thought. As the young detective looked at her dubiously, Takako forced a smile and tilted her head to one side. "Do you know Sergeant Takizawa well?"

"We used to be teamed up."

"Too bad you weren't matched up again this time."

"Yeah, actually I kind of hoped we would be."

That would have suited me fine too. Who in hell decided to make him my partner?

"He taught me a lot. I really owe him."

Well, bully for you.

"When we had time off together, he used to take me fishing."

Takizawa a fisherman? Who knew a man like him had any hobbies? Takako nodded slowly, trying to show interest as this fellow spoke warmly of Takizawa. How happy Takizawa seemed when they went fishing together, the different places they had gone, the kinds of fish they had caught. To Takako it was all a bore. She hated fishing. With all her working hours spent fishing for suspects in the murky waters of the city, she had no desire to spend her days off doing any kind of fishing.

"Taki was a lot thinner back then, and he had a lot more hair. Now that I think about it, he looks older."

It's more of a surprise to me to think he was ever young. I don't know, though—no matter how thin he was and how much hair he had on his head, his personality was the same, I bet. Rotten.

Her conversation partner, who hadn't bothered to introduce himself but who obviously knew who she was, drew a long breath. "Well, in the end—maybe Taki didn't want to have me for a partner."

"Why do you say that? You were fishing buddies."

The young detective seemed to hesitate, unsure whether to continue.

"You mean . . . it would bring up some memories?" She looked probingly at the young detective.

His gaze wavered indecisively. She sighed a little, deliberately. This was bait. The man muttered, "You could say so." Drunk fish were so easy to catch.

"Sure, it would bring up memories. Back then his wife was still living with him, and I was single, so I went over to their place all the time and she made me things to eat."

Faintly flushed, eyes a little glazed, he said this half-nostalgically. He was off his guard. It took little effort for Takako to act casual. Mustn't let the fish know he's been hooked. Fully conscious of Takizawa, although he was now out of her line of sight, she murmured, "Ah yes, his wife."

"I kind of took it personally, in a way. Sometimes I think it could happen to me—anytime my own wife might up and leave."

"Not as easily as that, surely."

"You never know. Taki's wife was a good woman. Not the kind in a million years who would take a lover and leave the family."

For a second she felt her chest constrict. The young detective swallowed the last of the saké in his cup and got up and went to look for more. Takako watched him go off and then glanced around to see if their conversation might have been overheard by anyone. Takizawa was off at a distance, engrossed in conversation.

His plastic cup filled, the young detective came back her way, passed her, and joined in a group of detectives deep in discussion, having forgotten he was in the middle of a conversation with her. After all, fresh drink, fresh people to talk to. Now was Takako's chance. She stood up without calling attention to herself, swiftly picked up her things, and said goodbye to the few she encountered on her way out. There was still time, barely, to make the last train.

Well, so that's it. That's what happens to a man whose wife leaves him.

Riding on the crowded train home, Takako's thoughts kept turning in the same direction. She felt she had finally begun to understand the reason for Takizawa's rigidity and hostility.

Well, who wouldn't leave a man like him? He probably never gave his family a thought, except to throw his weight around. Until now she had thought of his unseen wife with contempt, but now she felt like applauding her. Way to go. Take that, you loser. She wanted to feel that way, but her mind was cold and numb. She felt herself sliding into depression.

I wish I'd never asked.

It wasn't like she was dying to find out about his private life. Who cared what he did? Baloney. No way were they two of a kind. She *chose* to divorce her husband, of her own free will. His wife put an end to a bad situation. That was what she thought, and yet her spirits sank lower and lower.

I'm not a loser. I didn't get dumped.

She hadn't been able to take the jealousy. The husband she trusted and the woman who'd been an acquaintance of hers—one several notches below her, nobody she'd paid any real attention to: when she found out they were seeing each other, she tried to tell herself to stay calm, give him some space, trust him. But when she confronted him, he averted his eyes with a hangdog look, never looked her straight in the eyes again, never tried to patch up their relationship. Her trust vanished, never to return. The only thing left was for her to keep the wounds from infecting her life.

She didn't want the jealousy to tear her apart, and she didn't want to get into a mud-slinging contest. If the affair blew over, she didn't think she could love him again. He'd shown his true colors, slept with a woman like *that*; he wasn't the man she had thought he was. She couldn't bear being cast as the hysterical, jealous wife in another tawdry drama about adultery. So *she* drew the curtains and brought it to an end. She had been betrayed, but not dumped.

"What are you lookin' so sad about?"

All of a sudden, someone was whispering in her ear. Startled, she spun around, almost bumping into the face of a stranger pressed up close.

Who did this punk think he was?!

About twenty-seven or twenty-eight. She hoped desperately he wasn't one of her colleagues, but didn't think she had ever seen him before. The collar of his black cashmere coat was turned up, and he had a smooth white face, his hair combed back. Manager of a little shop somewhere, maybe. He certainly didn't have the aura of a cop, which was a relief. Takako studied the guy, who smiled amiably, as if Takako was someone he hadn't seen in ten years. He leaned in yet closer. The scent of hair gel, coupled with the alcohol on his breath, was nauseating.

"If something's bothering you, you can tell me about it."

She could have stopped it right then with a sharp "Don't be ridiculous." But a strange wave of nostalgia was washing over her. How long had it been since she felt someone's breath in her ear?

Was this how Teruo Hara seduced his women, whispering to them like this? For women tired in mind and body, that whisper must have been an oasis in the desert. They hadn't asked for much, those women. Just a moment's respite, perhaps. Teruo Hara had been a kind of savior.

"Come on, tell me about it."

Good grief. Did she look like those other women? Lonely? Needy? As if she needed someone—*anyone*—to lean on?

The man's arm was around her waist now. She pressed his hand back gently, then easily twisted it back behind him. He frowned, taken aback by the maneuver and her strength, but he drew his face down to hers again with an unperturbed half-smile. People around them probably thought they were together.

"If you want, I'll take you home."

The next station was announced as the train began to slow down. This was Takako's stop.

"I get off here."

"Then I get off here, too."

Takako looked at the man with distaste. "You really want to talk to me that much? What about?"

The man smirked. "Anything you want."

Takako sighed, smiled as sweetly as she could, and placed a hand on the man's chest. She lifted her face to his and whispered, "All right, then." As the man relaxed, she grabbed his collar, then swiftly jammed her hand into his Adam's apple, and squeezed until he started to gurgle. She looked him straight in the eye, their faces so close together it was hard to focus.

"Here's an idea—how about going to the police box in front of the station? It's warm there, and if you want, I can even arrange for you to spend the night. In fact, why don't you go on ahead and wait for me there?"

Just then the train doors opened. Takako let go of the man's collar, turned around, and got off.

5

Here, even the nightfall was orderly. The high-rise buildings, arranged with ample space between them in a display of smart contemporary architecture, were hushed and deserted; yet every other attraction of this manmade district—the groves of trees laid out at regular intervals to relieve the overall grayness, the boardwalk designed to impart warmth to people's hearts by reminding them that this little amusement area was made to face the sea, nature's gateway even if with stagnant water—was beautifully lit up. The illumination breathed life into the scenery, however false the breath. It was the sparkle of imitation diamonds falling on drab warehouses. It was a section of the city lacking life, where the flow of time was cut off from reality.

For a while Kazuki Horikawa stood between two tall buildings with the collar of his coat turned up and his hands thrust into his pockets, feeling the wind. It was past midnight, and the monorail between Hamamatsu-cho and Haneda had stopped running long before. The only way to get out of this manmade town was to walk to Shinagawa, or take a taxi. He couldn't quite make up his mind. His judgment was clouded by drink, and he was feeling a touch sentimental, not like his usual self.

He sighed, and his white cloud of breath was instantly swept away by the wind. He was reminded of what it used to be like to smoke. Standing here late at night, being buffeted by a dirty wind, if he had a cigarette in his mouth, that would complete the picture. Whatever happened to his old Zippo lighter anyway—the one he couldn't leave home without? Had he thrown it away? Given it to someone? It was a gift from an old girlfriend.

Somebody's wife by now, for sure.

Less and less like his normal self. Why tonight of all nights did he remember her? Was it because he couldn't think of even one woman he could go see? Had he gotten old without noticing? He wasn't a kid anymore. He couldn't go on frittering his life away like there was no tomorrow.

Taking a deep breath, Horikawa finally began to walk. He had no destination in mind. He simply wanted to be out in this cold wind a bit longer. He was getting more sentimental by the minute, and even if he woke up tomorrow morning feeling lousy, tonight he felt like doing some serious drinking, giving himself over completely to the blues.

It was the section chief's casual remark that had set him off tonight.

You weren't hired yesterday, you really know the ropes.

The comment had not particularly shocked him. He was surprised he could get excited over the remark of an insignificant man like that. He had always thought that giving your heart and soul to your job was the height of stupidity; stay cool, stay detached, call it quits when you can—that was good enough. But it seemed that all along he had been slowly transforming himself into a dreary workaholic. Without knowing it, he was staying late at the office alone, putting in hated overtime, and loathing himself more and more, until he took to drinking in hotel bars, alone. That was the story tonight.

I've turned myself into a common, pathetic stuffed shirt.

He used to laugh that the life of a salaryman was not for him—never imagined he would end up putting on a suit and tie every day and walking to work carrying a goddamn briefcase.

Looking up, he saw not stars but the winking red lights on the roofs of the high-rises. This was his daily scenery, this deadly section of town that he walked through without noticing on his way to the monorail station. It had the carefully planned perfection of a movie set as well as the dingy dust behind papier-mâché props.

Darkness spread before him. If he walked straight ahead and across the bridge, he would come to the Tokyo University of Fisheries. The darkness would grow yet denser. Could any part of the downtown area be this deserted, this black? If he was going to walk to Shinagawa, he would have to retrace his steps and turn right. And yet his feet kept on going straight ahead. He wondered how long it would take him to get to Hamamatsu-cho.

The wind felt good. However stagnant, the sea was the sea, the shore the shore. Damn it all, he wanted to see the unspoiled sea.

I'm not a workaholic. I hate workaholics.

He wanted to think of nothing but good times. No matter if people called him a kid or looked down on him for it, if life wasn't fun, it wasn't worth anything. That was his motto.

Suddenly Horikawa felt someone's eyes on his back. He stopped and turned slowly around, but there was no one. Of course not. The only people around here at this time of night were travelers on their way in or out of Haneda, and couples who used the night for romance. Either way, they wouldn't be out walking, they'd be snuggled in their hotel rooms.

No other reason to be on this reclaimed land at night; it's boring as hell.

Slowly he walked on, swinging his briefcase. He wanted to go home to bed, but at the same time he wanted to do something else, something to bring relief. Home to bed? That sounded real fuddy-duddy. Relief? Nowadays he didn't know where to start. No, not true. Anyplace would do once he got in the mood.

Suddenly, again, he got the queasy feeling that he was being watched. Once again he stopped, and this time he turned around warily. Nothing met his eyes but streets where the dry wind blew. Thanks to the overhead expressway, this area was dimly lit in the daytime, but now, because of the greater darkness of the perimeter, it was rather pale. The trees were trembling, either from the wind or from vibrations of the cars on the expressway. A taxi came speeding toward him with its vacancy light on. Before he could even think about hailing it, the cab was past him, only its red taillights in view. That option gone, once again Horikawa decided he had been imagining things. Nobody was around. The street was dead.

Like a huge stone coffin.

For some reason, this thought came to mind. The place wasn't squalid, it wasn't neat; it wasn't plastic, it wasn't organic; it wasn't old, it wasn't young; it wasn't pulsing, it wasn't still. It had no color and no rhythm.

No hopes or dreams either, as far as that goes.

Tonight was certainly the night for juvenile thoughts. Well, no harm in that, Horikawa thought, walking on again. If he were a young girl, he'd think twice about walking in a place like this. Dark streets at night, lechers on trains—these were the stuff the women at work always talked about.

Women, huh? Women.

They were different creatures. He used to yearn for them; lately they seemed more like a bother. His mother wanted him to settle down and get married, was trying to set up a meeting with a prospective bride.

An arranged marriage!

Actually, might not be such a bad idea. There were two kinds of women: the kind that made a good wife, and the kind that made a good lover. As long as you didn't get the two mixed up, you couldn't really go wrong.

Finally it dawned on him that he had no idea how far the Hamamatsu-cho station was. It was crazy to go to the station anyway; the trains would've stopped running before he got there. Take a taxi, get to Azabu. That's when he heard it: *skritch, skritch.* Instantly he was overcome by a feeling akin to fear. *There* is *someone behind me!* Before he could turn around, he found himself down on the pavement. His briefcase went flying. His knees were in pain, his palms were scraped, his jaw bloodied. His pulse was racing.

What the—

His ears were ringing. His face was on the sidewalk. He was pinned down. He tried to think. Suddenly he felt hot breath in one ear, got a whiff of something. It was the smell of . . . *an animal!* Too quick for him to know what was happening, a dull pain shot through his neck. He felt something warm and moist, teeth clamping down on his neck. A sickening sound echoed in Horikawa's head. It grew and grew, louder and louder. . . .

Until Horikawa lost consciousness. So that when his body was yanked over and he was ravished by the throat, it was as if it were happening to someone else. His body limp, the roar of his bloodstream echoed deep within his being. Horikawa felt nothing. This was mortal pain, so his oblivion was merciful. He never knew the searing pain, the biting into his flesh, the hot breath, the wetness, the sticky sounds, the coppery smell of blood, and then the odd prickling sensation, as living tissue was exposed to the cold wind. With a soft swoosh, warm blood spurted from his steaming throat. Had Horikawa's spirit been able to escape his body and look down on it, he would surely have averted his eyes and screamed.

His eyes stayed wide open, as if registering the carnage. Did his brain, still bearing a trace of life, process the two tiny round pupils in pools of pale green that were the creature's eyes? As its mouth dripped blood, the beast finished its grisly work, and detected the scent of death. Having ceased to feel anything, Horikawa's brain registered no fear and shut down without a flicker, never discerning his passage. His heart still beat, erratically, then more slowly, before vanishing into a flat line.

Horikawa's eyes were mere glass marbles now, open, seeing nothing. In the space of less than a minute, this unwillingly dedicated salaryman, who had just begun to contemplate taking his mother's advice and entering into an arranged marriage, had become a ragged corpse.

The blood continued to flow, gradually tapering off, puddling around the body, but in the darkness it was not evident. Overhead the traffic on the expressway continued without cease; now and again a taxi or truck would take the coastal road, but sidewalk shrubbery kept the body out of view. As earlier, Horikawa was left behind, alone, in this manmade environment. That he had been left behind for good was one more thing he did not know.

6

If he moved his head too fast, his brain was going to splash alcohol. Takizawa forced himself to take several deep breaths. His stomach churned. His back hurt where it leaned against the chair. Could his liver be swollen?

". . . and of all the chemicals handled in the lab today, organic peroxides are considered among the most dangerous. They belong to a particular class of chemical compound that demonstrates, if you will, uncommon instability."

This was the crime lab report they'd been waiting for, the results of the component analysis. But if it went on another thirty minutes, the contents of Takizawa's stomach were likely to have a chemical reaction of their own. Not that there was anything in there but alcohol. He faced forward, pleading silently for the speaker to make it snappy. There had to be five or six other guys who felt the same way: a bunch of them had been up all night drinking together.

"By uncommon instability I mean high sensitivity to shock, sparks, and other forms of incidental combustion. Organic peroxides are extremely sensitive to heat, friction, tremors, and light, to say nothing of strong oxidants and reductants."

The topic was actually of interest to Takizawa. You might not know it to look at him now, but at one time he had the brains for science and math. But damn—a lecture like this just didn't mix with alcohol in the blood. Taking yet another series of deep breaths, he tried to maintain the posture of an attentive listener. His breath reeked so strongly of alcohol that breathing in a lungful of it could get him drunk all over again. Technically this was no hangover; Takizawa was still bombed.

"The types of compounds known to generate peroxide include aldehyde, ether, allyl alcohol, and vinyl. In this case, the chemical on the device used to ignite the fire was a chemical compound with benzyl hydrogen. While it is impossible to be one hundred percent certain, it seems most likely to be in the benzoyl group."

At that point, the man from the Science Research Institute wrote BENZOYL PEROXIDE in large letters on the whiteboard. To the side, he wrote the chemical formula $(C_6H_5CO)_2O_2$. When he got out of here he had to go to a pharmacy and get some Sormak, thought Takizawa, calm the stomach down. Glancing beside him, he saw his goody two-shoes partner, proper as ever, busily taking notes. As long as she got everything down on paper, all he needed to do was sit here. She wasn't good for much else; let her knock herself out.

"The chemical benzoyl peroxide is a white, odorless crystalline powder formed when benzoyl chloride reacts with alkali and hydrogen or sodium peroxide. Because of its high oxidation effect, it is used to bleach flour, fats and oils, and tallow; it is an ingredient in pharmaceuticals and cosmetics and is widely used in the plastics industry as well. In this country, possession of benzoyl peroxide of 99 percent strength or greater is controlled. Usually it is used in the form of a 50-percent-strength paste made by mixing with oil or water, or a 25-percent-strength colloid. If you leave that mixture to dry naturally, then soak it overnight in methanol and then wind-dry it, you obtain a dry powder."

This SRI man might as well be delivering a lecture at the university, the way he's going on and writing stuff on the board. His eyelids feeling heavier by the moment, Takizawa forced himself to focus on the handwriting.

"This dry benzoyl peroxide spontaneously resolves at 103° Celsius; if you took a cardboard tube and packed in a kilogram of benzoyl peroxide, and lit it, you would get a three-meter-high flame. The fire does not burn as much as erupt, rather in the manner of a flamethrower."

A stir ran through the audience of detectives. Even with his drink-befuddled wits, Takizawa could see that here was a weapon of choice for a terrorist. An odorless white powder that exploded into flames. Easier, cleaner, more effective than gasoline.

"As I explained earlier, organic peroxides are among the most unstable of all organic compounds. Benzoyl peroxide is in fact safe if exposed to light, but it resolves at a low temperature and can be set off by shock or friction. While burning, moreover, it characteristically releases fumes that sting the nostrils and irritate the eyes, as well as a thick black smoke. After the fire burns out, a tarry substance is its residue."

Yes, it all fit the pattern of the fire. Instantaneous torching, thick black smoke, acute pain in the eyes. Takizawa thought back to the crime-scene investigation a week before. Who would have dreamed the case would take so many bizarre turns? And let's not forget him playing nursemaid to Otomichi.

"One chemical plant in Tokyo manufactured this chemical; in 1990 it was destroyed in an explosion and fire that claimed many lives. The greater the amount of the chemical, the greater the conflagration, it stands to reason; and the risk of such occurrence is significant. The tarry substance on the object recovered from the crime site, believed to be part of the belt the victim was wearing, has been determined to be residue of a fire caused by benzoyl peroxide."

His lecture done, the SRI man sat down, leaving the audience of detectives somewhat unsettled. The presentation had made it apparent, even to someone with a hangover, that the murderer in this case was not only cruel and exacting in his MO, he was also reckless, willfully endangering the lives of many innocent bystanders.

Captain Watanuki now stood up and cleared his throat. Through the wireless microphone his gravelly voice began:

"Until now this investigation has focused primarily on the victim—his lifestyle, means of employment, and surroundings. But no evidence or witness has shed light on the commission of the crime. As you are aware, the media have begun criticizing our approach, complaining that the investigation is likely to drag on without results. Now that the chemical used to start the fire has been identified and we have some insight into the mind of the perpetrator, we need to shift gears and renew our determination to make a breakthrough in this case. From now on I want you to concentrate your efforts on tracing the route of acquisition of this chemical. Let's all apply ourselves to this investigation with even greater energy than before."

Erasing the chemical formulas and terms that the SRI man had left on the whiteboard, the captain began to write out the new game plan. As he did so, the desk sergeants, exhaustion on their faces, passed out photocopied material. There was a newspaper article about the benzoyl peroxide fire in 1990, along with a list of chemical plants, pharmaceutical companies, university laboratories, and suppliers that sold chemicals wholesale in the Tokyo metropolitan area.

"Everybody who's been investigating the high school girls in the date club, or the women involved with the victim, should now switch over to work on pinning down the route of acquisition of this chemical. And everybody who was going door to door near the scene of the crime . . ."

Takizawa read the headline, but the print in the reduced copy of the article was too small. His eyesight wasn't what it used to be. True, the hangover didn't help either. He'd study it later. He looked at the list of chemical wholesalers and found prices noted in the margin: For benzoyl peroxide, it was ¥900/100g. Not that much, really. A three-meter pillar of flame would set you back less than ten thousand yen. That would cover everything, including ignition device and fuse.

". . . I know all of you are tired, but now is not the time to take a break. There are clues that—"

Suddenly Watanuki's voice broke off, and Takizawa lifted his head gingerly, so as not to rock anything inside, to see what was going on. Chief Wakita had come up to the podium and was conferring with Watanuki. Great, he thought; don't tell me somebody else got torched. Takizawa leaned back in his chair and stretched. By sitting perfectly still, he had started feeling better, his system working overtime to break down the alcohol.

Turning his attention back to the group, Watanuki cleared his throat and began again: "You may have heard about an incident that has been reported in the morning's papers and on the television news. If you missed it, let me bring you up to speed: Last night in Tennozu, Shinagawa Ward, a man was attacked and killed by what appears to have been a wild dog. The animal remains on the loose, whereabouts unknown. It has just come to our attention that this incident may have particular bearing on our case because the teeth marks on the Tennozu victim demonstrate a close resemblance to the bite scars on our homicide victim."

Now the room was buzzing. Takizawa moved his head a little too quickly, which made him feel like he was relapsing into drunkenness. What? Weren't we supposed to track down the peroxide? What's this with a wild pooch?

"We are in touch with the Shinagawa police and will check this new development out immediately. You will be notified of any pertinent results. In the meanwhile, proceed according to plan. Get your interim reports in by noon, everyone."

The meeting had lasted longer than usual, and it left detectives with a unpleasant sense of no movement having been achieved. By the time Takizawa left headquarters, the winter sun had lost the clarity of the morning, but when you were this hung over, sunlight, no matter how weak, was hard to take. Takizawa walked unsteadily. The assignment was for him and Otomichi to visit several chemical labs on the list.

A dog and blasting powder. Peroxide and a pooch. Wild dogs running around the city? Hard to believe. And in Tennozu?

"Where is Tennozu anyway?" Takizawa said the words half to himself. He had heard of the place, but that was all.

"The bay area." Otomichi spoke in a very calm, forthright manner.

Takizawa walked with his head down, and Otomichi's voice seemed to come less from his side than from diagonally above him. He lacked the energy to look up at her, but repeated her foreign-sounding response. "The bay area." The seaside, in other words.

"The monorail stops there on the way from Hamamatsu-cho to Haneda. It's the first station."

That part of the city was changing at a fast clip, Takizawa knew, but it was out of his circuit. Even if he spent all his time running around Tokyo, there were corners of it he had nothing to do with, knew nothing about. That included Shinagawa Ward and Ota Ward, the district known as Jonan, scene of the wild dog mauling.

"Sergeant Takizawa."

Takizawa wasn't feeling so well, and Otomichi wanted to talk just as he was thinking he needed to find that pharmacy, fast. "Yeah?"

"Do you think there is any connection between the Tennozu case and ours?"

"Damned if I know."

"Well, what if both victims really were bitten by the same stray dog?"

"You could never know that for sure," Takizawa said. He let a few seconds pass and then asked, "Have you ever been to Tennozu?" but didn't wait for her answer. They were just passing a pharmacy, and without any warning, he went in, bought some Sormak, and quickly swallowed it down. It was good stuff. Liquid medicine to calm the stomach, two bottles to a pack. He stuck the other bottle in his coat pocket and came outside to find Otomichi waiting for him.

"Uh, what were you saying again?"

"Sergeant Takizawa."

"What."

"May I have that, please?"

Takizawa looked up at Otomichi with a scowl, the sun in his eyes. "Have what?"

"The Sormak."

She was looking him straight in the eye, as surly and ungracious as ever. Takizawa took the bottle out of his pocket, feeling like a kid getting caught with something. Otomichi was removing her wallet from her purse. "Forget it, keep your money," he said, and handed the bottle to her. She accepted it, and walked off a few paces without a word. Sheesh, Takizawa thought, you think she's waiting outside, but she's got her eye on you the whole time. Doesn't miss a trick. Well, if she's always so keyed up, no wonder her stomach hurts.

He turned around in time to see Otomichi swallow the Sormak and toss the empty bottle into the trash before hurrying back. "Thank you," she said, as if everything was normal. "Sorry to impose like that."

"You feeling bad or something?" He did not want her sick or needing to rest, not while they were in the middle of an investigation. But come to think of it, she did look a little off color. She had fair skin to begin with, but today she looked deathly pale.

"I'm fine."

Just what little Miss Hardliner would say. As his own stomach began to settle, Takizawa's brain started to fire on all cylinders. What should he say back to her? He didn't want her to think he'd gone soft on her, but her tough act needled him.

"Well, I guess this case *is* kinda rough on the nerves for a delicate little thing like you."

This didn't come out quite as clever as he'd hoped, but never mind. He was beginning to feel pretty much like his old self; then he heard her reply:

"No. It's just a little hangover."

Hangover? Her? Thought she went home early last night. Did she go out drinking with somebody after that? Ten to one she was shooting off her mouth about me. Damn. I shoulda told her, buy your own Sormak.

7

WILD KILLER DOG? SALARYMAN ATTACKED,
SLAIN IN BAY AREA AT MIDNIGHT

At 2:30 A.M., an emergency 119 call reported a man found bleeding from the neck in Higashi Shinagawa 3-chome, Shinagawa Ward, Tokyo. Medical personnel rushing to the scene found the victim already dead, lying face up on the sidewalk of a tree-lined street near Tennozu Isle Station of the Tokyo Monorail line. Police from the Jonan Precinct of the Metropolitan Police Department established the identity of the man as Kazuki Horikawa, age 32, a company worker residing at 1 Nakamachi, Meguro Ward. Despite the injury to his neck, the victim's clothing showed no sign of a struggle. His briefcase was found nearby with his wallet intact.

Examination of the neck wound revealed an oval pattern of tooth marks bracketed with sharp fang marks. A large section of the victim's windpipe was missing, and his neck was broken. On his back, by both shoulders there was subcutaneous bleeding consistent with the claw marks of an animal. Police suspect that Horikawa's death resulted from an attack by a large canine.

The incident took place in a section of the waterfront that has undergone extensive development in recent years and is populated by many new highrises. Called Seafort Square, the area is filled with restaurants, theaters, and hotels, and is known popularly among young people as the "bay area." Horikawa was employed in a company located in an office building in Seafort Square. The neighboring area, which has many warehouses connected by canals, is said to be deserted at night; people are rarely seen walking dogs there.

According to Jonan police, if a dog was responsible for the attack on Horikawa, it must be of an extremely large breed. Since no households in the vicinity are known to possess a dog of that sort, police are working on the assumption that the dog is wild.

A wild dog.

Takako looked up from the evening edition of the paper from three days before. This was her first day off since the investigation headquarters was set up. On the low table in front of her lay a week's worth of newspapers, unread. Scattered alongside were an empty can of Coke and an empty container of instant ramen, a handkerchief that needed washing, and a pair of earrings. A pile of junk.

Last night when she went to bed, she had planned to spend her precious day off tending to her motorcycle and going out for a ride, but when she awoke it was already past noon. Too late to do anything. Besides, the sky out her window was cloudy and gray, with an icy cast. Thinking it might be nice to stay in and just rest, she made a cup of coffee, pulled out a newspaper from the stack, and the article jumped out at her. No wonder she didn't feel relaxed, even if it was her day off. The investigation was going nowhere. And now it looked like they were going to be drawn into this bay area death as well.

But thanks to all that's going on, I made it through.

Three days ago, the date of the newspaper article, was the day she'd been dreading. On that day last year she had affixed her seal to the divorce papers and moved out. It was her divorce anniversary, you could say. She'd been feeling downcast about it, wondering what she should do when the day rolled around, how she would get through it. But to her surprise, she was so busy she never gave it a second thought.

The day she moved into this new apartment had been cloudy like today, chilly enough for snow. She'd just gotten off all-night duty, starved for sleep, and the cold was punishing. When the movers were gone and she was left alone in a home where for the first time in her life she would live alone, the loneliness was overpowering. She was full of anxiety, wondering if she'd made an irrevocable mistake, if she would rue this day forever. What a fool she was, putting on such a show of strength and not asking anyone for help.

In retrospect it was good that she plunged back into work, leaving no time to wallow in sentimental regret. And now, a year later, she had managed to get safely past that anniversary, with too much to do to feel any foolishness. She would focus on the case. And then, one of these days, it would be spring. Sipping her coffee, enjoying its fragrance, she switched her thinking back to detective mode.

Was the attack a random event? Coincidence? Or intentional? If intentional, that was one helluva well-trained dog. A dog trained to attack humans?

The newspaper article was accurate enough, considering when it had been written. It was a little short on facts, however. And there were no follow-up articles in the next day's paper, nor the next, which was yesterday. The police had given out no further information.

The body was a ghastly sight, she'd heard. The article mentioned nothing about it, but Kazuki Horikawa had actually been bitten twice in the neck: first his neck had been broken, then his throat was ripped open. There were bites on his head as well, and an autopsy showed that the skull was crushed. Any of the three things could have killed him. There were no bite marks on the limbs or torso.

If it was a random attack, there was nothing to solve. If it was coincidence, it was a big coincidence. If it was intentional, well, whoever was behind it, the assassin—if that was the right word, whoever planned the attack—had done so with utmost care to ensure that the victim's life would be snuffed out. Chunks of flesh torn from the neck were found next to the body.

The wounds indicated that the dog was not only large, but had an extremely powerful set of jaws. To investigators, that in itself suggested intent to kill. The police were delaying the release of this information to the media because they didn't want to cause panic by suggesting that a savage dog was roaming the streets of Tokyo at night. Also, the connection between this case and the Tachikawa Timed Combustion Belt Homicide Case remained unclear.

The bite marks on Teruo Hara's legs also appeared to be the work of a fairly large dog, and the size of the teeth and position of the fangs were a match with the marks on the Tennozu victim. But comparing bite marks in cheese or an apple was one thing; this was quite another. It was all but impossible, they were told, to do a detailed comparison of tooth characteristics based on the marks left in human flesh. It could be determined whether the teeth marks were human or animal, and if animal, whether they belonged to a rat or a rabbit, or some larger animal like a pig or a dog; beyond that, results were bound to be uncertain. Yet in this day and age, it was odd to think that here in Tokyo there could be two attacks by wild dogs in such a short time. On the other hand, there weren't any reports of pets on the loose.

If a direct link between Teruo Hara and Kazuki Horikawa turned up, headquarters was bound to take over the investigation of the bay area case as well. It sounded like a hassle, but Takako wasn't alone among the detectives actually hoping it would happen. As it was, they were running out of leads on the homicide by chemical fire.

Headquarters had been eagerly awaiting the results of SRI's chemical analysis. But with those results in hand, all that had been learned, after combing through Tokyo, was the unlikelihood that benzoyl peroxide would ever lead them to a suspect.

Under the Fire Defense Law, benzoyl peroxide was rated a class-five dangerous substance, meaning that anyone handling more than ten kilograms of it had to file a written report specifying the amount, location, and purpose. Failure to do so was punishable by a prison sentence of up to one year and a fine of up to ¥300,000. But in fact, several firms had literally tons of the chemical illegally stockpiled. Annual distribution and consumption of benzoyl peroxide was immense; moreover, whether every firm kept careful watch on its supply was open to question.

Just as the man from SRI had said, the chemical was used in a wide variety of industries, from foods and pharmaceuticals to cosmetics and the manufacture of highly polymerized compounds. Often, since the chemical was used in a stable form mixed with oil or water, not everyone connected with its use was even aware of the danger involved. And at university laboratories and suppliers that sold chemicals wholesale, detectives found that, basically, anyone could get hold of benzoyl peroxide with ease.

These facts weighed heavily on the investigating team, who had hoped to find a clear trail of how the chemical was obtained. Certainly, some technical knowledge of chemicals was called for. And concerning the timing device, while the parts used were widely available, only someone with the requisite knowledge and expertise could have carried out the idea of enclosing it in a belt buckle. Yet no one in Hara's circle of acquaintances fit that description.

At last night's meeting, one after another, weary detectives offered their opinions. "I think we'd be better off doing a thorough search of the witnesses," one said. Everyone was frustrated. They had identified the victim. They had a pretty good picture of his occupation and his private life. They even had their hands on a key piece of physical evidence in the form of the timed ignition device.

Through their questioning of the high school girls in the date club, investigators had established that Teruo Hara was wearing a belt different from his usual belt, for the first time, on the day he was murdered. It was remarkable to have discovered all this without grasping any real leads. You'd think that by now they would have located somebody with a grudge against Hara, have gotten wind of some financial shenanigans or a love affair gone awry.

Clearly, the killer had set out carefully and methodically to do away with Teruo Hara. No one would pursue their target so relentlessly without a considerable motive. This had been no random murder or act of terrorism. The killer had gone after Teruo Hara with premeditation.

Even though Hara had a suspicious past, was using two names, and seemed likely to be up to his ears in serious trouble of one kind or another—likely, even, to have a person or two harboring murderous intentions toward him—so far they had found no one with even a grievance.

"We're missing something, that's all I can say."

"For one thing, we still don't know the victim's movements on the day of the fire. We haven't dug below the surface yet."

"If whoever did the initial investigation had put his back in it, we'd have known sooner that the victim operated a date club in the same building as the restaurant."

Takizawa was miffed when he heard this. Takako had glanced over at him curling his lip. She took the criticism to heart, reviewing mentally the faces of all those they had questioned. Had somebody been lying or suffered a memory lapse? Had the questioning missed something?

Mired in discouragement, the meeting had finally wrapped up with these words from Chief Wakita: "We are looking at the matter very carefully, and if it does turn out that the Tennozu case is connected with this case, then there's a strong chance of a breakthrough. I know you're all tired. Take the day off tomorrow, rest up, and let's start fresh the day after tomorrow."

There could be no doubt that the detectives' frustration was exacerbated by fatigue. The helpless sense that all their efforts had come to nothing was part of their collective misery. Getting a day off now would be a welcome break not only for Takako but for everyone, she was sure. And when they came back to work, maybe there would be a clearer understanding of the connection between the two cases.

But what if there isn't any connection? Then what? We'll have to keep going with the data we already have.

The thing was to find someone who had benefited from Hara's death. Who would that be? The women in his life? A business rival? The husband of an older lover? But all of this had been gone over already. Without exception, the married women whom Hara—no, "Takuma Sugawara"—was involved with had managed with great adroitness to conceal the fact of his existence. None of them had loved him wholeheartedly. None of them had shed real tears.

When you think about it, that's pretty sad. He was a pitiful man.

Perhaps Hara himself was the one who'd been toyed with. After all this time, his body still lay unclaimed in the cold city morgue. What had his life amounted to, in the end?

He was a fool. A foolish man.

* * *

She'd slept well, yet her eyelids were growing heavy again. Leaning back in the lone legless chair on the tatami floor, Takako took a deep breath. She wanted to clear her mind, think of nothing at all. Suddenly *men* came to mind.

She remembered the man who had come on to her on the train several nights ago. In the end the little weasel didn't have the guts to follow her off the train. She thought of Takizawa, the emperor penguin. And then she thought of her ex-husband, who on being confronted with his infidelity had acted almost defiant, but never looked Takako in the eyes again. Unbelievably, when he realized the truth was out, he had blurted, "It's got nothing to do with you."

Nothing to do with me? Then who was I supposed to be to him?

"You call yourself a wife? Then why don't you try acting like one once in a while?"

Where was he now, what was he doing? She had never heard rumors of him setting up house with that other woman.

Damn. She wanted to forget, but she couldn't keep the memories from flooding back. Takako opened her eyes. Wasting a perfectly good day off on thoughts like this was bad for her mental health. She'd be better off going back to bed and sleeping all day. Just then the phone rang. Headquarters? What now? She picked up the phone.

"Takako?" It was her sister.

"Tomoko, how are you?"

"I'm OK. Did Mom leave you a message on your answering machine?"

Takako had completely forgotten. She looked down at the telephone covered in dust and sighed. It suddenly occurred to her she wasn't so happy to hear the voice of her sister, who had been her closest friend during childhood. Instead of warmth and pleasure, what she felt was irritation.

"Sorry, I've been really busy."

"Yeah, I know. What about today? Are you on your way to work?"

"I have the day off. *Finally.*"

She put deliberate extra stress on "finally," but the implication of that was totally missed by her sister. "Great! Perfect!" said Tomoko excitedly. Tomoko worked for a government agency, doing little more than pouring tea and making Xerox copies. "So, can I come see you? I'll come to your apartment after work tonight."

"Um, sure. What's this all about?"

"Before you talk to Mom, I want you to hear my side of things."

Takako wiped the dust off the telephone with the tip of a finger, thinking that she would have to get out the vacuum cleaner. Since the case began, she hadn't done a lick of housework. Even if it was her sister coming over, she couldn't let her see this place the way it was now.

Boy, oh boy. Here goes.

Getting up with a creak, feeling ancient, Takako sighed and looked around the room. Then she turned on her CD player for the first time in a while, and started to clean up. A detective needed to be tough and agile. And tenacious.

A year ago, when she moved out of her old place, she left behind everything that might bring back memories of her husband. That meant leaving behind all but a few CDs. There were times when she regretted that decision, but she had done it for good reason. Now, she had an old Carpenters album on. These were songs that reminded her of her teenage years, long before she was married; they fell pleasantly on her ears and seeped into her heart. In those days, marriage and divorce alike had been just words.

She cleared away the old newspapers and clothes lying around the room, as well as the empty bags of sweets and unopened junk mail, and then did a once-over with the vacuum cleaner. Before her sister came she'd run a load of laundry, go to the dry cleaner's, and do some ironing. She'd have to clean out the refrigerator, too; didn't want her sister to see the spoiled vegetables.

As she was rushing around in jeans and a sweater, Takako was suddenly brought near tears. The song playing was "Yesterday Once More."

8

She'd just had a day off, but Takako hardly felt refreshed. Almost the opposite. Her sister came over after work, and they'd stayed up talking almost till dawn. Takako barely got a couple of hours of light sleep before it was time to get up for work.

Some day off.

So she wouldn't oversleep, Takako had stayed in the living room, dozing under the kotatsu, while her sister took the bed. As Takako was dressing, her sister awoke. "Are you leaving already?" Tomoko asked, her tone a little clingy.

"Yes."

"Sorry I kept you up all night."

"What about you? Aren't you going to work?"

"Not now. I'll take the day off."

"Can you?"

"It's nothing."

Must be nice, thought Takako. As she completed her toilet, she looked over at her little sister; her unmade-up face was still youthful.

"I'll leave you the spare key, so lock up when you leave. I'll get the key from you later."

"You'll think over what we talked about, won't you, please?"

Tomoko's grand idea was that she leave home and come live with Takako. At first she said she wanted to leave home because the commute from Saitama was so long and their aging father was getting increasingly irascible; but the main reason, it soon became clear, was that their parents had found out about the man Tomoko was seeing. Pouting, Tomoko said they'd hit the ceiling, and had even imposed a strict curfew.

"Tomoko, you're twenty-seven years old! I can't believe Mom and Dad going ballistic about a boyfriend."

Takako, the eldest of three daughters, had married at the age of twenty-six. The sister after her, now twenty-nine, was single still. Their parents had always told the daughters not to worry about their welfare, to go ahead and marry as they wished, so Takako couldn't understand why Tomoko having a boyfriend would upset them. As she asked more questions, the fuller picture emerged: Tomoko was seeing a married man. And her mother discovered the affair when she found the hospital bill for Tomoko's abortion.

Tomoko!

"Don't say anything. I know. I've been told over and over by Mom and Dad and Koko. But I couldn't help myself. I . . . love him. And I really trust him."

Takako was astonished. She still thought of Tomoko as a child; she had never dreamed she was leading such a life. She stayed up almost the entire night listening to her sister talk. She promised herself she wouldn't get emotional, and yet she felt sick and disconsolate.

"Please, Takako," her sister pleaded. "I'll do all the housework. I can pay part of the rent, too." Fully awake, Tomoko got up and followed Takako around the apartment like a puppy.

"Forget it. How many times do I have to tell you? You may think that once you leave home you can see him all you want, but believe me, nothing good is going to come from a man like that."

"Don't say that. I thought you'd understand. You're my only hope. And besides, he—"

"Yes, I heard. He gave you his word, right? Please. I don't have time to be listening to this."

"But you do understand, don't you?" Wearing Takako's pajamas, Tomoko padded around the apartment in her bare feet, pleading with Takako like a spoiled child. "Please."

"Absolutely not. I'm calling Mom, so go on home. Don't expect me to help you carry on an affair with a married man."

Tomoko had screwed up her face like an infant, stamped the floor and yelled, "I won't go back!"

My god. Involved with a married man. And an abortion, too.

Whatever had become of the sunny, wholesome child her sister used to be? What had gotten into her? As the youngest, Tomoko had been indulged by their parents, raised with every opportunity, fun to be around; now, to Takako, she was a stranger, someone separated from her by a great divide. Think how it feels to be the woman whose husband you're stealing, she wanted to say. Although the man, of course, was at fault: He was a married man, but that didn't stop him from seducing a naive girl, getting her pregnant, then aborting the child. The whole thing was his fault. Totally his fault.

What a bastard. And Tomoko is an idiot.

The train was packed, which only added to Takako's frustration, and she arrived at Tachikawa Central Station still feeling upset. Going straight to the rest room, she stared into the mirror as she combed her hair. Her eyes looked a little sunken. Well, another day alongside the emperor penguin begins. She better not let on about the weariness she felt.

As the morning meeting got underway, Wakita, looking himself rather healthier than two days before, spoke with a clear, ringing voice: "I trust you all had a good rest yesterday. Today we start afresh, and while we certainly have our work cut out for us, let's do our best to move this case along and get a suspect in custody as soon as possible. Now, as to the Tennozu case, there is a new discovery to report."

He's been to the barber.

"It is now believed that the tooth marks on the body of Kazuki Horikawa, the victim in the Tennozu case, were made by a large dog—or, possibly, by a wolf."

A wolf? The room swirled with mumblings. Takako stared at Wakita in disbelief. He was the picture of earnestness, looking stern as he nodded in confirmation of his announcement.

Actually his hair is cut too short; he looks like an anachronism, a soldier in the war.

"According to the report from the crime lab, the hairs found on the body of the victim are definitely not from a wild animal. They are from a male animal that's been well cared for, and yet they don't match any breed of dog. We are in the process of collecting samples for comparison, but at this point it seems quite possible that we are looking at a wolf. Two kinds of hairs were found, bristles and soft hair. The condition of the sebaceous matter, and the presence of skin tissue at the roots of the hair follicles, rules out any question of their coming from a fur coat. They are from the body of a live animal."

A well-groomed wolf? Somebody's pet? No one smiled. This was not a joke. It was inconceivable that the chief could be jesting.

"Examination of the area where the victim was found turned up relatively fresh prints in nearby shrubbery. They match the claw marks on the victim's back. The prints are thought to be from the animal's hind legs. They measure 10.6 centimeters by 7.5 centimeters, which would be enormous for a dog; moreover, whereas paw prints of a dog are normally fairly rounded, these tend toward oval. The savagery of the injury to the victim's head and neck tells us this must be an animal with jaws bigger and more powerful than a German shepherd or a Doberman pinscher. But the style of the attack suggests that the animal, whether dog or wolf, is not wild; it is a highly trained animal. These are only parts of the puzzle, but it seems safe to say at this point that we're up against something quite formidable."

After the chemical symbols and equations of the other day, which Takako had little understood, the image of the wolf in Takako's mind was very vivid.

"Now, the victim Kazuki Horikawa was employed as an ordinary salaryman, but in his university days he hung around Roppongi at night, lived in the fast lane. It seems to us more than a coincidence that many of the places he frequented at that time overlap with the employment of the homicide victim, Teruo Hara; we are investigating the possibility of a connection between Hara and Horikawa.

"There are many questions that remain, but because of the possibility that the two deaths may be linked in some way, headquarters has decided: We will be heading up the investigation of the Horikawa case as well as the Hara case. Both cases will be pursued in tandem."

Takako, with her notebook open, felt a vague dissatisfaction. Chase a wolf? She'd never done anything like that before. Of course, the ultimate purpose of the chase would be to round up whoever was controlling the wolf—but what did that have to do with benzoyl peroxide and a belt rigged to throw flames?

It was hard to call the latest development good news, yet the mood of the investigation, in the doldrums recently, had definitely perked up. They were bound to make some headway now.

Once again the teams and assignments were shifted around. In addition to the ongoing background check of Teruo Hara, the search for witnesses, and the investigation into the distribution of benzoyl peroxide, new teams were formed to look into possible connections between Hara and Horikawa, to search for new motives, and to track down the wolf. Takako assumed that again she'd be making the rounds of pharmaceutical companies, but to her surprise they were assigned to the wolf.

As the meeting was drawing to a close, Watanuki almost offhandedly announced: "Officer Otomichi, a word with you, please."

"Yes, sir," Takako replied automatically, lowering her head instinctively as she sensed the eyes of everyone, including Takizawa, on her.

When the meeting adjourned Takako first went quickly over to Takizawa, bowed, and said, "I'll be a minute."

His mouth in an ironic twist, he raised his eyebrows with a look of utter boredom, jutted out his chin, and said with exaggerated politeness, "Be my guest. Take all the time you want." Apparently, a day's R&R had only fueled the emperor penguin's ill nature.

Takako was led into a side room where various higher-ups were assembled, including Chief Wakita and the head of the Tachikawa Third Mobile Investigative Unit she belonged to.

"Otomichi, you are a lizard, is that right?"

Takako darted a glance at her supervisor and saw the approval in his eyes before replying, "Yes, I am."

"Lizards" were designated members of the mobile investigative unit who had served as motorcycle policemen or whose motorcycle skills were at the highest level; as need arose, they might be ordered to follow a suspect's trail alone on their motorcycle, departing from the usual pattern of working with a partner. While not exactly a code name, the term lizard was not in open use either. People Takako worked with were probably familiar with it, but here at investigation headquarters, few if any of those around her knew what it meant. Takako had started out as a motorcycle cop, and received the lizard designation after transferring to the mobile investigative unit of the Criminal Affairs Division.

"You're prepared to go into action at any time?"

"Yes, sir."

"That's all we needed to know. You may go."

Takako bowed deeply and left the room, wondering what that was all about.

"They say wolves run like the wind," a voice said from behind her. Takako turned find her supervisor following her down the corridor, grinning.

Ahh.

At the door of the meeting room, her supervisor stopped and motioned inside with his chin. "Looks like you've got your hands full," he said. Takako saw that he was referring to Takizawa sitting glumly in a chair, legs straight out in front of him. The room was empty except for the desk staff, and Takizawa was smoking a cigarette, stroking his jaw as if searching for patches of stubble he missed while shaving. Takako shrugged.

"One of these days you'll have a chance to show him your real stuff. Just hang in there."

"Thanks to him, I'm a lot more thick-skinned now. He—"

Her supervisor held up his hand, cutting her off; he understood, she didn't have to explain. Takako felt lucky to have colleagues like him for the most part.

"He's got a good reputation. You're just not used to each other. Think of him as the classic, old-fashioned type of cop."

"That's not the problem; the problem is he hates women."

"Then you two are a good match. The man-hater and the woman-hater."

"But I—"

"Don't tell me you're crazy about men. You aren't. You're not crazy about the human race in general. Anyway, main thing is, you do your job. Do what you can to get that wolf."

Takizawa had waited grumpily for his partner. As soon as she got back, he stood up with a cool, standoffish air. "Ready now? Is your important business finished?"

"Sorry to keep you waiting."

"Let's go. Time to round up the pooch."

As they left the room, Takizawa made a deliberate show of letting Takako go first, and even started to hum a little. "Yes, sir," he said, "gotta thank my lucky stars I'm paired with you. This way I get all the easy jobs."

Here we go again, thought Takako. She kept her eyes straight ahead, not wanting to get into it with him.

"So what was the big deal about?"

"Nothing special," she replied, not looking toward him. She could register his annoyance at this. That was one reason she disliked walking with a man her height. With his face so close by, she had to see his every little change of expression. Having Takizawa's scruffy face constantly in her line of sight was not a pleasant part of the job.

After a bit, Takizawa spoke up. "So where're we headed?"

Throughout their so-called partnership, Takizawa had called all the shots, deciding where they would go without giving Takako a say in the matter. What was this, she wondered. A test?

"Well, why don't we start by going around to the larger pet shops?"

"Good. What else?"

"As I recall, under something called the Washington Convention, trafficking in wolves is prohibited."

"Oh yeah?"

"At any rate, I think it would be best to start there."

"You do, huh?"

Takizawa evidently had no intention of taking her seriously, no matter what she said. What in the world was wrong with him? Had something happened to him on his day off? Well, same here. But, hey, we leave our private lives at home; you don't drag your misery to the office, especially if you're going to work with me.

"You think the wolf escaped from a zoo?" he asked.

"Has there been a report of a missing wolf?"

"You got me there."

"But a wolf in a zoo wouldn't receive any special training, would it? To have carried out an attack like that—"

Takizawa stopped in his tracks. Takako walked on a little ways, then stopped and turned back. Takizawa was standing with an unlit cigarette in his mouth.

"You really think there's a wolf out there?" he said.

"It's possible," she hedged. "That's why we need to check it out."

"You do it on your own, then. I'm out. It's too wacky for me." Takizawa lit the cigarette, disgusted.

Takako took a deep breath. "Tell me why."

"Look, all I want is to go after the human dirt-bag. Leave dogs to the dog-catcher. I can't take a kiddie assignment like that seriously."

"But the wolf is key to the case! It's actually attacked and killed someone."

"Yeah, well, for all we know, that case has zilch to do with ours. What I want to do is go back to the scene of the fire and start asking some more questions. I know we missed something the first time around. There's gotta be something we didn't ask, didn't see."

"Then why didn't you request permission? All you had to do was tell the chief." Takako watched as Takizawa blew a lungful of smoke in her direction. The smoke dissipated in the winter wind.

"'Cause I got paired with you, honeybun. They thought I didn't have what it takes to grit my teeth and go back for another try."

Takako tightened her grip on the strap of her shoulder bag. "Are you positive about that?" she said in a tense, quiet voice. Today was shaping into another chilly, overcast day. As long as she was walking, she didn't feel the cold, but standing here in the wind like this, she felt the cold creeping up from her ankles. She'd had enough. *I don't want to be paired with you either, buster.* "Maybe they just thought someone else should take a look from a fresh perspective."

Takizawa showed surprise at hearing this, but Takako plowed on without waiting for him to speak. "You find it supremely unpleasant to be paired with me, I know. I think I know why, too. But there's nothing I can do about the situation. I certainly don't think I've been given an easier job because I'm a woman."

"I'm sure you don't."

"If you want to continue the search around the crime scene, fine. You know your way around the area, and you were in on this case from the time the fire was first reported, so I know you want to catch whoever's responsible. But I'm going after the wolf. It's the job I was assigned to do. If you want nothing more to do with me, if you have no interest in pursuing the wolf, than I suggest you take it up with the chief. But today, I'm going to go after the wolf."

"How can you keep—"

"I apologize for being so blunt!" Having gotten that off her chest, Takako turned and started to walk away, purposely letting the heels of her shoes click loudly. Actually there was more that she could have said. But she felt a little better. She really had no intention of going up against Takizawa. He was the one who was out of line.

I'll track down the wolf myself. Hara's background and benzoyl peroxide have been dead ends. The wolf's the key, just watch.

Her insides were still seething with defiance and determination. She didn't want to lay eyes again on Takizawa's grouchy face or her sister's pleading face. Her supervisor said she basically hated people. She didn't think of it like that, but maybe he was right. What was there to like about people anyway? They were all selfish, wrapped up in themselves, didn't care about . . .

Today, when Takako exhaled, her breath actually came out frosty. Out here in Tachikawa, the temperature had to be a couple degrees colder than in the middle of the city. The cold air stung her eyes; suddenly she became aware of footsteps running up to her.

"At this hour, I bet no pet shops are open." It was Takizawa, whose scruffy figure had intruded into her field of vision.

"Well, department stores open at ten, and they all have pet shops."

Takako looked back at her partner, who had begun walking alongside her with a face curiously void of expression. His cigarette was almost down to the filter. With the usual ironic twist to his mouth, Takizawa mumbled, "After all, you and me are a team."

9

Right, left, right, left. From the outside of Mayo Uehara's pink sneakers you couldn't tell they were wet inside. In fact, her socks and her feet felt like they were soaked in tepid water.

It reminded her of when she was in kindergarten and wet her pants. Ugh. Her mouth tightened, Mayo walked on, face down. *Right, left, right, left.* Her feet were moving, but if she just focused on her shoes, there was the illusion that the pavement was moving instead. This was a magic trick her mother taught her for times when she didn't feel like walking.

Mommy knew lots of magic.

But Mommy was never coming back again. "Come and see me any time," she had said, but Mayo had never been over. It made Daddy sad, and besides, she thought maybe she wasn't supposed to see Mommy anymore. But at times like this she wished she could. She wished Mommy could teach her some magic way to cheer herself up. She wanted Mommy to stroke her hair and braid it for her. To listen to her troubles and help her find a way out. Daddy said, "If you have a problem, tell your teacher." But Miss Yokota didn't like her. She thought so before, but today she was sure.

Today the other girls in class hid her sneakers. During lunch hour, they came up and invited her to play with them on the horizontal bar. Usually they never asked her to do anything with them. They would stand off at a distance and say stuff loudly like "I hate mayonnaise!" or "Mayonnaise is like white poo." Just because her name was Mayo. So when they invited her to play with them today, she was thrilled. She quickly ate her lunch and went with them to the cupboard where the outdoor shoes were kept. But her sneakers were gone. Then the girls all laughed and laughed and laughed: You idiot. Your sneakers are so dirty, they probably got thrown in the trash. You probably came to school barefoot.

Mayo searched for her sneakers, tears running down her face. Even after lunch period was over, she kept looking, by herself. Finally she found one sneaker stuck in the toilet in the farthest lavatory stall. She kept on hunting until she found the other one, this time in a toilet in the boys' lavatory on the second floor. Mayo went back to the classroom holding a sneaker in each hand, dripping toilet water.

As soon as she walked into the room, Miss Yokota scolded her sharply. "Where have you been? Didn't you hear the bell ring?"

Trembling, Mayo tried to tell her teacher about the sneakers. Her humiliation. Anger. Sadness. But for second-grader Mayo, organizing all of that into a form her teacher could understand was impossible. Finally, with a supreme effort, she managed to say where her sneakers were—and then everyone in the room burst into derisive laughter.

"Uehara went into the boys' room!?!"

"Ew! She smells like pee."

"She stuck her hand right down in the toilet!"

They all jeered at her, every last one of them. Hoping that Miss Yokota would stop them, Mayo looked up at her expectantly. But on Miss Yokota's mouth there was the trace of a smile. The teacher hated her. Even the teacher thought she was dirty. Miss Yokota wasn't her friend. She was on the side of all the other girls, all the bullies. Mayo felt terrible. So she walked out. She never wanted to go back to school again.

Right, left, right, left. Mommy's magic trick still worked. Even after being jammed into the toilet, her sneakers glided smoothly over the pavement. If only she could keep on going till she got someplace far, far away. If only her sneakers would sprout wings and fly her up, up, and take her far, far away.

Would Miss Yokota call Daddy? Would Daddy be mean to her when he found out? Would he threaten to take her to Grandma's in Utsunomiya? Mayo didn't like Grandma in Utsunomiya. Grandma always said bad things about Mommy. But she said them about Daddy, too. She was Daddy's real mother, so how could she say bad things about him? Mayo couldn't understand. Grandma told her that both her mommy and her daddy were bad people. So Mayo, since she was their kid, figured she must be the worst kid ever. She should have never been born. So Mayo didn't want to go to Utsunomiya.

Right, left, right, left. When she got home, she was going to draw. She was going to imagine a world where she wanted to be, and she was going to draw a picture of it. In the yard there was a pony and ducks and penguins. She wanted to play with a big shaggy dog. The house had big windows with pretty pink curtains. Ponies and ducks couldn't go in the house, but the dog could. The dog was her best friend, so Mommy and Daddy said it was okay. Everybody was smiling. Then Mayo got the idea to draw a baby, too! A cute little baby, a cute little baby brother. She would draw lots of flowers, because it was warm, and on the table she would draw a big pile of cookies, and in a little stream by the house she would draw little fishies. Mayo wanted to invite lots of friends to her world.

Today I'll think up a name for my dog.

Mayo's big, warm, friendly dog. A nice, smart dog, who would come up to her and lick her face. If anyone was mean to Mayo, her dog would teach them a lesson. Mayo wasn't afraid of the dog at all, but all the kids that bullied her would be scared stiff. He was big and strong, and always stuck up for her. She wanted a dog like that.

She started up the hill. When she had a library book, she read it as she climbed the hill. That made the same magic as staring at her sneakers. But today she had no book. So, dreading the long climb, she sighed. If she stopped going to school, she wouldn't have to climb this hill ever again. She wouldn't go back, that's all. Why should she? There was nothing fun about school.

Unless she came up with some kind of regimen—like stepping only on stones at the edge of the pavement, or making the distance from here to the telephone pole in twenty steps—she could never make it to the top. Today she decided to walk up in a zigzag. She would go back and forth between the telephone poles at either side of the road, walking diagonally. If she kept her mind focused on walking, she wouldn't be sad. She wouldn't cry, and she wouldn't think of Mommy or anyone else.

Ready, go.

There was hardly any traffic. Depending on the time of day there might be a few cars, but you never saw anyone walking here in the daytime. One boy from her class lived part-way up the hill, actually, but she hardly said anything to him. They never walked to or from school together. She knew what his mother looked like, but his mother had never called out to her.

Deciding which telephone pole she would walk toward, Mayo started off. *Right, left, right, left.* When she lifted her face, the telephone pole that had seemed so far away before loomed right in front of her. Mayo was surprised, and happy. It was like playing tag!

Reaching her first telephone pole, she changed direction and headed off toward the next. She passed several poles this way, when up ahead of her, she saw someone walking. Someone wearing a coat halfway between pink and orange, a dark skirt, black tights, and pulling a dark blue shopping cart. She had wavy brownish hair and was moving very, very slowly, like it was painful. *That lady doesn't know any magic.*

Mayo stopped walking, gazed at the lady, then decided she'd copy the way the lady was walking, slowly, ploddingly, painfully. This was a stranger, and it might be someone she wouldn't like, so she stayed far behind. Just playing like this warmed Mayo's heart a little. It reminded her of walking with Mommy. But the lady was walking so slowly; Mayo had to fight the urge to run and catch up with her. She came to a thicket on the right, where the road leveled out a bit.

The lady got to the top of the hill and disappeared from Mayo's sight. Feeling suddenly lonely, Mayo walked faster. She had to get where she could see the other side of the hill; she didn't want to lose sight of the lady. When Mayo reached the top of the hill herself, she caught sight of the brown hair that was definitely the lady's. She was surprised to see how much the distance between them had shrunk. For some reason, she had the feeling she shouldn't get any closer. A cold wind was blowing at the top of the hill, drying the light sweat on Mayo's forehead. She had completely forgotten about her wet sneakers.

Mayo kept her eyes on the lady's back, allowing the distance between them to increase again, little by little. The lady seemed to be picking up speed, and now the distance between them was increasing faster than Mayo had figured on. If she wasn't careful, she might lose sight of her again. She started going straight forward—and that's when it happened. Something gray came leaping out of the thicket.

For a second, it stopped and looked at her. Mayo sort of gasped. It was a gray, dog-like creature. It was big, with standing-up ears and a long muzzle. There was black fur between its eyes and all around its forehead. From there to its big, black nose was a line of gray. The animal's eyes were small and shiny, and they stared straight at Mayo. Around the animal's neck was a ruffle of fur, and its body, which she first thought was gray, actually was kind of bluish. Around the long muzzle the fur was white, but everywhere else it was blue-gray, with a dull metallic sheen. The dog book Daddy gave her didn't have any dogs like this in it. Did the dog have a collar? She couldn't tell. But how beautiful it was! And how big! Its legs were really long. The dog stared at her and then, slowly, it blinked. In that instant, the creature that had seemed so magnificent, a canine king, became suddenly sweet and innocent.

Mayo wanted to run over and pet the dog. But before she could take a single step, the creature swung its head and walked away from her, as if it hadn't seen her. Mayo watched it go, fascinated by how it hung its head lower than its shoulders, how there was a black line along its back, how its long, bushy tail did not curl or stand up but stuck straight out behind. It stepped lightly, smoothly, fast, not bouncing along like an ordinary dog. Mayo stared at the creature, thinking it was sort of a dream.

The creature was going toward the lady with brown hair. Maybe it was the lady's dog. But the lady did not notice the dog any more than she had noticed Mayo. She continued to trudge along. The lady, the dog, and Mayo—the three of them not making a sound. But Mayo was still stopped in her tracks, and the creature was getting close to the lady. Mayo didn't want to be left behind.

Oh, what a beautiful, magnificent dog it was! At the moment that Mayo thought this, the creature leaped. Mayo had thought it was still a ways behind the lady, but in a single bound it landed right onto the lady's back. When it rose on its hind legs, just before it flew through the air, it was so tall that Mayo couldn't see the lady anymore. Then there was a *clank*. The lady's shopping cart toppled over. And in bewildered astonishment, Mayo dumbly watched everything that happened after that.

The lady put up no resistance. Even though a big creature like that had jumped up on her, she made no sound. The creature then crouched down by the lady's face and did something. The lady's body flopped around, and Mayo heard a crunching sound. Next, using its paws and nose, the creature rolled the lady over.

It didn't seem like the creature was playing. Mayo's knees suddenly begin to shake. She was scared. Something scary was happening before her eyes. It might have gone on for a very long time, or it might have been real fast. But the next thing she knew, the creature was looking back at her, one huge paw resting on the lady. It had something red in its mouth, and the fluffy fur around its neck, like a lion's mane only shorter, had red splatters. The lady with the brown hair was completely still.

"What did you do?" she murmured in a little voice. "You—"

Then the creature dropped what was in its mouth, bounded lightly over the lady's body, and ran. Even more nimbly and smoothly than before, like the wind. Its bushy tail swung back and forth, like a snow cloud come down to earth. It disappeared into the thicket without a sound.

Mayo could not be sure of what she had seen. From where she stood, she could see the lady lying and not moving. The legs that had been walking so very slowly were flung out at odd angles, like a broken doll's. Something warned her not to look, not to go near. Her heart pounded. The wonderful face of the animal when it gazed at her was burned into her memory. That was not a face that was mean. It was strong, and gentle, and dear. It had spoken to her: "This is our secret. Promise you won't tell." That was it, that must be it.

I didn't see anything. I don't know anything.

Saying the words to herself, Mayo turned toward the thicket the creature had disappeared into and nodded like they had a secret. It might be looking out at her from between the trees. Well, she'd promised. So now she did an about-face. Her legs were still shaking. But that surely was because her sneakers were wet. After all, she hadn't seen anything. She didn't know anything. Daddy said she lived in a dream world. *That's why the other kids make fun of you. You don't pay attention to what anybody says.* Maybe this was a dream, too. She hadn't heard any growling or howling. Or any other sounds. Just the *clank* when the lady's shopping cart fell over. But maybe that was her imagination, too.

A short way down this hill was a street branching off to the right. It was a narrow street, but it connected to another street, and even though it was a detour, it would take her home. Mayo decided to take the detour. When she got home, she would open her drawing book and draw a pretty, happy picture. A pony and some ducks and penguins in the yard—and a great big dog. Not one with shaggy fur, but silver, with big ears and a long face. A dog like that for sure was stronger than a regular white shaggy dog. It would watch over her. If anybody asked her about it, she would say she dreamed it. But nobody would ask. Daddy never looked at her pictures.

Mayo started running, running down the hill for dear life. All she wanted was to reach her front door.

10

Was everybody around him going mental?

Dad, you're always like that!

He thought of his older daughter's face glaring at him, eyes full of tears. This was the rage she turned on him last night, the daughter who never defied her parents, the one who looked after her younger brother and sister like a mother.

Always like *what*? What did I ever do? Except bust my butt day in and day out for the family and for a little law and order—wearing out my shoes, crawling around in the goddamn dirt?

The elevator reached the top floor. As soon as the doors opened, Takizawa was assaulted by the commotion of chirping birds and yapping dogs, along with the distinctive warm scent of animals. Otomichi headed toward the counter in long strides, her heels clicking loudly. Takizawa followed behind, remembering coming to places like this years ago, holding his kids' hands as they whined, we want a dog, we want a cat, and in the end buying them goldfish, as his wife stood smiling alongside.

Happy to let Otomichi do the talking, he wandered aimlessly around the cages of birds and kittens.

Go to hell!

Ever since yesterday, these words had been rising up into this throat time and again, and time and again he had forced himself to swallow them. He wanted to explode, bawl someone out. Yet he said nothing—not to his older daughter, not to her brother and sister who had both come to her defense, and not to the insolent, know-it-all Otomichi either. If he ever raised his voice to Otomichi, who was holding her badge in one hand and questioning the pet shop manager with great intensity, he'd get it back from her a hundred times over. He'd seen her menacing look. But if he didn't let some of this frustration out, sooner or later he might take a swing at somebody. He wasn't a hothead, but when he couldn't get somebody to listen, in the end his hand did the talking for him. The last person he hit . . . was . . . his wife.

As he was playing with a brown kitten that would roll around in its cage like a ball of yarn and grab at his finger, he heard Otomichi's heavy footsteps approaching him.

"Sorry that took so long. Let's go."

Her cheeks were slightly flushed, and her expression seemed animated.

"Did he say there's a place that sells wolves?" he asked as they walked along.

"No," said Otomichi with a shake of her head. "But get this." She turned to him. "There's a kind of breed known as wolf-dog. A cross between a wolf and a dog."

"A wolf and a dog? Yeah?"

"The more wolf blood it has, the closer it is to a purebred wolf. Some breeds are known to be ninety-nine percent wolf, he said."

Takizawa felt gloomy as he listened to Otomichi race on, talking nineteen to the dozen. Little dogs were OK, but he couldn't stand big ones. When he was out on a door-to-door search, they were a menace. He'd pooh-poohed the idea of a wolf, but if there were animals like a wolf-dog running around, the crime-scene unit that had examined the site of the Tennozu murder could be on to something after all.

"Who the hell would want to make a half-breed like that?" muttered Takizawa as they waited for the elevator, his lower lip sticking out. He wasn't looking for an answer. But he knew if he kept letting Otomichi ask the questions, afterward she'd only have more reason to chatter away to him. Before he knew it she'd be getting carried away, starting to act palsy-walsy. *Well, so what? Let her lose her guard, and then watch for your chance to take her down a peg.*

"So what's next?" he asked.

"Pet stores don't have wolf-dogs. The guy told me we should try places specializing in large breeds, look in magazines for dog lovers, that sort of thing."

"Large breeds." Takizawa nodded, in apparent good humor. Looking relieved, Otomichi boarded the elevator that finally arrived.

"Sergeant Takizawa, do you know much about dogs?" she asked.

"Unfortunately, I'm not a dog lover," he answered, trying to sound amicable.

She nodded, and then confessed, "I like dogs myself."

Sure she did. A kid like her with no experience to speak of wouldn't know about going out on a job and a watchdog coming and growling at you. She was in the mobile investigative unit. She rode in a patrol car.

"But I'd never heard of wolf-dogs. I wonder how they're different from Siberian huskies."

"Who knows. Huskies, those are the ones with the wolfish faces, right? Might be the same kind of thing." When Takizawa said this, Otomichi inclined her head doubtfully, but her expression wasn't contrary. As long as he was polite to her, she'd stay in a good mood.

"Before we go looking for a shop that specializes in big dogs, I'd like to stop by a bookstore."

"Great idea. Save time and trouble."

Otomichi spent the rest of the morning leading them from one bookstore to another, standing and reading for what seemed like ages. Then they visited a few pet shops in the Tokyo metropolitan area, and finally they were able to establish that the office for importing wolf-dogs was located in Ginza. Trailing after a policewoman who whipped from one place to the next without stopping for a moment's rest, Takizawa found his back beginning to ache. It was one thing to be in charge, deciding where to go and when, setting the pace; following someone else around wore you out.

When they finally stopped in a coffee shop for a bite to eat, Otomichi placed her order and then immediately slipped away to make a phone call. She came back full of energy and reported, "The person in charge will be back in the afternoon. I left a message that we'll be there at one. I said that we wanted him to tell us all he knew about wolf-dogs."

Takizawa's lower back and feet were killing him. It was all he could do to nod. Really, he was going to have to do something about his weight. He couldn't bear the thought of not being able to keep up with a young woman. He studied Otomichi, who was deep in thought; as far as looks went anyway, she was easy on the eyes.

When they called at the dog import office, thanks to Otomichi's phone call the guy in charge was waiting for them with an assortment of pamphlets. Otomichi greeted him with as bright a smile as Takizawa had ever seen her give anyone, bowed, and thanked him for taking the time to meet with them.

The guy was very smooth. "Wolf-dogs, as the name suggests," he started, "are a breed made by crossing wolves with dogs. In Japan and in the United States, however, wolf-dogs are not officially recognized by kennel clubs."

"What does that mean exactly?" asked Otomichi.

"Well, it means that the kennel club won't issue pedigree papers for them. And therefore they cannot be entered in any kennel club-sponsored shows or competitions. But wolf-dogs are by no means uncommon; in fact, there is a surprisingly large number of them. In France, they have official recognition."

Otomichi nodded and said, "I see," while scribbling something in her notebook. Takizawa hoped she knew that pedigree papers and kennel clubs had nothing to do with this case.

"What kinds of dogs and what kinds of wolves are crossbred to produce wolf-dogs?" Otomichi asked next. "There is, of course, the continental wolf or the Siberian wolf. Are they commonly used in breeding wolf-dogs?"

The import guy, who seemed a little nervous, nodded slightly at this and folded his hands in his lap. He had to be about the same age as Otomichi, thought Takizawa, and *not* the type to handle dogs; more like . . . one of those guys who show you around a model home. Guys like him—oval face, fair skin, businesslike and personable—gave the impression of being nice, regular fellows, but five would get you ten, below the surface they had their nasty, stubborn side.

"That's exactly right," said the guy. "There are all kinds of wolves. Our firm has a kennel in Alaska, and we import wolf-dog pups from there, in accordance with our customers' requests. The main kinds of wolves used for breeding are the arctic wolf, tundra wolf, timber wolf, and British Columbian wolf. The timber wolf, which is known for its large size and its resistance to cold, seems to be a popular choice for breeding."

"And they would be crossbred with . . . ?"

"They are crossbred with local dogs. In Europe, German shepherds are the dog of choice, but at our Alaskan kennel we generally crossbreed wolves with huskies."

Having gone through his spiel, the import guy now offered them some green tea that'd been brought in by a female employee. Otomichi acknowledged the tea with a polite incline of her head, then immediately resumed her questioning. Maybe constitutionally the woman just never got thirsty. She never wanted anything to drink.

"Do you know how many wolf-dogs there are in Japan now?" she asked.

"Well, let me think. . . ."

Takizawa studied a large photo on the wall. It was unmistakably a photo of a wolf, he thought, taken in a snowstorm. In the background was a dark grove of trees. Pelted by snowflakes and buried in a snowdrift up to its knees, the animal had white fur on its face, neck, and belly; the rest of its coat was varying shades of gray. It stood erect in the snowy expanse, face tilted skyward, as if howling. Its bushy tail hung low, its ears were laid back, its eyes were shut.

This was every inch a wolf, wasn't it? How could you call this a dog?

"... I can tell you the number of wolf-dogs imported through our firm. That would be approximately two hundred in all. There are probably some people importing wolf-dogs on an individual basis, and some of our customers have had success breeding wolf-dogs themselves, using stock purchased from us. I'm afraid I can't give you a more precise estimate than that."

"Is your company the only one involved in importing wolf-dogs?"

Takizawa was sitting back, sizing up the situation. How long this outfit had been in business he didn't know, but you had to wonder what kind of profit there was in importing two hundred wolf hybrids.

The import guy, as if reading Takizawa's mind, responded in the same mild tone: "This is not our primary business by any means. We deal mainly in food imports, including Alaskan salmon. While I wouldn't go so far as to say that importing wolf-dogs is something we do in our spare time, it is rather more of a sideline with us."

Takizawa raised his eyebrows and nodded, his mouth forming an "O," saying nothing. The import guy, who had been addressing Otomichi throughout the conversation, glanced over to confirm Takizawa's reaction, and then redirected his attention back at Otomichi. When the interviewer was a woman, did people always go out of their way to be this solicitous and oh-so-polite?

Takizawa sipped his tea, feeling a bit deflated, as Otomichi went on to her next question: What are the characteristics of a wolf-dog?

The man picked up the pamphlets lying beside him, took a sip of tea, and launched into another explanation: "By external appearance, wolf-dogs generally measure three and a half feet to five feet from head to rump, with a tail some 12–20 inches long. Their shoulder height is around 28–32 inches on average, so the head would come up to about here."

He placed his hand on his head, then slid it off to one side to demonstrate. For a moment, he stared into space as if an actual wolf-dog were in the room. Takizawa couldn't help feeling distaste at the whole concept. The import guy began another flowing explanation. With his head chock full of data, he was, yup, exactly like a salesman at a model home. Someone who gave the same spiel more times than he could count.

"Their weight varies quite a bit, ranging from around 45 pounds to 155–160 pounds for the larger subspecies. On average they weigh, I would say, about a hundred pounds."

A wolf-dog also had longer legs than regular dogs, and a more highly developed musculature, which gave it extraordinary powers of leaping; it could easily bridge a distance of five and a half yards. Wolf-dogs could run at full speed for twenty minutes; at a lower speed of twenty-five or thirty miles per hour, they could keep running for a considerably longer time. There were records of wolf-dogs covering 125 miles in a day; that's how tough they were. Unlike a regular dog's profile, wolf-dogs did not feature a hollow above the muzzle; a wolf-dog's muzzle, owing to its wolf heredity, was long and rather straight. The tip of its nose was large, and the sense of smell very advanced: they were reportedly capable of detecting the scent of prey one and a half miles away. The jaw was massive and highly developed, with biting power which—while no match for that of a tiger, puma, lion, or other large feline— was around twice that of a German shepherd, exerting a force of over 1,400 pounds per square inch.

If a pair of jaws that strong got hold of your skull, of course it'd be crushed.

Takizawa felt a chill come over him. Picking up a pamphlet distractedly, he was met by the face of a wolf-dog staring straight at him. What nut dreamed up the idea of crossing a wolf with a dog? If there were pets like these all over the place, what could be more frigging unsafe?

"While their bound and sense of smell are important distinguishing characteristics, what really sets wolf-dogs apart is the excellence of their memory and their intelligence. Presently there are wolf-dogs in training as police dogs, and I understand that they have a stellar record."

The guy went on talking. Next to Takizawa, Otomichi was leaning forward, all ears. Takizawa had gotten the point: wolf-dogs were great. Now he wanted his hands on the list of customers.

Otomichi spoke up. "If they are capable of undergoing training as police dogs, does that mean they have a tractable nature?"

The guy nodded eagerly. Oh boy. Now the conversation would drag on some more.

"Wolves are one hundred percent wild animals. Wolf-dogs are of course dog hybrids, but the greater the ratio of wolf blood to canine blood, the stronger that streak of wildness. It's better not to think of them as dogs; rather, think of them as a completely different animal. The ones that can be successfully trained as police dogs are those with a relatively weaker concentration of wolf blood, around eighty percent."

"What happens when the concentration goes higher?"

"Well, let's see . . . ," said the guy, smiling with pleasure. Apparently there was nothing Mr. Smooth liked more than the sharing the delights of wolf-dogs. "Wolf-dogs are highly intelligent, with a range of dispositions. In folk tales and fairy tales the wolf is usually cast as the villain, and we tend to think of them as savage and terrifying, but that's a mistake. Basically, wild animals are extremely cautious and timid. Wolves are the same. We call them 'shy.' They are fearful of strangers. They have delicate sensibilities, so they can also be friendly to humans who treat them kindly."

Wolf-dogs inherited these traits accordingly, again in proportion to the amount of wolf blood in their veins. Quite a few have been known to be human-hating and timid, unable to show affection to anyone but their owners, unable to turn into the sort of pet their owners wished for. Others, of course, have been known to be friendly and playful, even as, on the whole, they seem to live by their own rules. They aren't the kind of docile animal that people can mold into pets for their own purposes. Since wolves normally live in packs in the wild, wolf-dogs similarly require constant companionship and ample affection.

"Ample affection," repeated Otomichi.

"If you treat a wolf-dog as a member of the family, shower it with affection, and gain its trust, it is capable of great things. Wolf-dogs are physically very gifted animals. But, to repeat, a wolf-dog does not think like a dog—it does not consider the defense of a human being to be its greatest aspiration in life. It has great pride and great wariness. A wolf-dog has allegiance only to someone it knows and trusts."

"Who would want to take on a hassle like that?" Takizawa interrupted, unable to contain himself.

The import guy smiled knowingly and nodded. "I appreciate what you're saying, Officer, but I think that if you ever saw one of them you would certainly understand the appeal. They have such enormous presence, if that's the right word—a kind of splendor that I would say even borders on nobility."

Takizawa snorted. This was not his idea of a fun pooch, but thanks anyway, pal.

"Yet even with a dog as splendid as all that," Otomichi soldiered on, "if someone used it for ill purposes, there's no telling what could happen, isn't that right?"

The smile disappeared from the man's face. "Why exactly are the police interested in learning out about wolf-dogs?" he inquired, showing unease for the first time.

Otomichi threw Takizawa a glance. "Ah, yeah," Takizawa began in a meaningless preface, and then proceeded to outline the incident at Tennozu.

Hearing this, the import guy sighed deeply. "I've been paying rather close attention to that story myself."

"Why is that?" asked Otomichi, swift as a bat.

The guy seemed flustered, looking from her to Takizawa and back again, shaking his head. "Well, I just mean that being in this line of work, you naturally prick up your ears at bad news involving dogs." The import guy frowned, and dropped his voice in a tone of deep melancholy. "We take it upon ourselves to ask our customers not to ever, under any circumstances, train their wolf-dog to be an attack animal. The wolf-dog's powers are, if I may say, a two-edged sword. Unless care is taken to prevent it, a wolf-dog has the potential to turn into a monster beyond human control. Of course, this is not to say that any of our customers, who want a wolf-dog so much that they will order one from Alaska, would ever—"

"Do you have a list of the customers you have supplied with a wolf-dog?" Otomichi asked.

Silence.

Bingo. She finally asked the right question. Takizawa shifted his weight in the overly comfortable sofa and tugged on the hem of his coat. The leather screeched as he shifted position. With a doleful expression, the guy sighed and said, "I'll make you a copy."

"Tough crowd," Takizawa muttered after the import guy left the room. "Who the hell would want to keep an animal like that?"

Otomichi, her nose buried in one of the pamphlets, nodded without speaking. Just the way you'd brush off a kid who asked a dumb question. He itched to complain again, but since he'd decided to try a change of tactics with her, he bided his time.

Before long the import guy was back with a copy of the customer list. Looking at Otomichi, he asked in evident disbelief, "Do you really mean to tell me that that death reported in the newspapers was the work of a wolf-dog?"

"We can't be sure. But we do know that animal hair found at the scene of the crime doesn't match that of any known breed of dog, and that the victim was attacked by a very powerful animal. Also, tracks found near the scene of the crime were more wolf-like than dog-like. More oval than round."

Flipping through the pages of her notebook, she read aloud the measurements they'd been given in the morning's meeting.

The import guy now wore a look of deep sadness. "It's certainly true that the higher the concentration of wolf blood, the more a wolf-dog resembles a wolf in personality and appearance. It's not surprising if the tracks are more like those of a wolf than a dog. Tracks that big would have to belong to a fairly sizeable dog, and—if they really are oval—it's probably reasonable to assume that it was a large wolf-dog. Since, of course, there aren't any pure wolves in Tokyo."

"Could you tell us how to distinguish a pure wolf from a wolf-dog that's, say, ninety-nine percent wolf?"

"Hmm, with that high a concentration of wolf blood . . . Well, you know how there are fleshy pads on the back of the paw? In a wolf, those are black, but in a wolf-dog, they would probably be a different color."

"Would that be the only difference?"

"You like dogs, don't you," the import guy said, looking expectantly at Otomichi with a sense of simpatico as the conversation drew to a close.

"Yes, I do," she nodded.

If she likes dogs, I'm for cats, thought Takizawa dourly. Better yet, monkeys.

As they stepped outside, Takizawa stretched and looked at Otomichi. "So what do we do next? Check out the owners?"

Looking intently at her notebook, she said expressionlessly, "I wanted to talk to you about that. That would be one possibility, but—"

"Hold it." His cellphone was vibrating. It was headquarters.

"Where are you now?" the desk staff sergeant asked.

"In Ginza. We found something called a wolf-dog that's not exactly a wolf, but—"

Suddenly there was a new voice on the line. "Hello, Takizawa? Miyagawa here."

Takizawa answered tautly, "Yes, sir."

"A housewife has been killed in Kawasaki, same MO as Tennozu. I want you to go straight to the scene of the crime."

"Housewife in Kawasaki?"

"Report just came in. Other detectives are on their way. Get over there right away. Here's the address . . ."

Takizawa wrote it down, hung up, and hurried back to Otomichi. She was about to speak, but he grabbed her by the arm and said, "Let's go. Where's the closest station?" Damn, he thought, I hate the train.

"Sir?" Otomichi asked, flustered. "Where are we going?"

"To Tama Ward," he said as they hurried down the stairs to the subway.

"By way of Shinjuku, on the Odakyu line." His gut was making the dash a little hard on him, but he didn't slow down.

"I think the Chiyoda line is faster. Transfer at Omotesando," Otomichi shouted so he could hear. "The two lines share the same route."

Takizawa went through the wicket and was about to set off in one direction when he felt a tug on his elbow. For a moment, he was startled.

"Take the Ginza line. This way." Otomichi's voice was utterly calm, and she headed off in the opposite direction. Relying on the sight of her weaving with the fluid grace of a goldfish through the rush of passengers, Takizawa hastily followed her.

As they waited for the train on the platform, she leaned toward him and whispered, "What happened in Tama Ward?"

Takizawa, still agitated by the news, looked around to be sure he would not be overheard. "It happened again. This time it was a housewife."

Otomichi's expression underwent a transformation, hardening, toughening before Takizawa's eyes. He looked away reflexively. For some reason, in his mind her face overlapped with the image of the wolf he had seen in the Ginza dog-importing office. A creature that had gone back to its wild, savage state, silver fur around its neck, fleshy ears erect, tiny round eyes staring. Fuck you, Takizawa almost said aloud, don't look at me.

"I wouldn't want to be burned to death," Takizawa did say out loud, "but being mauled to death sounds worse."

11

The scene of the crime was on a street in a new residential area that had been created by leveling part of a hill. The neighborhood was relatively uncrowded, with new, prefabricated houses mixed in among older homes; squeezed in between these were low apartment buildings and dormitories for bank employees.

By the time they arrived, the body had already been removed, and here and there clusters of housewives stood talking. Markers placed by the crime-scene unit indicated the location of pieces of physical evidence, and a chalk outline showed where the victim had lain. But there was so much blood in the street that the markers were practically useless, and what seemed to be chunks of flesh were strewn about. By the edge of the road a shopping cart, with a bunch of green onions poking out, was flung on its side. The victim had been on her way home with her groceries.

Takizawa was spotted by a colleague inspecting the site along with investigators from the Kanagawa prefectural police. They greeted each other, and the colleague proceeded to brief Takizawa and Otomichi on the situation: "Victim was apparently attacked from behind. There were abrasions on the palms, knees, and jaw, the result of when she got knocked down. She was also bleeding from the head, and her neck was broken. Her windpipe was chewed out."

Takako felt her heart constrict. Secretly she was grateful that the body had been already removed. Hearing the report gave her a clear enough picture, and seeing the mutilated body would only be sickening. But more than anything, she did not want to be confronted with the evidence of what a wolf-dog could do.

"Same as Tennozu, huh?"

"Tooth marks look pretty big, manner of attack looks similar."

Takako stood a step back, listening to Takizawa and the colleague talk and feeling wretched; she did her best to go through the steps and make a careful inspection of the site.

"No witnesses," Takizawa's colleague was saying, "even in the middle of the day like this. Area is residential, quiet, little traffic. So far we haven't found anyone who heard anything—a scream, a bark, anything."

Takako contemplated the horror of the crime. Yet for reasons that she could not understand, she dreaded having to capture the wolf-dog that had done the deed.

". . . connection between the Tennozu victim and Hara now established. Seems they used to pal around, back in Hara's Roppongi playboy days. A woman paying Hara's bills back then identified him by his photo. A team is working on that angle now."

Takako turned around to join in the conversation. If this last bit was true, this was not an unrelated chain of incidents.

"Do we know the identity of this victim here?" asked Takizawa.

Before the conversation could go further, Captain Watanuki came hurrying by, looking grim. With him were two higher-ups whom Takako did not recognize, probably from the Kanagawa prefectural police. Watanuki greeted the group in his gravelly voice. "What do you think? See anything useful here?"

Before anyone could reply, Takako spoke up nervously. "We've picked up some new information today, sir." Her heart, constricted earlier, was pounding furiously. "I wonder if we could request the use of police dogs."

"Police dogs?"

Takako felt the eyes of everyone on her. She felt terribly nervous, but went on: "Sir, in our investigation we learned of a breed called the wolf-dog, actually a cross-breed between a wolf and a dog. The more wolf blood in the animal, the more it resembles an actual wolf in appearance and behavior. If a wolf-dog attacked this victim, its scent should still be here. It has a strong territorial instinct, and has probably marked the area at close intervals. A police dog could pick up the scent."

The captain gave a series of small nods, and turned to walk to his vehicle. Takako's heart was sore. Watching the crime-scene investigators go about their business, eagerly gathering evidence, she breathed deeply.

"Did that dog import guy say anything about marking?" Takizawa asked quietly.

Takako gulped. "It was in one of the books I read this morning."

Ever since their face-off outside headquarters this morning, Takizawa seemed to have undergone a change of attitude. He started to say something but held back, nodding only. He could be sympathetic, but Takako saw that his eyes were unsmiling. She knew better than to let her guard down.

"That explains how you were able to ask him all those questions. You did your homework."

"Had to. I didn't know anything about wolf-dogs," she said, her breathing still belabored.

Watanuki returned to say that, with the help of the Kanagawa prefectural police, a K9 unit would soon arrive. "But all I wish is that the perpetrator and his animal would keep running farther and farther away, and never stop." With this, the captain ordered two teams to remain at the crime scene, and the rest to begin a door-to-door investigation.

Takako wanted to stay and watch. When the police dogs picked up the scent of the wolf-dog, how would they react? She wanted to see with her own eyes what they would do.

As the day was drawing to a close, the police dogs arrived. Several intelligent-looking German shepherds on leashes went sniffing around the site, exhaling white breath. Takako watched with keen interest. *What do you say, fellas? Any trace of the scent of a bigger, fiercer creature than any of you? Which way did he come from, which way did he go?*

By then members of the media, with their own sharp powers for sniffing out a story, had gathered around. From all sides came the sound of someone speaking into a microphone. The scene was lit up so brightly that the police equipment was all but unnecessary. In the midst of all this commotion, the police dogs were divided into two groups and headed out in different directions.

Disciplined not to bark, the dogs did nothing but pace ceaselessly around the scene with their noses to the ground, glancing up occasionally at their handlers. Takako had expected no less, yet she felt half-disappointed as she watched. However smart they might be, the dogs had no words at their command; how could they possibly tell anyone, "This is no ordinary creature, this is a wild animal vastly more powerful than any of us"? They did not howl or show any excitement. These were not ordinary dogs either.

The meeting started at 10:00 P.M.

"As a result of tracking by a K9 unit, we were able to determine that the scent of the perpetrator remained strong at the scene of the crime. The dogs followed scent trails in two directions from the spot where the victim was found. One trail ended in front of the victim's apartment building, about three hundred meters away, and the other went into a deserted grove of trees."

Takako was exhausted, and so short on sleep that she felt she was losing the ability to regulate her body temperature. God, what a long day. The meeting had begun with a discussion of the link between the victims Kazuki Horikawa and Teruo Hara. The two men had hung out together in Roppongi, but because it happened over a decade ago, it was difficult to find anyone who could testify to their connection, and yet that arm of the investigation was said to be making gradual progress.

Next, the team assigned to Teruo Hara reported no new significant results. Depending on the day of the week, Hara slept at the date club without returning to his apartment, and accordingly was often seen in the vicinity of the building that burned down; and yet, there was no evidence linking him with anyone but the various women about whom the police already knew. The team would next interview people Hara had received New Year's cards from, and people listed in his address book.

The pharmaceutical team found no evidence of anyone attempting to purchase benzoyl peroxide from a university lab or other source in Tokyo and the surrounding prefectures. The investigation would move to companies using benzoyl peroxide, such as refining companies and manufacturers of cosmetics.

The team investigating the timed incendiary device reported that the structure of the device was actually quite simple; it was a remodeled pedometer. The pedometer in question, which was widely available at nationwide department stores and discount shops, could be switched to function as a digital watch; and it was that switch that was used as a timed trigger. The source of electricity was a micro-cell battery that passed through the circuit, connecting to a Nichrome wire used for ignition. With a chemical that had a high ignition temperature, a micro-cell battery could never trigger a fire, but given the low resoluble temperature of benzoyl peroxide, it was adequate to the task. The metal case used to disguise the device as a belt buckle had not turned up as a product widely available on the market, and the team opined that it might yet provide a lead of some sort.

Next, Takizawa reported on the wolf-dog. For Takako, it was quite a sight to see the emperor penguin discoursing earnestly with her report in hand, given his reluctance even to take the word "wolf" seriously that morning. He had apparently lost the inclination—or run out of the energy—to be snide and abusive; for the first time since they'd teamed up, he said to her, as he looked over her report, "Well done."

Takako was equally fatigued, as far as that went.

It was past midnight when the report on the new victim began. No trace of the one-day mini-vacation remained on anyone's face.

"Near the crime scene there are groves of trees and wooded hills, places where people don't usually go, but the scent was still present in those thickets—even across a fence 1.5 meters high. We found one place where the surrounding grasses and weeds were packed down, with traces of animal fur on the ground. Tests are now being run to determine if that fur matches hairs found on the body of the victim."

"Well, that would simplify the investigation, wouldn't it?" a detective suggested. "If there are only a couple hundred wolf-dogs in the country and you've got a list of owners, then you just go down the list until you find the guy with the dog that matches the hair. That should do it."

This idea made perfect sense. Yet Takako wondered if there weren't another way, a shortcut or a detour. But more also had to be learned about the day's new victim—Chieko Yoshii, née Inada, 28, a housewife married less than a year. And about all of the other threads in the case. If not, the list of victims might only get longer, and bloodier.

Trained to attack humans. But only certain designated targets.

Takako felt her mental energy ebbing. She had a feeling the answer was in front of her. But she couldn't think clearly. All that was clear was: They had to catch the animal. The animal, which wasn't the one to hate, would lead them to its human owner, who was the real culprit, the real killer.

I want to see the wolf-dog run. In full flight—across a vast plain.

Stop. Got to concentrate.

The husband of Chieko Yoshii seemed to know very little about the past of his newlywed wife. First thing in the morning, a squad would visit her parents' home to learn everything they could.

Have to keep the wolf-dog from killing again.

The animal didn't know the meaning of right and wrong. The owner did—the human who taught it to kill. Designing a belt with a timing device that turned it into a lethal flame-thrower would take scrupulous planning, but training a wolf-dog to kill like this could take years. Did the killer buy the animal in order to kill? How did the animal learn to recognize its victims?

Was this the work of one person with a lot of time on his hands?

As Takako's mind roamed, she heard Wakita ask: "If there is anything else you've noticed, speak up now." Reflexively, nervously, she raised her hand. She was beat. She wanted to go home and go to bed. Stretch out and fall asleep. Think about nothing. And yet here she was getting up from her chair, rising to her feet, with the eyes of all the male investigators turned on her.

"Wolf-dogs are extremely intelligent. Some owners train them like police dogs, and enter them in competitions. I realize the need to go through the list of two hundred wolf-dogs one by one, but it seems to me that no dog could carry out these killings without extensive training. Perhaps we should consider a visit to the training facility for police dogs?"

There, she'd said it. Seeing the chief nod with satisfaction, she sat down. In the end, it was decided to rework the direction of the investigation at tomorrow morning's meeting. It was nearly 1:00 A.M. when the meeting ended. Takako felt herself breaking into a cold sweat, or a greasy sweat, she wasn't sure which. She walked out of the investigation headquarters, striving to keep her composure.

So tired she was unsteady on her feet, she unlocked the door of her apartment, whereupon she was greeted by a cheery voice crowing, "Welcome home!" Tomoko, whom she had completely forgotten about, having assumed her sister would go back to their parents' house, was standing there with a smile on her face. Feeling all her strength ebb away, Takako looked at her sister and, lacking a word to say, stepped into the apartment.

"You must be tired. Are you hungry? I filled the tub for you, too. Hurry up and change, now."

Having grabbed her sister's shoulder bag and the manila envelope she was carrying under her arm, Tomoko walked around Takako's apartment with unconcealed pleasure, as if she owned the place. Not resisting, Takako went into the bedroom and collapsed on the neatly made bed. She could tell that her pulse was beating abnormally fast. There was a throbbing pain in the middle of her head, and her entire body, from her toes to the top of her head, felt as heavy as lead.

"You OK, Sis?"

She could not reply.

"Why don't you at least take a bath? You'll feel better."

In Takako's mind there emerged a picture of the wolf-dog she had yet to meet, steadily surveying the scene. Transformed to a wretched human-killing machine, it lived apart, in splendid isolation. Where was it now, what was it doing? Stalking someone else in the black of night?

"Come on now. Are you always this out of it when you come home?"

If the creature was going after designated victims at its owner's bidding . . . But could the wildness in its blood stop there? Was there a chance it could develop a taste for human flesh?

"Are you OK? Do you feel sick or something?"

"What are you doing here?" Somehow Takako managed to get the words out. No answer. She turned over on the bed and slowly opened her eyes. Her sister stood there, her lips pursed, a confused look on her face.

"I told you to go home."

"You know, you—"

"Someone else got killed today. I really don't have time to waste on your tawdry little affair."

Her sister's face contorted. Takako forced herself to sit up, using her last bit of strength. She felt hot.

"Stay tonight. It's too late to go home now, but tomorrow I want you out of here." Her breathing was ragged. She laid a hand on the bed and tried to stand up when vertigo nearly toppled her over. Tomoko quickly grabbed her by the arm.

"You've got a fever!"

Tomoko pushed her sister back down on the bed. After that, Takako obediently changed into pajamas and got into bed. As she lay dozing, with amazing speed her sister provided a soft fever-cooling gel sheet and some aspirin.

Nearly delirious, Takako managed to ask, "I had gel sheets in the house?"

"No, I bought them. You didn't have *anything* here. You don't even need that great big refrigerator."

Her sister's voice sounded like their mother's. Dimly aware of someone gently wiping the perspiration from her forehead, Takako fell asleep.

When Takako awoke in the morning, her fever had broken. Her sister was asleep on the floor under a blanket, her legs under the kotatsu. Having sweated profusely, Takako felt much better but she was ravenous. She stole into the kitchen. A pan on the stove turned out to be full of an appetizing curry. The rice cooker was on warm, the rice ready to eat. As she rattled around getting herself a meal, Tomoko woke up, sleepy-faced.

"It must be lonely when you get sick."

Sitting with a cardigan thrown over her shoulders, her mouth full of curry and rice, Takako looked up at her sister. "This still doesn't mean you're living with me, OK? I want you out of here today. Leave when I do—and go to work."

"*Please.*"

"Didn't you hear me? Don't make me an accessory to your extramarital affair. You know perfectly well why I got divorced."

"But your case and mine are—"

"They're *exactly* the same. Adultery is adultery. Unfaithfulness is unfaithfulness. You're in love right now, so you don't see that. But while you and he are off having yourselves a grand old time, somewhere else there's someone weeping bitter tears. And that person resents the hell out of you. Even if you end up living happily ever after, your happiness would be built on top of her pain and resentment. Don't forget that."

With barely another glance at her sister's pouting face, Takako polished off the rest of her curry and quickly went to take a shower. She had been too sick to study the list and pamphlets last night, but it was just as well; her brain needed rest. Having her sister around at such a time, she had to admit, was a godsend. Mustn't start counting on her, though. Even if they were sisters, they led very different lives. Tomoko needed to find her own way through her troubles.

Whichever path she chooses to take.

The wolf-dog, whose existence she had forgotten for a night, now roamed back into her thoughts. As the jets of hot water pounded her, Takako wondered fleetingly where she and Takizawa would go today, what they would see, what would unfold. She would still be with the emperor penguin, even if he seemed to be more decent to her. Must be careful he doesn't suspect she'd gotten ill. If she kept telling herself that, surely her temperature would stay down.

THREE

1

The following day, additional investigators were brought in on the case, doubling total manpower.

The morning meeting brought the news from forensics that the tooth and claw marks, as well as the animal hairs, found on the third victim were established to be from the same canine that had attacked Kazuki Horikawa. Hearing this plunged Takako into gloom. Mentally she addressed the unknown creature: *All this killing. Don't make it worse. Where in god's name are you? Stalking someone else at this moment?*

Even though Takako had never seen a live wolf-dog, its image from the brochures and books was vivid. She could picture it in the Alaskan wilds, running across vast distances, but in an overpopulated city lacking even the musky scent of earth, where would it hide? Takako's heart ached, which mystified her. The wolf-dog was nothing but a wolf with a little bit of dog thrown in, and yet she found herself becoming almost emotionally involved with the creature. Apparently, it had been trained to direct its violent tendencies toward certain specific individuals; but she was sure that around anyone else it would behave with natural timidity and reserve, not like the aggressive killer it had become. It was not the wolf-dog that deserved her hatred.

The morning report continued:

"Until her marriage ten months ago, Chieko Yoshii, maiden name Inada, lived with her parents in Ichikawa, Chiba Prefecture. Her father is employed by a paint company. The family is fairly well-to-do.

"The younger of two sisters, Chieko graduated from high school and went to work for a cosmetics manufacturer as a beauty consultant, leaving later for a job with a cosmetics outfit. Two years ago she met Tsutomu Yoshii, the son of the owner of the company, who personally manages two company stores along the Odakyu Line. He seems to be highly thought of. When their engagement was announced, her friends congratulated her on landing such a rich man."

On the surface, the young wife appeared to be a perfectly ordinary woman. The investigation learned, however, that soon after entering high school, Chieko went through a delinquent stage and was expelled from school. Her parents were at a loss to explain this behavior; but according to Chieko's sister, the father's philandering had torn the family apart, and the subsequent death of the girls' doting grandmother had also played a role. Chieko took to staying out later and later. She helped herself to money in the house, then started staying out all night, then on several occasions ran away from home. To this day, the family does not know who her friends were at that time. Then one day she announced she wanted to go back to school, and they rejoiced in her redemption without asking what prompted her change of heart.

"Naturally, given the unexpected turns this case has taken, we suspect a connection between this young woman and Teruo Hara and Kazuki Hori-kawa," said Wakita, grim-faced as ever.

With that statement, discussion was thrown open to the investigators, who were more somber and steely-eyed with now a third victim. What was the motivation? What was the connection? Was this the work of one lone perpetrator?

"So they knew each other more than ten years ago. Finding people who knew what was going on back then won't be easy."

"There's no evidence that the three victims were in touch recently, or even that they still knew each other. Their old circle could've broken up."

"Which means that if their connection has anything to do with the kill-ings, we're probably looking at a crime of revenge."

At the word "revenge," Takako inhaled sharply. Day in and day out, police officers encountered a wide variety of crimes, but those motivated by revenge were by no means common. The thought made the image of the wolf-dog come alive in her mind. She could almost hear his panting as he ran through the darkness, hell-bent on revenge.

"Anyway, we've gotta get a move on, find out more about their connection, see if anyone else was involved in their circle."

"If anyone else is being targeted, then if we can get to them first and keep them under surveillance, we could wrap this whole case up in one fell swoop."

A mood of peculiar excitement filled headquarters. When the meeting adjourned, the teams scattered quickly.

On this day, Takako and Takizawa headed for the Police Canine Association. This seemed the fastest approach, since the association dealt with all police dog training centers across the country. Teams assigned to finding the wolf-dog would continue the painstaking work of checking the list of owners, name by name.

At the Police Canine Association, located in the business district of Nihombashi, Takako and Takizawa were ushered into a reception room with a worn sofa and armchairs by a man entirely unfazed at the sight of their badges. He looked to be in his early sixties and casually lit a cigarette as he sat down opposite them. According to his business card, his name was Hatakeyama and he was executive director of the association. Takako suspected that he might be a retired policeman in a cushy second career; he had that air.

She opened her notebook, sitting erectly on the edge of the hard sofa, and looked directly at the man as she spoke. Takizawa was letting her handle this as she saw fit.

". . . and so," she concluded, "we thought you would be able to provide us with information on all the dog training centers in the country."

Hatakeyama looked at Takako with an expression of great equanimity. "Pardon me for asking, miss, but how much do you know about police dogs?"

Takako summarized: that canine units were brought in as requested by investigators, that the dogs received special training, that they were overseen by the Identification Division.

"Yes, I guess that would be all you would know." The man, who was about the age of Takako's father, spoke with one slightly raised eyebrow. Inside, Takako felt a grating sensation. She knew when she was being patronized. Hatakeyama went on, "That might be enough for an on-scene investigation. Particularly if you were with the crime-scene unit."

The man's every comment was barbed. Despite herself, Takako grew defiant. "Yes, well, that's why we're here, to find out more."

Hatakeyama let a scornful smile play around the corners of his mouth. "Let me tell you about police dogs," he said.

A police dog was one that had received special training for police work such as searches and protection. The training was designed to make the most of canine obedience, intelligence, and alacrity, not to mention a sense of smell three to four thousand times more acute than that of a human being. Police dogs came in two categories: those bred at prefectural police headquarters around the country, called department dogs, and those bred by private citizens, called contract dogs. The former currently numbered around 150; they were assigned to the Identification Division, and classified officially as "equipment," that is, consumable items like pencils and notebooks.

The MPD had no contract dogs. Its thirty-five canines, all of them departmental, worked an average of eight or nine years before being retired. Sometimes retired police dogs went to private owners as watchdogs, sometimes they spent the rest of their natural lives in a corner of the police kennel. Once their usefulness as "equipment" was over, new dogs were purchased and trained in their stead. There was no budgetary allowance for old dogs, so their handlers scrimped and saved to buy them food.

Of the half million canines registered as police dogs nationwide, contract dogs were the most able, having met the high qualifying standard; they were deployed on request to police working a particular case. Altogether there were some 1,300 in the country. A big advantage of this system was that it saved the police the considerable expense of breeding and raising dogs on their own. Also, it had great public relations appeal as a sign of police willingness to cooperate with the private sector and build good relations with the public.

The Saitama Prefectural Police Department, for example, had no K9 units of its own, and relied on contract dogs exclusively. Some contract dogs were trained by private individuals; more often, officially licensed handlers, ranked into three classes by the Japan Police Canine Association, did the training at approximately 2,300 training centers around the country.

Strictly speaking, the term "police dog" referred only to these two categories of highly trained dogs; in more general terms, it applied to any dog that was registered as a police dog and had undergone some police dog training. In addition to regional conventions, there were national events to raise the level and hone the abilities of police dogs; the two most important were the Japan Champion Trials and the National Police Dog Field Championship Trials. The Japan Champion Trials was something like a beauty contest. The seven breeds of dog eligible for registration as police dogs—German shepherd, Airedale terrier, boxer, collie, Doberman pinscher, Labrador retriever, and golden retriever—competed for the prize of best-looking dog in categories of adult, adolescent, young dog, and puppy.

While participating dogs were all highly trained, they were judged less on their intelligence and the fruits of their training than on overall appearance, muscle definition, teeth, and so on. All competitors had pedigrees and were things of beauty to behold; their owners lavished care on them, polishing them like precious gems. Champions brought their owners great honor, and great fortune as well, in the form of lucrative stud fees. Some people spent millions of yen to purchase likely champions overseas. It was a world where appearance was all, and people jostled to be noticed.

The National Police Dog Field Championship Trials, as its name implied, was a test of ability. Categories included protection, tracking, and search, with protection divided into the two categories of protection and detaining. Participants in this championship trials competed not on the basis of pedigree or appearance, but on performance alone, so the atmosphere was one of serious business. Participants, all of whom had completed a rigorous course of training, obediently walked or ran along prescribed routes, jumped over hurdles, barked at a suspect, engaged and held a suspect, selected an article of clothing belonging to the suspect, and tracked the suspect using the scent on an article of his possession. They were the very image of all that a police dog should be. Every dog wore a look of eager intelligence, happy beyond measure to show off its talents and earn praise from its human. Seventy percent of the dogs who placed in the upper levels of this contest were contract dogs.

Department police dogs, of course, were not entered in either competition. They didn't have the time; they needed to be ready to go to work at a moment's notice. And they were not allowed the luxury of mistakes. Any dog that entered the obedience event only to wander around in circles would never have been granted departmental status, but a department dog that did enter such a competition would be considered a shoo-in to win. They were professionals, and not the polished-gem type of professional dog either; no beauty contests for them.

When he had explained all this, Hatakeyama regarded Takako with a self-satisfied expression, not bothering to look toward Takizawa, who was not saying a word. "We're a private organization, but we do work closely with the police. You're still young, miss, but I suggest you try to keep this much in mind."

Takako said nothing, forcing herself to smile sweetly.

Hatakeyama's response in turn was to stub out his cigarette in an oversized ashtray with the brand of a pet food printed in gold, take a deep breath, and add: "But get this straight: We do not train dogs to attack and kill people. Period."

More than the words themselves, the tone of Hatakeyama's voice was aggressive. All but ignoring her, he went on to qualify his statement slightly: Attack dogs were indeed taught to engage and bite suspects, but exclusively on the arm or other non-vital part of the body; and the moment the suspect was felled, or clearly in no danger of escape, these dogs were trained to let go. No police dog would ever sink its teeth into anyone's throat, neck, or skull; the notion of a killer police dog was preposterous.

"Yes," said Takako, agreeing, "but by the same token, no dog could have carried out these crimes without careful training. No matter how high an IQ a dog might have, surely the services of a professional handler would be required for it to perform at that level."

"We have some wolf-dogs in training, I'll concede. Rottweilers also do exceptionally well in the program. As long as they have what it takes, we're prepared to accept dogs of any breed. We've even got Shiba and Akita dogs in training. But they tend not to make it through the final trials. They might have the brains, but not the stamina or strength. There must be both."

"Yes, and a wolf-dog—"

"What I'm saying is, police dog training is nothing like what you're talking about. With all due respect, the idea that any of our handlers would ever train a police dog to carry out a lethal attack is absurd. Besides, not all handlers are approved by us. Kennel clubs and other outfits also certify people as dog handlers."

This last statement was delivered with a look of contempt mingled with annoyance. And defensiveness. It seemed to suggest this: that here the Police Canine Association was dedicated to training dogs to be useful to society, and Takako had the audacity to suggest that an antisocial killer was a police dog in their registry. It might just be a rumor, or ignorance, but it was an outrage.

Takako refused to give up. "Thank you for explaining in such detail," she said. "What I'm asking now is whether you can assist us in this particular matter. Do you, for instance, have knowledge of anyone who trains wolf-dogs, or have you ever observed such training in progress?"

Hatakeyama scowled.

Takako continued: "True, such a person might not be a member of your association. But it seems possible that you might nonetheless know of such a handler."

"Possibly."

"Wolf-dogs stand out. Because they're part wild, I understand they have to be walked for hours every day. That makes it all the more likely that you might have gotten word of—"

"Nobody would come to me about anything so trivial." It was like he'd slammed the door shut.

Wondering if her instincts were off, Takako tried to think fast, casting about for another approach. She could feel Takizawa's eyes upon her. Ever since yesterday he'd been unbelievably deferential, listening in silence as she took the lead. But the eyes she felt watching her now were not full of warmth and admiration. They were saying, See, what did I tell you?

"Let me see if I have this right," Takako regrouped. "You're suggesting that the odds are good that someone trained the wolf-dog privately, on his own, is that it?"

"Yes."

"Well, then—" As she groped for words, behind her Takizawa cleared his throat.

And then inserted himself into the conversation: "Hatakeyama-san, how about this? You ever hear anything about someone who used to train dogs buying himself a wolf-dog, anything like that?"

"Now *that* I probably could ask around and find out for you."

Takako's mood began to sour as she listened to the two men rattle on.

"Handlers, is that what you call 'em? People who train dogs for a living. They must really like dogs, seems to me."

"Oh yes. In fact, they often treat their dog better than they do their own family." Hatakeyama's face suddenly softened. "I'll tell you," he said, "there's nothing more lovable than a dog that obeys your every command."

"I can see that," said Takizawa. "Must be a lot more lovable than some people. I'm no dog lover, mind you. I wouldn't know about that myself."

"Oh, you should get yourself a dog. You'd see."

"Not me. Are you kidding? On my salary, the best I could manage would be a turtle or a goldfish."

Hatakeyama laughed out loud, amused. When it was Takako asking the questions, he'd answered in a flat monotone, but to Takizawa he responded heartily. The problem was not the content of her questions, the problem was her; he didn't like her. In short, he and Takizawa were two of a kind.

"I'll bet someone like that never really settles into another kind of work," Takizawa said. "It's not a job you can do by halves, is it?"

"Neither is yours."

"True enough." Takizawa smiled broadly.

So Takizawa was heading in the same direction she was headed, asking the same questions she would have asked if he hadn't butted in.

"I've only seen wolf-dogs in photographs," said Takizawa, "but to me they look no different from wolves. One look and you can see it's no hound, it's a wolf, you know what I mean? And the more wolf blood they have, I bet the harder they are to train."

Hatakeyama was practically leaning forward, making appropriate interested responses as Takizawa spoke. Thoroughly soured, Takako listened in tight-lipped silence as he went on.

"The way we figure it is, since wolf-dogs are such wild creatures at heart, they'd never go after a human target without training from a handler who knew his stuff. Our two victims were done in by the exact same method. The second victim—a woman, just your ordinary housewife—was attacked in broad daylight, but nobody saw anything. Or heard anything either—no scream, no barking, no nothing. Getting a wolf-dog to pull off a trick like that had to take some serious training, if you ask me."

From where Takako sat, Takizawa was himself now leaning toward Hatakeyama, and he'd put on a disarming smile, something like the one he'd used on that young doctor at the hospital. He went on with such facility and smoothness, it was a wonder he had kept quiet all this time.

"So how about it? Maybe you know of a top-notch handler who hasn't been seen around a training center for the last few years?"

"Well, I could ask around and find out for you—but if you're talking about *really* skilled handlers, I would have to say there's no one better than the police. Somebody in the Identification Division, in charge of the canine unit."

Taken aback, Takako looked at Takizawa. His face seemed to have frozen for a second, too. The idea made sense—rather than go after all the handlers in all the training centers in the country, how much smarter, and easier, to focus on policemen training department dogs.

Acting impressed, nodding, Takizawa mumbled, "Aha, I see what you mean."

A policeman raising a dog for revenge: by no means unthinkable. All avenues had to be explored. Hatakeyama had mentioned there were no K9 units in Saitama PD. Then maybe the next step was to request the name of anybody who had retired early from the Identification Division in Tokyo, Chiba, or Kanagawa, somebody without a clear reason.

"Anyway, I'll get back to you if I find out anything," said Hatakeyama, as the three of them stood up.

Glancing sideways at the man talking to Takizawa with such easy rapport, totally unlike his attitude to her, Takako felt her chest constrict. Well, she would never see Hatakeyama again, and good riddance. No point letting every annoying guy get under her skin.

2

After putting in a request for the names of any Identification Division members who had resigned early in the last few years, Takizawa suggested the two of them make a visit to a police dog training center. After getting short shrift from the Police Canine Association guy just now, Otomichi was looking a bit peevish, but she walked alongside him without comment.

See there, I'm not the only guy who gets uptight dealing with a woman. That's what he wanted to tell her, but as long as she said nothing, he wasn't going to bring it up himself. Anyway, her hunch was right. He hated to think that someone who was on the police force would carry out revenge like this; but for both benzoyl peroxide and police dog training, it made sense, the easiest access to such specialized knowledge was for a member of the police force.

According to the materials they'd received at the Police Canine Association, there were nine top training centers in Tokyo, twelve in Chiba, twenty-two in Saitama, and fifteen in Kanagawa.

"You want to start here in the city?" Takizawa turned around to ask Otomichi. With her usual impassiveness she uttered only a single word, "Yes." Cautious by nature. Maybe she was on to his little plan to get her off her guard, let her get a swelled head, and then teach her a lesson, send her crashing to earth. Man, even after he softened his manner, her attitude had scarcely changed. Uncomplicated women were more appealing, he thought. Oh, well. He hitched up his belt and sighed softly to himself.

To teach a dog to attack a specific person, the first thing you had to do was to acquaint the dog with the scent of that person. One possibility was to train the dog to attack whenever it detected that scent, in classic stimulus-response fashion. That meant that the perp had to obtain an article of clothing worn by the target—which would suggest that he didn't live very far from the target. The perp could have followed his target around and stolen something belonging to him, or picked up a cast-off cigarette butt, or tissue, or other detritus. For sure he wouldn't do something like make personal contact.

Could a civilian pull off something like that? Still, no matter how knowledgeable a handler was about dogs, getting the dog to recognize the target's scent wasn't easy.

"Were any of the victims robbed recently?" Takizawa muttered this thought half-aloud as he sat swaying to the motion of the train.

Otomichi, who was sitting silently next to him, shook her head. "I haven't heard anything about robbery," she said. "Are you thinking that the perp may have stolen something to teach his wolf-dog the scent?"

The lady had read his mind. Smart. She got the point quickly—and that very fact got his goat.

"Obtaining something that belonged to the target, or something the target had on him, would mean contact, so it would involve some risk," she said. "Breaking into a residence would be even riskier. Do you think someone bent on carrying out a grand scheme of revenge would take such a risk?"

"If it was you, what would you do?"

"Well . . . I think it might be possible to take the opposite tack—attach a scent to the victim."

Made sense. Perfume would work, or anything else the animal had been trained to recognize. Takizawa rubbed his jaw, again feeling the whiskers he had missed while shaving; she was right, that would be easier. Even a civilian could handle that. "Either way," he spoke up, "we need to get the teams going down the wolf-dog list to find out the employment history of the owners."

Otomichi nodded, still looking as if she was thinking about something. Was she going to come out with another gem? But she kept quiet, eyes straight ahead, hands folded on the shoulder bag in her lap. She wore no rings or nail polish; the hands were pale and delicate, but her fingers were too long and too big for a woman

You never got a sense of how she lived her daily life. Once, while he was out drinking with the guys, he did some casual asking around, and found out she was single, lived alone in an apartment; no one knew more than that. He'd had her pegged as twenty-seven or twenty-eight, but turned out she was over thirty. Had staying single so long soured her personality, or was it her sour personality that had kept her from finding a husband in the first place? Takizawa felt mild curiosity on this point.

"Say—"

"You know—"

They both started to speak at the same time. Otomichi hastily caught herself. "Yes?"

"Nothing. You were gonna say?" Maybe it was better not to come right out and ask a thing like, *Not interested in getting married?* If he did, she might get the wrong idea, or think he was interested or even coming on to her. It was a funny thing, though. His own wife had run out on him; his married life ended in betrayal and ruin; he'd long lost any illusions about marriage—and yet when he heard of an unmarried young woman, he couldn't help thinking of her as a social misfit. "Let's have it," he said.

"I was just wondering if it was at all possible that the perp might work for our company."

That's what cops called the police organization, "our company." They used the expression to avoid attracting attention when talking among civilians, and it eventually became a habit. Hearing her say this, Takizawa had to admit they did share a bond.

"We can't rule it out. Or it could be someone who used to be with us."

"The best handlers are policemen, those who raise and train the department dogs, isn't that right?"

"That's what the guy said. Also you've gotta realize the perp hasn't left us any other clues to speak of. That right there suggests somebody who knows a thing or two about police investigations."

Otomichi's mouth tightened, and she sighed. Takizawa started to say he didn't want it to be true either, but in the end all he did was sigh also.

They got off at Asagaya on the Chuo Line, and went first to the police box in front of the station for directions to the dog training facility. Takizawa contacted headquarters, requesting the employment history of all the wolf-dog owners.

Leaving the police box, they passed a bank where Takizawa remembered he had investigated a robbery ten years back, then down a street with wide sidewalks, heading toward Ome-kaido Avenue. As they walked along, Otomichi suddenly said, "God, I hope it's not one of us." A dry breeze swept past them. Her short bangs, tousled by the wind, changed her expression in a variety of ways.

"There're all kinds of cops," said Takizawa, walking along at his usual brisk pace.

It was true. Even among his fellow cops there were plenty of pricks, good-for-nothings, and greedy bastards, as well as clowns, homosexuals, and losers that made you wonder how they ever got to be guardians of the law. Decent fellows had them far outnumbered, of course, so the department maintained face. But the presence of so many different types undoubtedly lay behind the brass's frequent exhortations to "overcome your differences and work together." Between lifers and non-career guys, there was another difference.

And from his perspective, this female was another queer fish in a class all her own. And yet she had a sense of pride and camaraderie as an officer of the law; otherwise why would she have made that remark just now? It galled him to admit it.

They crossed Ome-kaido Avenue and walked another fifteen minutes through a quiet residential neighborhood before arriving at their destination. It was an old-fashioned style of house, unremarkable, and not in the best of repair. Behind a concrete block wall about four feet high were tall evergreens, interspersed with camellia bushes. There was a carport, where two station wagons were parked. The black paint on the iron gate was peeling; in spots rust was showing through. The only evidence this wasn't like every other house in the neighborhood was the classic calligraphy—POLICE DOG TRAINING CENTER—on the doors of the station wagons and the collection of dog collars and stout leather leashes hanging on the wall of the carport, alongside hoses and car-washing equipment.

"Can they really train dogs in a place like this?" Takizawa wondered aloud as he pushed the buzzer at the gate. Instantly there was the report of dogs barking frantically. Their barks were so deep and so loud, he could imagine how big they were. Turning to Otomichi, he said uneasily, "You don't think they'll jump over the wall, do you?"

She blinked in surprise, then giggled, almost childishly, "Heavens, no."

Go on and laugh, Takizawa thought bitterly. All I want to do is ask what we came here to ask, and then get the hell out. Why in god's name do we have to spend all our time visiting these dog joints anyway?

In short order, a man appeared, dressed in sweats and sandals. His short, graying hair had a permanent wave, and his face was deeply tanned, like a workman of some sort. Takizawa pulled out his badge and showed it to the man. Immediately, he was all smiles.

Here's a switch, a guy who smiles at a cop.

"Hello, officers, welcome," he said, pulling open the gate, delighted to see them. The dogs kept up their cacophony. From all the commotion there had to be more than three of them. "I heard from the Police Canine Association that you might be dropping by. Come in, come in."

The man beckoned them to enter, but Takizawa, who saw a weed-grown lawn with patches of bare dirt, could not bring himself to budge. Seeing his nervousness, the man smiled again and said reassuringly, "It's all right. They're in a cage."

No choice now, he'd have to go in. Smiling vaguely, Takizawa gingerly took a few steps. The guy went first, leading the way across stepping-stones to the yard around back. Takizawa hastily intervened, "No, right here is fine." The handler turned around with a disappointed look on his face. Just like a doting parent, thought Takizawa. Dog-lovers never could fathom the feelings of dog-haters.

As the barking went on, the man asked, "So are you here about the dog that's been attacking people?"

Takizawa nodded, distracted by the clamor of the barking and thinking what a nuisance to the neighborhood. "Yeah, we figure the dog's got to be a very well-trained animal."

Even as he said that, the barking grew more agitated. Takizawa now heard a clattering, as if the dogs were throwing themselves against the walls of their cage. Could they jump out over the top? If they leaped up on him, he'd be mauled. The barking was so unnerving that Takizawa had just about lost interest in asking any questions. He glanced over at Otomichi, who was standing beside him as cool as ice.

Catching his signal, she crinkled the corners of her eyes in a little smile, looked at the dog handler, and said: "And so we'd like to ask you a few questions. We've already asked the Police Canine Association representative the same question, but in theory it would be possible to teach a dog to attack and kill a particular individual, wouldn't it?"

"Yeah, but I hate to think anybody would train a dog to do a thing like that." The guy was agreeing, but shaking his head at the thought. "What breed are we talking about? A Doberman, for instance, is an aggressive dog to start with, so it might be more suited to training like that."

"We think that it may be a hybrid, part dog and part wolf."

"A wolf-dog?" He widened his eyes in surprise, looking first at Takako and then over at Takizawa.

Fighting the urge to put his hands over his ears, Takizawa watched the guy as he repeated, "Well, well, a wolf-dog!" Didn't the barking bother him in the least? Can't you shut those dogs up? he wanted to say.

"Yes, we'd like to ask you about that," said Otomichi.

"Go right ahead."

"Do you have any knowledge of someone who's been training a wolf-dog, or have you heard any rumors to that effect?"

"That *would* be a challenge, training one of those. They have a lot of wild blood. I've heard of wolf-dogs running away from their owners."

"You have?"

No sooner did she say this than the man strode toward the back of the house and yelled, "Hey!" The barking and growling instantly softened into whines. Impressive, thought Takizawa—but if you've got 'em that well trained, why let 'em raise such a ruckus to begin with?

"Sorry about that. It's almost time to take them out. We only have adolescent dogs here now."

"Whaddaya talking about, wolf-dogs running away?" asked Takizawa, who was getting his interest in the job back.

The man thought for a few seconds, then nodded to himself with satisfaction. "It was last year or the year before, I think," he began. "This is all just a rumor, I don't really know for sure."

"What kind of rumor?"

"They said a wolf-dog got loose in Saitama. A woman there had two."

"*Two* wolf-dogs?" Otomichi exclaimed, stepping forward. "What happened to the one that got away?"

In a tone that was both reluctant and somehow pretentious, the man responded, "As I say, it's all a rumor. It ran into the hills—"

"And was never caught?"

"An animal like that is no good for women and children. Turns out it wasn't the first time it got away; neighbors were complaining. Wolf-dogs are supposed to be timid and quiet, but how many people would know that at a glance? You'd think they were wolves, plain and simple." The man took a moment to let things sink in. "Anyway, what I heard was she kept the dogs in a narrow space under the eaves, no bigger than this, behind a fence that was more like a screen. My jaw dropped when I heard that. I don't know how the woman could think she cared about dogs. She only had a flimsy lock, too."

"So about the escaped wolf-dog, did you hear what happened to it?" Takizawa asked as he felt his spine grow cold. He knew if the creature ever came charging out of an alley at him, he'd be scared shitless.

"The story was, it took off into the mountains, went feral. A dumb dog is easy to capture alive or lure out, but wolf-dogs are smart, you know what I mean? It went deep into those steep hills around Chichibu, and now it's the leader of a pack of wild dogs. That's the word anyway."

For a dog as sturdy as a wolf-dog, getting from the wilds of Chichibu to the city center would not be hard. But why would a wolf-dog gone feral seek out particular victims in the city? Inconceivable. So, interesting as it was, this particular information had no bearing on their case. The possibility of a connection seemed extremely low.

"Where'd you hear this rumor?"

"Let me think. I guess it was when a bunch of us from the training center got together. Somebody was talking about it."

"Any other stories about wolf-dogs?" pursued Takizawa. "Someone bought a wolf-dog or saw someone training one, anything like that?"

When it came to these vital questions, the man only shrugged. Something set the dogs barking again. When one started up, the rest joined in, as if in response.

"What are they?" Takizawa asked with a frown, jerking his chin in the dogs' direction.

"We've got six German shepherds. Another three are retrievers, but those don't bark."

Hearing this, Takizawa's indignation faded. Still, fully trained police dogs working a crime scene were bearable, but no way was he going near those growling monsters in the back yard. He looked at Otomichi, who seemed bizarrely warmed by the barking; the desire to go see the dogs was written all over her. But as soon he finished his questions, Takizawa held up a palm and said, "Well, thanks very much." Give me a break, he was thinking. The last thing I want to do is go look at a cage full of humongous dogs. Besides, he suddenly noticed as the wind shifted, he didn't like their smell either.

"Very helpful. If you think of anything else, give us a call." Takizawa said his goodbyes to this fellow, who, if you met him on the street in that getup, would be a dead ringer for a yakuza, and then he turned his back on the training center and hurried away. Otomichi's footsteps followed quietly behind him. Even after he had managed to get fairly far away, the sound of barking still rang in his ears.

Through the window along the staircase, beyond the iron fence painted light green, he could see waves of steam rising into the winter sky. The steam, coming out of the kitchen chimney, sparkled in the morning sun before disappearing into the atmosphere.

When the steam disappears, it will be spring, thought Funatsu, sticking a hand under his white hospital coat and fishing out a bunch of keys from the pocket of his pants. The key ring was fastened to his belt with a chain. Either Funatsu was too short, or the chain was, because once he had selected the right key, he had to twist his body and press his right hip up against the door in order to get the key into the keyhole. One thing he had to do, as he made his rounds from floor to floor, was to make absolutely sure the doors were locked; this requirement added a certain accent to the routine.

"Doctor!"

As soon as Funatsu opened the door, he was submerged in the loud voice of a patient and in the warm air rushing outside.

"Good morning, Aki!"

Aki, who would soon be forty-six, was standing right in front of the door in a pale pink jersey suit. Swiftly locking the door behind him, Funatsu smiled at her.

"Doctor, you know what I've been thinking?"

"No, what?"

"I've been thinking about *kurabayapunikuria*."

"What's that?"

This flaccid-faced woman, once an ordinary housewife, now pouted unless called by her girlhood name. At Funatsu's question, she looked at him with a smile that bore a discernible touch of triumph.

"I already told you!"

"You did? I forget—what was it again?"

"When I met you in *konidera*, I told you about it along with *merahon*."

As Aki spoke, several other patients noticed that the doctor had arrived and began drifting his way. Others continued to shuffle up and down the corridor, their posture tilted forward, oblivious to everything else.

"Don't you even know that, Doctor? I told you about *yunmashuin*, too. . . ." Aki continued to chatter.

A patient, about the same age as the woman, came up alongside her and burst into shrill cackles. "Doctor, never mind her! This lady's plumb crazy. Honey, nothing you say makes one bit of sense."

Aki showed no reaction to this; she just stood vacantly still. The cackler was an old-timer on the ward. She had no symptoms of neologism, the coining of new words that was a symptom of schizophrenia. Instead, she was in the grip of a delusion that more than a decade of treatment had done nothing to dissolve: she was convinced her real mother was an American and she herself was a former first lady. She didn't stop there: she had Austrian royal blood, descended from Russian nobility, and had come to Japan on a special mission. For the sake of world peace, she was to explain cosmic principles to select foreign visitors.

"Hey, Doctor, my legs hurt. Below the knees they're stuffed with voices screaming, 'Let me out! Let me out!'"

"Got any cigarettes, Doc?"

As he stepped forward, a swirl of complaints, requests, and pleas poured forth from all sides. Funatsu walked straight down the corridor, making simple replies to everyone, as he headed for his office. Here again, he had to open the door with one of the keys attached to his belt; but the nurses inside had seen him coming and opened the door for him.

"When is it ever going to warm up, huh?" he said with a grin, and the nurses and clinical nurse specialists nodded in agreement: "Not soon enough for me," and the like. Within this limited area, ordinary conversation took place in an ordinary way. Funatsu inquired if there had been any significant change in the patients in his care and asked how the newly committed patients were doing. Then he asked about a sixteen-year-old girl who had had an episode the day before and was now in a special cell.

"It's only been a day. Once she comes to, I'm afraid she might get agitated again," one CNS replied with a sigh. Even a young girl could exhibit ferocious strength if she became agitated and violent. It took two or three grown men working together to subdue her. Funatsu listened to the CNS, thinking that the girl probably ought to stay where she was for another week.

"And Emiko," he said. "She's going home for a week starting tomorrow, no problems there?"

One of the nurses shook her head as she smiled and said, "She's really looking forward to it."

"I wish I could transfer her to an open ward."

"Since she's been able to go for visits home, she's calmed down so much," the nurse said. "It's because that dog means so much to her."

Funatsu remembered the dog that the girl's father always brought with him when he came to pick her up. He himself, along with the other members of the staff, looked forward to seeing the dog again. It had been coming by for a couple of years now, as he recalled, and had won everybody's heart. It was an ideal pet in all respects: handsome looks, gentle disposition, trained superbly. Funatsu had never seen a finer dog. As the nurse suggested, there was no doubt that the dog, whose name was Gale, had a positive influence on Emiko. In the last two years her symptoms had undergone no worsening or complication.

"All day long she's been asking what time her father is coming to pick her up."

"I'll go check on her," Funatsu said as he prepared to return to the ward.

Several patients were waiting outside the door for him, and as he walked down the corridor, they trailed along behind him, with nothing to say, rather like seaweed.

The hospital where Funatsu worked treated many patients, most of them suffering from schizophrenia or alcoholism. Housed in this closed ward were patients whose symptoms were in flux; patients with poor orientation skills; and patients who, if returned to an open ward where they had freedom of movement, would be at risk of running away or engaging in unsafe or anti-social behavior. Their symptoms being severe, many patients were prescribed strong medication that left them semi-conscious all day; most were therefore unaware that they had been forcibly cut off from society and deprived of their freedom. Even so, those who followed Funatsu around were in better shape than the rest. Others stayed in bed all day or sat alone facing the wall or lay motionless, as if dead. What was going on inside their heads, what voices they heard, what visions they saw, all were beyond Funatsu's power to understand—even if the patients frequently confided in him and even if he had spent years observing their behavior.

When he unlocked one of the tatami-mat rooms that accommodated twelve patients, Funatsu observed a patient, with the covers pulled over her head, being repeatedly jabbed by Emiko from the next bed. When Emiko saw the doctor, she moved hastily away from her neighbor, sat up straight, and lowered her head politely. Her gaze wandered, and she appeared suddenly ill at ease.

Funatsu slipped off his sandals and, stepping onto the tatami in his stocking feet, went over to Emiko and knelt down on one knee in front of her. She put her hands behind her and fiddled with the straw matting while twisting her body around.

"Emiko, you know your father's coming for you tomorrow, right?"

"Yeah, I know."

"And you know that this time you'll be away for a whole week?"

"I said I know."

Funatsu could not help but think how Emiko looked like a mollusk, though it was terrible of him to think so. Her body kept wriggling as if without spine while her head swung loosely back and forth.

"Heh-heh-heh," she laughed uncertainly.

"Are you glad?"

"Sure, I'm glad. I can play with Gale. Go to the river, take walks, and stuff."

"Be sure to dress warmly. Don't go and catch a cold."

"Gale's always warm. He's warm and furry!"

Some of her pronunciation was hard to figure out. She was wearing a sweat suit that was pilling almost everywhere. It looked like it hadn't been washed in a while, limp, the ribbing in the collar all stretched out. Her shoulder-length hair, which had been tied back in pigtails, probably by a nurse, was oily, dandruff showing.

"OK, I want you to take a bath today, all right? You want to look your best for your father, don't you?"

This seemed to make Emiko laugh, and she nodded her head. In the next moment, she suddenly turned toward Funatsu and began to bow over and over. "If I take a bath, can I go home?" she asked obsequiously, trying to read his expression with the air of a crafty adult.

"Yes. If you get all clean and fresh, you can go home."

"Goody!" Her body still twisting, Emiko reverted to a laughing child.

Funatsu gently stroked her head, and got up to leave. But just before he got out the door he heard Emiko say, "Hey!" Thinking she was calling him, he turned around, but her attention was on the patient in the next bed, whom she was jabbing all over again.

"*Nah-nah-na-nah-nah*," she was going on. "Gale's coming tomorrow. I'm going home with him and my dad."

When Funatsu was around, Emiko was on her best behavior, but the second he took his eyes off her, she would pick on other patients, sometimes get a little rough. Her movements, though slow, were jerky and clumsy. She was unable to stick to doing one thing, and would sometimes behave with astonishing coarseness. Even so, compared with nine years before, when she was first hospitalized, her symptoms had eased dramatically. But considering that roughly seventy-five percent of all speed addicts required only five or six months of treatment, Emiko's hospitalization had gone on for an exceptionally long time.

She was, what, twenty-six now? thought Funatsu as he unlocked the iron door with a key chained to his waist, went out on the landing, and locked it again. Emiko, whom Funatsu had had charge of since shortly after coming to work here, was once the youngest addict in the ward. At seventeen, her face was paper-white and wasted, and she had suffered from paranoid delusions as well as visual and auditory hallucinations. In addition, she had gonorrhea, and she was pregnant. She looked so frail that if you held her down too hard you worried she would snap in two; and yet she used to howl, "I want *shabu*. Gimme *shabu!*" *Shabu* was the street name for amphetamines, her drug of choice.

Be nice if she could go home permanently.

From the recovery period, when indications first show improvement, through the anchoring period, when progress slows, Emiko had displayed an amazing range of symptoms typical of chronic amphetamine abuse. As a rule, the condition does not cause dimming of consciousness or forgetfulness. It begins with apathy, fatigue, lassitude, inactivity, absence of initiative, and progresses to restlessness, hypokinesia, catalepsy, negativism, tonic hyperactivity, . . . There are also symptoms of pseudo-dementia and paralogia.

Even so, Funatsu and other residents had expected her to be out of the hospital and back functioning in society within six months; she might well drift back into drugs and have to be re-hospitalized, they knew, but that was the kind of life this girl was going to live. Yet, after all this time, she was still here. What should have been the best, most radiant season of her life—a time when, if not for amphetamines, she might fall in love, marry, become a mother—was spent locked away behind iron bars. Time for Emiko flowed differently than it did for others: persistent childishness was definitely one of her behavior patterns. She had not so much reverted to childhood as remained a child; she lived in a dimension removed from the passage of time.

Emiko's father came the next afternoon, arriving in a big station wagon as usual, the dog along for the ride. Funatsu and as many of the nurses who could get away trooped outside, less to see Emiko off than to catch a glimpse of the wonder dog.

"Gale! Gale, Gale, Gale!"

As soon as she stepped out the front door of the hospital, Emiko, whose movements were ordinarily sluggish, started running toward her father, who was standing beside the car. Emiko ran as fast as she could and threw her arms around the bundle of fur sitting patiently next to him. The dog's head, larger than Emiko's, was almost a meter above ground. Clutched and pummeled by Emiko, the dog closed his eyes in seeming bliss.

"Oh, Gale, I missed you so much!"

Normally Emiko's emotions and expressions were flat, her reactions dull; but at times like this, her voice was eager, alive. As if he understood everything Emiko said, the dog licked her face, slowly and tenderly.

"She's been quite stable, so I don't think there's anything to worry about," said Funatsu, going over to the man whose sunburned face had broadened into a smile. "I can't get over the power that dog has over her," he added, thinking how he'd like to pet the animal himself. "No matter what we do, we can't get Emiko to laugh like that."

Emiko's father was a squat, taciturn man with a low center of gravity. Watching his daughter embrace the big dog, he smiled calmly. His profile was chiseled. The days and years flowed by for everyone, Funatsu was given to think, but this man had had a lot to bear.

"Emi, won't this be nice? A whole week with Gale!" a nurse called out.

Emiko nodded happily and answered "Yes!" in a voice even more animated than before. But the concept of a week was something Emiko could not understand. Just because she could carry on a conversation did not mean she comprehended it.

"Emiko, could I pet Gale, too?" another nurse asked.

"Yes, if Gale says yes," said Emiko, who, with this magnificent dog at her command, was the picture of mental health.

"Oh. Well then, would you ask him?" said the nurse, who along with her colleagues, was so taken with the dog that all thought of work seemed forgotten.

At this request, Emiko looked happily up at her father, smiling with an almost theatrical simplicity. With her gaze on him, her father slowly nodded.

"Gale, want to play with the nurses?" whispered Emiko in the dog's ear.

The dog's ears were bigger and thicker than most dogs', and his body fur was dense and rich. He held himself up with a kind of intelligence, shifting his ears continually to gather information from all directions. When Emiko whispered to him, he twitched his ears and tilted his head, then wagged his long, bushy tail.

"It's all right; he's perfectly harmless."

Reassured by Emiko's father, the nurses gathered with delight around Gale, then cautiously began to pet him. Thinking what an apt name "Gale" was, Funatsu strode over with studied ease and stroked the dog's muzzle. When he had first seen the dog, he'd been afraid it would bite; but in striking contrast to its formidable appearance, the creature was extraordinarily gentle and patient.

"You're a great help," he told the dog. "Take good care of Emiko." Whether or not the dog remembered him from previous visits he had no idea, but as those intelligent, contemplative eyes met his, he found himself addressing the dog the same way he would a human being. All the while, Emiko and the nurses continued to stroke Gale on his back and chest. Despite all the people surrounding him, fussing over him, Gale remained utterly calm and unperturbed. He seemed to possess greater composure and maturity than all around him.

"Never fails to amaze me. Teaching a dog such discipline must be awfully hard," Funatsu mused aloud.

"A hell of a lot easier than with people, you might say."

Funatsu was making casual conversation, but the father's reply seemed anything but. He was normally so stolid, but the accumulation of strain seemed to show through today. He had no one else to look after things. No matter how helpful a dog might be, it couldn't keep house. If the father was feeling low, Funatsu thought, maybe it wasn't such a good idea for him to take Emiko home. But even if Funatsu voiced his concern now, the father was hardly likely to call off this long-awaited treat. Besides, Emiko had been counting the days.

Suddenly Emiko looked up at the doctor and asked, "Are you going to talk to my dad some more?"

"A little bit more," Funatsu answered, knowing that it would be a good idea. Out of the corner of his eye, he saw relief cross the father's face.

"Then can we go play over there? Can we?" Emiko jumped up in delight and pointed to the hospital playground. The girl did not always listen, but as long as she was with the dog, Funatsu did not worry. He knew that a single word from his master would be enough to bring Gale rushing back like the wind in the sky. Emiko would not then dally and sulk.

"Dad, Dad, get Gale's toy!"

At his daughter's urging, the father got out a red ball from the back of the station wagon. Emiko took it from him with a happy smile, then tottered off to the playground.

"Gale, go!" her father said, in a voice that sounded almost solemn. The dog, which had until then remained motionless on its haunches, now leaped up and flew after Emiko. However many times he saw it, Funatsu never got over it. The nurses all followed the pair over to the playground.

"Did you have his vocal cords removed?" asked Funatsu, as he watched the dog catch up with Emiko in the blink of an eye and then walk alongside her, tail wagging.

For a moment Emiko's father looked taken aback, but then he understood and shook his head: "No, that's a trait of a wolf-dog. They don't bark needlessly."

"The weaker the dog, the more it barks, they say; maybe it's true after all, then."

"Not many big breeds are noisy. German shepherds are barkers, though."

"But if Gale doesn't bark, he can't be much of a watchdog, can he?"

"No, he isn't. But you've got to realize this isn't a dog that lives to serve people's needs. He makes up his own mind about what he wants to do."

This fellow's tongue loosened only when the topic turned to dogs, apparently. Even his face lit up. He comes to see his daughter faithfully, so he can't be faulted there, thought Funatsu; and I'm not in his shoes, so who am I to judge? Still, he had often thought that if only this man had given his daughter half the affection he lavished on that dog, her life might have been different. She had no genetic predisposition to illness, nor had her condition popped up out of nowhere. If Emiko had stayed away from drugs, she would have lived a perfectly normal life.

"Gale is just like Emiko. It's not a question of being useful or not. He's family."

Even from a distance, the wolf-dog romping around in the field chasing the ball looked huge. His athleticism was in a class of its own. Ever since first laying eyes on Gale, Funatsu imagined owning a wolf-dog himself someday. He liked the way Gale had eyes only for this father and daughter, for no one else. The wolf-dog was well trained, and he showed no aggression toward anyone petting him, since his master forbade it. But Funatsu was also well aware that Gale had no ears for commands issued by anyone else.

"What would you say if we released your daughter from the hospital sometime soon?" Funatsu broached the topic that had been on his mind

Emiko's father stared at him in surprise. "Would it be all right?"

Consternation rather than joy. Well, that was certainly understandable. "I've noticed that her spirits improve considerably when she's with Gale, which makes me think she might be better off at home. Her symptoms aren't going to show much improvement down the years, and it's still impossible for her to focus on one task for very long. But seeing that you live alone, I can appreciate that it wouldn't be easy."

At this, the man sighed deeply.

"Of course, it wouldn't have to be right away," continued Funatsu. "You have your own matters to attend to, I'm sure, and I'm certainly not suggesting that we're anxious to turn her out—nothing of the kind. But if she herself wanted it, and if there was no likelihood that she would create more problems than she does now, I'd like to see her have a chance to get out and breathe the fresh air more often."

"But she can't even be transferred to an open ward."

"That's because she runs away; she says she wants to see Gale."

The father was silent.

"If she were with Gale, she'd have no reason to run away. I'm sure she hasn't the slightest desire now to go back to her old way of life, you can be sure of that."

The father's expression remained clouded with doubt. The sound of Emiko's laughter came to their ears. They turned to see her in the act of tossing the ball, her movements unsteady. Facing Emiko, who was obviously wobbly on her feet, the bundle of gray fur eagerly wagging his tail did indeed look like her bodyguard. No matter how erratically she threw the ball, Gale would make one of his magnificent leaps into the air, bound after it, catch it in the twinkling of an eye, and return it to her. Even when the nurses called out to him or pet him on the back, Gale seemed to see no one but Emiko. Yet, at the same time, Funatsu could sense the animal retained close attention to his master's presence.

"I find it amazing that they get along so well when they see each other so rarely," he commented.

"Gale has a strong sense of responsibility. He's made up his mind that it's his job to protect Emiko. When we are alone at home, we're just a couple of carefree bachelors, but whenever she comes home for a visit, the way I see it, that dog does everything he can to be good to her."

The words were full of praise, and yet the man's tanned, leathery profile appeared sorrowful and bleak. Funatsu nodded and said, "I see." For some reason, he, too, felt a twinge of sorrow.

"No, no, Emi, stop that!"

"Emi, you mustn't hurt Gale!"

Suddenly they heard the nurses shouting. Funatsu turned to see Emiko standing firm with her legs apart, the ball under one arm, the other arm holding on to Gale's ear.

"Emi, that hurts poor Gale. Let go!"

Emiko was probably pinching the animal's ear. Funatsu glanced over at the figure beside him, but the girl's father remained calm, watching the scene without comment. Gale made no sound. Before long, as Funatsu watched, the girl put her arms around Gale and hugged him, then toppled over on the ground still clutching him. Even after she had pushed him over with her arms wound tightly around his neck, Gale's tail, the long-haired fur shading subtly from black to gray, kept on slowly wagging.

Funatsu could not keep back a cry of admiration: "They completely trust each other."

This was evident. Someone watching this might think Emiko was treating the dog with deliberate malice, but then the dog seemed also to be enjoying it. It was as if Gale asked for no greater happiness on earth than to accept Emiko's whole being with his whole being.

"As long as that dog is around, it seems to me she'd do OK, even out of the hospital," said Funatsu, returning to the topic.

The father's expression remained dubious. "But I have to go to work in the daytime, and—"

"No need to decide right here and now. Why not just give it some thought?"

Somewhat stiffly, the man nodded and said, "I'll do that." Then, turning toward the playground, he called out, "Come!" The wolf-dog, who until that instant had seemed thoroughly focused on Emiko, now snapped his head and began running toward his master at full tilt. He flew over the ground with such intensity and drive that if Funatsu hadn't known better, he would have thought the wolf-dog was coming in for the kill. But the moment Gale reached his master, he sat down in front of him, wagging his tail.

"Dad, are we going home now?"

"Yes, we are, we're going home!"

"Emiko's going, too!"

The twenty-six-year-old Emiko had evidently bathed yesterday, as instructed by Funatsu. Her hair neatly combed and bound in a pink rubber band, she came running back happily, if unsteadily. Yellow cardigan, green plaid skirt. Everything she owned had been purchased by her father.

"Say goodbye to the doctor. Tell him we'll be back next week." As her father said this, Emiko turned to Funatsu and bowed her head again and again, persistently. All the while, Gale watched them silently, lying down. When the back of the station wagon was opened, he quietly scooted into the car without being told.

"Call me if anything comes up," said Funatsu, after they were both buckled up. The father smiled and Emiko said brightly, "OK!" in a tone suggesting that nothing could ever go wrong.

"Bye-bye, Gale! See you!" the nurses, standing together, called out to the gray dog, whose face poked between the seats. Emiko was all smiles. The car started off.

"Brr, it's cold," said Funatsu. "Let's go back in."

Spring was supposedly just around the corner; yet as the sun now clouded over, the group found themselves standing in a chill. The car rolled out the hospital gates and disappeared from view. Funatsu leaned his face down to blow warm air on his cold hands, and caught a whiff of dried grass and fur. The smell of that big, goodhearted wolf-dog with fur like a winter cloud.

What a splendid dog, thought Funatsu, as he stuck the hands still smelling of Gale back into his pockets. Then, grabbing on to the bunch of keys by force of habit, he went back into the building.

4

On the night of the third day since they'd begun making the rounds of police dog training centers, having spent the entire day going to centers in Kanagawa Prefecture, Takako and Takizawa returned to headquarters with little to show for their efforts. The farther away the places they visited, the longer it took just to get there and back. It couldn't be helped, but it made them feel less efficient. Lit up by whitish fluorescent lights, headquarters was enshrouded in cigarette smoke and tired sighs. Always drab, tonight the place seemed positively unwholesome.

Tedious tension.

To tell the truth, as the case dragged on, something of that nature was building up inside Takako. She was definitely keyed up. The situation allowed for not a moment's delay. The police had announced that Kazuki Horikawa and Chieko Yoshii had been attacked by the same large canine, but word that the two victims had known each other and that their assailant was a wolf-dog was being withheld. But the media were doing their own investigations day by day, and writing up all sorts of supposition and rumor. They had fallen silent about the "Tachikawa timed combustion belt homicide case," preferring to write about what had been dubbed the "killer dog case." In response, there had been a flood of reports from the citizenry, and the phones at headquarters were ringing off the hook:

"Lately there's been a stray dog in our neighborhood."

"The neighbor's dog keeps running away."

"A friend of mine took a circular to someone's house in the neighborhood, and got bitten by the dog there."

"I saw a dog walking around with a bloody piece of meat in its mouth."

"At a house nearby there always used to be a big dog, but now all of a sudden it's gone. I bet they abandoned it somewhere."

And so on and so on.

Every tip had to be followed up on. But the connection never panned out. All they had to do was ask one question: what kind of dog is it? *A collie.* Nope. *A bulldog.* Nope. *A mutt.* Certainly not.

How long would she have to go on subjecting herself to this tension? Where would it get her in the end, walking around strange neighborhoods with a partner who might be her ally but would never be her comrade? Even now, over and over again, her imagination was filled with nothing but pictures of the wolf-dog racing through the night. Ever faster, ever silently, and in the end, striking with violence.

Detectives, working to finding the wolf-dog's owner, had told her about the various wolf-dogs they had come across: power, presence, and beauty; sensitivity, timidity, fear of strangers, and nervousness; highly individual temperaments—melancholy, stubborn, tolerant, amiable. Wolf-dogs were as varied in personality as humans, it seemed, and just as individualistic. Some were friendly, while others hung back shivering and wouldn't come out of their doghouses; others only gave the investigators judicious looks. What about the wretched wolf-dog that had been forced to kill two people in accordance with its master's command—what sort of character did it have? Perhaps they should be thinking of it less as a dog and more as a being with a personality of its own; perhaps they should be trying to analyze that personality.

It seemed a long time ago that the brass had verified with Takako her status as a lizard. A motorcycle cop who pursued suspects by stealth, blending into the darkness, hiding her identity, trailing after them like a shadow. What good was that now? These days she was more like a newt, crawling around on her belly.

A police officer couldn't fear fool's errands, had to have the patience and tenacity to keep doing the same thing over and over without complaint; this she knew perfectly well. All the same, she couldn't help feeling a certain uselessness, that all her patience and tenacity were getting her nowhere. Her powers of concentration could not hold up forever either. Just keep your eye on the ball and keep moving in that direction, people said—but the ball itself was increasingly out of focus.

As she was slowly preparing to write up the daily report, sighing, a man came bounding into headquarters and called Takizawa's name in such a loud voice that everyone turned to look. The head of the wolf-dog unit, whose name was Umemoto, came hurrying over with great strides.

"That was a great lead you gave us!" he exclaimed.

"Huh? What was?" drawled Takizawa.

Takizawa truly disliked dogs, it seemed. Ever since they'd started visiting canine training facilities, he'd begun to look drained. He could hardly manage to answer when Takako spoke to him, let alone zing her with his usual snide comment. As he followed Takako around, he seemed less fed up with the investigation than barely able to hang on. Back at headquarters, there was none of his old arrogant insistence on writing up the reports himself. Just now, he had been sitting with a lit cigarette between his fingers, letting the ash grow long, his mouth hanging open as he stared up blankly at the ceiling; then, hearing Umemoto call his name, he turned around with a dull expression on his face.

"We found him, just like you said," said Umemoto excitedly. "There's a former member of the Yamanashi Prefectural Police Department, somebody from the Identification Division, who owns a wolf-dog. He was in charge of training police dogs, too."

Takako's mind had until then been foggy and vague; she hadn't been able to think of a way to start writing the report. Now she was all focused attention. She twisted around in her seat to look at Umemoto. With a smile like that of a neighborhood grocer, businesslike yet friendly in an unpretentious way, he nodded at her. The other members of the wolf-dog unit were also there, crowding around.

"We had a tough time finding him, though. His name wasn't even on that list you got from the importer. He bought a pup that was born in Japan. Not directly from the owner, but through an intermediary. We might never have found him. It just happened by coincidence."

Umemoto, who was in his forties, was a personable, round-faced little man. Having delivered that announcement, he licked his chapped lips and took a deep breath. Umemoto's partner, an officer about Takako's age, now added, "The intermediary was a breeder. Of other dogs."

Umemoto nodded his head in agreement.

"That kind," said his partner. "You know."

"Huskies."

"Right. Siberian huskies."

They seemed in perfect tune, almost able to read one another's thoughts. Both were tanned, with deep crow's feet, with a similar aura. Ideal partners. Takizawa urged them to get on with the story, and Umemoto bit and pulled his lower lip expressively, nodding to himself and saying, "Well." A dimple appeared in one cheek.

"It was awfully suspicious. This guy—name of Katsuhiro Takagi—left the Yamanashi Prefectural PD twelve years ago as a sergeant. Where he went after that, no one seems to know. Officially he retired for personal reasons, but Yamanashi PD said it was due to an illness in the family."

That in itself was not implausible. Twelve years ago was a good long time, too. Still, Takako was shocked to hear that a retired police officer was among the wolf-dog owners in the area. The sense that this might be it, the joy at a potential breakthrough, was swamped by other feelings.

"Yes, and besides . . ." Takako had said the words aloud without meaning to, which caused everyone to look at her. She went on: ". . . twelve years would match the time when Hara and the others were living it up together."

Several detectives nodded in agreement. With slowly mounting tension, Takako forced herself to think hard. Roppongi nights. Kids wandering around, out on the town. A retired police officer. Revenge, revenge . . .

"Yamanashi PD say he was one of their top handlers," Umemoto picked up the thread again. "We haven't heard anything more yet. But this broker says he sold Takagi a male wolf-dog pup about three years ago. Takagi never said anything about his job—never gave any indication he'd been a cop—but he did say he knew how to train the dog himself." Umemoto was excited and triumphant at all this. But Katsuhiro Takagi's name was new; they would now have to dig around to find him.

"How come nobody knows where he is?"

"When he worked as a cop, he lived in a little house in Kofu with a wife and three children. Right after quitting the force, he left there. We have yet to find anybody who knows where he went after that. When he bought the wolf-dog three years ago, he said he was living in Fujino, in Kanagawa Prefecture. But the broker said he had no contact with him after that."

"Fujino? Out by Lake Sagami?" Takizawa asked.

Umemoto nodded, excited still.

"How old is this Takagi?"

"He was just forty when he quit the Yamanashi PD, which would make him fifty-one, fifty-two now."

"Give or take," chimed in the partner.

Takako could not feel very optimistic. She wondered what sort of life a man would lead after leaving the police force at age forty. For an ordinary salaryman, changing careers at that age involved considerable hardship. It would have to be even more wrenching for a cop, although some were able to pull off the transition by capitalizing on police-related skills. A cop who'd been assigned to fight organized crime, for example, might take a job as bodyguard or bouncer, while a cop with accounting skills who'd been working on intellectual crime might become a broker or something similar. Such cases were not so unusual.

Takizawa's face had regained some of its old animation. "You never know, you never know. Maybe he's our guy. I have a feeling he's our guy."

Deep down, Takako felt more relief that Takizawa was looking and sounding like his old self than she did that a suspect had finally emerged in the investigation. Then she caught herself. *Yuck. Heaven help me. Why should I care if this papa penguin feels better?*

"We never would have found him if you two hadn't gone around to the Police Canine Association and the importer. That list did the trick."

"In that case," Takizawa replied, "the credit goes to Otomichi. She's dedicated when it comes to wolf-dogs." Takizawa said this with a smile that seemed not so very ironic. Caught off guard by the praise, Takako was not sure how to react, and just smiled vaguely.

Then from behind them came a purposely loud voice, sighing theatrically. "Must be nice. Some guys get all the breaks!"

The investigators, who were gathered around Takako and Takizawa, all swung their heads in that direction. Members of the chemical unit and the incendiary device unit were also gathered together, looking over at the wolf-dog unit with melancholy expressions.

"What's the matter, no results yet?" Umemoto said sociably.

The man sitting back in his chair with his hands clasped behind his head, stretching, spoke up. "You got that right. Day after frigging day. Hey, Otomichi."

An officer about Takizawa's age whom she had never before spoken to, with oddly pale skin and eyes shaped like persimmon seeds, was looking right at her. "Um, yes?" she said.

"Wolf-dogs are superior to regular dogs, right? Even to police dogs?"

"It depends on the quality of training they get, but yes, they have the potential." She didn't know his name, but one look was enough to tell her that Persimmon Seeds was not her type. He was nervous and calculating. Looked like he would be nagging and annoying, too. Besides, she didn't like the look of that skin, so pale it was hard to believe he spent time walking around in the sun every day.

"I get it," he said, and nodded. The motion was purposely exaggerated and slow, as if he were rocking in a rocking chair. "I just wish a wolf-dog would come along and sniff out our chemical for us. We could sure use the help."

The longer an investigation dragged on, the more complaining there was. The idea was to solve the case through group effort, not the exploits of a few; and yet when your own unit was feeling low, it didn't help to hear that the one next to you was bubbling over with good news. Takako understood this.

"Hey, Taki." This time Persimmon Seeds, twirling his ballpoint pen, called out to Takako's partner, sitting next to her.

Takizawa's usual "Yeah, what?" rang out, loud and hoarse.

"How about spreading a little of your luck this way?"

"My luck?"

"Come on, you know what I mean. Don't you have a little too much luck for one guy? First, you get to spend all day every day with a good-looking babe, then you score like this. You've got it made."

Takako's pulse was speeding up. She could feel the blood draining from her face.

"Now if the doggy just turns up, you'll *really* have it made, eh? But what about the timed incendiary device? I think we oughta change the name of the case, don't you?"

"Knock it off, Kanai." So Takizawa knew Persimmon Seeds.

Kanai put on a craven smile and said, "Joking, just joking." But he still looked ticked off.

Keep your temper, Takako told herself, and turned back to the report still waiting to be written. She knew how the others felt. She hadn't exactly had a fulfilling time of it so far herself. When she glanced over at Umemoto, she saw a tinge of blood on his lower lip, as if he'd bitten it too hard.

"Must be nice," Kanai muttered. "Instead of getting stuck goin' around with a scruffy dude hunting for white powder, you go out every day with a young chick doing god knows what together—"

"Lay off, Kanai!"

"Now now. You're getting the fucking job done. Who's complaining?"

"Fucking is right," said the guy next to Kanai, snickering.

Bent over her report, Takako knew her face was crimson. *Mustn't get angry. That just plays into their hands. Let them say whatever they want. Nothing they say bothers me.* As she was desperately telling herself this, she heard Takizawa's voice on edge:

"Hey."

Oh no, she thought. Now he's going to chew me out in front of everybody.

But instead, Takizawa went on: "Kanai. Listen up. Don't say anything to upset my partner. Got it? You can say whatever you want to me, but her you treat like a lady."

"Ain't that sweet. Looking out for your little partner, are you? Taki, I didn't know ya had it in ya."

"I know you feel like blowing off steam, but knock it off with the bullshit. It only reflects badly on you. People will just think you got no character."

More detectives were beginning to file into headquarters. Some stopped, wondering what the loud exchange in one corner of the room was all about. Someone teased, "Don't get jealous, now."

"Character?" Kanai said. "Never had any to start with."

"Isn't that too bad. Guess that's why you're no judge of people."

"I don't know. I can tell you're a perfect gentleman, and she's a perfect lady. With a stinking secret."

Kanai spat this out, twisting the edges of his mouth, and Takizawa rose from his chair. Just then Chief Wakita came into the room and announced, "Let's get started, people." Sounds of coughing and throat-clearing echoed around the room as the men took their seats, and finally silence ruled.

Takako could sense that Takizawa, beside her, was seething. "Sorry about that," she whispered.

"Ssh!" he responded. His face was apoplectic, eyes focused straight ahead, "Don't say a word," he hissed through clenched teeth. "They watch everything we do."

Takizawa, letting out several jagged breaths, seemed to be struggling to regain his composure. Takako was reminded what an annoying bunch of people she was surrounded by. Whoever she'd been teamed with, it wouldn't have made much difference. If it was Persimmon Seeds, it might have been Takizawa who made those ugly insinuations. It was that sort of world. Really, her whole adult life, she had almost never had occasion to be glad she was a woman. She was past frustration, past wretchedness and anger; she was just appalled.

". . . concerning the tenants of the building, most have found new addresses. We have heard about disputes with the owner about being evicted. Some tenants are seeking compensation . . ."

The meeting began with reports connected to the Tachikawa timed combustion belt homicide case. Desperate for some sort of lead, the detectives were trying to delve into Hara's background from every conceivable angle. While Takako and Takizawa had been shifted first from the neighborhood door-to-door search to the chemical unit and now to the hunt for the wolf-dog, these others had been plugging steadily along on the same assignment all this time.

"Even if the wolf-dog killings of Horikawa and Yoshii were crimes of revenge, it's more logical to assume that Hara's death wasn't connected to them, that it was carried out by someone else."

"Since the canine attacks on Horikawa and Yoshii succeeded so perfectly, how come Hara got just a couple of bites? Doesn't make sense."

"No one with a motive has appeared so far. Maybe we need to focus on finding someone who would benefit, directly or indirectly, from Hara's death."

Teruo Hara. It had all begun with his pitiful, charred body; had his remains been claimed and taken back home yet? That man who had traded on his nihilistic smile was the sole link between benzoyl peroxide and the wolf-dog. But his catching on fire, writhing in agony, and dying felt like it'd all taken place a long time ago. Tedious tension. The danger of giving into the impulse to say, That's it, I'm sick of it, who cares what happened to him anyway! The temptation to throw the whole thing aside. Awash with these conflicting emotions, Takako sat and steadily took notes. She wished she could get on her motorcycle and ride off to the sea.

5

From somewhere beyond the border of her consciousness came the harsh ringing of a bell. She stuck a hand out of the covers and groped unconsciously in the dark until finally her fingers found the cold smooth object.

But wherever she touched it, however she hit it, the ringing would not stop.

"What gives?"

Her eyes still closed, Takako frowned, groaned, and squeezed the metal object hard. The feel of it was real; this was no dream. The moment she realized that, she dropped the alarm clock, sat up in bed and reached for the telephone.

"Sorry to disturb you at home. I have a message from Chief Wakita."

The voice was unfamiliar. Ordinarily investigators received no emergency messages, but on hearing Chief Wakita's name, Takako made an immediate effort to banish the fog of sleep.

"Is this Officer Otomichi?"

She had to say something, but could manage only a croak. Before she could answer properly, the voice went on: "There was a fire about three hours ago. Your presence is requested at the site."

After clearing her throat a few times, she was finally able to speak: "A fire?"

Takako peered into the darkness. No need to look at the clock; dawn was far away. No need to ask further questions. She had been notified precisely because the fire was connected with the series of incidents already under investigation. But her head was still so fogged that she could not think beyond that.

"Sergeant Takizawa is your partner, is that right?"

"Yes."

"I have other calls to make, so would you mind phoning him with the news? Do you have his number?"

"Yes. I mean no."

Quickly she switched on the bedside lamp, got out of bed, and found a pen. Only then was she able to read the numbers on the clock face. 4:20. She'd gone to bed after one, so the three hours' sleep was going to have to do. She wrote down the number that the desk staff read her, repeated it back, and then reconfirmed the location of the fire.

"Haijima-machi, Akishima. Got it. The Chuo Expressway to Hachioji Interchange. Then Route 16 north. Toward Yokota Air Base?"

"Not that far. Take a left when you come to the New Okutama Kaido, and you'll see it."

Takako had a general picture of the location in her head. It was right across the Tama River. What was it this time? Arson? She sat back down on the bed and let her mind go vacant just for a second. It was taking a bit to resist the temptation to lay her head back on the pillow. She raised her chin as high as she could, stretching her neck, took a deep breath, and reached out for the receiver she had just set back in its cradle. Dialed the number she had just jotted down. After three and a half rings, she heard a "Hello." The thin, high voice of a girl.

"Um—" For a moment no words came out.

The girl, a teenager from the sound of her voice, said "Takizawa residence," and Takako hastily said who she was.

"You're my father's partner, right? Nice to meet you. Wait one moment, please."

The girl's telephone manners were impeccable. Takako realized how tense she herself was. At the other end of the line was the unknown universe of Takizawa's home life. A house with no mother. A child trained to answer the phone. Holding the receiver between chin and shoulder, undoing pajama buttons in the cold, Takako listened to the on-hold music-box melody issuing from the receiver. So the emperor penguin was somebody's father—a girl's father, at that. Unlikely thought. The melody played over and over. "Home Sweet Home," that was it. After a while, there was a gruff "Hello?"

"Sorry to call in the middle of the night. This is Otomichi."

"Ah."

This was the first time she'd heard her partner's voice over the telephone, and it sounded deeper than it really was, almost like a growl. It was like the voice of a total stranger. Takako briefly filled him in.

"How are you getting there?" he asked.

"At this hour, I'll drive."

"Then could you stop by and pick me up on the way? I'm a little . . . I'm not in shape to drive right now."

His voice was now extremely hoarse. Takako put two and two together. He'd been drinking. He'd drunk himself into a stupor, and he hadn't sobered up yet.

"I can meet you at the station near my house," he said slowly and meekly, almost despondent.

Was it because of the earlier flap with Kanai, when he was on the verge of grabbing the loudmouth by the collar, or because after all this time it still galled him to be stuck with her, be the butt of jokes about her? After she hung up, Takako quickly began changing her clothes, again feeling put-upon. Why did *she* have to go pick up the emperor penguin? Easy: she was his partner. Maybe this was a sign of a new level of acceptance?

She remembered the furious look on Takizawa's face a few hours before when he stood up in Kanai's face. Had Takizawa been angry on his own behalf, or was he trying to protect her?

No, mustn't go there. Don't ever let down your guard. Nobody who spends his whole life immersed in a male-dominated society is going to change his ways overnight. Safer by far to assume this.

4:30 A.M. Ten minutes after she'd received the phone call, Takako was ready to go. She'd put on minimal makeup, got her clothes on, slipped on her shoes. Outside, to her surprise there were snowflakes coming down. She had attributed the quiet to the pre-dawn hour, when it was the peculiar quiet of snow falling. Paved areas gleamed with dark wetness, while the perimeters of small gardens and the rooftops of houses were getting covered in white. Well, this snow ought to help her wake up.

Hurriedly she went back into her apartment and grabbed an umbrella. The hushed hallway rang with the clang of the iron door, followed by the soft click of the lock.

By the time she reached the parking lot at the side of the building, she was completely awake. The car she was too busy to use much these days was awaiting her in the rear of the lot; there was a light dusting of snow on it. She climbed into the frigid car and immediately turned on the ignition; the engine sprang, gratifyingly, to life. She let the engine warm up for a few minutes while she checked her appearance in the mirror and applied lipstick. She looked all right. Her eyes were a little bloodshot, but the circles beneath her eyes were hidden, and she didn't look too sleepy.

As she punched the CD player on and eased out of her space, she suddenly remembered: Once, long ago, she'd driven somewhere before dawn like this. The sense of haste, the need to get moving quickly was the same; but that other time hadn't involved work.

"Oh yeah—that was it."

She'd gone to pick up her husband. He'd gotten an emergency call, and he was at his parents' for some reason, so she dashed out to get him. She'd been tired herself but hadn't minded, bothering only to throw a sweater over her pajamas. She remembered it well. It was back when they hadn't been married long; she'd been foolishly earnest about everything, and had derived enormous pleasure from her own foolishness.

This was a heavy, moist snow. It didn't sweep lightly from the windshield the way powdery snow did. It stuck fast. The wipers changed the snow to drops of water and flicked them away. The music on the CD was Sade's first album, which didn't seem appropriate for snow. Takako hadn't seen the CD around recently, and no wonder—it had been stuck in the car here. Everything she did, everything she heard, was connected to some memory. Was that what happened as you got older? Was that what life meant, filling yourself with memories of times you didn't even want to remember?

The roads were empty. As if to leave her memories behind her, Takako stepped hard on the gas. The snowfall was light, dissolving as soon as it hit the asphalt. As a result, though she expected it would take longer, it was not yet 5:10 when she arrived at the pick-up spot stipulated by Takizawa. The trains were not running, and there were no cars or taxis waiting for fares in the rotary in front of the small station. Switching off the CD player, she turned into the rotary, and her headlight picked up a round little figure. He had evidently gotten here ahead of time. Responding to her toot of the horn, he dropped his cigarette and crushed it.

"I called back to confirm. One person dead," he said as he climbed into the front seat. No hello, no thank you. The smell of alcohol filled the car. Takako opened the back windows a crack as she pulled out of the station. So she'd been right.

"First a person on fire, then a wolf-dog, and now a red cat."

"A what?" Hands on the wheel, Takako glanced over at her passenger, and did a double take. Not only was Takizawa's voice different this morning, so was his face. The only illumination was from streetlights, so she couldn't be sure, but as she turned her eyes back on the road, Takako thought, *He's been in a fight.*

"Red cat—never heard of the expression?"

"Um, no."

"That's what we always said. A red, or a red cat."

"So what does it—"

"It means an arsonist. I guess nobody says it anymore."

Takako made a polite response, even as she wondered why this fire should involve a red cat. She traveled west on the Koshu Kaido, and got on the Chuo Expressway at the Chofu Interchange. Here Takako sped up and eased into the passing lane. The snow was coming down harder, almost like a live thing, dancing madly and trying to avoid the windshield wipers.

"So it's arson?"

"That's what I heard."

He still reeked of liquor. But although his voice was hoarse, his tone was milder than usual.

"There's gotta be some connection. Could be that chemical. But then why would *we* be called in?"

"The CSI won't be in till after dawn, right?"

"Right. And you and me are assigned to the wolf-dog search. Who knows."

Takako felt her nervousness spike. They were just west of Tokyo, and the snow was coming down hard now. If it snowed any more, she'd have to put on chains. Had she ever come this way for work before?

"Pretty wild driver, aren't you?" said Takizawa after a short silence. "Careful, or the swerving will make me sick. I'm already drunk."

Unusually for him, this came off sounding a little whiny. She cast a glance at her partner, who seemed oddly cramped in his seat even though her car was not particularly small. Sure enough, his face was swollen. On the side of the mouth, and up along the cheekbone. His mouth might even be bleeding on the inside. Was that why his speech sounded so meek?

They passed Kunitachi Fuchu, and seconds later the sign for the Hachioji exit came into view. If she got off the expressway there and took Route 16 north for ten minutes, they should be at the site.

"I'll bite," she said. "Why do they say 'red cat'?"

"A cat goes in and out of the house from under the veranda, right? In the old days, when they set fire to a building from outside, they threw something under the veranda. The flames would leap out suddenly, like a cat. People said other things, too, though—red dog, red horse."

Whether true or not, the explanation sounded convincing. In the old days, cops used all sorts of colorful jargon. Some of the words were still in common use—like *deka*, for cop, supposedly a transposition of the first and last syllables of *kakusode*, which was the square-sleeved coat they used to wear; Takako used to think it came from *dekai*, meaning "huge," as in policemen having huge egos, lording it over others. For the most part, though, people of Takako's generation didn't use jargon. She had never expected to hear about it from Takizawa.

"Sergeant Takizawa?"

"Yeah."

"Your face . . ." From the corner of her eye, she could see his thick hand reach up to his face. He made a sound that could have been a moan or a reply. "Is that from drinking?" she ventured.

"No."

She couldn't bring herself to ask more than that. She fell silent, and when the Hachioji exit came up, she put on her turn signal, changed lanes, and got off on the sloping curve of the exit ramp. There was still no sign of morning.

"The little shit pasted me one good," Takizawa said in a half mumble.

"Someone you know?"

"Yeah. My son."

A deep sigh scattered the smell of saké in the car. Takako reopened the back window, which she had closed earlier, and sighed, too. The sound of the daughter's voice answering the phone was still in her ears.

"You have two children?"

"Three."

She said nothing.

"Honestly. Whaddaya gonna do?"

Having no idea how to respond to this, Takako again said nothing. She had no brothers, and found it hard to imagine how a quarrel between father and son could get so heated. For it to come to blows. For the son to have left a mark on his father's face—no thin-skinned face by any means. It must have been some fight.

When they got off the expressway, their surroundings were blanketed with snow. Takako headed north up Route 16, and soon came to the Tama River. The road was slightly frozen.

"Just our luck."

"Pardon?"

"The weather is shit and they drag us all the way to Akishima in the middle of the night."

She turned left at the intersection of New Okutama Kaido and drove another six hundred yards before spotting the red beacon of a police car. As she pulled over, a uniformed policeman with snow on his coat and hat approached them. He saluted when he saw her badge, and with frosty breath explained where the fire was. She was to turn left, then take a right when she saw another police car. From there she couldn't miss it. Since even Takizawa and she had been called out, Takako expected a crowd.

"When they see I came in your car, they'll start in with the jokes again." As they went slowly down a narrow street in a residential area, Takizawa offered this comment in a self-mocking tone.

"It doesn't bother me."

"That's good. 'Cause I don't give a shit either."

They saw the second patrol car. As expected, by now there were cars all over the place. Takako pulled up behind one of them. Fat flakes of snow were falling fast, at a slant. Oh no, why hadn't she thought to bring a pocket heater? Takako turned off the engine.

"One good thing is, you're no blabbermouth," Takizawa said as he reached for his coat in the back seat. Failing to understand, Takako turned and looked at him. The swelling was worse than she'd imagined. The right half of his face was untouched, but the left side was a pitiable sight. Apparently he'd been punched especially hard just beneath the eye, which was blood red.

"Pretty awful, isn't it."

"Does it stand out?"

He scowled, turning his head to show her the left side of his face. Takako nodded slightly, thinking that even after the swelling subsided, the bruises would remain.

"You'd better have it looked at."

"I already treated it. Soaked it in alcohol."

Whether he was laughing or bitter she couldn't tell. Imagine having your own son beat you up like this.

As they got out of the car, he said: "I know I can trust you. Don't tell anyone, OK?"

So he did trust her, to that extent. She answered briefly, yes, of course, and stepped out on the snow-covered road. Then she had a sudden thought: "Do you want to take the umbrella?"

"No."

"It might hide the bruises a little."

It was a woman's umbrella, but plain navy blue, so it wouldn't seem ridiculous. When she held it out, Takizawa started to say something, but then silently accepted it. She turned up the collar of her coat and walked quickly ahead. She had not the slightest desire to walk side by side under an umbrella with Takizawa, like a pair of lovers.

6

As his partner marched off alone, Takizawa tried to wake up and to follow her. Maybe he shouldn't have drunk the booze after all. It felt like his heart had moved into his face. He hadn't felt pain like this in a long time. If it weren't for the prying eyes all around, he would have lost the umbrella and let the snow fall directly on his raw face, but he didn't have the nerve of a kid who didn't know better.

Damn that kid, doing this to his old man.

He wasn't actually that mad. The kid had sucker-punched him, all right; but the fact that he could hit his old man this hard just showed he was growing up. Still, Takizawa was going to have to teach the kid not to mess with him again, that if he did, he might get some of his own medicine back. Punching out on your own father was an outrage. Even if the son was technically in the right. Even if Takizawa's own high-handedness brought it on himself.

As he walked along, head down, a terrible burning smell drifted by. There were clusters of people rubbernecking. It's cold, everybody, go on home, he thought. Another two or three hours and they'd be commiserating about the sleep they lost because of the fire. They didn't know how lucky they were.

When he got to the scene of the fire, by now extinguished, Inspector Miyagawa was already in command. So the top guy had shown up in person, and early to boot. "People say they heard an explosion," Miyagawa told him, "followed immediately by clouds of thick black smoke and an acrid smell. The seat of the fire is around back, by the kitchen door. But it wasn't the gas stove, which wasn't in use at the time. We have testimony from a material witness that after the explosion the fire started on the outside before spreading into the house."

"So it was that same chemical, is that what—"

"Can't say for certain. We'll have to wait for it to get light."

As Miyagawa spoke, he caught sight of Takizawa's face and was on the verge of commenting, then seemed to reconsider. Turning away, he told a young officer next to him to go get Chief Wakita. Relieved, Takizawa went to stand next to Otomichi and look up at the remains of the fire.

The wreck of a building that had only hours ago been the setting for daily ordinary life stood cruelly exposed in the snow. You could tell it had been a two-story wooden house, but parts of the roof had caved in, leaving nothing but beams and pillars thrusting upward in the shadowy darkness. The life of the house had been extinguished.

"Do your eyes sting?" Otomichi asked in a low voice.

"Can't tell. Everything from the nose up hurts," he answered, his voice similarly low.

He looked at her. Her hair was already covered in snow, with drops of water clinging to the bangs. Silently he held out the umbrella. She gave him the usual impassive look and said, "I'm OK." Then, her breath coming out in white clouds, she gazed on up at the site. Curt as always. He couldn't very well go on standing next to her and be the only one using an umbrella.

Quietly he folded it. The snow felt pleasantly cold on his smarting face. He took out his white police gloves from his coat pocket, and Otomichi quickly retrieved hers from her bag.

The house was surrounded by a tall fence, on a lot that was a good 450 to 500 square yards. Next to the house was the skeletal steel framework of what was once a garage. The station wagon sitting inside was half charred.

"What happened to you?" asked a colleague passing by and seeing Takizawa's battered face. Takizawa said nothing, only waved slightly. The place was turning into Grand Central Station, with investigators from the local police, backup from the head office, and now their colleagues from investigation headquarters, likewise woken up by telephone, all arriving in a steady stream. Amid the crowd, several of his colleagues, upon seeing his face, would gape. "At your age, you should know better!" one guy kidded him.

Five minutes went by before Chief Wakita made his way through the crowd to where Takizawa and Otomichi stood. Coming up to them, he gestured with his chin that they were to follow him, and led the way through the burned gate. They entered the property, passed the house, and headed for the carport. Walking single file between the fence and the car, they got to the backyard, where running along the wall that surrounded the house, a steel cage, about two meters tall, had been constructed. It was covered with mesh.

"What do you think?" Wakita asked, turning back toward them. Takizawa inspected the interior of the cage. Part of the bottom of the cage was an extension of the concrete garage floor; where there was earth were several large potholes. There was an airless basketball and a beat-up tin basin. And at one end of the cage was a shed, approximately twenty feet long.

Before Takizawa could say anything, Otomichi spoke up: "Is it the wolf-dog?"

"Possibly. Once CSI gets here, they can give us a better idea. Anyway, take a look at this."

Takizawa and Otomichi now peered into the station wagon, its windows shattered, and saw a leather dog leash, a dog collar, a softball, and other items numbingly familiar from their rounds of the last few days. In addition, there were several objects resembling scarecrows. Strange-looking things stuffed to resemble human form, wrapped round and round with cloth. Takizawa leaned farther in for a better look. One had been ripped at the throat and on the head.

"This clinches it," Takizawa growled. Otomichi, who'd gone to the other side of the car, could only clear her throat, as if she'd lost the power of speech. Training in murder. Practice targets.

"Neighbors never saw anything unusual going on. Some knew that there was a dog living here, but that was it."

"What about the head of the household?" Takizawa asked, drawing his head out of the car. Wakita looked in turn from Otomichi to Takizawa and then took a deep, resolute breath.

"Judging from his age and appearance, the man taken to the hospital was the head of the household. He was suffering from severe smoke inhalation, and may still be unconscious. This house was rented. The former tenant went by the name of Takagi—"

"Takagi? Then—" Otomichi began to interrupt. Wakita forestalled her with one hand in the air.

"But the current resident is named Kasahara."

"Kasahara? Not Takagi?" This time it was Takizawa who spoke.

Chief Wakita wrinkled his forehead and nodded soberly. "Kasahara. Katsuhiro Kasahara."

"Katsuhiro? That's the same first name," Otomichi said. If it was Katsuhiro Takagi, this was their man, but Katsuhiro Kasahara? Was this someone else? Or an alias?

"What about the victim?" Takizawa asked.

"Not yet identified. A woman."

"A woman." Trying to process this information, Takizawa repeated the words to himself.

"Where's the dog?" Otomichi asked.

She's more worried about the damned dog than she is about the name of the owner.

"No sign of it. No body. When the fire department got here, the cage was open."

"So he let it out?" Every time she spoke, a white cloud of breath swirled around her face.

Looking up, Takizawa thought the eastern sky was beginning to lighten, but with all the snow you couldn't tell.

"Hard to say. We have to wait till Kasahara comes to." The furrows in Wakita's brow deepened, and he clucked his tongue slightly. "We have witnesses who say they heard some kind of barking after the fire got started. Not the usual barking, but deeper in pitch, kind of gruff, but not for long. Some witnesses say they heard howls."

"Howls . . ."

In his mind Takizawa started to review what he'd learned about wolf-dogs: they didn't bark needlessly; they didn't make good watchdogs; they weren't really dogs, but wolves with some dog mixed in . . . And now this animal was on the loose.

"As you can see, he kept the animal in such a way that it couldn't be seen from outside, and if he took it out of here by car, no one would have known. We have no witnesses who've ever laid eyes on it."

The owner had exercised extra caution. Had he sneaked the animal away from here and trained it somewhere else? Where he trained it to rip out the throats of specific human targets?

"If the animal has gotten away—"

"That's why there's no time to lose." Wakita's expression grew still grimmer. His eyes kept wandering back to Takizawa's bruised face. Every second counted—but they were after a wolf-dog, not a human being. The usual tracking methods did not apply.

"He had no family?"

"We don't know. According to the neighborhood records, the guy lived alone."

A detective, head of the chemical teams, approached Wakita to say he was needed elsewhere at the site. Recognizing Takizawa and Takako, he raised a hand in silent greeting.

The dawn was approaching. Takizawa thought back to the picture of the wolf-dog in the snow in the dog importer's office. Was this wolf-dog doing the same thing? Was it running through the landscape, breath coming in white puffs, its body blending into the pale gray atmosphere? Big question: Where was it running to?

"This is what I want you to do," Wakita said firmly to Takizawa and Takako. "Go straight to the hospital. As soon as the burn victim comes to, begin your interrogation, I don't care how bad off he is. Find out about this wolf-dog."

As they exited the property, Wakita went off to speak to other investigators at the site, but then stopped and called Takizawa to him. Laying a hand on his shoulder, he drew Takizawa close to him and spoke quietly. The man was a good four inches taller than Takizawa.

"I hear you and Kanai got into it. Is that what happened to you?"

Reflexively, Takizawa drew back, straightened up, and looked at the chief. "No, sir," he said. "This was a personal matter."

Though a gleam of mischief appeared in Wakita's eyes, he spoke with authority. "You've gotten this far, I don't want any blowups. I put you with Otomichi because I was confident you could handle it."

"I understand, sir. But this really is another matter. It's . . . actually . . . domestic violence." He had no choice but to confess. Otherwise this other suspicion would never go away.

"And after that you hit the bottle?"

"To kill the pain, sir. Also, alcohol is a disinfectant."

Wakita's eyes widened momentarily; then he let out his breath with a sound and clapped Takizawa on the shoulder without another word. Next he called Otomichi over.

Takizawa moved off, savoring the chief's expression of confidence. From a little distance he watched as the chief spoke to his partner. It was a gray morning. There were spots all over Otomichi's stockings where she'd been spattered by snow and mud. Her head, nodding now and then slightly in response to the chief's words, was soaking wet.

Easy for him to say. Thanks for nothing.

Why he in particular should have inspired Wakita's confidence he had no idea, but there was no doubt that Otomichi was bad news. And now if it got around that he'd been in a dustup with another cop over her, he'd never hear the end of it.

"Let's go."

Their talk was over. Otomichi came striding his way across the mucky ground. They ducked under the rope at the perimeter of the site and headed back to her car. Takizawa lit a cigarette; he'd been dying for one all morning.

"So what'd he want?" He expected her to brush the question off: "Oh, nothing." Instead, with her eyes fixed on the ground as she stepped carefully along, she said, "He told me not to cause you too much trouble." So the chief didn't believe him? The possibility was upsetting. But sooner or later Wakita would talk to Kanai, and then he'd get the story straight.

"You think Kasahara and Takagi are the same man?" she asked.

"I dunno. All we can do is ask the guy himself."

"Would he tell the truth?"

Otomichi's car was lightly coated with snow. He was frozen to the bone. Lucky thing he'd listened to his daughter and put on his long johns.

"It's up to us. At this point, we can't afford to go easy on him."

Going round to the passenger side of the car, he started to discard his cigarette, but Otomichi stopped him: "I don't mind if you smoke in the car."

For crying out loud, lady, why didn't you say so sooner? The whole way here, he was craving a cigarette, but he'd gone without in deference to her. He slid onto the seat, saying nothing. What he really wanted to say was "I'll drive." He didn't like to ride with a woman driver. But if he could just warm up a little, he could doze off. At least for the ride to the hospital.

"I'll wake you up when we get there. Go ahead and rest," Otomichi said, expressionless as usual, as she started the car.

She'd done it again. Every so often, the woman said something that made it seem like she read his mind. This was very unnerving. But he lacked strength to say anything. He smoked his cigarette nearly down to the filter, threw the butt out the window, and reclined the seat a bit. Warm air from the heater blew against him. OK, you talked me into it. Sweet dreams.

"If Kasahara is still unconscious, I'll leave my car at the hospital and go back to headquarters; I'll get a company car and be right back."

He was dimly aware of the car beginning to move, of someone next to him speaking, but no more. Takizawa fell fast asleep. His face hurt like hell.

7

It was the first heavy snow in a long time. When four inches piled up, the city of Tokyo ceased to function. Now the forecast was for continued snowfall till the middle of the night, with the city center due for at least eight inches. This meant that Tachikawa, Akishima, and places farther west in Tokyo, with the hills of Okutama close by, would get an even greater accumulation of snow.

For Tokyoites, a weather disaster. For the wolf-dog, a perfect day for flight.

Takako felt guilty for even thinking such a thing, but on a day like this it was sure nice not to have to do actual legwork. In a police car fitted with radial tires, she drove through the snowy streets back to the hospital where Takizawa was waiting. The crime-scene unit on their way to the fire site had a rough day ahead of them. Getting rousted out of bed in the middle of the night was nothing compared to having to dig through wet, cold fire ruins. At least she could get around by car, and until Kasahara came round, she could spend her time inside a warm building.

If that was a wolf-dog that ran away, then he's our man.

A flood of questions went through her mind: Who was this Kasahara guy? What happened to Takagi? Where was he? Pretty weird, two guys sharing the same first name mixed up in the same case. Who was the young woman who died in the fire? What was her connection to the dog? Assuming this

Kasahara guy had something to do with the string of wolf-dog attacks, and his house was set afire with the chemical, then he couldn't be the one with the benzoyl peroxide. So, two killers? What was their link? Hara. The one victim they had in common. Hara—the date club manager, the guy with a past, the guy bitten by a dog. He knew the other two victims. What had they done to deserve such a cruel death? What happened?

Loping through the falling snow.

Her thoughts kept returning to the wolf-dog. Why, though she'd never seen an actual wolf-dog, was she so drawn to the creature? She couldn't explain it. She couldn't forget the eyes in photographs. Eyes with an almost mystical power, eyes that bespoke a lofty intelligence, eyes brimming with life and light, personality and individuality. Eyes that expressed feelings richer by half than those of the human heart, eyes without a trace of savagery, eyes that took in everything they saw, accepting it on its own terms.

She wanted to follow those eyes. She wanted them to look at her, into her. The desire haunted her.

She crawled along roads jammed with traffic because of the snow, finally getting back to the hospital at 9:00. Despite the inclement weather, the dimly lit first-floor waiting room was packed with outpatients waiting to see a physician. The room was punctuated with dry coughs. In one corner, a large TV console was set on NHK. Many of the patients were elderly. If it wasn't a life-threatening emergency, wouldn't they be better off staying home? As their reward for coming out today, they were likely to catch cold, or fall and break a bone.

Takako went down a long corridor, turned and walked through a small connecting passageway, and then her surroundings grew noticeably brighter. Here, in what seemed to be a new wing, there were no outpatients, only long cream-colored walls.

She kept going, referring to the signs hanging from the ceiling to help her find her way, until she came to a corner where a uniformed police officer stood. Before he spoke, she showed him her badge. Still in his early twenties, perhaps, with a trace of boyhood in his features, he tightened his expression and said, "Straight ahead." She walked past with a nod, and kept on.

There was another policeman at the next corner. This one looked a couple of years older than the other one. Even after she showed him her badge, he continued to regard her with suspicion. Already brainwashed, she thought. Taught to think of police as an exclusively male fraternity. Why couldn't he at least give her a proper greeting, she fumed, as she turned the corner.

Finally she came to the door of the ICU. As she drew nearer, she began to hear something that sounded suspiciously like snoring. Green vinyl benches lined both sides of the empty, spotless corridor, and on one bench there lay Takizawa, sawing away. She wondered if she should wake him, but soon gave up the idea. Here in the corridor where the air was filled with the sound of nurses' shoes stepping briskly back and forth, the sight of her partner lying asleep as if dead, his arms folded and his mouth half open, was in stark contrast to everything going on around him. To the patients and doctors in life-and-death struggles in the ICU, Takizawa had to seem inconsiderate and offensive.

A woman would never get away with this.

Times like this were when you had to call on your reserves of strength. The saying that a cop had to be able to sleep anywhere, anytime, to catch what sleep he could, really applied only to men. People said women were the weaker sex, that they couldn't handle physically challenging assignments— and yet in the end, it was women who invariably had to push themselves harder than men.

She went to get a cup of coffee from the vending machine, and was sitting blowing off the steam when a middle-aged nurse came up and smiled. "Out like a light. Are you with him?"

From force of habit, Takako quickly drew out her badge from the inner pocket of her jacket and showed it to the nurse. Nodding as if she'd already figured that out, the nurse said, "He told us you'd be coming. You know, your work must be awfully hard."

The nurse was wearing a dark blue cardigan over her uniform and held a clipboard tucked under one arm. She had a kind smile, and her eyes twinkled behind metal frames. Takako simply nodded, realizing what a long time it had been since she'd had a conversation with another woman. The nurse looked at Takizawa again, and laughed. The nametag on her cardigan read HEAD NURSE TATSUKO SAWAYAMA.

"I told him he ought to get that face looked at while he's here. But he insisted he couldn't go anywhere until you got here. He tried hard to stay awake, until just a little while ago. What happened to him? Something at work?"

Takako glanced down at Takizawa and made sure his breathing was regular before replying. "I think . . . it's . . . a personal matter," she whispered. Nurse Sawayama looked startled, and then smiled again.

A smile—something she'd forgotten existed. "How's the patient?" Takako asked.

They were supposed to file frequent reports to headquarters; similarly, whenever headquarters acquired new information, one of them would be contacted. She wasn't here as a family member; this was her job.

"It's still too early to say. The doctor says he'll pull through if he regains consciousness."

The man who had been pulled alive from the fire was, for now, listed merely as an unidentified key witness. The nurse added that the extent of his burns was not life-threatening, but that he had inhaled a great deal of smoke and was probably suffering from carbon monoxide poisoning.

"We treated him with hyperbaric oxygen therapy, so his blood density should have gone down by now. But because of the burns, his blood has a tendency to thicken, and the amount of blood in circulation is also down."

Takako wasn't sure what symptoms that might cause. "Is he out of danger?"

The veteran nurse, still calm-faced, said quietly, "No, his life is still in danger." Then, as she looked at Takako, her expression grew troubled. "I suppose you won't tell me, but did he do something bad? I mean, he's not just another burn victim, is he?"

"It's really too soon for us to say. We have to wait until we talk to him."

"And you're sure this is Katsuhiro Kasahara?"

"For now, yes."

At this response, the head nurse looked dubious and was about to say something when a young nurse came scurrying up, her rubber-soled shoes squeaking. She murmured something to Sawayama, then turned and hurried back into the ICU. The head nurse's expression remained tranquil, but she shifted her position.

"In any case, whoever he is, it's our job to save his life. But the minute he regains consciousness, I'll let you know."

With that, she too hurried into the ICU. As she went in, a nurse in a surgical garment came tearing out. The area was full of sudden activity. Then came the sound of a gurney trundling this way, IV tubes and container swaying, bearing another patient to the ICU. Sawayama came back out. Standing back to avoiding the gurney coming toward them, she said in a crisp tone, very different from the one she had used before, "Family members wait here." Several doctors and nurses passed, pushing the gurney and leaving behind a lone woman of about forty.

Takako scanned the woman's appearance. She was wearing a dark red windbreaker and light brown slacks with an elastic waistband. Her short hair was wet and so utterly bedraggled that although she'd evidently had a permanent, the effect was lost. She must have walked through the wet snow without an umbrella. Her brown shoes, of manmade material, were waterlogged and stained. She looked dazed. From her mouth came the low entreaty, "Oh, please." Then her gaze wandered, as if in search of something to cling to. Takako quickly looked away.

Roused by the commotion, Takizawa now dragged himself to a sitting position. He started to rub his face, then realized anew that he was hurt, and looked around cantankerously.

Catching sight of Takako, he lurched sleepily over. His left eye was completely bloodshot, the area below purplish and swollen. His mouth was badly bruised, too. The total effect was to give this face, which was far from beautiful to begin with, a lurid intensity.

"Any change?" he asked, his voice huskier than ever.

Takako shook her head, and motioned with her eyes toward the woman. Takizawa blinked several times and swung his head around. On the bench catty-corner from him, the woman was staring with undivided attention at the door. They could not hear her voice, but her lips formed the words "Please, dear god," over and over.

Praying for someone she loved. Was the patient her husband? Was this a sudden illness, or had he already been hospitalized and just now taken a turn for the worse?

"Kasahara is still unconscious," she reported. "The burns themselves are not so serious, but he's got carbon monoxide poisoning."

Takizawa yawned again, took out a cigarette, and then, realizing there were no ashtrays around, got up with a muttered comment she couldn't catch and walked down the corridor. If you want to smoke, go on and do it by yourself, she thought, watching him go off, but midway down the corridor he stopped, turned around, and looked back at her. She had no choice. Rising with the cup of now-cold coffee in her hand, she followed after him. His coat flapping open in front, Takizawa walked on with his bandy-legged gait to the end of the corridor. Spotting a smoking lounge ahead, he stuck the cigarette in his mouth and lit up.

The smoking lounge had ashtrays and a beverage vending machine in one corner. No one was there. Takizawa went over to the window and blew out a cloud of cigarette smoke, clearly savoring the taste.

"Look how it's piling up," he said.

Beyond the window, large flakes of snow fell thickly, blotting out the scenery.

8

"They've started the crime-scene analysis, I suppose?"

Takako stood beside Takizawa looking out at the snowy, gray scene.

"They've asked someone from the SRI to look in, too. They'll send us the results of tests on the animal hair ASAP."

Cigarette in mouth, Takizawa nodded slowly. Takako drank her cold coffee and then threw the empty cup in the trash. Short on sleep as she was, standing still made her feel lethargic. Just then her cellphone rang. She exchanged glances with Takizawa before pulling it out of her skirt pocket. It was investigation headquarters.

"The test results are in," Chief Wakita said. "The animal hair we collected from that house is from the same dog that was on the last two victims."

Takako turned back to face Takizawa. "It's a match," she said simply, and saw the uninjured half of his face stiffen slightly. She herself felt a suffocating sensation.

"What about the burn victim?" asked Wakita.

"Still unconscious."

A sigh of frustration came over the line. Then: "Now, this is not yet confirmed—although we're working fast on it—but we've had word from a hospital in Saitama."

"Saitama?"

"They're telling us they believe the dead woman could be an inpatient of theirs. The patient's name was Emiko Takagi, age twenty-six. She had gone home for a one-week visit with her father."

"Takagi? Her name was Takagi? Then—"

"We're asking the Yamanashi PD to check on it. Anyway, as soon as the patient comes to, find out all you can."

The atmosphere at headquarters was almost electric. Takako could sense her own heartbeat quickening. The face of Takizawa, who'd come up next to her and was watching her impatiently, entered her view. He was breathing right on her, with breath that reeked of alcohol and cigarettes.

"What about the dog?" she said into the phone. "Any sign of it?"

"We've notified all police stations in Tokyo and surrounding prefectures. Nothing yet."

"And the media?"

"We're not releasing any information yet. No point in stirring needless panic. Right now it looks like our chances of finding the dog are pretty slim unless Kasahara—or Takagi, or whoever he is—wakes up."

The chief was talking uncharacteristically fast. But when she thought the conversation was ending, he added this: "One last thing. We've arranged for the motorcycle for you. In this weather I don't think we're going to want you on it too soon, but it's ready for you. For now, whatever you do, get the burn victim to talk. We're counting on you."

With that, he hung up. Takako looked down at what she'd scribbled in her notebook: "Emiko Takagi, 26." Wakita's encouragement wouldn't make the patient wake up any faster. Perhaps they should say a prayer for him to recover, like that woman in the corridor.

"Who's that?" asked Takizawa impatiently, pointing to Takako's notebook. He listened to her report, then muttered, "Why didn't they call *me?*"

"Maybe they thought that if they didn't call me once in a while, I'd get jealous." Not the cleverest response, but better than "They thought you might be asleep on the job." Takizawa still looked peeved, but he said no more. Earlier this morning at the fire scene, Wakita had taken Otomichi aside and told her to be prepared to go out on her motorcycle at any time; Takizawa knew nothing about this, and she didn't say anything about it either.

Finding the wolf-dog was a daunting task.

For starters, wolf-dogs were meant to live in a cold climate. For Japanese owners, unless they lived up north in Hokkaido or Tohoku, a big concern was always how to get their wolf-dogs through the hot summer months. So this wintry weather was ideal. By now, if it had a mind to flee, the wolf-dog had probably left Tokyo far behind, gone off to safety in the wooded hills to the north.

No. He won't go so far. He's just wandering around in the snow, somewhere nearby.

Because wolf-dogs were "one-master dogs," never forming attachments to anyone but their original owner. A dog that needed extra affection, one that opened its heart only to a select few—what had gone through its mind as it fled that scene of horror, watching its home go up in smoke and flames?

From beside her came the murmur, "So it was his daughter." Takako shot a glance at Takizawa's profile. The red eye appeared to be weeping. Her ill-natured partner, who could be slightly paranoid, scowled as he took out another cigarette. "If her name's Emiko Takagi, then her old man was one of us."

"It does seem that way."

Takizawa looked even more aggrieved. Cops esteemed their colleagues above all else. There might be sexual discrimination, outright betrayal, and ugly recriminations on almost a daily basis—yet to them, all this was in the nature of the family, no more. A closed-off world, perhaps; but then nobody likes having strangers stick their noses in private, family matters. Confronting a former colleague who had gone over to the other side aroused a welter of conflicting emotions. When news of a wayward cop aired on TV, Takako and the fraternity of cops experienced an awkward embarrassment, as if a family member had gone and made a damn fool of himself. Among themselves, the discomfort and misery were so great that they could barely speak of it.

"What was wrong with the daughter?" asked Takizawa, not looking at Takako.

"Don't know yet. They're still checking her out."

"Rotten luck for her, getting dragged into this just when she goes home for a visit." He sounded despondent. The sound of Takizawa's daughter saying "hello" on the phone echoed in Takako's ears. It seemed forever ago, and yet it was only this morning. A father beaten up by his son and then awakened by his daughter: that was her partner.

"Whaddaya think?" he asked abruptly, turning toward Takako. "If those are crimes of revenge, what's it all about?"

His weird-looking face stared straight at her. Once they pieced together the past connection among the victims, detectives had surmised that these were crimes of revenge, an assessment which Takako had no quarrel with. But what connection could there be between a former cop and a bunch of playboys who'd frequented the same watering holes? Takako paced, trying to think. "The daughter in the mental hospital, hmm, not the same age as the other victims, but close enough—close enough to hang out with them. Young girls in their teens can be very impressionable."

Takizawa's eyebrows lifted; his partner had seen a thread. Young daughter hangs out a bad crowd, goes off in a wrong direction, father seeks to level the score—not implausible. What had Emiko Takako been in the hospital for? If she was home for a week's visit, must have been long-term hospitalization. Had the father turned into a demon bent on revenge, all because of her?

"Twelve years ago, she was fourteen. A middle school student." The word "rape" sprang into Takako's mind. But wait, one of the victims was a woman. Then what else could it have been?

Again, Takizawa nodded. "They did something to her. What was it?" His thoughts seemed to be on the same track as hers, his expression bitter. What terrible thing happened to the cop's daughter?

"Why didn't he take legal action?" she said. "It seems logical that a cop would do that before taking things into his own hands."

"That's why I'm asking you. You went to college, right? You're a helluva lot smarter than me."

There he goes again.

Still trying to pick a fight, after all this time. She gave him a look—but found surprisingly little hostility in his eyes. Instead, somehow, he seemed pathetic and forlorn, the emanating loneliness not merely the effect of his facial injury.

"I only went to junior college," she said. "Never liked to study."

"Never liked to study but went to junior college anyway, eh? So, what'd you study?"

"Child care. It was what my parents wanted."

Takizawa expressed surprise. "What your parents wanted?" he repeated. "Huh. That's the way it goes." He took out another cigarette. "Parents always have their own ideas about their kids. If they wanted you to study child care I guess that means they never thought you'd end up a cop, huh?"

"Especially my mother. She hated the idea," Takako said, her candor surprising herself. Somehow she felt the urge to mention it, didn't want to pretend otherwise. She was willing to meet him halfway. Yet she didn't want to discuss details of her private life either. If she didn't get the conversation off this personal stuff, soon she'd be telling him about her divorce and revealing her ex's last name. She cut back to the chase.

"You think we'll catch the wolf-dog?"

"We got no choice."

"Takagi was a trained handler of police dogs. Someone like that has to love and respect dogs. How could he have used his own wolf-dog to carry out murder?"

Takizawa crossed his arms over his paunch and said, "Who knows? No matter what case you're working, no matter how much one-on-one you do with a suspect, no matter how fair his story sounds, whether it's true or not is one thing you'll never know."

Takako was silent.

"Our only job is to do what we're told and nail the suspect. Isn't that right?"

"Is it?"

"Even if there is some other truth, it's not our job to go look for it."

She'd heard this point made many times before. Each time, she was unconvinced.

"We've got enough to do. There's no end of bad guys out there, and the crimes just keep coming. Our job is to get a reasonable explanation out of a perp and gather enough evidence so it'll hold up in court. Even if it's not the truth with a capital T, as long as it holds together, what else can we do? The prosecution and the defense sure as hell don't know what the truth is. Especially in a homicide. I mean, who's gonna say what the victim's truth was? Dead men tell no tales. Even if the perp swears he's telling the truth, and maybe it is the truth, it's only his version of the truth. The truth it suits him to tell. In other words, it's a waste of time to think about it."

The more experience people had on the force, the more they sounded like this. Once Takako's boss said to her, "If you want to know the truth that much, go out and commit a crime yourself. That's the only way you'll ever know." That was probably true, she had to admit. How could one lone investigator hope to fathom the truth of a case, or the mind of the perpetrator behind it?

Especially when they were dealing with a dog.

She was aware that she was becoming too emotionally involved. Private feelings had no place in an official investigation. She knew this.

It's a dog, for heaven's sake.

A dumb, pathetic excuse.

For a while she and Takizawa continued to stand in silence, watching the snow fall thick and fast. Time passed slowly, uselessly. Takizawa went back to sleep on the bench. Takako paced up and down the corridor and drank two cups of coffee to fill her empty stomach. Better not eat anything now; it would only make her sleepy. She watched the hands of the clock crawl and the snow pile up. It was just nearing 1:30 in the afternoon when she heard busy footsteps coming her way. Sawayama, the head nurse, reappeared.

"Oh, here you are. The patient is starting to regain consciousness."

Until then Takizawa had been snoring with almost arrogant loudness, but at this announcement he jumped to his feet. "Can he talk?"

Caught by surprise, Sawayama mumbled, "Well . . ."

"We can see him now, right?"

He was on his way. Takako hastily got up and followed. From the corner of her eye, she could see the head nurse standing bolted to the floor, surprise still on her face.

9

The ex-cop was wearing an oxygen mask, with tubes up his nose and inserted into other parts of his anatomy. His head, arms, and torso were wrapped in bandages and he lay gasping for breath. Around him were the sounds of a compressor and the electronic beep of a heart monitor. The room was peculiarly inanimate, a world of machines—including, it seemed, the man stretched out on the bed.

Wearing sterile gowns over their uniforms, Takizawa and Takako stood beside the man's bed. The attending physician viewed them somberly. "The patient is not fully conscious," he said. "With all the smoke inhalation, his trachea was severely burned. So even if he comes to fully, he won't be able to speak."

Takizawa nodded absently and looked back toward the bed. Unlike earlier, when they had elicited testimony from people in the hospital, Takizawa wasn't wasting any effort on warm smiles. "We've gotta talk to him, one way or another. By writing is fine—that'd be OK, right?"

The doctor gave a brief nod, and instructed the nurse to bring a board with *hiragana* symbols. "He can use this to communicate," the doctor said. Taking the board from the nurse, he handed it to Takako. Then he knelt beside the bed and took hold of the patient's hand; the upper arm was swathed in bandages. "Kasahara-san, Kasahara-san," he called out gently. "Can you hear me? Kasahara-san, if you can hear me, squeeze your right hand."

The man in the oxygen mask moved his head from right to left in seeming pain. No other reaction. Takako stared at the gnarled hand, limp, half open.

Then Takizawa, standing next to the doctor, thrust his face forward and spoke: "Takagi-san, Takagi-san. Can you hear me?"

The doctor turned to Takizawa in surprise. Takako quickly transferred her gaze back to the man's right hand. Where at first it had just lain there, now it moved slightly, then slowly it squeezed the doctor's hand. Takizawa looked at Takako, who nodded back at him. Breathlessly they looked at the patient's face. The lower half was hidden by the oxygen mask, but she could see that his face was oval-shaped, with thick eyebrows. Deep wrinkles were etched into the forehead, and around his eyes were lines that could make him look merry when he laughed. There was white netting on his head, through which hair poked here and there; his hair was white. If this was Katsuhiro Takagi, he was fifty-two years old. He looked older.

"Takagi-san, this is a hospital," the doctor spoke again. "Do you understand? You are Katsuhiro Takagi, is that right?"

The man squeezed the doctor's hand again. Now the doctor said, "Open your eyes." The man's eyelids twitched; he seemed to summon all his strength, and opened his eyes. They were unfocused, swimming in space, and started to close again. He was able to resist the impulse, however; the lids trembled but remained half open. His lashes were sparse and wispy.

"Remember?" whispered Takizawa. "There was a fire."

The man's eyes opened wide. He looked around desperately. When his eyes locked onto Takako's, she was unsure what look to give him, and only managed a small reassuring nod.

"It's OK, you're safe now," whispered Takizawa, taking the man's hand from the doctor and holding it in his own. The man turned pleading eyes on Takizawa, and then his gaze swam again. After a moment he pulled his hand away and shakily pointed up.

"If you want to say something, here, use this," Takako said, holding out the *hiragana* board to Takagi. He blinked several times, moving his hand, pointing to different squares: *e . . . mi . . . ko.*

"Emiko? Is that your daughter?" asked Takizawa. At these words, the hand that had fallen back on the sheet in exhaustion squeezed his hand again. Stronger, harder than before: Yes.

"She was in a hospital in Saitama, right? She'd just come home for a visit?"

Yes.

"She's twenty-six."

Yes.

The man looked at Takizawa again, then motioned for the board. *Bu . . . ji . . . ka.* Is she safe? Takako looked at Takizawa. Takizawa pretended to stare at the board. What to do. Tell him the truth? What effect would that have on the interrogation? He could go into shock and that would be it. He'd never talk with them again. Yet they could not rightfully conceal the information from him either.

"She's in critical condition," Takizawa answered. The man looked at him sideways, as if weighing the truth of these words, then closed his eyes. His chest swelled, he heaved a sigh. Of relief? Or despair?

"You probably know this already, but we're police officers."

Yes.

"Is Kasahara your real name?"

Yes.

"It was Takagi before?"

Yes.

"Divorced? You had your wife's name?"

Yes.

"Ah. Well, we'll call you Kasahara then. This morning we saw your house. Burned almost to the ground."

Yes.

"No sign of the dog."

No response.

"What happened to the dog?"

No response.

"The wolf-dog. The one that belongs to you."

No response.

"We knew about it. It was just a matter of time. If we'd gotten to your place a little faster, neither you nor your daughter would've ever been in that fire."

Kasahara slowly opened his eyes. They looked troubled, as if trying again to weigh the truth of Takizawa's words. His eyelids trembled.

Takizawa went on in the gentlest of voices, as if talking to a little child—a voice Takako had never heard before: "It's OK, Kasahara-san. I know you had your reasons. You had to have reasons, right? Once upon a time you were a cop like us."

Yes.

"So you know we have our job to do. When you're able to talk, you can take all the time you want and fill us in."

No response.

"Right now, tell us about that dog that meant so much to you. You let him go, didn't you?"

Yes.

"A wolf-dog, right?"

Yes.

"Male or female? What's its name?"

The hand reached for the board. Takako held it out and watched intently as Kasahara's fingertip pointed in succession to *ha . . . ya . . . te.*

"*Hayate.* Gale?" she said, interrupting. "Like the wind?"

Takako's mouth tightened. Kasahara nodded weakly, then indicated the wolf-dog was male.

"Where's Gale now?" asked Takizawa.

No response.

"No idea?"

No response.

Takako peered intently at Kasahara's face. He was shaking his head, the movement barely perceptible. It wasn't that he didn't want to answer, his eyes said that he did not know.

"You don't know where he is, do you?" said Takako softly.

Yes.

"But you trained him, didn't you?" said Takizawa. "Trained him to attack people."

Slowly Kasahara gripped Takizawa's hand and squeezed it: yes. Then he seemed to fall back, exhausted. The doctor, who had been watching wordlessly in the background, now stepped forward and said, "Better make this all for today."

"All right. Just one more question." With his trademark persistence, Takizawa, called out to the former cop, who was drifting back to sleep: "Kasahara, Kasahara!" He had dropped the *san*. "Who burned down your house?"

No response.

Takizawa didn't give up: "Kasahara! Hey!" After a few moments, once again Kasahara's hand moved feebly.

"You know something about that fire?"

Yes.

"Then tell us! A place, a name, anything!"

Again, no response. Frustrated, Takizawa called Kasahara's name again and again.

"That's it. He can't take any more of this," said the doctor, but Takizawa ignored him, bellowing, "Kasahara! You give me a name! Who burned down your house? You know, don't you?"

Weakly, Kasahara's eyes opened. Sought the board. Takako, scarcely able to bear watching, held it out once more. The shaking hand struggled to find the letters it sought. From the corner of one eye a stream of tears fell. Was this pain, or remorse, or sadness?

"That's the way, come on, give us a name!"

A strange cheering section. Still, as if encouraged by Takizawa's voice, Kasahara's hand moved across the board: *o . . . ga . . . wa.*

"Ogawa? Somebody you know?"

No response.

"I have to insist. That's all for today," said the doctor. "Tomorrow he'll be stronger."

This time Takizawa meekly withdrew. Takako studied Kasahara, who lay as if dead, unmoving, eyes shut. Not knowing that his daughter had perished, he himself hovered between life and death. Using a wolf-dog named Gale, he had brought about the deaths of two people. Yet how weak and helpless he was now. Even for a burn victim, his eyes trembled with such sadness. The lines cut in his face, the white hair poking through the netting, all made him look at least ten years older than he was.

"Call headquarters," Takizawa, taking out a cigarette, barked to Takako as they left the ICU. Takako pulled out her cellphone, imagining the wolf-dog flying across the snow like the wind which was his name.

Gale.

She had a feeling they would never catch him. Part of her even wished they wouldn't. But she was going to try.

"Good work. Meeting starts at four. You'll be back by then, right?" Chief Wakita rattled off to her, even more rapidly than usual.

After she hung up, Takako went back over and stood next to Takizawa, feeling so exhausted she could collapse. She had to get something to eat, had to get some rest.

"With this weather," Takizawa said, "we'd better get an early start. Let's head back."

The uniformed officers standing at every bend of the corridor had all been replaced by the next shift. Outside, the snow was falling a little less, but it was still coming down. Takako and Takizawa wandered around the parking lot before finding the unmarked police car Takako had driven over, now piled high with snow.

She was opening the door to the driver's side, when Takizawa stopped her. "Forget it. With this much snow on the road, your driving would scare the hell out of me."

He took the key from her and lost no time jumping in the driver's seat. She climbed into the passenger seat uncomplainingly. Hunger and tension had combined to drive away her drowsiness, but she was so cold she couldn't stop shivering.

"Damn, it's freezing in here," Takizawa said as he punched on the heater and switched on the wireless radio. Out of the radio came a stream of police messages transmitting back and forth in the area; out of the fan came a stream of warm air.

"Now, if only we were done for the day." Waiting for the engine to heat up, Takizawa let this thought escape. Takako smiled wanly and looked out the window without comment. Finally Takizawa pulled out of the space, but once out the hospital gate, they were stuck in a traffic jam. On all sides were drivers who had set out despite the morning's snow, never thinking it would pile up to this extent.

"Guys in the Traffic Division will have their hands full today," Takizawa said with a wry smile, looking out at the cars. He didn't seem in much of a hurry, inching the car along. As if remembering something, he looked over at her. "You've got dark circles under your eyes."

"I do?"

He twisted one side of his mouth in a wry grin and said, "Don't knock yourself out. I won't attack you or anything; get some sleep until we get back to the station. Lack of sleep is bad for your looks, I hear."

"I'll be fine."

"I knew you'd say that." This time he laughed out loud. "You ladies can't lie down and catnap anytime you want, the way we can. Go ahead and be stubborn if you want, but if you collapse when the crunch comes, others will catch the fallout. I'll tell you something: A woman who's always got something to prove isn't exactly adorable."

"Adorable is not my style."

"I noticed." Takizawa turned his gaze back to the road.

I may have circles and bags under my eyes but what about you, face covered in bruises? Hah! We're like a couple of panda bears.

Still, he meant well. He was trying to look out for her. But she'd resolved she wasn't going to let her guard down. Besides, she couldn't let go of what she'd witnessed in the ICU just now. That was the most pitiful suspect she had ever encountered in her entire career.

Come to think of it, Kasahara was younger than her father, who would be sixty next year; yet Kasahara seemed far older, like a very old man. No peaceful, golden years for him. He faced arrest, indictment, trial, sentencing—and a long time in jail. Even if he was sentenced to death, it would take years before the sentence was upheld, the Minister of Justice affixed his seal to the papers, and the execution took place.

Gale.

Just as Kasahara would never see his daughter again, he'd never see his wolf-dog again. Even if they managed to capture the animal, the two of them would never live together again.

"Sergeant Takizawa."

Hearing his name, Takizawa looked at her in surprise. "What, you're not asleep?" he said.

"You think Kasahara has any other family?"

"I dunno. Probably somebody's checking it out."

"What will become of Gale—the wolf-dog—after he's captured?"

Takizawa folded his hands on the steering wheel and rested his chin on them. "Hmm," he said. "If we ever catch the dog, I suppose it'll be destroyed. The thing's killed two people."

She was silent.

"The wolf-dog is important evidence, so they'll probably keep it alive till the trial's over, at least."

Then let the trial be a long one, she thought hazily. In killing two people, all Gale did was follow his master's orders. He was innocent. If there was anyone willing to take him in, let him live.

"Ogawa. . . . Damn. Who's this Ogawa?" This slipped out from Takizawa.

As she looked out the window at the snow-blanketed scenery, Takako slowly relaxed into drowsiness. On the verge of sleep, her eyes popped open. "Does the name mean something to you?"

"I'm tryna think," Takizawa said. His swollen profile facing her, he still rested his chin on the steering wheel. Ahead, a flashing red light came into view. As their car slowly approached the scene, they could see that it was a police car. At the side of the road were three cars involved in a collision. Takizawa leaned over toward Takako's side of the car, checking out the accident and clucking his tongue in vague amusement.

"There's always a joker who causes an accident like this. You can bet on it."

Takako looked out at the uniformed officers walking around in leather coats and snow-covered caps. She didn't recognize either the officer with a measuring tape, his breath coming out in white puffs, or the officer talking to a driver. Small wonder. The MPD alone had 45,000 police officers. They were divided among eight different divisions—the Traffic Division, the Daily Life Safety Division, the Public Security Division, the Criminal Investigation Division, . . . as well as adjunct institutions like the police academy. There had to be five thousand officers in each division. Nobody could remember that many faces.

192

"It's not an uncommon name. I just have this nagging feeling like I've run into it recently." His interest in the accident quickly waning, Takizawa went back to muttering: "Ogawa, Ogawa . . ."

Please, let it not be another cop, thought Takako. Listening to Takizawa repeat the name over and over like a Buddhist chant, she grew sleepy again. A heavy, clinging drowsiness that made it hard to breathe. It wasn't supposed to be like this, she thought hazily. Once they identified the suspect and started to close in on the wolf-dog, her spirits were supposed to rise. She had been waiting for this moment. She had endured this emperor penguin of a partner for this moment. But now that they had come this far—and learned the name of the wolf-dog—her spirits were sinking.

10

The identity of the man named Ogawa was cleared up at the 4:00 meeting. One of the detectives who had been working on the background check of Teruo Hara said, "I wonder if that isn't Masanori Ogawa. He ran a company that manufactured and sold health equipment in the same building. He's the tenant that's been hounding the maintenance company for compensation for forced eviction."

Takizawa slapped his thigh. That was it. Right after the investigation head-quarters was set up, when they'd gone to the building maintenance company to check on the other tenants, he'd seen the name. It was one of the building tenants with no contact information posted on the door. *Son of a bitch. I shoulda gone to see him. I mighta smelled something.*

"Do you know where this guy is now?"

"The last time we talked to him was, let's see, two weeks ago."

"What was your impression of him then?" Chief Wakita's voice was even, devoid of emotion.

"There was nothing that struck me. He didn't talk too much or too little, and he acted calm. He said he thought he might have seen Teruo Hara before, but he had no idea there was a date club in the building. A skinny guy, kind of high-strung."

"Masanori Ogawa . . . ," muttered Wakita, and looked at Takizawa. He had already heard the report that the burn patient in ICU identified himself as Kasahara, admitted to releasing the wolf-dog named Gale, and claimed his house was burned down by somebody named Ogawa. Naturally, the chief also knew that they didn't have a first name.

Before Takizawa could say anything, Otomichi spoke up: "We'll go back to see Kasahara tonight." Looking at her erect posture, the profile gazing straight ahead, Takizawa quickly nodded in agreement.

"We'll find out all we can about Ogawa," he said.

"Do that," Wakita decreed matter-of-factly. Then he looked over at the Teruo Hara unit, standing dejectedly with their shoulders slumped as if responsibility for the time it took to come up with a suspect's name fell on them. Gently, he told them, "Go back over Ogawa. Find out the financial condition of his health equipment company, his history, his friends and family, anything you can. And of course, I want you to zero in on any connection he might have with benzoyl peroxide. I'm counting on you."

Those four words—"I'm counting on you"—were a lifeline to the demoralized team members, as Wakita well knew they would be. The leader of the unit, a sociable, friendly guy named Matsushima, who kept the drinks poured at parties, now stood tensely and said, "Yes, sir!"

Just then the door flew open and two detectives who were on the wolf-dog unit entered the meeting room. The train had been delayed by snow, they explained, still wearing their coats, bowing to the investigation leaders.

"Katsuhiro Kasahara was adopted into his wife's family to carry on the wife's family name." With that one statement, it was clear that they had successfully traced Kasahara's identity. As they took off their coats, Takizawa realized that they had just gotten back from Kofu. Even if they were only doing their job, to go that far on a day like this was no simple jaunt. From all around came murmurs of appreciation.

Without a chance to catch his breath, the team leader launched into his report: "Besides checking the police records, we were able to talk with several of Kasahara's former coworkers in the Identification Division, as well as with his ex-wife. It's a depressing story."

This Sergeant Tada, who was good at karaoke, was a man like himself, thought Takizawa, with one difference. Where Takizawa was a bumbling speaker, self-conscious in front of others at meetings like this, Tada loved to speak in public; he had a lively style, like a storyteller. Having thus prefaced his remarks, Tada pulled his jacket down in a show of smartening his appearance. Then he began to relate Kasahara's history.

Katsuhiro Kasahara, formerly Takagi, was from Akishima, Tokyo Prefecture, and the house that burned down was his family home. He was the youngest of four siblings, two brothers and a sister; the two brothers were deceased and the sister was in a hospital, in the final stages of terminal cancer. On graduating from high school he had taken the qualifying test for the MPD and failed; the following year he passed the test to join the Yamanashi Prefectural Police Department. At age twenty-three he had a formal meeting with his boss's daughter, as her prospective groom. Because she was an only child, and Kasahara was the third son, it was agreed that he would be adopted into the Takagi family, thereby taking their surname as his own. Any children born to the couple would thus carry the wife's family name.

"We spoke to many people, and we got the distinct impression there was nothing remarkable about him, that he had a very unassuming disposition. People were surprised he wanted to be a cop in the first place. They described him as relatively bland, not hot-blooded at all, even kind of a weakling, although they said when you got to know him he had a good heart. Overall he was the type who liked to plug away at things by himself. Not a ruffian. In short, a very serious type. Some called him eccentric. Everyone who knew him was in shock. They said, to the one, they couldn't believe he would do something like this."

Tada looked down at his notebook with a small sigh. Even with small gestures such as this, the man's timing was perfect, thought Takizawa. As he listened, he thought he might try to imitate Tada's style the next time he had to speak in front of a group. Next to him, Otomichi was scribbling notes assiduously. For almost an hour before the meeting started, she had disappeared. When she came back, the circles under her eyes were gone. Aware he was looking at her, she had moved her prim, cold mouth in the shadow of a smile, as if to say, Well? Nothing about me to betray weakness now, is there? Yeah, whatever. That's what makes dames so scary, he thought. They disguise themselves expertly. He had shrugged his shoulders at her.

"Taking all this into consideration, it seems almost inevitable that Kasahara would request a job in the Identification Division. He was diligent and something of a perfectionist, someone who could be relied on to do his job. When he was twenty-nine he was put in charge of the canine unit, and he kept that position until he quit the force."

He quit for personal reasons; that was all anyone knew. But finally one of his coworkers spoke up and said it was because of Kasahara's daughter. When she was in middle school, she developed a rebellious streak and went off the rails, turned delinquent.

"I have to say that it was not at all easy interviewing members of our own profession. They understood what we have to do, of course, but they weren't willing to open up. Even though it was more than ten years ago when they knew him, they still felt a brotherly bond with him, and I'm sure they hated to drag the Yamanashi Prefectural Police Department through the mud, too. . . ."

Whether from an excess of self-confidence or self-awareness, Tada's report contained a lot of such unnecessary comments. Get to the point, Takizawa was thinking, when beside him he heard a little sigh. He looked over surreptitiously and saw Otomichi's long-lashed profile, her eyes staring down at the notebook in front of her. That alone was enough to make him feel uncomfortable. He remembered stealing looks at her sleeping face in the car a short while ago, as he drove through the snowy streets. Asleep, the stubborn lady cop had looked like any ordinary girl.

Her long neck, wrapped in a light-colored scarf, had seemed uncannily white, as if lit by the glow of the snow. Her exhausted, colorless face was turned away from Takizawa, her eyes closed as if she was dead. Even though he had done nothing wrong, Takizawa began to feel like he was imposing a terrible burden on her, asking impossible things; for no reason he felt guilty, disgusted with himself. When you came down to it, however you looked at her, Otomichi was a woman. He could only think that before she was his partner, or a cop, or an investigator, or anything else, she was a creature utterly unlike him: a woman.

What can you do?

Muttering the words to himself, Takizawa had gripped the wheel with a pang of peculiar sadness. This was why he didn't want a woman for a partner in the first place, damn it all.

Now her lone sigh had revived all the awkwardness of that moment.

". . . Kasahara had three children, of whom the youngest, a girl named Emiko is—as I think you all know now—a key figure in this case, it's fair to say. Emiko's name is written with Chinese characters that can be read 'laughing child,' a meaning that has turned out to be ironic."

As Tada promised, this was getting depressing. For Takizawa and everyone else, too overworked to spend time with their families, the topic hit uncomfortably close to home. It was especially hard for Takizawa to sit through this, given that his face still bore the marks of his son's punch the previous night.

It's because you're like that—that's why Mom left!

The kid didn't know what the hell he was talking about, shooting off his mouth like that. Anyway, don't call her Mom, he thought. Whatever made her do it, that woman walked out on her three children to be with another man. A real mother would give her life to protect her children, but she leaves them with me, like I don't have enough to do already, and whines, I want to be happy, too. The reason I bawled out my kid in the first place was—*hold it, you're at work now.*

Takizawa hastily banished his son's voice from his thoughts and tuned back in to the report.

". . . and so she followed what you might call the typical path, first dropping out of school, then getting high on paint thinner, followed by shoplifting and then acting out physically at home. Time and time again she ran away from home, and in the end she was taken into police custody. She was also seen with the local gang of hot-rodders. Kasahara may have thought that these difficulties at home made it impossible for him to go on with his career as an officer of the law, and so he made the decision to request early retirement. That's the impression we received, at any rate. Now—"

"Okay," interrupted the chief, "another unit will be reporting on Emiko Takagi, so skip the rest about her. Anyway, there's no doubt that Kasahara is Katsuhiro Takagi, is that right?"

Looking somewhat disappointed, Tada was forced to nod, and then rustled the pages of his notebook as if to reestablish his self-importance. "Yes, there's no question. Katsuhiro Kasahara, a.k.a. Katsuhiro Takagi, took the surname Takagi through marriage, becoming the adopted son of his wife's father, and then got divorced, thereby reverting to his original name of Kasahara."

Takizawa had thought this Tada guy was similar to him, but he'd been wrong. Nobody this pompous and theatrical could resemble him in the least.

"Takagi reverted to the surname Kasahara three years ago, which was after his purchase of the wolf-dog. But it was only one year after leaving the police force that he separated from his wife and children."

According to Kasahara's ex-wife, Akiko, after retiring from the police force, her husband became a different person. He couldn't settle into a new job, quitting time and again in a matter of months; nothing he put his hand to lasted; he started drinking; and, in the end, he had bouts of violence with greater and greater frequency. His father-in-law, who was also his former boss, spoke to him more than once; but even if Kasahara bowed his head at the time and apologized, afterward he went right back to drinking and being physically abusive. While this was happening, his youngest daughter, who had calmed down for a while, ran away from home again, and this time they didn't find her right away. Kasahara had scolded his wife viciously, blaming her for everything—even for his having to quit his job.

"He was out of control, his ex-wife said. So she took the other two children with her back to her parents' home. Emiko was found after that—but more on that later. Anyway, one day about nine years ago, without so much as a word to his ex-wife, Kasahara moved off somewhere by himself. She never heard from him again until suddenly one day, this would be three years ago, divorce papers arrived in the mail."

It was enough to break your heart. The record of a cop's disintegration, the picture of slow degradation. The more you blamed someone else, the more it only came back to haunt you. You ground yourself to bits working for your family and for justice, and in the end what did you have to show for it? Content like this he would rather hear presented like business, thought Takizawa; lose the drama.

"His ex-wife, Akiko, is a rather tall woman with fair skin, and seems to have a quiet personality—"

"That's enough. We're not finished with your report, and already it's turned dark," said Wakita with a wry grin. None of the detectives felt like looking the others in the face. Awkward laughter rippled around the room as everyone had the same thought: *Man, that could be me!*

Takizawa had been hearing that the job of a police dog handler was not something you were fit for if you thought of it only as a job. You had to raise the dogs from the time they were pups, literally eating and sleeping with them. Three hundred sixty-five days a year, holidays and all, you had to be around the kennel, dispensing affection and discipline, putting the dogs through training. It was rewarding work for anyone who loved animals, but those with families paid a stiff price: you had to give up family trips as an impossible dream; you had to worry about the dogs more than about your own kids; you had to memorize each dog's personality and quirks.

It wasn't hard to imagine how much passion Kasahara poured into the job of handler, a man who was a hard worker to begin with and not very sociable. Nor was it hard to visualize the resulting pattern of a child in the neglected family building up resentment and ultimately losing her way, taking the wrong path.

"The report on Emiko Takagi is about ready, too, isn't it?"

Thus encouraged by Chief Wakita, another detective got up. He was a kid of twenty-six or seven, with a dismal look on his face before he ever said a word. "My partner Officer Takeuchi has laryngitis, so I'm going to make the report instead of him."

Good grief. Here it was time to go capture the suspect, and the atmosphere at headquarters was getting downright depressing. Takizawa took a deep breath, closed his eyes, and folded his arms. He thought of Takagi—even though the guy's name now was Kasahara, Takagi was the name he had responded to—as he had last seen him in the ICU. As soon as he came to, he was searching the room for someone; Takizawa couldn't forget the look in those eyes.

"Officer Takeuchi and I went to a hospital in, um, Ogose, in Saitama. The hospital where Emiko Takagi was. It's a . . . a mental hospital."

In striking contrast to Tada's smoothness, this guy spoke haltingly, nervously. At the words "mental hospital" Takizawa could not keep his mood from getting gloomier, although he'd known this fact before. Kasahara's eyes, the burned house, the empty dog cage—the face of his partner as she handed him her umbrella in the snow.

"Emiko was in the hospital there for more than eight years. Before that she'd spent time in several other hospitals. The diagnosis was always the same—mental illness caused by chronic dependency on stimulant drugs. When she was seventeen—when she came to the present hospital—her face was white as a sheet and she was completely delusional, totally . . . unable to respond to doctors' questions."

By putting together her medical records from the other hospitals, accounts from her family members, and things that Emiko herself told them, little by little personnel at the Ogose hospital were able to establish that she started sniffing thinner when she was thirteen. At first she tried it for kicks, but after a time she lost interest in school and stayed shut up in her room. In the beginning her mother concealed what was going on, not wanting the father to know. After a while Emiko stopped going out in the daytime, out of fear of being seen by schoolmates, and would only go out at night, to convenience stores and other places where she made new friends with people not from her school. She first spent the night away from home because she stayed late at a friend's house and it was too much trouble to go home; but the next day when she got home, her father found out what happened and gave her a severe tongue-lashing.

"As if to pay her parents back for that, she stayed out again, and was hauled home and scolded again. This went on for some time, and Emiko's delinquency got worse."

Finally, one day, she ran away to Tokyo. She wandered around with no idea where to go, and eventually met a young man.

"He took her to a disco, and that night he put her up in his apartment and they sniffed thinner together. But the next day a woman came to the apartment and threw a fit when she saw Emiko, so Emiko got scared and ran away."

Children roaming the city that never sleeps. They were a dime a dozen, even now. To Takizawa and the others it was pretty clear where they were headed; the kids flew around like moths to a flame, until one day they grew dizzy and, just like that, got sucked in.

As generally happened, Emiko progressed from thinner to speed, *shabu*. By the time she'd been away from home for three months, she was a full-fledged addict and had even moved on to prostitution to support her habit.

"When she was brought to the hospital, Emiko was infected with gonorrhea; she was also pregnant. She didn't know she was pregnant, and soon after arriving, she had a miscarriage."

Takizawa slowly opened his eyes. An oppressive quiet reigned in this large room. After this he would have to go see Kasahara again, an almost unbearable thought. It probably wasn't so wild a guess that the guy who introduced Emiko to speed was Teruo Hara.

"This contradicts the earlier report, but from what we learned at the mental hospital, Emiko's mother became hysterical in front of the doctors and nurses, accusing the father, telling him it was all his fault, everything that happened to Emiko."

Kasahara then disappeared from Kofu. But he went to see his daughter in the hospital two or three times a month, without fail. Her mother and siblings never went once. Then around four years ago when Emiko's symptoms started to stabilize, her father applied for permission for her to spend nights away from the hospital periodically. He would pick times when she was doing well to bring her home, first one night at a time, then gradually for longer periods.

"They couldn't tell us anything about Emiko's personality or her feelings for her father before her addiction. But she came to live for these visits home. She'd tell the doctors and the other patients, 'There's a big dog in my house,' or 'I want to go home and play with Gale.' She was extremely childish, probably an effect of the *shabu*. In many ways, she never left the mental age of a middle school student."

Takizawa could hardly breathe.

By the time father and daughter were reconciled, she was no longer herself. Most of her life was wasted in rebellion against her father and addiction to speed; and in the end, she died in flames. It really was like Tada said: the name Emiko, "laughing child," was painfully ironic.

To Takizawa, Kasahara's motive was all too understandable. But the law didn't allow vendettas. The goddamned fool. He'd gone and let loose that wolf-dog, too. A living lethal weapon. If they didn't capture that dog, then even if Masanori Ogawa was their other suspect and they managed to arrest him, they still couldn't quit. Takizawa felt a hot lump rise in the back of his throat, and quickly swallowed. He took a deep breath. If he could, he sure would like to toss down a quick one before going to see Kasahara again.

FOUR

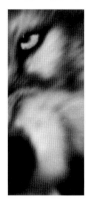

1

It was morning two days later, and most of the snow that had blanketed Tokyo in white was gone without a trace. Like the day before, and the day before that, Takako and Takizawa were on their way to visit Kasahara in the hospital when the radio in the patrol car rang. Takako picked it up for Takizawa, who was driving, and heard a woman's voice say, "There was a call for you, Officer Otomichi, on an outside line."

"An outside line?"

"It was your mother. I told her you'd call her right back."

This voice doubtless belonged to the policewoman who was the lone female on the desk staff. Partly because they were both so busy, their paths rarely crossed, and even though they were the only two women around, until now they had barely spoken. Thanking her politely, Takako hung up. What could her mother want at a time like this, she wondered, irritated. Then she realized that her family had never before called her at work, and her mind flooded with awful premonitions. Was it an accident? Illness? A fire? What's happened?

"What was that all about?" asked Takizawa, his glance flickering her way. The swelling in his face had clearly subsided from two days before; only the bruises remained.

"A personal call."

"Oh, a personal call," he rejoined with ironic displeasure. But Takako kept her eyes straight ahead. She didn't want him seeing the anxiety she felt. Besides, she had no idea yet what the trouble might be. And anyway, at a time like this she could not just drop everything and run home, no matter what the problem was. From Takizawa came a gruff snort. Perhaps her reply had been too abrupt.

"It was from my mother."

"Your mother? What does she want?"

"I don't know. I'll call her back later."

This time Takizawa nodded with a trace of satisfaction. "We'll be at the hospital soon," he said. "Where do your folks live?"

"In Urawa. They were originally from the older section of Tokyo, but they moved a few years ago."

"Urawa. That's not so far away, if you needed to go."

Takako answered noncommittally, knowing that even if it did come to that, it was unlikely she could. Her mother was as aware of this as anybody, and still she had called. This was no casual dinner invitation, no reminder of an upcoming class reunion. She began to feel jittery. Really, Mom, not now. This is not the time to burden me with some family difficulty. All I can think of now is Gale. I have to find a wolf-dog, who could be anywhere, and catch him before they shoot him to death. That's all I want to focus on now.

When they got to the hospital, Takako stepped aside and phoned home. To her surprise it was her father's voice that came on the line: "Takako, is that you?" Two days before, nothing but a gray blur of falling snow had been visible from the window in the smoking corner; today she could see piercingly blue sky. She wished Takizawa would go on ahead to Kasahara's room, but instead he was here puffing away, waiting for her to finish her call.

"Are you busy?"

"Yeah, pretty busy. I got a message somebody called."

"Oh, it must have been your mother."

Her father's voice sounded no different. He was usually reticent, rarely chatting with his daughters, but the fact that he was home on a weekday morning raised a red flag.

"Is Mom there?"

Instead of answering, her father sighed, and then murmured, "Ah. Busy, huh?" Speaking in a louder voice, he continued, "She probably wanted you to come home."

"What's going on? Did something happen to Mom?" Without meaning to, she let a note of exasperation creep into her voice.

"Nope," said her father, and sighed again. "Not to her." Takako was about to ask, "Then who?" when her father said, "It's Tomoko. She took some pills."

"Pills?" In that moment, Takako felt all her blood congeal. Oh god, she didn't want to hear this. She couldn't deal with it now. "How is she?"

"This morning she was late getting up so Koko went to wake her, and found a bottle of pills lying by the bed."

The investigation was nearing its climax. Everyone expected things to come to a head in the next day or two, and despite near exhaustion, they were spurring themselves on. Thinking only of the pleasure of toasting each other once the case was solved, they had been out till late last night, slipping and sliding on frozen snow, and up again early this morning. The chemical unit, which had little to show for their previous efforts, were especially fired up. Right about now they would be piling into the house of Masanori Ogawa's in Tokorozawa.

"Is she all right?"

"Yes, for now. Her life isn't in danger."

At this reply, Takako's heart, which had felt as if someone had grabbed hold of it, resumed beating at a furious pace. "Why?" she said under her breath, and felt a wave of anger rise from the pit of her stomach. Why now, of all times, did her sister have to pull a stunt like this?

"We were afraid she might try something like this. She'd been acting strange the last couple of days."

"Well, anyway, she's in the hospital now, right?"

"Yes. Your mother and Koko are staying with her. Koko's taking it all right, but your mother is a nervous wreck. That's probably why she called you."

Takako felt the strength drain from her shoulders. Her mother's condition weighed on her mind. She thought of the woman who had stood rooted in front of the ICU, out of her mind with worry, the first day Kasahara was in the hospital. What happened to her, that woman who was whispering the words "please, dear god" over and over again? What became of the patient?

"I wish I could go to see her, too, but I can't, not right away. We don't have any time off."

When Takako said this, her father answered, "We know." After the two nights she'd spent in Takako's apartment, Tomoko had gone back home with some embarrassment, and evidently reported how busy she was. Tomoko sounded worried about her health, her father said.

"If she was that worried about me, why would she do such a thing to herself?"

"I don't know. You heard what the problem was, didn't you?"

"Yes, I did. But she didn't seem to be taking it all that hard. I mean, I thought she seemed kind of happy-go-lucky. The things she said sounded awfully childish to me."

"That's why she thought of doing a thing like this—because she is childish!"

For the first time, there was anger in her father's voice. Takako thought of the time when she had told her father she wanted a divorce. Then, too, he had taken the news with perfect calm, listening to her without getting emotional. "Is the marriage unendurable?" he had asked; when she answered, he said, "Then it can't be helped." Finally he had said caustically, "Just forget it ever happened." Only then did she realize what she had done to him. Feelings of a father of three daughters toward his only son-in-law, feelings aroused by her news, were contained in the loneliness of his retreating figure.

"So tell me," said Takako, lowering her voice, as Takizawa stood innocently at a nearby window, "did you find anything like a note?"

"No. I took a look around, but there wasn't anything like that. The room was the usual mess."

"Well then, you don't know if she really meant to kill herself."

"Yes, but—well, never mind. We'll take care of it. Your work is more important." He told her to look after herself, and to focus on work without worrying about Tomoko or her mother, because he and Koko were there.

"As soon as I can, I'll come home," Takako promised before hanging up with a heavy heart. She was so mad she could hardly see straight. She walked over to Takizawa, thinking her sister was the worst little troublemaker imaginable.

"Are you ready?" Takizawa asked flatly. Takako nodded silently. "Then let's get to work." He started down the hall, his paunch leading the way. "Life's full of surprises," he said.

Takako studied Takizawa's head, the scant oily hair plastered down; he had been listening, after all. In her mind she was still irritated with her sister. "That little fool," Takako grumbled. A picture of her came to mind: wearing Takako's pajamas, stomping her foot like a spoiled child. But Tomoko had also bought fever-reducing gel for Takako that night, and had prepared a curry dinner for her; she had always been Takako's baby sister, someone with whom she had felt a bond. Yet that same Tomoko had fallen in love with a married man, gotten an abortion, and now, to top it off, had overdosed on sleeping pills.

If Tomoko were a stranger, Takako would be tempted to say, "If you want to die, suit yourself." But her sister, she knew, had no idea how much trouble and anguish she would cause, how far from romantic and beautiful such a death would be. If her death were ruled not to be due to natural causes, her body would be stripped naked and handled by strangers, subjected to an autopsy, treated like an inanimate object. This reality was beyond Tomoko's imagination. God, what a little fool she was. Takako felt like heading right over and slapping her face. But since Tomoko was going to be all right, maybe she had better let it go? Hold her hand, smile, say, Glad you're fine.

Today, any hand-holding she did was going to be with someone else. Takako slipped into a sterile gown, went into the ICU, and sat with Takizawa beside the suspect's bed. She held the hand of this man destined to be carried off to prison as soon as his injuries healed sufficiently. He was out of the worst danger, but his fever was still high, his consciousness dim.

"Kasahara, how're you doing?" said Takizawa. "Do you know me? Can you hear me, Kasahara?"

They were allowed fifteen minutes at a stretch. From beginning to end, Takizawa spoke to Kasahara incessantly, and Takako held his hand. After Takizawa called his name repeatedly, finally Kasahara's eyelids opened and his eyes looked dully out at them. When he recognized their faces, he slowly squeezed Takako's hand.

"We're looking for Ogawa now. We'll get the guy who did this to you and your daughter, don't you worry."

Weakly, Kasahara signaled "yes" with his hand. Sensing the reaction, Takako looked up at Takizawa and nodded.

Based on Kasahara's testimony, investigation headquarters had declared Masanori Ogawa, who ran a health equipment business in the same building as Hara's date club, their prime suspect.

"I spoke to him first." Yesterday, in shaky, disjointed fragments, Kasahara had begun his story in simple words: While he was out training Gale, he saw Ogawa setting experimental fires in the riverbed, and in the course of stalking Hara, he had seen Ogawa hand him something in the underground parking garage of the restaurant.

"I wasn't going to say anything. Because Ogawa acted for me."

Ogawa had not been home since the fire at the Kasahara residence, and he'd made no contact with his family. His business, furthermore, had been going downhill for several years, and he'd taken out substantial loans from non-bank sources.

They would have to wait for the chemical analysis to be sure, but around Kasahara's house there was a telltale tarry substance suggestive of benzoyl peroxide. The investigators were strongly of the view that this arson case was connected to Hara's murder. If they could come up with concrete evidence linking Ogawa to this incident, they were ready to arrest him on a moment's notice.

"With only fifteen minutes a day, I can't ask all the questions I need to ask. Well, when you get better, you and me'll have a good long chat, OK?"

Takizawa's tone was gentle. As she held Kasahara's damp hand, Takako looked back and forth between the faces of the two men.

"But there are some things that can't wait," Takizawa was going on. "You understand me, right? You know you're not just a helpless victim here yourself. You admit what you did was wrong, right?"

The answer was a weak "yes." Takako was looking at Kasahara's profile; his eyes were closed.

The image of Tomoko angrily stomping her foot popped up again in Takako's mind. Ever since that girl was little, she always whined to get her way, always turned to Takako when she needed help. If she so much as caught a cold and took to her bed, she became needy and clingy; she'd cough on purpose, cry, and do all she could to keep Takako and Koko from doing things without her. This one time Takako had refused to play her game—was that why she ODed?

"Depending on the way you look at it, some people might even say you got what was coming to you," continued Takizawa.

Kasahara's fingers jerked as if a weak electric current had gone through them.

"There's not much difference between you and Ogawa when you come down to it, now is there? You both took someone else's life without getting your own hands dirty. You had your reasons, I'm sure. I've got a couple of young daughters myself—I'll tell you about that some other time."

The man's heavily bandaged chest moved, barely, up and down. Kasahara's eyes, surrounded by deep crows' feet, opened slowly and he gazed up at the ceiling.

What was Tomoko doing now? Maybe Takako should have at least asked for the name of the hospital where she was.

"Anyway, the main thing we need to know now is about that dog you let go. Gale."

The eyes closed again. Under the lids, Kasahara's eyeballs were in restless motion. Then Kasahara's throat curved up and he let out a groan from deep inside, twisting his face. Reflexively, Takako squeezed his hand hard. His large, gnarled hand moved weakly in hers and went limp.

"Got any idea where Gale might've taken off for?"

No response. Instead, as if he were experiencing sudden pain, Kasahara's face twisted in agony and his breath came in ragged spurts. The doctor, who had been standing a ways off, quickly came forward.

"Step back, please. He can't be subjected to any more of this." The doctor peered into Kasahara's face and checked the various tubes and cords connected to him before giving the nurse an order. Until then she had remained in the background, but now she sprang into action. Takako was struck by the realization that this was their place of work, not hers; feeling awkwardly in the way, she stood and yielded her spot to them. Takizawa, however, was not so willing to give up. It irked her to realize it, but this was one area where she could learn from him. Even if people resented you for it, you had to get the job done. That was a detective's first duty.

"Can you give him something to calm him down? There are things we absolutely have to ask him."

"Can't you see the state he's in? I think you should leave."

"How many minutes till I can talk to him again? I'll wait outside."

The doctor did not answer Takizawa's question. Even so, Takizawa did not give up, appealing to him several times before finally turning away.

"We gotta have more than this before we contact headquarters," Takizawa grumbled as they left the ICU. The words were no sooner out of his mouth than the ring of a cellphone went off. He and Takako looked at each other, and reached into their pockets at the same time. Before Takako could check hers, Takizawa murmured, "It's mine. . . . Of all the times to pick to call."

His face was already a sight, half purplish with bruises; now, twisting his features in a scowl, he looked like the angry demon on a temple roof. Takako came dangerously near laughing, but controlled the impulse, telling herself sternly, "No time for silliness." As he squared his shoulders defiantly, walking with phone in his ear, she followed after him.

Tomoko. This is how everybody lives. Even betrayed by their husband or wife or child, even double-crossed, they go on living. They may live only to be sad, only to experience pain, but they go on living. . . .

Looking at Takizawa's back, for the first time Takako felt a true partnership with him. That clumsy emperor penguin probably spent all his time talking inwardly to other people, as Takako was doing now, while he went about his daily business. Pursuing cases that involved the lives of strangers while the confused mess of his own family life went on. Despite this ironic fate, he got through the days. His face might get bruised and swollen, but all he could do was go back to work, with no time to hide the damage.

She was starting to feel a slight lump in her throat when Takizawa suddenly turned around. With a queer look on his face, he handed her the phone wordlessly. In her ear came a crisp voice: "Ask your partner to fill you in on the details. When you're finished there, the Takizawa team is hereby disbanded. We have a new job for you, Officer Otomichi."

Takako answered perfunctorily and hung up. She turned around to look for Takizawa, but he was gone. She spun around quickly, and caught sight of him disappearing back into the ICU they had left only minutes before.

2

Pushing his way through the doctors and nurses blocking his way, Takizawa went back over to the bed. Kasahara's face was a mask of agony, his breath coming in gasps; he was oblivious to Takizawa's presence, his eyes tightly shut. The guy was seriously ill, a pitiful sight. Right now he didn't have the strength to fight a baby.

"Can you hear me, Kasahara?"

The only sound was jagged breathing. Takizawa crouched down beside the bed, put his mouth up next to Kasahara's ear, and called his name again. But there was no response. His dried, cracked lips half open, Kasahara went on gasping for breath. Next Takizawa grabbed his wrist, joggling it lightly as he said his name again. Just then Otomichi came scurrying in. With a confused look on her face, she came and stood next to Takizawa, her slanting eyes wide open for a change.

Takizawa's ears were ringing with the order just handed down from Watanuki: "The Takizawa team will be disbanded as soon as you finish your questioning. Officer Takizawa will be assigned a new partner to carry on this assignment with. We have new orders for Otomichi."

Why dissolve their partnership now, after all this time? Had she put in a request? His mind swirled with questions. But there had been no time to think of them while he was on the telephone. The news from Captain Watanuki had come like a new punch in the face.

"Look, I know you're suffering. But I have to ask you some questions. Can you open your eyes?" Still joggling the man's wrist, he squeezed a bit harder, lifting the unresisting arm. For a second, Kasahara's gasping stopped. Behind him, Takizawa could sense Otomichi's nervousness. None of your looks now, he thought. I gotta do what I can to clear this guy's head, whatever it takes. Glancing up, he saw her offering Kasahara the *hiragana* board. Thoughtful, smart of her, even if . . . Independent judgment, acted on swiftly. And calmly. Whatever may be going on in her family he didn't know, but she had the strength of mind to lay it aside when it counted.

"Can you hear me, Kasahara-san? If you can hear me, open your eyes!" Perhaps in response to the sharp female voice, Kasahara's eyelids fluttered open. Damn, lady cop or no lady cop, she was good. But today would be their last day together.

"You with me, Kasahara? Listen up. You know a guy named Mizutani? Taku Mizutani?"

Kasahara's hand trembled, and his eyes opened wide. His bloodshot, watery eyes wandered before turning toward Takizawa.

"You know him, don't you?" muttered Takizawa. "That's right, Mizutani from Takenotsuka, in Adachi Ward."

Kasahara's eyes wavered. Takizawa leaned forward so Kasahara had no choice but to look at him squarely. Then, loud enough so Otomichi could hear, he said, "He's dead." For a moment Kasahara lay still, as if his breathing had stopped. But his eyes remained wide open.

"They found his body this morning in a temple compound not far from here. His throat was torn out and his skull was mangled." Even as he spoke those words, Takizawa felt a chill travel down his own spine. The agitation in Kasahara's eyes was clear. His gaze roved about as if seeking salvation. From beside him came the whisper, "Is that true?" Without taking his eyes off Kasahara, Takizawa nodded, though barely, and then lowered his face even closer to the patient.

"It was Gale, wasn't it?"

Kasahara focused on Takizawa's face again, staring back as if to test him. Takizawa sighed and said, "You don't believe me?" Instead of a reply, Kasahara blinked once. "Unfortunately, it's true."

Takizawa told Kasahara to blink once for yes, twice for no, and repeated the question: Did he know a man named Taku Mizutani? After a second's hesitation, during which he looked from Takizawa to Otomichi and back again, slowly Kasahara blinked a single time.

"Well, it's good to know that dog you trained just doesn't go around attacking random strangers. That's something. That's what had me worried."

Once again, Kasahara's gaze wandered. His eyes, already reddened and watery from fever, seemed actually to tremble, tears oozing from the corners. This was not the place for tears. But unlike a woman, when a man shed tears during an interrogation, it meant he'd come around. Takizawa leaned farther forward and asked, "How'd that happen? Here you are, lying in a hospital bed. But Gale out there went and found Mizutani on his own. How'd he pull off a trick like that?"

Choking on tears, Kasahara raised a shaking hand. Without a moment's delay, Otomichi offered him the board. The wretched man craned his neck to see it and then, with frustrating slowness, his hand lacking strength, he spelled out his message:

We checked him out.

"You taught him to recognize Mizutani?"

Found out where he lived, followed him.

Was that enough for the animal to remember Mizutani? Could it be that smart? We're talking about a pooch here, thought Takizawa. No matter how well trained, there had to be a limit to what a dog could do. Obeying an on-the-spot order was impressive; but if he could remember and carry out an assignment even when separated from his master, he was practically human. Was that what they were like, these wolf-dogs?

"So Gale could carry out his mission even without you around?"

Never thought he'd take it so far. As Kasahara stared at the board, seemingly frustrated with his slowness, there was definite fear in his eyes. *Gale has strong will. Won't act unless convinced.*

"OK," said Takizawa, thinking, My god, what kind of creature have you created? "Who else did you teach him to recognize?"

No response. For the first time Takizawa spoke roughly, thrusting his face before the other man, intimidating him: "Tell us! Who else is Gale hunting?!"

Kasahara's wrinkled eyelids moved feebly in a double blink.

"'No' doesn't mean nothing. I'm asking you who he's hunting!"

The eyes wavered anxiously again, and the soundless lips barely moved.

"What?" said Takizawa, putting his ear down by Kasahara's mouth. "What is it, goddamn it?"

Otomichi spoke up, her tone severe: "If you have anything to say, Kasahara-san, please use this."

The lips moved vainly again, but finally he gave up and used the board.

No more targets.

Takizawa was about to say, "No more, huh?" but Otomichi clutched his arm to stop him. Kasahara's wobbly hand was still not finished.

Gale. His breath was coming unevenly. Tears rolled from his bloodshot eyes as he stared at the board.

"What about Gale?"

"Take your time. Take as long as you want." Otomichi spoke in a subdued tone. Still holding on to Takizawa's arm, she bent over and said encouragingly, "Go on, please. You can do it." Not the sort of thing people usually said during an interrogation. What was the point of sympathizing with a suspect? But in this case, when they needed to debrief a bedridden suspect, it was the best possible thing. And no male cop would ever have uttered those words.

Would not attack ordinary people. But maybe Ogawa.

As the finger painstakingly traced out these words, through the sterile gown covering his arm Takizawa felt Otomichi's grip tighten. Son of a bitch, he should have asked the captain where Ogawa was. But the captain hadn't said anything, they must not know.

"With that dog's determination, if he can find Ogawa, he'll attack."

In answer to this mutter, Kasahara's eyelids feebly blinked once. Separated from his master, left alone to fend for himself, had Gale ceased to be a dog and become the next thing to a real wolf, hunting down Ogawa in a full display of lupine prowess?

"Is that what you want him to do?"

No response.

"I told you we're gonna catch Ogawa, right? You still want Gale to kill him?"

No response. Slowly Kasahara closed his eyes, struggling to get his breathing under control. His carotid artery was pulsing. Tears flowed without end. Takizawa stared down at the ex-cop with irritation.

Otomichi spoke up: "Don't you care about Gale? He killed those people for you. Is that the only reason you raised him, as a tool of vengeance? The reason he trusts you so completely—isn't it because of the unconditional love you've always given him?"

Fresh tears flowed from the corners of Kasahara's eyes. Takizawa looked from his face to Otomichi's profile and, scarcely realizing it, pulled slightly back. She had her own questions to ask. She was trying to use a woman's tactics to get Kasahara to talk.

"I don't want Gale to die. If it's at all possible, I want to capture him alive."

At that, Kasahara's eyes opened again. Mingled weakness and obsession, indecision and regret, loneliness: all that was concentrated in his gaze.

"Tell us—how can we capture Gale when he isn't tame with strangers?"

The silence went on so long that it seemed like the clock had stopped. She never moved a muscle, just stared intently at the man's eyes. New orders, thought Takizawa. He never even knew that Otomichi used to be a motor-cycle cop. There was silence except for the raspy breath of this pathetic, voiceless, injured man.

"Isn't that your duty, as his master? Or are you willing to abandon him now? Now that he's accomplished your goals for you, he can just go wild, is that what you want?" Silence. After a pause, Otomichi took a deep breath and asked, "Isn't he family?"

Kasahara looked at Otomichi for a while and then, after many seconds had gone by, finally he moved his hand.

Emiko's things. Her scent.

"Emiko's personal belongings? Are you saying that if he detects her scent, he'll come out of hiding?"

Slowly, one blink. As he looked at the man's rigid expression, Takizawa could tell: The guy knows his daughter was burned to death.

Her things are at the hospital.

"Ogose Hospital? We can use whatever is there? OK, but where should we go? Where would Gale go to hide?"

Little by little, she was talking faster. She seemed far more composed than Takizawa, but inside she had to be frustrated, too, up against the wall. And from now on she'd have a solo assignment. Be in the forefront of the hunt for the wolf-dog. Imagine that—the princess is a lizard! It wasn't just her being a woman; apart from her gender, there was something basically mysterious and unknowable about her.

Home.

"Home?"

"Your old house, you mean, the one that burned down, in Akishima?"

Kasahara blinked slowly, once. Seeing Takizawa nod with understand-ing, he closed his eyes again. There was so much more Takizawa wanted to ask. But for now they had to catch that pooch—although plainly, this was no ordinary mutt, he had to admit. Anyway, while they did that, Kasahara should concentrate on getting better so he could answer questions more eas-ily next time around.

Gesturing to Otomichi, who was frowning, Takizawa thought: "The wolf-dog's got no place else to go. He's bound to go back and search for Kasahara and Emiko." Then he moved away from the bed. Behind him, he heard her say, "We'll find him. I promise we'll find him."

As he left the ICU, walking fast, Takizawa spoke without looking at Takako, "You heard what the captain said?"

Her answer, a soft "yes," followed behind him along with the sound of her shoes. With that, he clammed up. He rushed out of this depressing place, where it felt like you'd get sick just walking around, and jumped into the unmarked police car to escape the flock of reporters who had somehow sniffed them out, even though there had been no official announcement.

Apart from the report he filed over the phone as they started for headquarters, Takizawa said nothing on the ride back. He didn't know what he was supposed to say to this female cop he would be done working with now, and she was silent, too. What, she couldn't manage a simple "Thanks, it's been nice"? Or was it possible that despite her calm exterior, on the inside she was panicking?

When they were almost there, she finally opened her mouth. "Sergeant Takizawa." Until then, the car had been filled only with the sound of transmissions from headquarters; now, finally, the atmosphere lifted. Taking care to keep his voice no different from usual, Takizawa answered, "Yeah."

"Would it be all right if I asked you to write up the report this time?"

"No problem. After all, you've got better things to do, don't you?"

Damn, he'd done it again. He hadn't meant to be sarcastic at a time like this. He clicked his tongue. But see there? Just when there was an opening for conversation, she closed up again and didn't say boo.

3

That afternoon, Masanori Ogawa was put on the nation's most wanted list. The morning search of his residence had turned up tools like a tabletop milling machine and a belt sander; a circuit tester, an oscilloscope, and other measuring instruments; a printed circuit board and Nichrome wire fitted with an aluminum block, a vinyl chloride sheet, a crystal oscillator and a timer IC; plus copper rivets, cables, and more. His family explained that the storeroom, where this evidence was found, was used by Ogawa to develop new health equipment. However, among the various chemicals—including methanol—was a white, odorless, dry powder. Although it had to be tested, headquarters felt confident that among the chemicals taken from Ogawa's residence they'd find benzoyl peroxide.

"No doubt about it, Ogawa's our guy."

Takako heard about all this while sitting in the car on stakeout. The sun had set hours before, and darkness had set in. It was two days after the fire, but a stench still emanated from the charred ruins of Kasahara's house, which was surrounded by investigators watching not for a human suspect but for a canine.

"What about Ogawa himself?"

"Missing since the fire." It was Takizawa who said this.

After their partnership ended, Takako had assumed she was through with the hassle of conversation with the grumpy sergeant; but Takizawa had also been assigned to hunt down the wolf-dog, to perform the special role as Takako's backup.

"He left his home in his car," Takizawa was saying. "They know the model and license number, and they've checked everywhere he's likely to go: his parents, relatives, and friends."

"Then it's just a matter of time till we find him."

"Maybe, maybe not. If Kasahara's right, it's a race between us and Gale. Who's gonna get to him first?"

Takizawa scratched the back of his neck with a finger fat like a caterpillar. Even in the dim light, she could see what looked like flakes of dandruff fluttering down. Takako was sitting in the back seat. Up front next to Takizawa was his new partner, Imazeki, who was about Takizawa's age and had an aura of stubborn earnestness. While Takizawa and Takako talked, he stayed mum. Somebody like this was a more suitable partner for the emperor penguin, she thought. Anybody on the street looking at them would think she was an ordinary bike rider hauled in for a traffic violation.

After a brief silence, Takizawa twisted his short, thick neck with effort and looked back at her. "How long does a person's scent last?" he asked.

She tilted her head speculatively and said only, "I wonder."

Headquarters had obtained a pair of pajamas worn by Emiko Takagi from the mental hospital. The pajamas had been placed atop the fence in front of the Kasahara house in hopes that Gale, when he came back in search of his master, would catch the scent and relax his wariness. However ridiculous it seemed, they had to try everything.

"When's it ever gonna warm up?" Another mumble from Takizawa. Then, without turning back to Takako this time, he added, "What a night for a bike ride, eh?" Takako looked out the window without replying. She had a feeling that at any time, a pair of eyes might shine out of the dark. But Gale was surely too cautious to appear this early in the night, an hour when people were still hurrying home from work.

"She's young, that's all there is to it." At last a comment from the shotgun seat. "I used to ride for fun myself, but I gave it up about ten years ago." Imazeki had joined the team as backup from the neighboring precinct; his style of speech was more polite than Takizawa's.

"Oh, I dunno. It's more than her being young. She's gotta love it, right? Wearing the leather outfit, and then *zoom*."

Earlier that evening, on seeing Takako dressed in her leather motorcycle suit, Takizawa had gone goggle-eyed with astonishment. And then, his face showing a complex blend of emotions, among them embarrassment and discomfort, he said, "Look at you! Pretty cool."

"Maybe," said Imazeki, "but riding in winter is harsh. No matter how much she might like it, still—"

"Well, nothing we can do about it, is there? That's Officer Otomichi's assignment. Hey, Otomichi, why don't you catch a few winks while you can? You know that wolf friend of yours isn't going to show up until the middle of the night."

Holding her helmet in her lap, Takako obediently leaned back and closed her eyes. Whether she would be able to sleep or not she didn't know, but it would be easier this way than when she was alone with Takizawa.

Headquarters had come up with a plan for capturing Gale alive. If the killer were human, they would have him red-handed, but since Gale was an animal incapable of testifying, he constituted important physical evidence. Eventually he would have to be destroyed, but they intended to keep him alive at least until the trial, so that they could demonstrate to the judge his remarkable abilities. This decision had come as a great relief to Takako. The thought of her leading the troops to Gale for the sole purpose of killing him was heartbreaking.

"Who'da thunk it? A lady lizard."

She overheard this muttered comment from Takizawa. He must have thought she was already asleep. He was showing unusual solicitude, for him, in lowering his voice so far; yet the very quietness of his whisper had roused her.

"She's really persistent. You two must have been great partners."

The barest suggestion of a snort. Then Takizawa said sarcastically, "Is that what you think?"

Go right ahead, thought Takako, say whatever you like; get it off your chest. Don't mind me. Once Gale shows up, I'll be rid of you once and for all.

Some of the brass, she had heard, were of the opinion that even if Gale was shot and killed, the bite marks, dog hair, and tracks together would provide enough evidence to prove he had committed the crimes. They wanted to deploy snipers from the riot police. Inspector Miyagawa was against the idea. Instead of snipers, he turned to a private hunters' association. Hunters assembled in response to his request were now standing by, each armed with a tranquilizer gun.

"This is gonna be a long night."

"Why don't you get some shut-eye, too, Takizawa? I'll stay awake."

She could hear the two of them talk. She listened, then drifted off. She thought about Tomoko, but stopped herself. She was about to go after Gale; she couldn't let anything distract her. Clad in her leather suit, her gloves still on, she slept fitfully.

In the end, Takako never had a chance to get on her motorcycle that night. Dawn arrived without Gale showing up; the seat of Takako's CB400 Super Four, parked in front of the patrol car, was covered in frost.

Takako crept out of the car and was brushing off the motorcycle seat when Takizawa came out, yawning. Imazeki was still asleep in the shotgun seat.

"We may be in for a helluva long wait," said Takizawa.

"I wonder if everyone is too close in," said Takako. "Not good to let him see we have the place staked out."

"Good point," Takizawa agreed. "He's supposed to be smart, after all."

When the sun was up, the three of them let the next shift take over and went back to headquarters. Since they might have to go back out at any time, and the motorcycle might be indispensable, it was decided that Takako would not go home after the meeting, but would sleep in the station to save precious time.

The other investigators, resting at last after a long night's stakeout, spent time watching television and reading newspapers, in the process learning how the story was playing out.

"Says here Ogawa had a lover. She wants to tell the world how she feels!"

"This one is speculating that Ogawa belongs to a terrorist organization."

Media coverage of the case was heating up. For the past few days, reporters had been camped out in front of Tachikawa Central Station. As always happened when a sensational case like this broke, people connected with the main figures—at the moment, Kasahara and Ogawa—were hounded by the media. Sometimes the TV screen was filled with a montage of faces, while commentators blabbed on. A parade of experts no one ever heard of before made their appearance on television shows, were quoted in the newspapers; there were social critics, chemistry professors, veterinarians and zookeepers, all giving every conceivable opinion on every conceivable topic.

"This guy says the animal is probably hiding out on Tsukuda Island."

"This one says the animal's gone up north to Tohoku: 'There have been sightings of an animal too big to be an ordinary dog.' Hah."

As they read the newspaper accounts, the detectives found themselves half-amused. For the media to talk up the case was fine, but for them to provoke a panic was only going to make things worse. To prevent this from happening, the police released details only sparingly, but the media went ahead and published any old thing they liked.

"The humane society is coming here to protest!" an investigator exclaimed. There had been a flood of complaints from citizens demanding that police capture or kill the dog immediately. At the same time, the humane society was getting into the act: once the dog was captured, they wanted it released to their custody, or returned to Alaska.

It was a circus. And the detectives knew to treat it that way. In the real world, on the other hand, Gale was moving through the landscape with nimble caution, unseen. And going from his home on the western rim of Tokyo all the way to Adachi on the eastern end, traveling by night, he had brilliantly carried out his master's wishes.

"This is weird. Says here the latest victim Mizutani was an honest man leading a sober life."

"Slip 'em the real dope—that he was a crazed drug addict on his way to becoming a street slasher."

"Who, me? No way. I don't want them coming after me."

Regarding Mizutani, however, the fact of the matter was this: Finding any connection between him and Teruo Hara, whether a dozen years ago or more recently, had not been easy. But Mizutani's own past was somewhat checkered. At the time of his death he was employed at a food storage company, but in his twenties he spent two years in prison for drug possession; and on the arms of his common-law wife there were some telltale tracks.

As far as anyone could tell, Gale had cut straight through the densely populated city center to go after Mizutani. In terms of distance, it was not that far; but how did the wolf-dog manage to avoid highways and make his way through a city with almost no empty space? They'd never find out, supposing they ever caught him.

"You don't think he already got to Ogawa?"

"Maybe. You never know. He might be biding his time, waiting for his chance. I bet he's got that much savvy."

On learning that Gale had continued to go after his targets even while his master lay in the hospital, headquarters had dropped its dismissive "it's only a dog" attitude. They would never catch Gale as long as they thought of him as a dumb animal: he was a creature of the wild, something no one on the investigation team had ever faced before. A wolf possessed mystic abilities; and even if the animal had a certain percentage of dog genes, the balance of its genes was still a wolf's.

That was clear to Takako who, rather than stand around chitchatting, decided to call and check in with her family. Today it was Koko, the middle sister, who picked up the phone.

"How's Tomoko?"

"So-so." Koko was almost the opposite of Takako in personality and in fact seemed to harbor some hostility toward her older sister. It was as if they weren't cut from the same piece of cloth, or were on different wavelengths; whenever they were together, there was a strained awkwardness. Even now, Takako found Koko's response irritating.

"What do you mean, so-so? Is she better?"

"Yes, she's better. It's everybody else who isn't."

"Oh. Well, that's good to know."

Conversations with Koko never seemed to go anywhere. "Um, is Mom there?" she asked.

"Hang on."

"What did you say to Moko?" Those were her mother's first words to Takako when she got on the phone.

"What do you mean?"

"Onee-chan, didn't you talk to her?"

Moko was Tomoko, and Koko was Kouko, the first "o" stretched out; but Takako was forever *onee-chan*, "elder sister." Takako was not sensitive about it, but her mother did treat her differently. Sometimes this worked to Takako's advantage; more often it was a channel for her mother's emotions, so Takako would end up as the mediator between her parents and sisters—or, as now, the villain.

"You have important work to do, I'm sure, but I'd like to know how a person who won't lift a finger to help her sister when she's in trouble thinks she can go around keeping society safe from criminals. Tell me that."

"Just a minute—"

"I left a message, didn't I? You never called back. Moko wanted to ask your advice, that's why she went to see you, and I was sure you'd be a good sister and help her. I was *counting* on you."

Her mother's tone was sharp and annoying, and Takako's nerves were fraying. She listened silently to her mother, who clearly had not yet recovered from yesterday's shock. Takako could think of no words to respond with.

"Do you understand me? You came *this close* to letting your precious sister die. I don't care how blasé you are now about people dying, since you see dead bodies on the job every day—"

"Who could be blasé about a thing like that?"

"But you are. Yesterday you made one little phone call, and then you washed your hands of her."

What Takako regretted was that she had bothered to call now. She didn't have time or energy to listen to her mother go on and on. She had to stay on an even keel in case she needed to climb on her bike. She needed to conserve her strength.

"I don't know what keeps you so busy day in and day out, but if your job prevents you from rushing to your sister's side when her life is on the line, then maybe you better quit. That job is why your marriage fell apart—"

"Um, I only called because I wanted to check on Tomoko's condition. I'm still in the middle of work. So, how is Tomoko? Has she regained consciousness?"

There was a brief pause. "Yes, she has. Of course she has—if she hadn't, it would be terrible!"

Takako sighed loud enough for her mother to hear, and then murmured, "That's good to hear." Having managed to suppress her mother—who might have gone on in a torrent of words like a burst dam—and having learned all she needed to know about Tomoko for now, Takako attempted to end the conversation. But her mother was not about to let her go so easily.

"Moko relies on you, you know that, don't you? We thought that if she wouldn't listen to us, she'd listen to you, that you'd be able to talk sense into her. And instead, you—"

"I told Tomoko to leave that guy. I told her not to ask me to help her commit adultery. And as I told Dad yesterday, when she came over, she didn't seem all that depressed. She's not a child anymore. She can think and act for herself."

"Nonsense. If she thinks for herself and takes an overdose of pills, it is unbearable. Onee-chan, you—"

"Look, if you want to make this whole thing my fault, go right ahead, but—"

"Don't give me that sulky tone of voice. All I'm saying is, I do not understand how you, the oldest child, could make one phone call and think you've done enough."

"I'm not sulking. I—"

"I know, I know. You're up to your ears hunting for some criminal. But why does it have to be *you* who does it? Isn't there anybody else who could do it? You're Moko's only big sister."

"She's got Koko."

"Koko is Koko, and you are you."

What a hopeless conversation. Takako dared not say anything more about her work, because her mother was sure to start going on about how a woman ought to live—which did not include being a cop. She just held the phone.

"When are you coming home?"

"When things come to a stopping point."

"When will that be?"

"I don't know. I'm doing all I can."

"I'm sure you are. So when will it be?"

"All I can say is, when things come to a stopping point." Feeling like her chest was leaden, Takako used her mother's most hated excuse—"I'm busy, I have to go"—and hung up the phone. *Thanks, Tomoko. Thanks, Mom. What a wonderful family. Love getting my divorce thrown in my face.*

But what could she do? To keep her mother from worrying, Takako had never offered anything but the vaguest explanation of her work. Even now, if she said she was standing by to lead the hunt for a wolf-dog that killed three people, her mother's eyes would narrow in anger, her blood pressure would shoot up, and she was certain to say something like, "Are you crazy?! Don't do it! That's nothing *you* have to do, is it? You're a woman—there should be something safer and easier for you to do." Yes, Mom, I know. But I want to ride my motorcycle. Even if it wasn't an order, I want to find Gale, myself, on my bike.

Peeved by the conversation, Takako turned around to find a detective standing nearby. Takako stiffened, fearing that he'd listened to the entire conversation.

"Your boyfriend?" the detective, who looked to be in his mid-thirties, asked, smiling. "He can't see you lately, and so he's giving you a hard time, eh?"

Takako smiled evasively back. Don't think about extraneous things. Rest, so you're ready to do the job at any time. Tomoko, just because you put me through all this, you're getting well whether you like it or not. And you're breaking up once and for all with that jerk. Got it?

Entering the sleeping room, she was in such a foul mood that if not for the other people there, she might have kicked something. Even so, she was physically exhausted, and no sooner did she lie down on the thin bedding than she was fast asleep.

4

It was the color of a dirty rag. At first, Teruko Iohara thought it was a patch of dirty snow from the snowstorm a few days ago. She hadn't done anything with the garden for some years now; the trees were overgrown, and so many of them were sasanqua, fatsia, and evergreens that the garden was never bare, even in winter. As the sun didn't reach all the way to the ground, snow didn't melt quickly.

When is this cold weather going to end?

Teruko sighed as she stepped casually out into the accumulation of snow. This was her first time out in the garden since the storm. Usually she took a turn in the garden once a day, but fear of slipping and falling had kept her indoors until now. Really, she needed to call in a gardener and have the shrubbery trimmed. But living alone on a fixed income, she couldn't afford it, and finding a good gardener was so much trouble. All the workmen she used to know—not just the gardener but the tatami-maker, the house painter, the joiner, and the plumber—well, she didn't know them anymore.

So be it. This house and I could just molder away together.

And yet she couldn't sit back and let the garden go to seed. Stray cats might move in, and who knew what people were going to throw over the wall. People were a disgrace, the way they tossed empty cans and cigarette butts and whatever else they felt like getting rid of. Just because the garden was unkempt didn't give them the right to treat it like a garbage dump. How rude.

"Honestly, folks today haven't got a lick of manners," she said aloud.

As she surveyed the garden of this house where none of her four children, nor any of her grandchildren, ever came to visit, Teruko's gaze was drawn back to that spot in the snow. There was something funny about it. The whole garden was covered in white. How come that one spot wasn't? Maybe it wasn't snow, maybe it was something else.

"Mercy! I almost fell. The ground is so soft and muddy."

Carefully, she picked her way through the garden. She was wearing heavy socks over her tights, and a pair of old slip-ons. Usually she scarcely noticed it, but there was no doubt that her steadily worsening cataracts were affecting her vision.

"All I need to do is fall here and break a hip. I'd never get up again." When you lived alone, your health—the ability to get around without any problem—was a main priority.

"If I remember right, there used to be a stepping-stone right around here."

Here it is! Under the snow, covered over with dirt so you could hardly tell it was there. She hadn't so much as swept a leaf these many years, so that wasn't surprising.

Eyes on her feet as she made her way slowly toward the dirty patch of snow, Teruko wondered if it could be a sandbag. Except who would be able to throw a sandbag into the middle of a 600-square-yard plot of land? If it was near the wall, maybe, but not this far . . . they'd have to climb over the wall first. If someone was pulling a prank like that, harassing her, she might have to do something about it.

"Land's sake. Why do these things have to happen to me?"

Coming finally to the edge of the shrubbery, Teruko cautiously straightened her back. If she moved too quickly, the way she used to when she was young, she could throw her back out of joint. That reminded her; she'd been putting it off because of the snow, but today or tomorrow she needed to go get an electric massage. She looked around, beyond the ferns and *omoto* lilies and the daffodils just starting to come up.

There she saw something that dumbfounded her. How much time had gone by while she stood there, just looking at it without a word? This was astonishing. Something akin to fear crawled up her spine. But another emotion had her even more strongly in its grip.

"Now how did you get in here?" she muttered in a gruff, low voice. The lump of gray, still curled in a ball, stared at her, unmoving. It looked like a pile of dirty snow with a black nose and round, greenish eyes. But on top was a pair of big, triangular ears, and beneath the pointy jaw there were undoubtedly legs. "I asked you how you got in here!"

Of all things. Imagine a stray dog this size, here in the middle of Tokyo! More than astonishment or fear, Teruko felt anger. An irresponsible owner had abandoned his dog here.

"Where's your master, eh? This is *my* house. You have no right to be here."

She'd had dogs of her own before. Never one this big, though. When the children were little, they were always bringing home a stray dog or cat, and she'd had Shibas and mixed breeds for watchdogs, too. Around back somewhere there was still a long-abandoned doghouse, gone to ruin. "I'm talking to you."

Teruko ventured farther along the mucky ground in her sandals. Only then did the animal rouse itself from its curled-up position and sit up. Teruko's eyes widened at the size of it. The head was high off the ground. And what sharp, intelligent eyes it had. She didn't know what kind of dog it was, but the nose was big and black, the muzzle was long, and come to think of it, it looked like a wolf. The thought crossed her mind that if a dog like this attacked her, it could easily kill her.

Better not raise a fuss. Instantly, she made this judgment. Wasn't that what you were supposed to do if you ever came across a bear in the mountains, make no fuss, show no fear, never look away for a second? What worked for one animal had to work for another. Besides, there was a strange power in those eyes that was irresistible. Teruko could barely turn away from the animal's gaze.

Well. We can't stand here staring at each other forever. What to do? Finally, coming to herself, Teruko began to worry.

First thing was to get away safely. Then, she could find a stick or something to chase it off; or would it be better to call the department of health? Staring into the small round eyes, Teruko wracked her brains—and then she happened to see the animal's feet. The mud-covered forelegs, planted on snow and dead leaves, were trembling.

It being a dog, its expression did not change. The relatively small eyes shone as if there was an inner light. Teruko thought the dog had fine eyes, possessed a fine dignity. And yet those stout, solid forelegs were trembling. Where had it come from, how had it gotten here? Cleaned up, it would be a good-looking dog, she thought, because from jaw to chest it was covered with a reddish-black, muddy-looking substance.

The words "Are you cold?" formed in her mind. Preparing to say them, she moved her hand a fraction of an inch, and instantly the dog began shaking all over.

"You don't have to be so scared."

She wasn't going to bite. A big dog like this was more likely to attack her than the other way round. And yet it just sat there and shivered, looking at a little old lady like her. What a pathetic creature.

"It's all right. Lie back down." After observing it a while longer, this was what Teruko told the dog. It wasn't barking or growling, just shivering; no point in waving a stick at a dog like that. "Brrr, it's cold. I'm going back inside."

With that, she turned quietly on her heel and began to walk away, beside herself with apprehension that the dog might attack her from behind; when she had taken five or six steps, she turned and saw the gray dog hadn't moved, was watching her from between the leaves of the fatsia bush.

Just as well. It'll go off before long anyway. Probably it got separated from its master and wandered in here, exhausted. She didn't really mind letting it rest in her garden for a while. Besides, this wasn't some smart-mouthed person she was dealing with; it was a silent, shivering dog.

"Oh, that's better." When she got back to the living room, Teruko sat on the floor and warmed her legs under the kotatsu. When was the weather ever going to get warm? From where she sat, she poured hot water over the tea leaves she used for the last cup, and sipped the weak tea. She started to think again about the dog in her garden.

"He's in the garden, all right, but how did he get in?" The gate was always shut. Before, she used to open it in the daytime, but so few people came by, and she found it so intimidating to have to go outside at dusk to lock it again, that now she never opened it except when she herself went out.

Then maybe it jumped over the wall? The wall was made of *oyaishi* stone and was as tall as a grown man; not so easy to jump over. Maybe to a dog, a jump like that was nothing; even so, Teruko felt uneasy as she sipped her tea. There were so many trees now, this room got less light than it used to.

Wrapped in silence, alone in the twilight, she couldn't help worrying about that dog. How long would it stay?

After staring off into space for a time, Teruko clucked at herself and got up from the kotatsu. Going through the frigid entranceway and then a formal room she once used as guest room, she carefully slid open the *shoji* door and went out into the corridor. If all the shutters were open, it was a pleasantly sunny hallway, but lately she only opened one or two shutters. The messy corridor, with its piles of old cardboard boxes and whatnot, was damp and even colder than the rest of the house. Teruko stood by the one window with open shutters, and surreptitiously opened the curtain.

The grayish lump was still among the trees. Perhaps it was curled in a ball; she couldn't see the face. Nevertheless, it was definitely there in the same place as before.

"I wonder if it's injured."

Teruko began to worry the dog had come here to die, an unbearable thought. Yet even though it was shivering, the animal didn't look famished or weak. As long as she didn't go outside it would leave her alone, and if she returned the favor, sooner or later it would go away. Coming to this conclusion, she moved away from the window.

Or maybe it was hungry.

Settling back into the warmth of the kotatsu, Teruko reconsidered. The dogs she used to have had been fond of rice gruel. She would throw in leftovers from a meal, sometimes a bit of boiled fish or tempura, and give it to them. Dogs always felt closest to whoever fed them. Remembering the old days, Teruko considered pouring a little miso soup on some leftover rice and giving it to the dog.

"No, not on your life!"

What if she was kind to it, and then it settled down and wouldn't go away? A puppy might be one thing, but she couldn't keep a great big dog like that. It would eat her out of house and home.

She ended up peering out at the garden every hour. Every time she looked, the lump of gray was still there. As the sun sank, the wind moaned in the trees. When she closed the shutters, the animal was still there, ensconced in the shadows.

That night Teruko ate alone as usual. Her false teeth didn't fit right, and she had little appetite, so she ate a simple meal in less than ten minutes. Afterwards, there was little to do. She made preparations for breakfast, then walked around locking up the house. She laid out her bedding and changed into her nightclothes. Before turning off the lights, she switched on the television. Whether a program was interesting or boring, she always watched television till eleven. The television was now Teruko's greatest pleasure, and her best friend.

Peeling a tangerine, she half-watched the news. Teruko's days passed by changelessly, but out in the world, all sorts of things were happening.

"Next, early this morning in the compound of a temple in Takenotsuka, Adachi Ward, the body of a man in his thirties was found bleeding from wounds to the head. Tokyo police have determined that the victim was apparently bitten to death by a large canine. The victim has been identified as Taku Mizutani, a nearby resident of Takenotsuka. Investigators say . . ."

Teruko knew from watching the news that there had been incidents of fatal attacks by dogs recently in the city. Tonight, however, as soon as she heard this report, she felt her heart jump into her throat. A large canine. Nothing in the least unusual about that, she knew, and yet . . .

"The dog that is thought to have attacked Mizutani is a male wolf-dog roughly three feet in height, dark gray in color, one of very few such dogs in Japan. Wolf-dogs do not ordinarily attack humans, but sources indicate that this one has received special training. Police are conducting an all-out search for the animal."

Dark gray, three feet tall, wolf-dog: these words were compressing Teruko's heart until she could hardly breathe. It couldn't be! But the description matched the dog out in her garden exactly, the dog that had looked her coolly in the eye.

"Oh, my. What shall I do? It's a killer dog, they're saying."

She felt a chill. Should she call the police? This might not be the dog they were looking for, though. After all, it had been trembling. How could a dog that shook with fear at the sight of Teruko ever attack and kill anyone?

Suddenly she remembered the reddish-black mud on the dog's jaw and chest. What if that wasn't mud? What if it was gore from the deadly attack? The dog had attacked and killed someone, and then, tired out, it had sneaked into her garden to hide and rest. When this thought came to her, she began shaking uncontrollably. She wanted to open the shutters right away and see if it was still there. But no—if something went wrong, it might attack her. Berating herself for her foolishness in even thinking of giving food to such a dog, Teruko debated whether or not to call the police. But what if the police came rushing up this late at night with their sirens going full blast? What would the neighbors think? The dog might be gone by then anyway. If only it would just disappear. She didn't want to get involved in anything.

"Just go away somewhere. I don't know anything. It's got nothing to do with me."

She didn't feel like watching the television anymore. She switched the news program off before it was over and crawled into bed. She'd lived alone for so many dozens of years now that she was completely used to it, or so she thought; yet tonight this house empty of other occupants, filled only with memories, struck her as eerily large.

5

It looked like a shaggy gray cloud.

It was before dawn when headquarters radioed them the information and they found themselves racing from the stakeout in Akishima to the house in Nerima Ward.

"Are we sure it's Gale?" Takako asked Takizawa, frowning. She had no desire to leave the vicinity of the Kasahara house. This was no time to spend chasing a bum tip.

"Who knows. But the lady who called sounded convincing, so we have to check it out. She says the dog's neck and chest are covered with gore."

"With . . . gore?"

"That's what she says. And come without sirens, please, to keep from disturbing the neighborhood. Of course, sirens or no sirens, the second that animal senses danger he's gonna make a run for it." Takizawa looked unenthusiastic. But you couldn't ignore orders.

Takako had gotten on her frost-covered motorcycle and sped off for the address in Nerima Ward, near the Saitama border.

It was a fairly old residential neighborhood, with what might have originally been farmhouses. Most of the houses sat on large plots of land, and many of the trees in the gardens were conspicuously large. But would Gale pick a place like this to hide in? Doubtful, Takako watched as some forty riot police surrounded the house. A debate was underway as to whether they should wait for the members of the hunting association to arrive, or try to corner the animal first. The chief was trying to elicit information from the lady of the house. Suddenly, something gray came flying over the fence about as high as Takako's head and floated to the ground.

It's him!

Standing next to her motorcycle, she had chanced to be looking back unconcernedly when the creature flew noiselessly through the air. The riot police and other officers standing around didn't even cry out, it happened so fast, so quietly. Barely nine or ten feet ahead of her, Gale stood firmly on the asphalt road yet untouched by morning sun.

"Gale."

Takako said his name softly. Instantly the atmosphere around the animal underwent a slight shift. Long, pointy face, large ears. Legs longer than an ordinary dog's, dense fur. The thick, shaggy tail standing straight up in the air. And the eyes. Deep-set eyes, the likes of which Takako had seen only in photographs, now stared directly at her.

So this is Gale. The dog with wolf blood in his veins.

He was just as she had imagined he would be. The commanding presence, the dignity, the intelligence. She was swept by an impulse to go up to him. For a brief second, she forgot about the people he had attacked and killed. He conveyed neither the peculiarly woebegone look of a criminal, nor the murderous look of someone cornered, nor violence, nor malice, nor savagery. Like a cloud hovering between mountains at dawn, Gale was simply there. He didn't snarl. The calmness of his face bore no suggestion of anger or hate.

How could he be so calm? What was this aura of nobility that he exuded? Just as Takako started to waver, thinking it might indeed be possible to walk up to him, from behind her came the cry, "He jumped the wall!"

As if hit by a stone, Gale started running. He tore alongside the wall he had just sailed over, and headed off to the left. Only a moment later, when he was out of sight, did Takako come out of her trance and get on her bike. She had to go after him. Blood raced to her head. She gunned the engine and took off, accelerating a little too fast. Where he had headed left, she veered left. She was prepared to follow him to the ends of the earth—but he had vanished.

"Huh?"

He had rounded that corner only moments before. He couldn't be far. Now she was even more excited. For a while she kept going straight, trying to look on both sides as she rode. But like a sudden gust of wind or a gray phantom, the figure of the wolf-dog was nowhere to be seen.

"Find him! He may have gone back in the garden!"

When Takako reported having lost the animal, police fanned out over the neighborhood. Others poured back into the garden where he had been hiding for the last two days. Takako joined them.

A little old lady with a shawl around her shoulders was pacing nervously. She looked to be in her late seventies. Her thin, mostly white hair was loose and undone, her eyes were sunken, and she looked exhausted. Completely at a loss, she had been wandering among the investigators saying, "Excuse me!" Then, catching sight of Takako, the only one dressed differently from the others, she came mincing over. "Was that really the killer dog they've been talking about on the news?" she asked. "Is it still in the garden?"

"I don't know," said Takako. "They're checking now."

The old woman looked up at Takako in surprise. "Oh, my!" she exclaimed. "Are you a *woman*?"

Takako put on a smile and bowed her head, then inquired briefly about Gale.

The old woman recounted her story of discovering the animal in her garden. "But I have to say, it was an awfully quiet-looking thing. When I went up to it, it didn't bark or growl at all. Do you know what? It was actually shaking."

"Shaking?"

The old woman nodded once, her face wreathed in tiny wrinkles, and then pulled her shawl up around her nose to warm herself. "Shaking and shivering. So I thought it might be a cowardly dog, even though it was so big. The garden is huge, as you can see, and I've just been letting it go to rack and ruin. Really, I was thinking I would just let the poor thing stay. And then I heard about the dog on the news! Who could believe it was a terrible dog like that?"

Wolf-dogs were nervous around strangers, never warmed to anyone but their master. So even a little old lady was, from Gale's point of view, a total stranger.

It was Gale, it had to be.

And after flying by them like a burst of strong wind, he was gone. While the neighborhood search continued, the town woke up and traffic increased. In the end, Takako and the rest returned to headquarters empty-handed.

"At least we know he's in the city. He'll show up at Kasahara's house. It's just a matter of time. Nothing to do but continue the stakeout. Whatever happens, we want that wolf-dog captured alive. Understood?" Those were the words of Chief Wakita, his appeal to a group of tired, impatient detectives.

Gale's figure, which blended into the gray, pre-dawn sky, was imprinted on Takako's memory. She longed to see him again. To get closer to him. That longing would only grow stronger with time. She didn't need to be reminded by her bosses; however long it might take, she told herself, she would find that wolf-dog and bring him in.

6

But that night and the next, Gale did not show up in Akishima. Neither were detectives able to find Ogawa.

Among the chemicals taken from Ogawa's house, however, analysis was able to identify benzoyl peroxide in a twenty-five percent paste and in dry powder. This made it definite: Ogawa was their prime suspect.

But where the hell is he?

Day by day, frustration had grown. Investigators were haunted by the suspicion that they were too late, that Gale had already found him and done his worst. But smart though he might be, Gale was nothing but a wolf-dog. There was certainly no way that he could hide the body of someone he had mauled.

Takako continued to blame herself. She was furious. How could she have lost him? When Gale was in the garden of that old lady, they should have surrounded the place with more care, so that even if he did make a run for it, as long as they knew the direction he'd gone, they could be on his path. But they underestimated him. They might be professional man-hunters, but as dog-hunters they were rank amateurs.

For one thing, no one anticipated that the dog had such superb leaping ability, making fools of them by virtue of his uncommon lightness and supple grace. Of course, based on all he had done, they knew that the animal was anything but common, but the reality had far surpassed their imagination. Even for Takako, it was true. Gale had been far more beautiful, more wonderful, than she had envisioned. For one second, she had forgotten her assignment, had wanted nothing more than to gaze on at him, rapt. Perhaps that was the strange power of wolf-dogs. Like magic, they mesmerized people, locking their gazes and immobilizing them. Anyway, once they found either Gale or Ogawa, the other could not be far away. With something like a prayer that this was true, the search split in two, half the force looking for Gale, the other half looking for Ogawa.

"Kasahara insists that Gale will come back," reported Takizawa. "He says Gale will use that house as home base, and will stop by once every few days to see if Kasahara is there."

There was nothing to do but take Kasahara at his word. And to sit and watch and wait. An endurance contest between the wolf-dog and the police was underway.

This was the fifth night since they had begun staking out the house, a Monday. Today Takizawa was riding shotgun. Squirming uncomfortably in the cramped car, he declared peevishly, "The thing about a stakeout, it's murder on your back."

"You can say that again," said Imazeki, in the driver's seat. "When I was in my thirties, I slipped a disk, and my back's bothered me ever since."

"A slipped disk, ugh. Happened to me, too."

As far as Takako could tell, when these new partners were together they talked about nothing but their health problems, didn't matter who spoke first. Listening, Takako learned for the first time that the man she once beat the pavement with suffered from corns and athlete's foot, that five years ago he had a stomach ulcer, and that any time now he expected the symptoms of hay fever to set in.

"Maybe you should try wearing a corset for that back," suggested Imazeki.

"Not with a paunch like this. Too painful."

God, what a depressing conversation. But on a stakeout, when they had to keep their eyes peeled, there wasn't much else to do. To keep from getting bored, to keep awake, it was better to talk about anything than to sit silent. In any case, she could be grateful that for a stakeout lasting days on end like this, she didn't have to be alone with Takizawa. What blessed relief. Here was a whole new reason to be glad she was a lizard.

On the other hand, if the two of them had had to do this on their own, that might have been fun in its own way. As long as he didn't make uncalled-for remarks.

It was now after 2:00 A.M. The darkness was deepening, the temperature dropping. Takako sighed quietly and looked vacantly out the window of their unmarked police car. On the side of the car was her red motorcycle, completely tuned, languishing alone again. She found the CB400 Super Four a comfortable machine—easy to handle, quick in response. It was of classic racing style with a smooth engine, and its power, the sense of control she had while riding it, was huge. It lacked a strong personality and was often used as a training vehicle for novice riders, but it was good for both short hops and long-distance rides.

Rather than sit here listening to these men talk about their backaches and neuralgia, she wished she was out riding it. But until Gale appeared, she was trapped. Perhaps he wouldn't show tonight either. The cold wouldn't likely bother him, but what was he doing for food? Just as these thoughts were going through her mind, suddenly a voice came over the radio.

"West Tachikawa 47 calling MP 22."

MP 22. The call sign for the microbus that the command officer was in.

"West Tachikawa 47, come in."

"We have spotted a large dog. The location is the confluence of the Tama River and the Aki River. The dog is walking downstream in the river bed. Over."

Automatically, she picked up her helmet. Sensing the accelerated beating of her heart, she held her breath and listened.

"This is MP 22. We read you. Can you make out any characteristics of the dog? Over."

"It's dark, so it's hard to see, but it's a fairly big animal with a pointed muzzle and long legs. It has a smooth gait. It's moving at a pretty fast clip. Over."

It was Gale. Takako zipped up the blouson she was wearing over her leather suit, and put her gloves on. Takizawa turned to look at her. "You going?"

"I'll listen to the rest of the dispatch through the radio on the bike. I want to warm up the engine."

Takizawa signaled approval with his eyes, as Imazeki secured his seat belt. Takako quickly got out of the car, put on her helmet, and strode over to her bike. Her warm breath steamed up the shield in an instant. The bike had been sitting here since early evening, and the engine would be cold. Swiftly she inserted the key, pulled out the choke and pushed the ignition button. Having checked that the engine fired up with a slightly higher sound than usual, Takako switched on the wireless radio on the bike.

"MP 39 calling MP 22."

"MP 39, go ahead."

"Got him with the infrared camera. He's walking down the riverbed. His body measures about five feet three inches. The tail is long and straight, and the ears are huge. He's in front of Ryugahara Athletic Ground. Over."

"You mean the south side of the riverbed? Over."

"Yes. He's walking on the Hachioji side."

"Copy that, over and out. MP 22 to all units. We have located the wolfdog. Stand by."

The bus carrying Captain Watanuki was stationed closest to the Kasahara house.

"MI 17 to MP 22."

"MP 22 here, what is it?"

"Subject has just passed Haijima Suidobashi. He has stopped. He's looking around. Now he's going across. He's crossing the river, heading your way."

"West Tachikawa 3 to MP 22. We have a visual on the animal. Looks like Gale all right. Over."

"MP 22, copy that. Don't lose sight of him whatever you do. Don't let him on to you!"

Her heart beating fast, Takako climbed on the 400 Four and pushed the choke back in. With the engine idling smoothly, she refastened the strap on her helmet. Then she brought the tiny microphone attached to her helmet close to her mouth.

"MP 22 calling MP 447."

Takako's heart leaped. MP 447. That was the call sign for the wireless on her bike.

"This is MP 447, go ahead."

"Are you ready?"

Pressing the transmission button on her handle grip, Takako answered, "MP 447. Ready. Over." Her voice was shaking a bit, but that was due to the cold. Next the command vehicle's radio called Takizawa's vehicle and confirmed that they were ready to follow Takako.

"West Tachikawa 10, copy that."

Takizawa's voice came through the small speaker embedded in her helmet. For a change, he spoke crisply.

"MI 16 to MP 22. Animal is crossing the riverbed and heading for the end of the boardwalk."

"MP 86 to MP 22. The hunting association is not going to be ready in time. If he leaves the riverbed now, we'll lose this chance."

"MP 22 calling MP 86. Nothing we can do about it. Stay on him. Let him go where he wants, as far as feasible. Don't forget, he may know where Ogawa is. Over and out."

He was coming. Finally, Gale was on his way here. This time she wouldn't let him get away. Takako smoothed on her gloves once more and listened intently to the barrage of messages. Somewhere inside, she didn't want Gale to come. Part of her wanted to tell him, Now's your chance, run! But when she thought of everything that led to this moment, the people who were killed—even if they were slime—she knew it was sheer sentimentality. I've paid my own price for this, she thought. My skin is chapped, I'm chilled to the bone, I can't ever go home, I can't even visit my sister in the hospital, I had to hear that garbage from my mother.

"MP 86 to MP 22. We have a visual, too. Animal is walking by the Haijima High School athletic field, heading to the middle school next door. He really is huge. Over."

Did Gale sense anything? Did the scent of Emiko's pajamas, placed in front of the ruined house as a lure, carry to him, wherever he was?

Come on out where I can see you. This time I'm running with you all the way.

She revved up the engine a little. The needle on the right meter quivered slightly. At 2:30 A.M., the area was dead quiet.

"MP 22 calling MP 447 and West Tachikawa 10. Proceed to the park entrance and stand by."

Right. She grasped the clutch lever and stepped on the gear pedal. The sensation of being in low gear went from the soles of her boots to the entire machine. She put on her turn signal, twisted the throttle a bit, and at the same time slowly opened her left hand little by little. With a low hum, the 400 Four began to slide out. Soon she saw the headlights of the car following in her rearview mirror.

"MP 447 to MP 22. I'm in position, over."

"MP 86 to MP 22. Animal is heading from the middle school to Okutama Kaido Avenue. Over."

"MP 22 to MP 447. He should come into sight any time now. Follow him, but keep your distance. Over!"

The wireless transmission was loud and clear. Still gripping the clutch, Takako held her breath. The beam of her headlight cut straight into the darkness. She thought of sports competitions she participated in as a child: the tension just before a race as starting time drew near; the sound of the pistol, the cheers, the music blaring from speakers. But in the moment of maximum tension just before the starting signal, her ears would hear nothing at all. This was exactly like that. She had never been this tense even at a competition among motorcycle policemen.

"MP 14 to MP 22. Animal has crossed the road. He's just in front of the Daishi bus stop."

"MP 8 to MP 22. Gale is in sight!"

It happened just after that: a creature leaped into the beam of her headlight. Swift and soundless, it appeared with sudden nimbleness. Takako gasped in admiration at the sight. Finally face to face, again.

I'm not letting you get away this time.

His eyes shone green. A big, black nose. The fur on the muzzle and around the eyes was white, surrounded by black. From the back of the ears and around the neck, a short silver mane framed the head. The stance—head slung below the shoulders, forelegs slightly apart—was not that of a dog, but of a wolf. His figure was perfectly still, seeming to absorb the flow of time. No murderous intent, no hostility. Only the eyes shone with fierce light.

This was the creature that killed three people. The dog that was on the hunt for Ogawa, remembering Kasahara and Emiko. Yet strangely, Takako felt no fear. Once again she felt an impulse to dismount and go up to him—but at that very moment, Gale, who had until then remained motionless, whirled and leaped. His motion was caught not in the beam from her motorcycle, but in the headlights of Takizawa's car behind her. Reflexively, she rotated the throttle.

"MP 447 to MP 22."

"MP 447, go ahead."

"I'm with Gale. I'm following him. Over."

By the time she finished speaking, Gale had rounded a curve fifty yards ahead. Takako shot forward, after him. When she made the turn, she could see Gale running, farther ahead than before. What incredible speed! He ran with a light, flowing motion, almost as if gliding on the surface of a cloud.

"West Tachikawa 10 to MP 447."

"MP 447, Otomichi here. What is it?"

"I don't know where Gale is going to turn off. I want you to report where you are. Over."

"Got it."

"We're right behind you. Don't worry."

With Takizawa's loud, hoarse voice sounding in her ear, Takako sped after Gale. In her rearview mirror she could see the lights of Takizawa's car. There was no siren, but she could see its flashing red light.

Gale, this is the opposite direction from your house. Is that OK? Didn't you catch the scent of Emiko, the woman you love?

But Gale ran on without a backward glance. His long tail streamed out behind him, waving slightly, drifting in the wind. His ears lay slightly back. His stride vastly larger than any dog's could be, his running fluid and smooth. Hitting Route 16, he headed south without hesitation. Takako wove between the scant cars, went through a red light, and turned right at a no-turn corner. Gale was running in the lane for oncoming traffic. Even if traffic was light, if he turned right again, it would be difficult for her to follow. She could hear Takizawa informing the command car of their position.

"MP 22 to MPD."

"MP 22, go ahead."

"Request restricted roads in the direction wolf-dog is proceeding. Over."

"Copy that, over and out. MPD to Traffic Control."

The tension of a few moments earlier, so intense that her heart had felt twinges of pain, was gone. In its place was a tremulous happiness welling up from the center of her being. Now she was pursuing Gale. The 400 Four responded directly to her touch on the throttle, carrying her along faithfully and obediently. I'll follow you anywhere, she told the wolf-dog. I'll never let you out of my sight. She clenched her knees, drew in her chin, and fixed her eyes on Gale as he continued to run. He was doing around thirty miles per hour. She could easily match him in speed and power.

"West Tachikawa 10 calling MP 22. Gale is running on the wrong side of the road. He's crossing Haijima Bridge."

The Tama River that Gale had splashed his way across before, he was now crossing on a straight bridge. Then, just as oncoming cars had tapered off, he crossed diagonally over to Takako's side of the road. It was like he was making her pursuit easier, or issuing a challenge. His stride was so easy that it seemed impossible he was running so fast.

"MP 447 calling West Tachikawa 10."

"MP 447, what is it?"

"Did you see that? He switched over to my lane."

"This is West Tachikawa 10. Roger. We see him."

A strong crosswind began to blow. The wind whistled, coming through the gaps around her helmet shield. She could almost hear the sound of Gale's footsteps. Soon they approached the bypass. Without a flicker, Gale went sailing by it. Scarcely looking at her rearview mirror, she left everything behind her to Takizawa and his partner, focusing only on Gale. If he should turn down an alleyway, it would mean trouble. If he turned too many corners, there was a good chance of losing him, even on her motorcycle. Just as she was thinking it might be a good idea to shorten the distance between them, the entrance to Chuo Expressway came into sight. Showing no hesitation, without slowing down in the least, the wolf-dog made a beeline for the slope of the Hachioji Interchange.

"West Tachikawa 10 to MPD. Please close entrances to Chuo Expressway. Animal may proceed to the Metropolitan Expressway. Please prepare to close all routes. Deploy units in the opposite lane as well!"

"MPD here, copy. MPD to Traffic Control. Request closure of all ramp exits east of the Hachioji Interchange on the Chuo Expressway."

"Traffic Control, copy that. Will have full compliance within eight minutes."

Although she herself was involved, she listened to the radio exchanges as if a fictional drama. There seemed a strange disconnect between the tense voices on the radio and the figure of Gale before her eyes. The wolf-dog bore himself with a kind of dignity. Ever since he first looked levelly into Takako's eyes, he never looked her way again, not even when crossing over to this side of the road; now he continued to run at a fixed speed along the expressway. Takako, who was in the cruising lane, now speeded up slightly, trimming the distance between her and Gale.

"West Tachikawa 10 to MP 447! Otomichi, do not approach too closely. Danger!"

The voice of Takizawa, who was more than eighty yards behind, made her eardrums ring. She answered, "Roger," but continued to gain steadily on Gale. She wanted to watch. To see him up close, this creature running his heart out. Under the pale, bluish highway lights, Gale's entire body was vibrant with life and energy; it was luminous. The fur from the midsection of his back to his tail was a dark gray, nearly black, and the closer it was to his belly, the more silver it seemed. With no regard for whoever might be pursuing him, the wolf-dog ran with his eyes fixed on an invisible point.

He's not running away.

Suddenly she sensed it: Gale was not fleeing from her. There was no terror in his heart. His running was brimming with confidence, free of all tentativeness. After a while, from below the trestle she heard the wail of a siren. So as not to lose Gale wherever he got off the expressway, a patrol car was following along on the arterial road below. But Gale seemed unperturbed. The speedometer on Takako's motorcycle registered 30 MPH.

"He passed the Kunitachi Fuchu Interchange. Still running at the same speed."

"Could be heading for the Metropolitan Expressway."

"This is MPD calling MP 22. All expressways in the metropolitan area have now been closed."

"This is MPD calling MP 22. The riot police are ready to move in."

In Takako's ears, exchanges between the different investigators flew by with the wind. But Takako herself could not say anything to either the command car or to Takizawa's car, following close behind. How could she ever tell them: "This is lovely; I'm having a marvelous time"?

Inside her helmet, she called to Gale in a loud voice: "Go wherever you want!" And then she laughed aloud. Riding alone, she often talked to herself; comfortable in the knowledge that no one could hear her, she would call people names, sing songs, carry on monologues. Never had she found riding with someone this much fun. As long as the road went on, she wanted to keep running with Gale. To chase this shining, silvery creature.

7

Closed to all ordinary traffic, the Metropolitan Expressway in the middle of night was an uncanny space, seemingly part of a near-future world. With his left hand clutching the grip on the car door, Takizawa held the wireless transmitter in his right hand, eyes straight ahead. He could see a small gray ball. And like a laser mark, the red taillight of Otomichi's motorcycle gleamed just behind it in the dark.

"West Tachikawa 10 to MP 22."

"West Tachikawa 10, come in."

"They passed the Shibaura Interchange. They're on the Haneda Route, heading toward the airport. Over."

"Roger."

"MP 22 to MP 447, do you read me?"

"MP 22, loud and clear."

"Everything OK?"

"Everything's OK. Gale is not slowing down. It's like he decided where he was going right from the start. Over."

The voice coming over the radio sounded so cheerful and energetic, it was not easy for Takizawa to connect it to the cold-looking figure on the motorcycle ahead. It sounded like riding made her happier than anything, like chasing the wolf-dog was fun, for god's sake. Usually when she was with him her expression was stiff and brooding. This voice was worlds away from that sullen young lady.

"She's really going." His hands on the wheel, Imazeki muttered, "Amazing."

Takizawa shot a sideways glance at this new partner of his, who was so devoid of idiosyncrasy that no matter what you said brought no satisfying response, who seemed as clean and flavorless as water. He grunted a noncommittal reply.

"I mean, here she is in the fore of the entire investigation, leading the way. She was a patrol officer so I guess it's only natural, but she rides as solid as a rock."

This was true. A young woman in the lead, grown men following after her with their sirens going full blast; when you thought about it, it was a pretty funny spectacle.

Takizawa continued to file reports: "They've passing Haneda. We're now on the Yokohane Route, heading toward Hamagawasaki. . . . They're past Hamagawasaki. Heading toward Shioiri."

The wolf-dog had gone from the Chuo Expressway to the Shinjuku Route on the Metropolitan Expressway, then taken the Inner Loop and bypassed the city center. Past Haneda Airport, heading for Yokohama. Otomichi was right: he was running with a specific destination in mind, running without hesitation or wasted effort. He tore along the complicated, intertwining web of metropolitan expressways, with its tunnels and radial routes, as if he owned it.

"What a fantastic animal," Takizawa said.

"You can say that again," said Imazeki. "He lives up to his reputation, all right."

Nodding silently, Takizawa kept his eyes on Otomichi's back, her blouson blowing in the wind like a sail. For some reason, he was falling prey to a peculiar illusion. It seemed to him as if Otomichi and the wolf-dog were running in synch, their minds attuned to one another as if there was a special connection between them. It even seemed as if the wolf-dog and the motorcyclist, running neck and neck down an expressway from which all other traffic was barred, were in their own private world. They weren't hunter and hunted, they were two creatures with a shared destination, enjoying themselves. But surely they weren't fellow travelers?

As these thoughts flitted through his mind, Otomichi's voice came over the radio:

"MP 447 to West Tachikawa 10."

"Come in, MP 447."

"We're at Namamugi. He turned! He's heading toward Daikoku Pier."

No sooner did the words register than he saw Otomichi's motorcycle, small in the distance, flash its turn signal. Imazeki speeded up to keep her in sight. Takizawa reported his position and the position of the wolf-dog to the commander. Where would the wolf-dog leave the expressway and take to the streets below?

"He's not going to do something crazy like take a flying leap off the Bay Bridge, is he?"

"No."

As they considered this possibility, Gale turned in the opposite direction from Yokohama's famous Bay Bridge, and started down the Bayshore Route in the direction of Kawasaki. What a route—a complete tour of the local expressways. Come to think of it, Gale's first attack had been at Tennozu, which they just passed. Maybe Kasahara had brought him to this area before. Maybe Gale remembered every road he had ever traveled. Then maybe he was running the exact route that he had gone over with Kasahara before. This was a dog capable of attacking the next targeted victim without a direct order from Kasahara. A dog who—wherever he had been hiding—returned to the site of his home, exactly as Kasahara had predicted he would.

"This is a new road, huh," Imazeki said, half to himself. The beautifully paved and well-outfitted road stretched out straight before them, gently dipping down before rising back up. After a while, it entered a long tunnel. Without glancing at the map, Imazeki said, "Must be under the sea." Takizawa felt an unpleasant, suffocating sensation, but he kept his eyes focused straight ahead. There in the distance was Otomichi's back, and still farther ahead he could make out the figure of the ceaselessly running wolf-dog, lit up by the orange lights of the tunnel.

"It's the Bayshore Route, the Bayshore Route!"

"It's possible they could swing back to the city center!"

Over the radio, people were excitedly calling back and forth. Yet Takizawa and Imazeki, as well as the two shadows in front of them, were wrapped in a silence far removed from those exchanges.

Surely a creature like Gale could ask for nothing more than to run like this, for all he was worth. After undergoing harsh training to attack and kill, the rest of the time he'd lain low, living in hiding; he must never have had a chance to run so freely before. So go ahead, run your heart out, he told the wolf-dog. And when you're tired, rest. We won't kill you right away.

This newly completed road circled Tokyo Bay, connecting the Yokohama area with Chiba. The scenery before them was so different from the part of Tokyo that was Takizawa's usual beat, it might have been a different city altogether. If this was Tokyo, what would you call that place where he and Otomichi used to stomp around?

"MP 22 calling West Tachikawa 10, tell us your position. Over."

"MP 22, come in. We just crossed Ramp 13. Maintaining the same speed. Headed toward Ariake. Over."

"OK. Everything all right with Otomichi?"

"Yes. She's going at the same speed as the dog, sticking right behind him."

After one interchange there would be several exits, then the next interchange. She must be nervous as hell whenever they came to one of these, wondering if Gale was going to change his course; and yet, from his vantage point anyway, neither Gale nor Otomichi showed the slightest sign of nervousness or hesitation. The pair passed Ariake and Kasai, coming at last to Urayasu. On the right was Tokyo Disneyland. Over the radio, the command car and MPD headquarters were discussing whether or not to bring in the Chiba police. There was no reason yet to ask for cooperation. The question was, would this end up a mere transit point, or a new stage?

"Passing Chidoricho Ramp and the Ichikawa Interchange."

* * *

It was now 4:00 A.M. The coldest time of night. This pursuit without hurdles, carried out at a steady speed, began to fill Takizawa with a peculiar tedium and a disagreeable impatience. That was no ordinary dog. Maybe it was planning something; maybe it intended to keep running straight until the cars ran out of gas. For the first time, his mind began to fill with thoughts like these.

"This is West Tachikawa 10 calling MP 447."

"This is MP 447. Go ahead."

"Are you cold?"

"Yes, I am. But now that we're on the Bayshore Route, it's a little better. Over."

Otomichi's voice sounded cheerful and excited. She's actually enjoying this, thought Takizawa in amazement. It wasn't the rush of cornering a criminal that excited her, it was the pleasure of running side by side with the wolf-dog. I'll be damned, he thought. A new thought struck him: She's not urging the wolf-dog on? The name of the expressway had changed from the Metropolitan Expressway to the East Kanto Expressway.

"What is the animal's condition? Over."

"Unbelievable. His speed never wavers, and he doesn't seem tired in the least. It's like he just started running. Looks to me like he could go all the way to the end of the line. Over."

The other cars could hear their conversation. The officers following behind Takizawa and Imazeki, and on the streets below, had to be wondering where in hell this would end up.

"We're at the Narashino toll booths."

"OK."

Takizawa heaved a big sigh, and realized that he felt a slight pressure on his bladder. Not that, please. His kidneys and his liver were weakening, he'd been told. What if this went on all night? They couldn't shut down the whole highway system forever. And they couldn't call the whole thing off just because the sun came up.

The sign for the Wangan Narashino Interchange came into sight. If they kept on like this, they'd come to Miyanogi Junction, where the expressway intersected with the Keiyo Road, going on as far as Itako.

"Let's hope they don't go into a golf course," mumbled Imazeki.

"You're right, that area's full of 'em."

"If he takes the Keiyo Road, it could be a possibility."

Damn it, this was no joke. If Gale ran into a place like that, full of hills and trees, it would be too much to take. They meant to surround him, but there was only so much they could do. Just then Imazeki cried out sharply: "Ah!"

And at the same time, Otomichi's voice came over the radio: "Gale is getting off! At the Wangan Narashino Interchange. Over."

"MP 22 to West Tachikawa 410. Keep Otomichi and the animal in your sights."

"OK!"

His mood was instantly taut. Takizawa sat up straight and leaned forward. No sign of Otomichi. She'd already gotten off the expressway.

"We're off the expressway, going straight ahead on the street below. Passing under the viaduct now."

"Roger! Watch that curve."

Their car had finally left the expressway, too, at the Wangan Narashino Interchange. Over the radio, the supervisor was telling headquarters to notify the Chiba prefectural police.

"We're at the second traffic light—he went straight ahead. I can see the entrance to the Wangan Chiba Interchange."

"Don't tell me he's going back on the expressway," muttered Takizawa.

As he said that, Otomichi's voice came in: "Gale turned. Turned right at the third traffic light."

Takizawa leaned forward, peering out through the front windshield. He had lost sight of her red taillight.

"There's a building on the right, looks like a school. The road curves left in front of it. There's a school on the left."

Otomichi's reports were growing more detailed. Imazeki was frowning as he kept his foot on the accelerator. Takizawa held on tightly to the grip over the door, preparing for a sharp turn, and for the first time felt like praying: Don't let me lose sight of her. Soon the tiny red light of her taillight came into view. "That's her," he said, and at the same moment the light disappeared from his line of sight.

"We're going under what looks like an overhead railway, curving along with the road."

"OK!"

Hastily he glanced down at the road map spread out in his lap. It had to be the Keiyo Line. Gale was headed for the sea.

"There's a thicket on the left, a park, I think. Ah—"

"What happened?"

"Gale went into the thicket. I'm going in after him."

"Is it safe? Hey!" He yelled so loudly into the transmitter that spittle flew from his mouth. Going into the park? Riding through trees? "Otomichi!"

No answer. Imazeki, who had been driving parallel to the expressway, now swung sharply to the left. Sure enough, something like a park spread before them. But nowhere in its dark expanse was the shining red taillight of her bike visible. Ahead of them was only the vast, deserted road, shooting forward like the boom of a cannon.

As Imazeki started to slow down, Takizawa bellowed, "Keep going! Don't leave Otomichi on her own! If she gets attacked while we're slowed down, that'll be the end!"

His blood was boiling. His palms now sweaty, Takizawa concentrated every ounce of his being on staring on into the darkness.

8

Gale bounded lightly over the park shrubbery. Takako, from force of habit, had lowered her speed after they left the elevated expressway and now, back on the ground, she felt Gale's energy anew; seeing him fly through the air above the shrubbery, she couldn't hold back the thrill, the wonder. But beneath her, her tires were spinning. There was no way she could run the way Gale did, oblivious to expressway or a road, on grass or over dirt. So she roared after him like one possessed. If she so much as glanced away, he disappeared—but the next moment he would reappear, running through the trees, entirely in his element, where he belonged, in a forest.

"Otomichi, where are you?"

In her helmet, Takizawa's voice sounded. But she could not afford to reply. Not now. No matter how good her motorcycle skills were, this sort of delicate handling required full attention. For now, she needed to focus on getting through the park, racing through the woods ahead. And that was when her tires slipped in the mud.

Oh no!

The thought came too late. She lost her balance, and her left foot touched the soft ground. She thought she might be able to pull out of it, but this motorcycle, not made for off-road adventures, was too heavy: in a split second, her CB400 overturned. Instantly, with a kick at the motorcycle, she rounded her body protectively. She was not pinned beneath the machine, but thrown off. Her back slammed against the base of a tree, and she rolled over. For a second her breath stopped, her mind went blank. Above her was a sky full of stars, waiting for the dawn.

Beautiful.

She wanted to close her eyes and go on lying there. She felt tired, overcome by a sudden fit of drowsiness. But the next moment, she came to herself: *Get up! What in god's name are you doing?*

Tentatively, she took a deep breath. Good, she could breathe. She'd landed on soft dirt; she wasn't injured. Realizing this, Takako hurriedly got up and righted her overturned bike. The darkness of night was profound. In the air was the smell of winter decay, and the barest hint of spring. She mustn't get anxious now, she knew, and yet she could have wept with frustration.

After coming so far!

She pushed her bike along until she came out of the muddy patch before sitting astride it again. Then, her hands shaking with fatigue and tension, she switched the engine back on.

"Otomichi, come in!"

Mud and dry grass were all over her shield, obscuring her view. If she tried to rub them off, that would only make it harder to see. There was nothing to do but ride with the shield raised. She turned on her headlight.

"Otomichi, what's happening?! Have you lost him?"

"No, I haven't lost him. He's still here in the park." She said this into the microphone, staring suddenly straight ahead in disbelief. Gale was standing in the cone of light from her headlight, looking directly at her. He was not thirty feet away, his green eyes shining just as they had several hours ago.

Why?

His breath streamed white. Faint steam seemed to rise from his body. Why didn't he run? Or was he—? No. While Gale was breathing hard, the expression on his face seemed peaceful. He showed not the slightest sign of intent to attack. Rather, he seemed to be viewing her with sympathetic interest, as if asking: Are you quitting?

Is this a test?

His gaze held her transfixed. In his eyes she read immense pride, stern intolerance of lies and betrayal, isolation. The look in his eyes was peaceful, remote.

"Gale."

She whispered his name, and the large, erect ears pricked slightly. With a doubtful look, he tilted his head the tiniest bit. Takako held her breath, continuing to gaze into his eyes. As long as he didn't move, she couldn't either.

Yet it was clear: Gale had been waiting for her. After she'd run with him from his house in Akishima across the expressway and all the way here to Maku-hari, he had, for whatever reason, waited for her.

He wants something.

Sudden pain filled her heart. To be called by name, to be accepted for himself, to know peace of mind. Kasahara, whom he had trusted from the bottom of his heart, and Emiko, who had remained a little girl even in adult-hood: no doubt he was continually seeking, continually waiting for them. Takako could feel it. Why was he left alone? Why did Kasahara never come for him? Why must he be hunted down? Who are you? With his single-minded gaze, Gale poured out these questions to her.

"Otomichi, do you read me?"

Takizawa's voice again. But Takako could not reply. Gale's eyes had her trapped. I am alone, they said. If you want to come up face-to-face with me, then you cannot turn to anyone for help. I do not want to fight, nor do I ask for single combat. I want answers to my questions. Why was I betrayed? Why was I abandoned? Why—

"Officer Otomichi, come in. Where are you? Are you all right?"

Now it was the captain's voice. Still Takako remained silent, face-to-face with Gale. She had no explanations to offer. She could not offer him safe harbor. It was not her that Gale had chosen anyway, she knew. But no lie, no deception could get past those eyes.

"Otomichi! Do you read me?!"

Resignedly, she pushed the transmit button on her radio. "I'm all right. I'm—"

At that moment, Gale turned, and the next thing she knew, he had taken off again, darting swiftly among the trees. Takako hurriedly squeezed the clutch lever. Good, the bike seemed unharmed, too.

"What happened just now? Officer Otomichi, come in!"

"I'm giving chase. He stopped for a moment, but now he's started running again. Ahead I see high-rises."

As she made her report, she felt a strange guilt. For a second, Gale had given her a chance. He had tested her to find out if she was someone he could trust. That was all she could think. But Takako had not been able to respond. Gale, I *have* to pursue you. I *have* to catch you.

The park came to an end. She was on the alert, thinking Gale might swing back this way in a U-turn, but he tore through the park shrubbery and emerged on pavement.

"We're on the street. On both sides of the street there are tall buildings, and straight ahead is a pedestrian overpass."

Under the streetlights Gale ran on, with never a backward glance. She hadn't noticed it before, but now she felt throbbing pain from shoulder to hip, and in her elbows and knees.

"He's turned left at the pedestrian overpass. On the left I can see . . . the New Otani Hotel. On the right is Makuhari Messe."

Further on was the sea. Where was Gale headed? As Takako sped along with the shield on her helmet raised, the wind on her face slowly grew moist. From all sides came the sound of patrol sirens, like waves. This artificial town known as Marine New City Center was as devoid of human life as a miniature architectural model.

"On the right I can see Chiba Marine Stadium. Gale is running straight ahead."

"If he keeps on, he'll hit the ocean."

"I can't see the ocean from here. But there's a dark patch of woods."

Another pedestrian overpass came into view. Gale tore along with no letup in speed. Takako could now feel gritty sand beneath her wheels. No! she thought. If I have to make a sharp turn here, I'll spill again. But Gale kept straight on. Without swerving, he entered a small unpaved road. Just as Takako was thinking that this surface was no easier to ride on, before her eyes Gale sprang. With inconceivable lightness and power, he seemed to hang motionless in the air. The next instant, Takako saw the barbed wire. This land, being prepared for development, had been fenced off. She jammed on the brakes and just managed to pull up safely, her rear tire skidding.

"Gale! Wait!"

Ahead was a pine woods. Gale vanished into its black depths.

"This is MP 447 calling MP 22, come in."

"This is MP 22. What's going on?!"

"He went into the woods next to Marine Stadium. It's fenced off. I can't follow."

"Roger. Good work! We'll take it from here."

She said nothing. Her face was frozen. Vacantly, she sat astride her motorcycle, staring into the darkness. Now the scream of sirens came closer, surrounding her. The air echoed with slamming car doors, shouts, footsteps.

First to come up to her was Takizawa. "Hey, you had me worried back there in the park."

While internally reproaching herself, for the life of her she could not frame a coherent reply.

"What happened to you? All that mud!"

She looked up, half dazed, and saw Takizawa, the captain, and other investigators standing there before her. With an effort, she reached to shut off the engine, lowered the kickstand, got off the bike. It was too soon to let the tension drain away.

"I ran into a patch of mud in the park." Good, her voice was steady.

"You mean you fell?"

"Yes."

"Lucky thing you didn't lose sight of him."

"Gale . . . waited for me. He waited till I picked up my bike and got back on."

Their faces registered skepticism. Takizawa alone nodded. I must look horrible, she thought. My lip is split and my face is a wreck, I'm covered with mud, I'm exhausted. Yet unaccountably, Takizawa's eyes looked on her softly, calmly.

"Doesn't surprise me," he said, and gave Takako's shoulder a light pat. She immediately cried out in pain, scrunching her face.

"What, you're hurt?" Sharp concern on his face.

"I'm fine," she said. "I just got bumped around a little." With that, she paced nervously off. What was the next step?

Watanuki's orders, however, were: "You can rest now. We've got him surrounded."

"Yes, but maybe Gale knows where Ogawa—"

"Don't worry, we're checking all parked cars and all hotel guest registers."

There was nothing she could say. Finally Inspector Miyagawa arrived, increasing the tension; the streets of what had been a ghost town now overflowed with uniformed police officers. Takako felt ashamed to be among them in her mud-spattered leather suit. With no other choice, she started to limp off out of the way, dragging one leg. The wind was strong. Clouds blew in from the sea, one after another.

"If you want to, go rest in the car."

She heard the captain's voice behind her and, turning slowly, motioned, no thanks. He nodded and turned quickly away. She felt a peculiar alienation. It was she who had led everyone else here. Were they showing such consideration for her because she was a woman? Was it perverse of her to think so?

I loved every minute of it.

Gale's figure was burned into her consciousness. She would never forget his face as he stood in the park emitting white clouds of breath, staring at her. If only she could look into his eyes forever. Not as his pursuer, but face to face, one on one. She climbed the stairs to the pedestrian overpass that hung over the broad T-shaped intersection. When she got to the top, she looked down in surprise.

What a peculiar sight met her eyes. Beyond the woods where Gale had taken refuge was a string of lights from the industrial district surrounding Tokyo Bay. Boso on the left and Keihin on the right, and lights of factories that never ceased operating, day or night. Turning around the other way, lining the wide avenues that symbolized this artificial landscape she could see a completely inorganic collection of tall hotels and skyscrapers, rising up to the amazingly wide sky. Nowhere a breath of nature. A world where everything was immaculate and supervised.

He would never come here by choice. Who would?

Leaning against the round railing of the overpass, Takako watched the figures beneath her rush busily to and fro. She yearned for a cup of hot coffee. She wanted to warm her frozen body. Yet she couldn't budge. Hunters with their hunting dogs were on the move. All around were the red lights of patrol cars.

"Hey, go rest in the car already." It was Takizawa, rushing up the overpass stairs. His scant hair, blown about in the strong wind, looked dreadful. She stood idly, letting the wind blow against her. "You've got to ride that motorcycle back, too, you know," he said.

"I want to watch," said Takako.

Takizawa moved his mouth slightly as if he wanted to say something, but chose not to. Then he stood beside Takako and looked around.

"Almost morning."

"Yes."

"They found Ogawa's car."

Takako quickly looked up.

Takizawa nodded slowly, adding, "Just a bit ago."

Until then Takako had been chilled to the core, but now something hot stirred within her.

"That's some dog," Takizawa said. "He knew where Ogawa was the whole time."

She was silent.

"They're going over this place with a fine-tooth comb. To keep Gale from killing again."

"What can I do?"

"The captain said rest, so go on and take a load off. Take a look—there's plenty of manpower."

Even her sigh was swept away with the cold sea breeze.

Takizawa was shaking a cigarette out of a pack. "I have to say . . . ," he started to speak, turning his back to the wind and managing somehow to light his cigarette, "you looked like you were having a ball." He squinted his eyes and blew out a mouthful of smoke.

Takako nodded but didn't say anything.

"Watching you . . . ," Takizawa paused, taking another drag on his cigarette, "I could tell."

She tried to explain. "Funny to say, but I felt as if Gale . . . appreciated me."

"Too bad you didn't meet under different circumstances," said Takizawa, and then left. Same old emperor penguin, striding away. Feeling a sudden choking sensation, Takako followed his retreating figure with her eyes. Her shoulder and lower back hurt like hell. It was cold enough to need to stamp the ground to stay warm, and yet she did not move.

If only . . . under different circumstances.

The sky was growing light. While she was riding, the sky had been clear, but now thick clouds hung low overhead. She turned around and saw a drifting cloud beginning to be reflected on the mirror-like façade of an all-glass high-rise hotel. The hotel gave off a dull light as it rose up, piercing the gray sky. Gradually the cityscape began to emerge in outline, spacious and irritatingly vapid. An eerie oppressiveness in a thoroughly calculated, thoroughly supervised environment. In this place less suited to Gale than anyone she could imagine, dawn came.

"It's morning, Gale," she whispered.

The woods that had been a part of the night now came into outline as well. From the top of the pedestrian overpass she could make out the zigzag silhouettes of still-young pine trees reaching up to the gray sky. The hunters must have been waiting for morning light.

Never again would the two run together. Never again would she look into those eyes.

No human being has eyes that expressive.

Slowly, steadily, the day broke. The lights of the industrial district now blurred. Her body felt clammy. Were the waves real at an artificial beach? At the very least, this stagnant sea water wasn't fake, probably. Involuntarily, in the bitter cold, she found herself stamping the ground when there came something like the sound of the wind. The wind? A flute? Takako held still and listened carefully. A high, resonating sound. It stretched out mournfully, riding on the wind.

The howl of a dog.

It could only be Gale. The howl stopped the officers roaming the area in their tracks; they stood still, listening, remarking on it to one another. Takako felt her heart grow cold. Why would Gale do such a thing—tell them where he was, give away his hiding place? Or was he deliberately trying to communicate? To say, here I am. But however he called to them, neither Kasahara nor Emiko could ever come. Gale surely knew that. Then whom was he calling to? Was there anyone else he knew? Suddenly the vision of Gale, gazing at her amid the surrounding darkness, came back to Takako. Gale had waited for her, spattered with mud as she was; without fear, without attacking, he had stood his ground quietly, looking straight at her.

No way.

Such a thing wasn't possible. But she agonized as she listened to the long, drawn-out, mournful cry. If she called to him, would he come obediently to her? Could he be captured without a shot fired, even if from a tranquilizer gun? She made up her mind: she would head in the direction of the officers and call Gale herself. That was when, over in a corner of the grove, she saw fire break out.

Takako leaned over the railing and yelled: "Fire! Over there!"

The officers, who had been listening to Gale's howls, immediately looked up at her. In the next moment, shouts rang out, along with the frantic baying of hunting dogs. Takako watched, frozen in the direction of the flames. People started running. Only Takako, without a radio, cut off from everyone, had no idea what happened. Clouds of black smoke billowed into the bright morning sky.

The howling grew more intense. Immobilized, Takako stared in the direction of the fire. It was not a big fire. At first she had thought it had great momentum, but now the clouds of smoke were clearly bigger than the flames. Benzoyl peroxide maybe? Ogawa's doing? And then she heard it: the dry, small pop of a rifle. Her hands flew to her mouth. She knew what it was. Yet, instinctively, she knew that if she did not cover her mouth, something might slip out that was unprofessional and unbecoming to a police officer:

Perhaps the scream of "No!" Or perhaps an unintelligible, strangled cry.

Otomichi's figure riding in front of Takizawa and Imazeki, under the low-hanging bank of gray clouds, looked exceedingly small and cold. Mixed in with the neat line of police cars no longer on the chase, her motorcycle sped through the chilly air, its license plate spattered with mud.

Imazeki, his hands on the steering wheel, murmured again in admiration: "Even a man would get worn out, riding around that much in the middle of the night. And in this bitter cold, too." He may or may not have been aware of Takizawa's sidelong glance, but he went on, "Bravo. She's got real guts. I can see why you look out for her so much, Taki."

"Look out for her? Me?" Takizawa shifted his position, letting his paunch expand. Watch it, buddy, he thought. That's not even funny. But this upright colleague of his seemed convinced that Takizawa and Otomichi had been on the best of terms from day one of their partnership, or even before.

"I can tell just by watching. She does so much, and yet just because she's a woman, she gets a lot of grief. You see that going on, Taki, and that's why you protect her. That's why everybody says you're a sweet guy."

There was nothing Takizawa could say in reply. The woman had really earned herself some Brownie points. She'd walked off with all the credit, and now people were congratulating him just for being her partner.

Well, what of it. Let it go.

A sweet guy? Him? Well, he'd been called worse things. Actually, it wasn't so bad, not as much as he would've thought. His eyes on the figure of Otomichi on the road ahead, Takizawa let out a small breath. The woman was in a state of near-total exhaustion. She was injured, her complexion, fair to begin with, drained of color, and yet she gritted her teeth and stood and watched as the tranquilized wolf-dog was carried out to a van. Seeing how close she was to tottering, even he had sympathy.

"Still, there's not the feeling of accomplishment we were looking for, is there?" said Imazeki. "I mean, basically, it was the wolf-dog who took Ogawa down."

"Better than having the case drag on and on. At least now it's wrapped up."

"True enough. All that's left now is to write up the report." Imazeki let go of the steering wheel momentarily and cracked his knuckles.

Takizawa felt put off: The guy was actually eager to get going on this most annoying part of the job.

That afternoon it snowed again. Takizawa trudged through the snow to visit Kasahara in the hospital. Kasahara was slowly, steadily gaining strength; although still unable to speak, on hearing that Gale had been safely apprehended, he let out a deep sigh of relief.

"Looks like Gale was on Ogawa's trail the whole time. Once you get your voice back, you've got to sit down and fill us in on how that dog was able to target Ogawa and find him. The animal sure isn't going to tell us anything."

Two days earlier, Takizawa had broken the news of Emiko's death to Kasahara. After being told she was in critical condition and then hearing no updates, not even the name of the hospital she was in, this former policeman had prepared himself for the worst. Lying in bed scarcely able to move, he wept silent tears. Takizawa in turn gazed wordlessly at Kasahara's sunburned face, somehow so familiar that it seemed they must have known each other, and watched the crow's feet around his eyes grow moist with tears. Takizawa, himself a father of daughters, understood.

"It was a near thing. An instant later and Gale would've been at Ogawa's throat. What a fine specimen! Man, when you see him up close like that, he's a huge son of a gun."

Kasahara nodded slowly at Takizawa's words, and reached for the memo pad beside his pillow. In the days since they last talked, Kasahara had regained some use of his hands, and conversation flowed more smoothly with a pen than with the *hiragana* board.

"What about the policewoman?" Kasahara wrote.

Looking at the scribble, Takizawa exchanged glances with Imazeki. He didn't know what she was doing on this snowy afternoon, freed from her solo assignment. Had she gone to the doctor for her injuries, or gone to headquarters to file her own report, or gone home?

"She . . . ah . . . she was the one who chased after Gale on her motorcycle. Ran with him all the way from your house to Makuhari."

Kasahara's face registered surprise.

Takizawa nodded and said, "Quite a feat, all right. Along the way she took a spill; she actually says that Gale stopped and waited for her. She was all right, but she got herself covered in mud."

After a bit, Kasahara picked up the pen and wrote: "Gale must have a sense about her. He knows when there is no fear. His instincts are sure, he knows trust. Not like with family. But he recognizes trust."

Takizawa couldn't disagree, and he nodded slowly. With his own eyes, he had seen Otomichi and Gale race together through the night like they owned it. It was hard to understand, but the two of them had looked happy together. In his own way, Takizawa could sense the bond between them.

"It's great you've recovered so much movement with your hands," Takizawa said. "As Gale's master, maybe you could help us out a little. For one thing, how the hell did Gale know where Ogawa was?"

On that note, he left the hospital. With the suspect under arrest, the only work left was the unexciting business of taking down his story and gathering corroborating evidence. But it was by no means as easy as it seemed, preparing the documents to build a case, one that lawyers for the defense could not overturn in court. There were a million matters to ask the two perps about: Gale, Emiko, the connections between the people Gale killed, Ogawa's background and motives, the method of acquiring benzoyl peroxide, construction of the timed ignition device, the relation between Kasahara and Ogawa, . . . At the same time, they had to interrogate others in order to verify the facts of the crimes. Get more eyewitness testimony.

"Think we'll get any more snow this year?"

"Has there ever been a year when it snowed after the cherry blossoms came out? God help us."

The heavy, moist snow dissolved as soon as it struck the windshield. Takizawa was remembering the last time it snowed—already it felt so long ago; he'd been out bouncing around in Otomichi's car, face freshly swollen. But this night, instead of getting started on Ogawa's interrogation, the investigators drank a toast at headquarters and went home early.

"Thanks for everything." On her way out, Otomichi had said this to him in a small voice, her expression as stiff as ever. She had apparently had her injuries tended to in the afternoon: when she came up to him, she smelled faintly of medication.

Takizawa raised a hand lightly in greeting, saying only, "Oh." He had wanted to say something more; but in the end he couldn't. He'd thought he would find a chance to say something the next day—but that ended up being the last time he saw her.

The patrol unit, with its greater mobility, was generally involved only in the preliminary stages of investigation; even if its members were assigned to an investigation, once the subject was in custody, they generally took no part in the subsequent tasks of writing reports, interviewing material witnesses, and digging up corroboration. Otomichi and the other members of the Mobile Investigative Unit were taken off the case the following day and returned to their normal assignments.

"How's it going? Lonely now?"

When Takizawa got back to the familiar, all-male environment at Tachikawa Central Station, all sorts of people came up to him. Everyone had the same thing in mind.

"Taki, did you know your partner was so accomplished?"

Realizing the keen interest they'd had in his partnership with the policewoman, Takizawa felt for the first time a glow of satisfaction. But without that brusque-mannered girl around, the place seemed suddenly drab and cheerless.

"Motorcycles—is that all she's good at riding?" one guy said.

"I'd like to be *her* motorcycle any day," said another.

Comments like this could now be bandied about openly, without restraint. Working with a woman was stifling, after all. Drab and cheerless or not, a workplace was easier to take when you could say whatever you felt like, without worrying about what some dame would think. Takizawa was sincerely happy, he decided, that life could return to its old rhythms at long last.

10

The next day, Ogawa's interrogation began in earnest.

Ogawa testified that he had slept in his car while moving from place to place in the city, and that for three days prior to his arrest he had hidden in a shed located in a grove of trees by the sea in Makuhari, facing an artificial dune. He did not know the wolf-dog was after him; but that morning, hearing the sudden screaming of sirens, he figured he'd been found and surrounded. He decided to use the two kilograms of benzoyl peroxide in his possession to start a fire, and then try to escape in the commotion.

"What's with that dog?"

Those were Ogawa's first words when the investigators grabbed him.

He was able to start the fire as planned. He placed a lit cigarette upright, like a stick of incense, in a plastic bottle filled with benzoyl peroxide and threw it out the door of the shed. As the bottle flew through the air, the highly flammable chemical danced around, coming into contact with a spark from the cigarette. That was all it took. But then, just as the bottle exploded into flames, the wolf-dog appeared and had just started to leap.

If a shooter from the Hunting Companion Society had not spotted Gale in time, Ogawa would have been dead on the spot.

Ogawa confessed to the arson of the Kasahara house, adding: "After I set the place on fire, I thought the dog was dead. So I was caught completely off guard." He gnashed his teeth about having been "tracked down by a damned dog." He spoke as if it had completely slipped his mind that he was on the most-wanted list.

Ogawa would have been all right if only he had kept the unglamorous lab job he got right out of college, working for a food manufacturer. Instead, he let himself be cajoled into developing health equipment, getting so wrapped up in it that he eventually quit his job and started his own company, only to go bankrupt.

His statement read in part: "There I was, going through all that trouble to try to improve people's health; I couldn't understand why wealth always goes to people who do things half-heartedly, just for fun." And so, when his business venture went south, Ogawa came up with a plan. Rather than skip town in the middle of night to escape his creditors, he would put up a last, desperate fight. He didn't want an inordinate sum of money—a million yen, two million tops, enough to bring himself back from the brink of ruin.

His big chance was insurance money. But people who took out life insurance policies on others and then murdered them were always caught. Better to go for money that was a sure thing, even if the amount was smaller. So he figured he'd start a fire in the building where his company was located. He knew better than to underestimate the power of a police investigation. If they found anything suspicious about the fire, they would go over the site with a fine-tooth comb. If they thought it was arson and started poking around, they might wise up to him. Setting fire to the building or the company would be a dead giveaway; better to set fire to something moving, something alive. That was Ogawa's reasoning.

"I decided a guy like Hara didn't deserve to be alive. He was a filthy piece of shit. So I chose him."

Ogawa knew Teruo Hara by sight; to his mind, Hara was a slimeball who made an easy living by preying on young girls. Every time Ogawa saw him, Hara was with a different woman, always dressed in flashy clothes, thumbing his nose at society. Ogawa was doing his damnedest to make a sober, decent living; it was sickening how a low-life like Hara could get everything his own way.

He devised a way of setting fire to Hara using a health belt of his own design, one implanted with a pedometer as well as crystal beads to improve the flow of blood. He wired into the pedometer a timer function that could be manipulated by a command sequence so that, at the designated moment, a Nichrome wire inside the belt would heat up. Then all he had to do was pack the inside of the leather belt with the proper chemical—one that would ignite with the heat produced by a tiny, micro-cell battery and produce a spectacular blaze. The most likely candidate was benzoyl peroxide. In small increments, he acquired the chemical from various places around the city. There was little difficulty in purchasing benzoyl peroxide as a paste with twenty-five percent water. He could dry the paste at home, leave it to soak overnight in methanol, then let it dry outdoors to produce a dry, white crystalline powder.

Ogawa's plan appeared to succeed. It was the acquaintance he formed with Kasahara, in the course of his numerous experiments on the deserted riverbed in the upper stream of the Tama River, that proved fatal in the end.

For his part, Kasahara spent his days training Gale as an attack dog and alternately tracking down everyone who had corrupted Emiko and ruined her life. "There were many times I came close to stopping the insanity. It was my daughter who had been foolish. And it was my own fault she turned delinquent. I alone was responsible for turning my back on my family."

Before he regained the use of his voice, Kasahara wrote this confession in a letter, according to Takizawa's instructions. When he was able to speak again, he filled in the details. It started with a chance remark by Emiko. Back when she was first hospitalized for abuse of stimulant drugs, she was literally insane; but as her condition improved and she became capable of rational speech, she told Kasahara bits about her life when she ran away from home:

"I really wanted to come back home, but I couldn't because I knew you hated me. Everyone I met was really nice to me. They said if I used the injections to lose weight and make myself pretty, you'd like me again. It was kind of true, wasn't it? See how nice you are to me now."

Recalling this, Kasahara broke down and wept. These were the sobs of a man who had remained silent even on learning of his daughter's death.

But when his daughter told him those things, Kasahara swore he would get revenge. That was all he could do for her. On her good days he would ask her, little by little, about the crowd that got her hooked on amphetamines. Taku, Kazu, Chieko, Mizu-kun. Emiko referred to them by their nicknames, and talked about them with eager pleasure. She described them as "nice people." To the end she believed they were kind to her, were fond of her.

Kasahara questioned his daughter about the people she hung around with later, people she got mixed up with when she escaped from the hospital to the seedy area of Kabukicho; but among them, Emiko had been a mere faceless "buyer," and she had nothing to tell.

In the beginning Kasahara never intended to use the wolf-dog in his grand scheme, but having spent so much of his life training police dogs, even after retiring from the force he kept gravitating to dogs. He worked at pet shops and kept dogs of his own. "When I found out about wolf-dogs, I had to have one. When I finally got my own wolf-dog, I was blown away by his personality and brains."

He had acquired Gale by sheer chance, and Gale exceeded anything Kasahara dreamed of. Of course, since wolf-dogs came in all varieties, not all would have been like Gale, so their encounter was like destiny. Even though Gale saw Emiko rarely, he developed a bond with her, and was even able to understand her speech. When they went on walks together, if children made fun of her, from the time he was a puppy he would bare his fangs menacingly. Seeing Gale so protective of Emiko—almost as if he was reading Kasahara's thoughts—Kasahara decided to train him: "From the start, he seemed to understand that this was his mission, his role as a member of the family."

As Kasahara proceeded with the training, sometimes Gale's prodigious intelligence did not surprise him so much as disturb him. "Wolf-dogs grow amazingly fast. I got Gale when he was three months old, and I started training him two months later."

Gale had a strong will, and was not content to obey meekly. His intelligence made up the difference. He did not seek constant praise from his master; rather he seemed to be thinking of ways to smooth and cement the relationship, ways to receive unfailing love. There was no need to train Gale in the basic points of good behavior that most dogs needed to work on: to come immediately when called, to walk at the same pace as his handler, not to howl unnecessarily, and so on.

"He had a vulnerable side, too. If you scolded him too hard, he would be down in the dumps for a day or two. He seemed to be worrying, what if he doesn't trust me anymore, what if I've lost his affection?"

Gradually, Kasahara trained Gale in the same ways he had trained police dogs: obedience, alarm, search, and so on. He began with "sit" and "heel," then moved on to obedience training using commands of "stay," "fetch," "down," and so forth. This Gale seemed to find tiresome, although he enjoyed vigilance training with commands like "guard" and "track." Usually in the police dog training center, dogs were trained to attack by setting up a third person as suspect; the dog would express anger and excitement before attacking, and stay engaged until the command "stop." But Kasahara taught Gale to carry out attacks on designated targets without excitement, and without hearing the command "stop." Also, he often had him practice using the sense of smell to follow a trail or to select one item out of several. His goal was to get Gale to attack in response to a particular scent.

"Gale's disposition has both a hard side and a soft side. He's proud and obstinate, but he's also very sensitive. You can't force him, and he's temperamental, not like a German shepherd, for instance. In the beginning I had my share of troubles with him."

But he was just as often pleasantly surprised. The animal's superb memory, tenacity, and stamina surpassed anything in Kasahara's experience; often he found himself profoundly moved. But in the end he appropriated Gale's abilities for his own purposes of revenge. As one year went by, then two, he began to feel that this was what Gale, too, wanted.

"The time I really saw what unusual ability Gale had was about six months ago, when I took him to visit Emiko. When we got out of the car at the hospital, he ran off and didn't come back. Yet when I arrived home that night, he was there, lying in his pen. Gale had abilities that can't be learned through training. He was able to think for himself, act on his own volition."

Exceptional powers of memory, exceptional composure and discretion, exceptional strength. In all of these ways, he was completely reliable. To Kasahara, Gale was far more trustworthy than the average shallow human. And while they were stalking Teruo Hara, whom Kasahara had finally found, Gale had also grown familiar with the scent of Ogawa, who worked in the same building.

Hoping to learn more about Hara, Kasahara had spoken to Ogawa when they met by chance by the riverbed. One time only, they had stood and talked. Never suspecting that this man out walking his dog recognized him from elsewhere, Ogawa responded with friendliness and willingness to chat, in order to cover up his chemical experiment. Neither man had had any idea what the other was up to.

"The only reason Gale failed to kill Hara on his first attempt, when he attacked him as he was walking down the street late at night, was because at that very moment a car came flying out of a nearby alleyway."

Hara had jumped out of the way, startled not by Gale but by the car. Gale, too, had been surprised, and was momentarily sidetracked. Even then, he resumed his attack on Hara's leg, but Hara screamed as another car pulled out on to the street, and Kasahara, who was watching, commanded Gale to stop. That was the only time he rescinded an order to pursue and kill. Kasahara decided then and there that Gale should not bother with a target's legs, and he retrained Gale to go straight for the jugular.

Several days later, in the underground parking garage of the restaurant, Kasahara saw Hara and Ogawa exchange greetings in passing. Then Ogawa had called out to Hara, and handed him something. That was the belt with the timed incendiary device planted in it.

As Ogawa testified: "Telling him it was a new product I was putting on the market, I handed Hara the belt. He was quite pleased. He said now that he was in his thirties, he wasn't getting as much exercise as he needed, and he was a little worried about his fitness. I talked him into putting it on right away. Then I told him, 'Just to see how it works, try checking how many steps you take today, and how many calories you burn up that way.' Then, pretending to show him how it worked, I punched in the command sequence on the pedometer, and set the timer on the ignition device."

Ogawa established from this conversation that Hara would be in the building until around midnight that night. "I never thought the device would go off in that restaurant. I didn't need anything near as big a blast as that was. All I needed was for my office to burn."

From Kasahara's perspective, Ogawa had saved him the trouble of killing Hara. As the outlines of the fire at the family restaurant emerged through television and newspaper reports, he realized Ogawa had done the job for him.

"I assumed Hara had other enemies. And then, even though I didn't bring about his death myself, I decided to go look at the place where Hara burned. I went to see the building after the police stopped talking to people there, and happened to run into Ogawa. I blurted out a hello, wanting to thank him."

Don't worry, I won't rat on you, thanks for saving me the trouble: Kasahara wanted to tell Ogawa these things. They shared something in common, both after the same man. For all Kasahara knew, they shared a similar motivation, too. Kasahara suggested he and Ogawa have a cup of coffee, and on that occasion hinted to Ogawa that he knew who was responsible for Hara's death.

Ogawa said: "I broke out in a cold sweat. I thought he wanted to blackmail me. But he acted like a decent guy and never said another word about it, not even when we split up that day. I was creeped out, and so nervous I couldn't sleep that night."

Kasahara said: "To tell the truth, I was worried about what people were thinking. Ogawa knew I owned a wolf-dog. I wanted to find out if he had made any connection between me and these attacks starting getting to get media attention."

Kasahara's own overdriven, workaholic life had helped turn his daughter into a delinquent and a drug addict—and now one careless, rash action ended up costing her life. Once again he broke down and wept uncontrollably before police investigators. His grief contrasted starkly with the carping of Ogawa as he bewailed his ill fortune and his inability to finish the wolf-dog off in the fire.

Kasahara continued: "There was this terrible blast, and the inside of the house burst into flames. The first thing I did was let Gale out of his pen. I just told him, 'Go!' It wasn't an actual command; it was the first word that popped out of my mouth in desperation. There are all sorts of commands I could have used—'Search,' 'Follow,' 'Run'—and I think they were all rolled up in that one single word. For a moment Gale studied my face, but the fire and smoke were so intense that he instinctively sensed danger, I think, and took off. Then I went to get Emiko, but the fire had spread quickly and the smoke was so blinding, I couldn't keep my eyes open. It got so bad I couldn't take another step. Looking back, I have no idea why I didn't go to my daughter first. But maybe I wanted to entrust Gale with something.

"Of course, no matter how developed a dog's sense of smell may be, once Ogawa got in his car and sped off, his scent would be gone. But with his strength and speed, Gale could cover a lot of ground fast, and since it was snowing that day, the car was held up in traffic; following it might have been pretty easy for Gale. He must have learned to recognize Ogawa's car."

After Hara's death, Kasahara was able, merely by repeated pointing, to indicate to Gale his next target, and get him to attack on his own. Kasahara would follow the designated victim around for days on end, establishing a pattern of movement and searching for a place where he or she would be easy prey. As they tracked different people together, Gale soon learned whom they were after and became quicker than Kasahara at finding the target, issuing a slight growl when he picked up the scent. Kasahara observed the attacks from inside his car, and then drove home alone. Gale unfailingly returned by himself, morning at the latest. He used the Akishima house as his home base—a style of territoriality that was one more sign of the wolf blood running in his veins, as wolves normally roam widely through their territory. According to Kasahara, wherever Gale went, his movements centered on the house, as if he were always recalculating his direction and distance from home.

"Normally this would be unthinkable, but I have the idea that after getting separated from me, Gale remembered following Mizutani around. That dog had such a strong bond with his family, and he hated being alone so much, he must have felt lost without me. It kills me to think of it. Maybe all he could do was to concentrate on me, and the places he and I had gone together, and go back there in hopes of picking up some trace of me. And all the while he must have been turning over that word 'Go!' in his mind, trying to figure out what it meant."

Ogawa reasoned that, even if Kasahara made no threat, sooner or later Kasahara would come after him. So one day he followed Kasahara home from the pet shop where he worked and found out where he lived. He made up his mind to do away with him. He knew that the investigation of the case of the timed incendiary device had stalled; police showed no interest in talking to him about it. This meant that if he used the same chemical as before, he didn't have to worry. This time he made an even simpler explosive contraption, using a plastic bottle. First he cut out the bottom out and then, using a cheap watch and a battery, he attached a timing device using only a spring and Nichrome wire. Then he reattached the bottom of the bottle, and filled it with dry benzoyl peroxide. He made several of these firebombs, and placed them at regular intervals on the perimeter of Kasahara's house.

"I never thought it was an attack dog. I'd seen it a bunch of times, but it never howled at me, and that night, too, it never made a peep. I had my own problems; those 'dog bites man' stories didn't interest me. Then at Makuhari the animal came flying at me out of nowhere, and my heart just about froze."

This was Ogawa's account. There was no appreciable difference in the testimony of the two men, it was adjudged. As the investigation proceeded, detectives devoted themselves to compounding evidence and interviewing witnesses, creating a paper whirlwind. Investigation headquarters was disbanded the day after Masanori Ogawa was formally indicted for murder.

Over two months had passed since the death of Teruo Hara.

EPILOGUE

It was almost cherry blossom season. The sunshine had more sparkle, and along railroad tracks and on little embankments, yellow rape flowers were in blossom.

"Dead? When did it happen?"

"About two weeks after he came here—no, more like three. Not long after his master's indictment."

This was the MPD kennel for police dogs, located in the Tama Identification Center. Freed from the rigors of her previous assignment, lately Takako had been spending all her time on the case of a serial street slasher. The scrapes and bruises incurred during the spill she took while chasing Gale having healed, she decided to spend her day off enjoying the feel of the spring breeze against her skin, and set off again on her motorcycle. Once she was out riding, for the first time it unsettled her to realize that she had no destination in mind. That never used to matter. Before, she would always just ride and ride to her heart's content before deciding on a destination. Now the idea that she didn't know where to go, didn't know what to aim for, made her anxious.

And then, the next thing she knew, she was heading here. Headquarters had wracked its brains over what to do with the wolf-dog that attacked and killed three people. Unable to send it to the pound or put it in the zoo, they decided to shelter it in a police dog kennel. She didn't have to see Gale, she just wanted to hear how he was doing.

"What did he die of? Was he sick?"

"No, he wasn't sick." The officer assigned to care for Gale was an unassuming man of about forty. Something about him reminded her of Kasahara.He twisted his mouth awkwardly and sighed. "He just wouldn't eat."

Takako stared at this man who was smaller in stature than herself. When she'd first shown up on her 1200cc bike, wearing her leather suit, he looked askance at her; but after she showed him her badge, he nodded in

265

comprehension: "Oh, you're the one." The story of the motorcycle police-woman who chased the wolf-dog over Tokyo expressways that night had spread even to this backwater, far from the noise of the city.

"He was important material evidence, so I did all I could for him," said the man. "I checked with his master about what he was used to eating and bought the same brand of dog food, and I took him to the vet time and again."

"There was nothing physically wrong?"

The man shook his head, and sighed again with evident regret. "I figured maybe he didn't like me, and tried having someone else take over for me for a while. Even brought in something with his master's scent on it to put in his cage. He didn't seem either ill or depressed; more like he'd just made up his mind he wasn't ever going to eat again, and that was that. You could say he was firm in his own mind."

Suicide. The word floated into Takako's mind.

"Are you saying he deliberately starved himself to death?"

"We gave him fluids, did what we could."

"IVs and injections didn't work?"

"He was smart. It worked the first time, but after that the sight of the vet set him off something fierce. He'd snarl and bare his fangs."

That day, when six men carted Gale off before her eyes, he'd been knocked out with tranquilizers. The eyes that had stared into hers were closed, and the muscles that had rippled so magnificently beneath the dense fur lay unmoving. His legs and body were muddy, and while his expression was of course unreadable, he gave off an air of exhaustion. In front of the others she had struggled fiercely to maintain control, but tears had never been far. Had Gale never taken in another mouthful of food?

"Ordinarily he was completely self-possessed, so to speak; even when other dogs barked or people came by, he was as quiet as you please. I mean, the idea that he could ever attack anyone seemed preposterous to me."

"He was that quiet?"

"Only the IVs set him off. We tried a different vet, but it didn't make any difference. That dog knew. Seeing that, I felt dread. Because for a dog like that, ripping someone to pieces might be nothing after all."

"And then he just died?"

The officer sighed again, and nodded. "He had enormous—I don't know what else to call it—mental strength. He just stared off into space, like he was thinking about something, or waiting for someone. That's what I thought."

"And he lasted nearly three weeks?"

"That's right. One morning when I came in, he was already cold. When we weighed him, he'd lost over twenty pounds."

Takako could not imagine a Gale that was wasted away, cadaverous. Dazed, she left the Identification Center. Gale, with all his life force, all his fierce energy, was gone.

Where should I go?

As she got back on her motorcycle and rode, she felt her shock increase. She was bewildered, rattled, about to lose it. Devastated, she rode on through the halcyon spring sunshine. Under a sky so soft and warm that, after the harshness of midwinter, even the honking of horns sounded gentle, on and on she rode, blending aimlessly with the flow of traffic.

With the passing of days, her impression of the hours spent running with Gale blurred into something of a dream or a vision. Everything about that bitterly cold night had been fantastic and unreal. Only the strange joy and satisfaction she felt as she flew along behind Gale was unforgettable. That, and the look in Gale's eyes when he had stared into hers, was etched indelibly in her mind.

Yes, you had no alternative. What other course could you have chosen?

Yet, what a quiet death it had been—maybe, in its way, a sublime death. How strange that the death of a dog should affect her so deeply. As she rode blindly on, Takako wondered if Gale had not planned on ending his own life from the first. Once he had carried out his last mission and killed Ogawa, he would die: Gale was certainly capable of thinking that way. He was that human, that single-minded in his devotion.

Then they should have let him carry out the attack.

This stunning thought suddenly seized her. Ogawa would face a long trial now, to be followed by conviction and a harsh penalty, without a doubt. Murder, attempted murder, arson of an inhabited structure accompanied by the burning of neighboring structures, unauthorized use of a controlled substance for antisocial ends. He had all these crimes to answer for. Prosecutors would certainly request the death penalty.

Ogawa and Kasahara might confront one another in court. When that happened, Takako wanted to be there. Anyway, there was talk that she might need to take the stand as the legally appointed officer who went after Gale. It would be some time before the events of that night could fade to the far reaches of her awareness.

She'd been heading west, yet at some point she'd gotten on the expressway—and then, before she knew it, she found herself back on the Bayshore

Route. The spring sun was high in the sky, and its reflection on the line of cars on the crowded lanes before her sparkled. The same road; but what different air, what different scenery from that day, flew past. In her mind's eye, Takako had a vision of Gale: a wolf-dog tearing through the darkness with bounding lightness and fluid grace.

Suddenly she thought of the emperor penguin. Come to think of it, perhaps the only reason she'd been able to race along with her mind focused solely on Gale that night was because she knew she could count on Takizawa, behind her. She had imagined herself alone in Gale's presence, but unlike him, she had had backup. She had ridden this long way with Takizawa there, watching after her, the whole time. That was how he could come up to her afterward and say, "You looked like you were having a ball."

She'd never seen him again since then, no chance to say a proper goodbye. Rumor had it he was troubled about his daughter's upcoming marriage. Supposedly he was tearing his hair out because, although barely twenty, she was bent on getting married right away. "Even for a woman, it's not like marriage is the only thing in life," he had groused to his coworkers.

Her former partner probably knew that Gale was dead. But he hadn't been able to tell her. *Maybe he never told me because he wanted to spare me.* That's the way he would think. Without him around anymore, she found herself thinking nostalgically of the emperor penguin. Her memory of him as he said only "Oh," and walked off with a wave of his hand was strangely warm. Still, she had no desire to be paired with him ever again.

She passed the Ichikawa toll booth and saw the Wangan Narashino Interchange coming up ahead. She put on the turn signal of her old friend, the XJR1200, and changed lanes. Still in a sentimental mood, she decided on the spur of the moment to visit her parents' home in Urawa.

She would check on Tomoko, who had taken up Chinese breathing exercises, and stay for dinner, putting up with Koko's malice and her mother's complaints. Talk of love and marriage was now off limits at home, so there would be no carping about her divorce. After a while her father would come home. She'd see him, hear him say as usual, "Sure is a big bike you got there," and then go back to her apartment. Days off were few and far between. Might as well make the most of this one.

Her thoughts turned to the case she was currently assigned to. The suspect remained a mystery. Even after hearing eyewitness testimony, she had no clear image of the attacker. What sort of man would go after defenseless young girls, slashing them from behind, she had no idea; there was something cheap and disgraceful about such behavior. Damn it, there were no decent men around, any way you turned. Though indeed, if she should ever find one with a long, bushy tail, she might follow him to the ends of the earth. Thinking this, she stepped three times on the gear pedal, then veered down the gentle curve of the ramp.

Acknowledgments

I am indebted to the following people: Paul Heineck, for expert advice on biking terminology; Kahon Wada, for checking chemistry terms; my editor, Elmer Luke, for helping to make this a "sweet ride"; and my husband, Bruce, for once again tolerating my odd questions and odd hours.

—Juliet Winters Carpenter

（英文版）凍える牙
The Hunter

2006 年 10 月 30 日　第 1 刷発行

著　者　　　乃南アサ
訳　者　　　ジュリエット・ウィンターズ・カーペンター
発行者　　　富田 充
発行所　　　講談社インターナショナル株式会社
　　　　　　〒 112-8652　東京都文京区音羽 1-17-14
　　　　　　電話　03-3944-6493（編集部）
　　　　　　　　　03-3944-6492（マーケティング部・業務部）
　　　　　　ホームページ　www.kodansha-intl.com
印刷・製本所　　　大日本印刷株式会社

落丁本・乱丁本は購入書店名を明記のうえ、講談社インターナショナル業務部宛にお送り
ください。送料小社負担にてお取替えします。なお、この本についてのお問い合わせは、
編集部宛にお願いいたします。本書の無断複写（コピー）、転載は著作権法の例外を除き、
禁じられています。

定価はカバーに表示してあります。